THE RUNAWAY PRINCESS

RH
GRAPHIC

THE RUNAWAY PR

Johan Troïanowski

Translation copyright © 2020 by Makaka Editions
Cover art and interior art copyright © 2015, 2016, 2017, 2020 by Makaka Editions

All rights reserved. Published in the United States by RH Graphic, an imprint of Random House Children's Books, a division of Penguin Random House LLC, New York. The titles in this work were originally published in three separate volumes in France and in the French language by Makaka Editions, Saint-Etienne-de-Fontbellon as *Rouge, Petite Princesse Punk* by Johan Troïanowski in 2015, copyright © 2015 by Makaka Editions; *Rouge et la Sorcière D'Automne* by Johan Troïanowski in 2016, copyright © 2016 by Makaka Editions; and *Rouge L'île des Gribouilleurs* by Johan Troïanowski in 2017, copyright © 2017 by Makaka Editions.

RH Graphic with the book design is a trademark of Penguin Random House LLC.

Visit us on the Web! rhkidsgraphic.com • @RHKidsGraphic

Educators and librarians, for a variety of teaching tools, visit us at RHTeachersLibrarians.com

Library of Congress Cataloging-in-Publication Data
Names: Troïanowski, Johan, author, illustrator. | Smith, Anne Collins, translator. | Smith, Owen (Owen M.), translator. | Troïanowski, Johan. Rouge, petite princesse punk. English. | Troïanowski, Johan. Rouge et la sorcière d'automne. English. | Troïanowski, Johan. Rouge l'île des gribouilleurs. English.
Title: The runaway princess / Johan Troïanowski; translation by Anne and Owen Smith.
Description: New York : RH Graphic, [2020] | Originally published in three separate volumes in French by Makaka Editions, Saint-Etienne-de-Fontbellon, in 2015–2017 under the titles Rouge, petite princesse punk, Rouge et la sorcière d'automne, and Rouge l'île des gribouilleurs.
Identifiers: LCCN 2019018080 | ISBN 978-0-593-11840-5 (trade pbk.) | ISBN 978-0-593-12416-1 (hardcover) | ISBN 978-0-593-11842-9 (ebook) | ISBN 978-0-593-11841-2 (lib. bdg.)
Subjects: LCSH: Graphic novels. | CYAC: Graphic novels. | Princesses—Fiction. | Adventure and adventurers—Fiction. | France—Fiction. | Fairy tales—Fiction.
Classification: LCC PZ7.7.T76 Run 2020 | DDC 741.5/944—dc23

Designed by Patrick Crotty
Translation by Anne and Owen Smith

MANUFACTURED IN CHINA
10 9 8 7 6 5 4 3 2 1
First American Edition

A comic on every bookshelf.

This book was drawn with India ink and a nib pen on 180g a4 sheets of paper, then colored directly with crayon and inks. This edition was lettered with Stanton ICG.

For Mathilde, Lou, Camille, and Pome

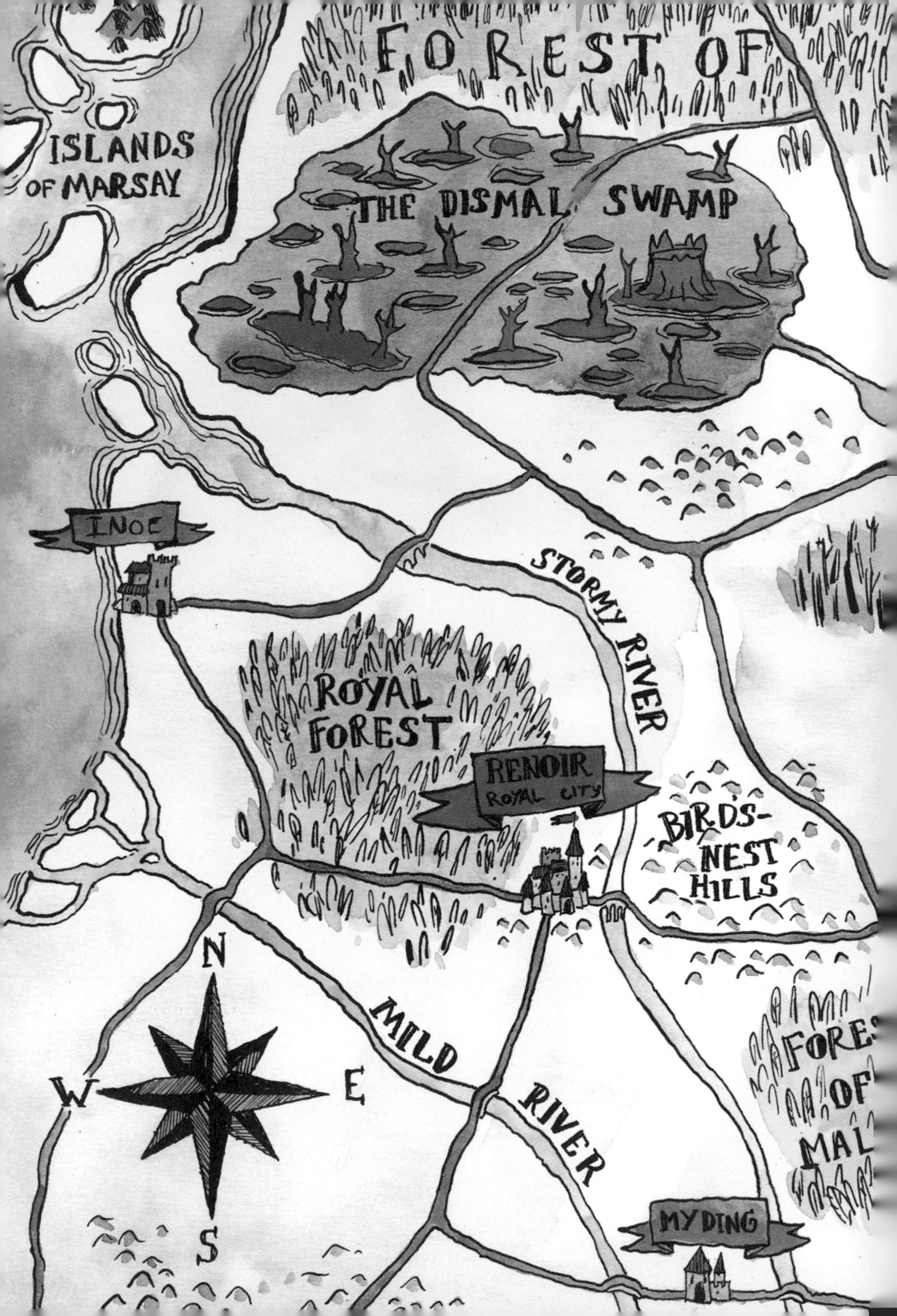
FOREST OF
ISLANDS OF MARSAY
THE DISMAL SWAMP
INOE
STORMY RIVER
ROYAL FOREST
RENOIR
ROYAL CITY
BIRDS-NEST HILLS
N
W
E
S
MILD RIVER
MYDING

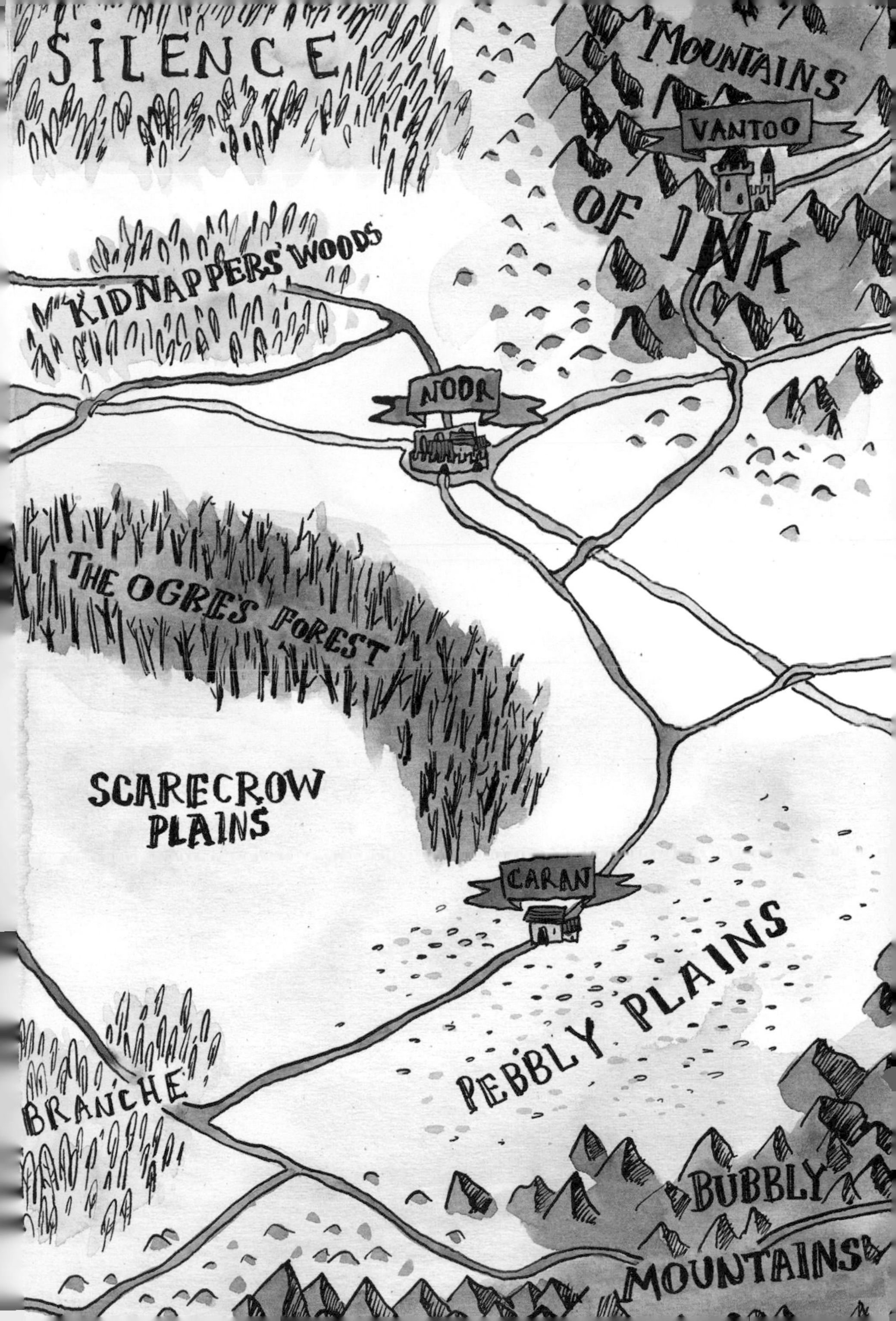
SILENCE
MOUNTAINS
VANTOO
OF INK
KIDNAPPERS' WOODS
NOOR
THE OGRE'S FOREST
SCARECROW PLAINS
CARAN
PEBBLY PLAINS
BRANCHE
BUBBLY
MOUNTAINS

THE PRINCESS RUNS AWAY

(AND MAKES SOME FRIENDS)

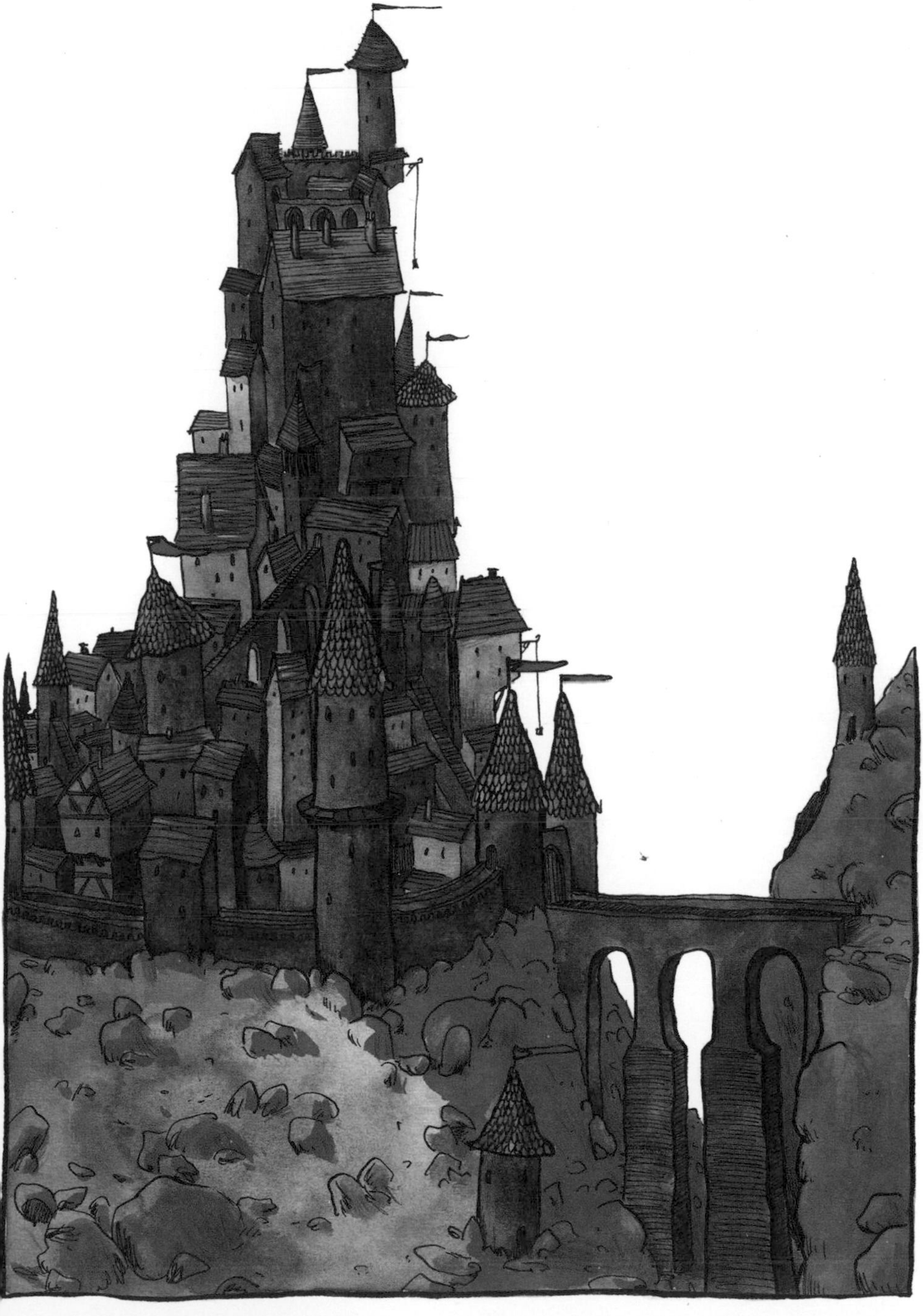

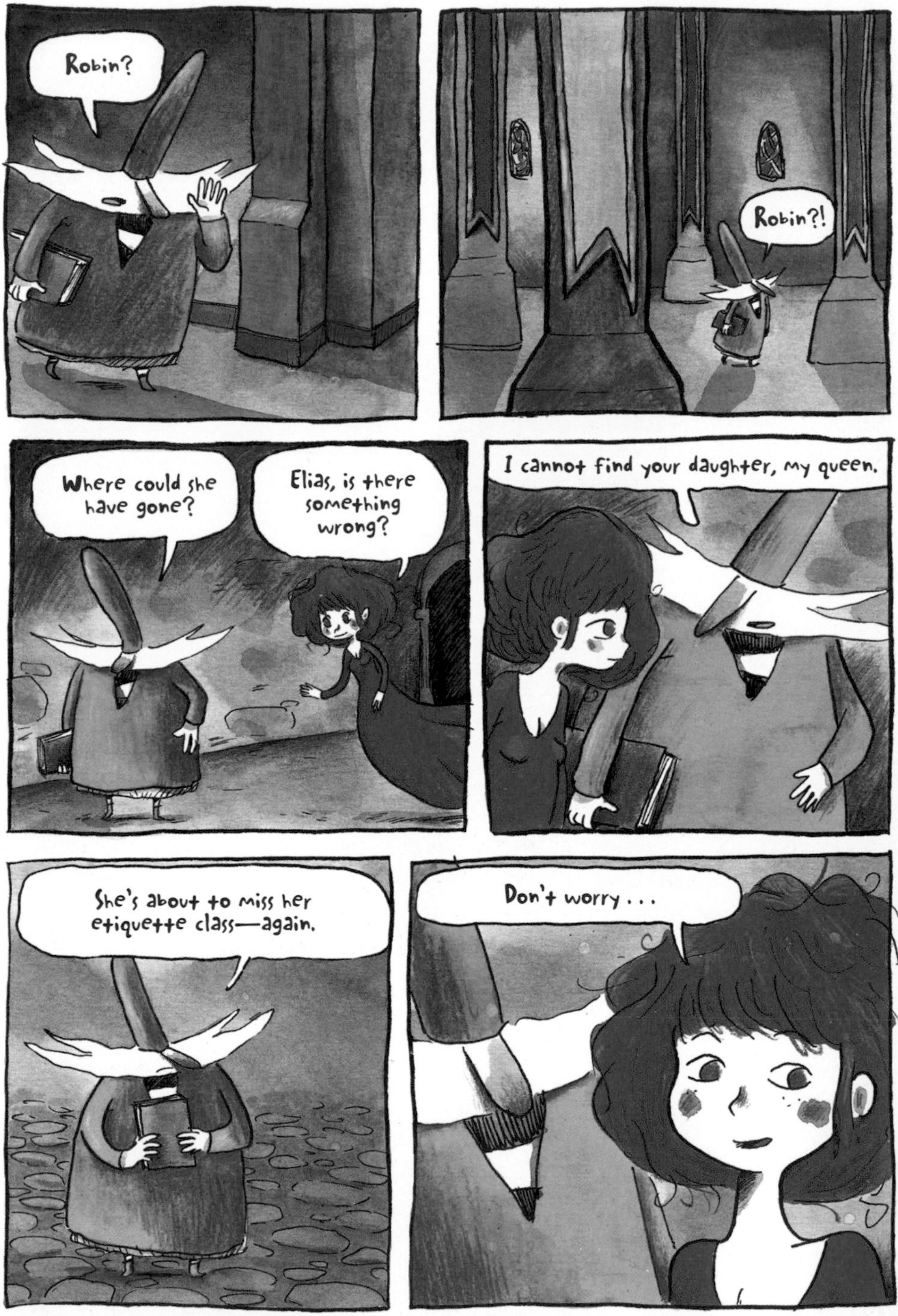
Robin?
Robin?!
Where could she have gone?
Elias, is there something wrong?
I cannot find your daughter, my queen.
She's about to miss her etiquette class—again.
Don't worry . . .

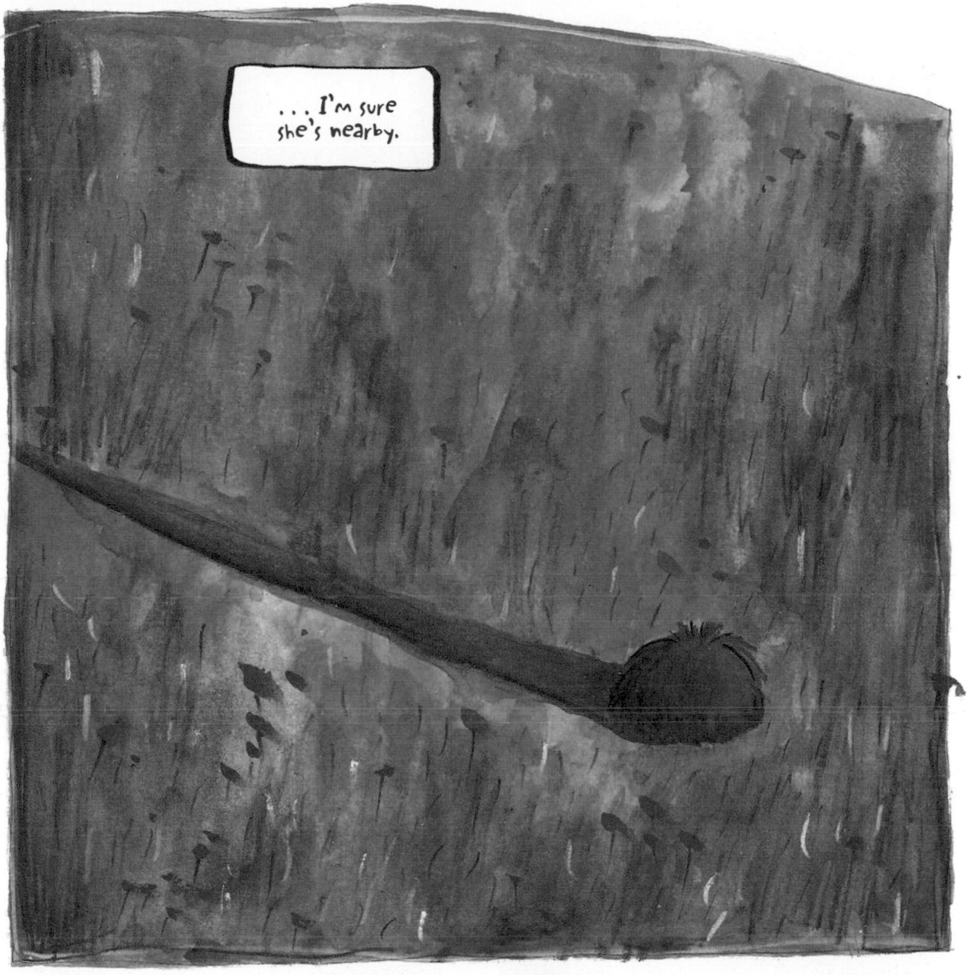
. . . I'm sure she's nearby.

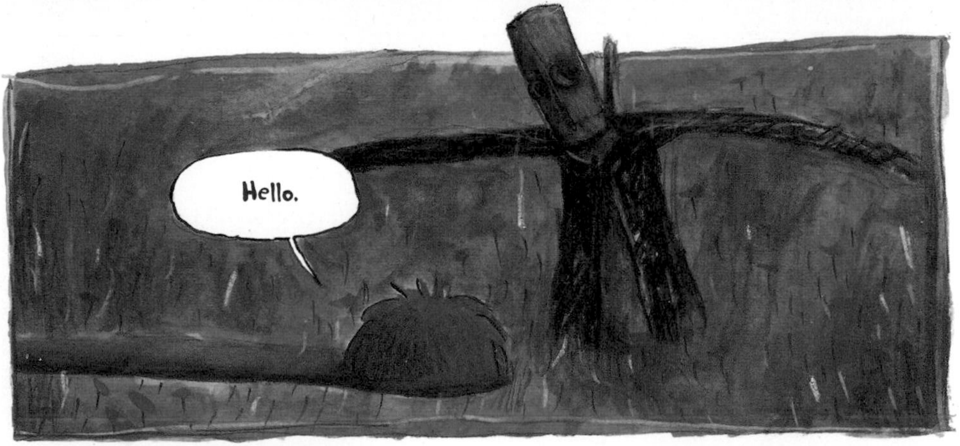
Hello.

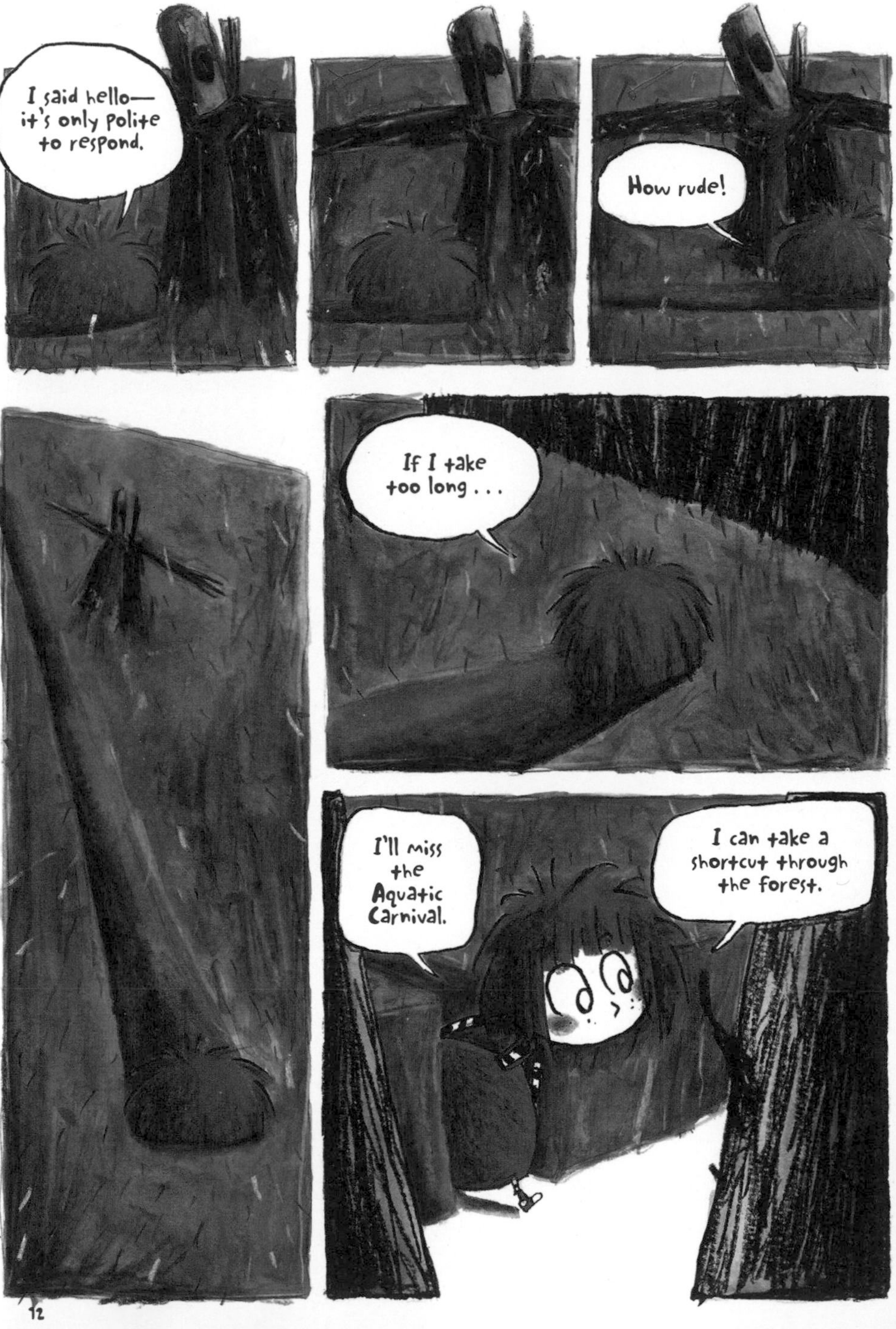
I said hello—it's only polite to respond.
How rude!
If I take too long . . .
I'll miss the Aquatic Carnival.
I can take a shortcut through the forest.

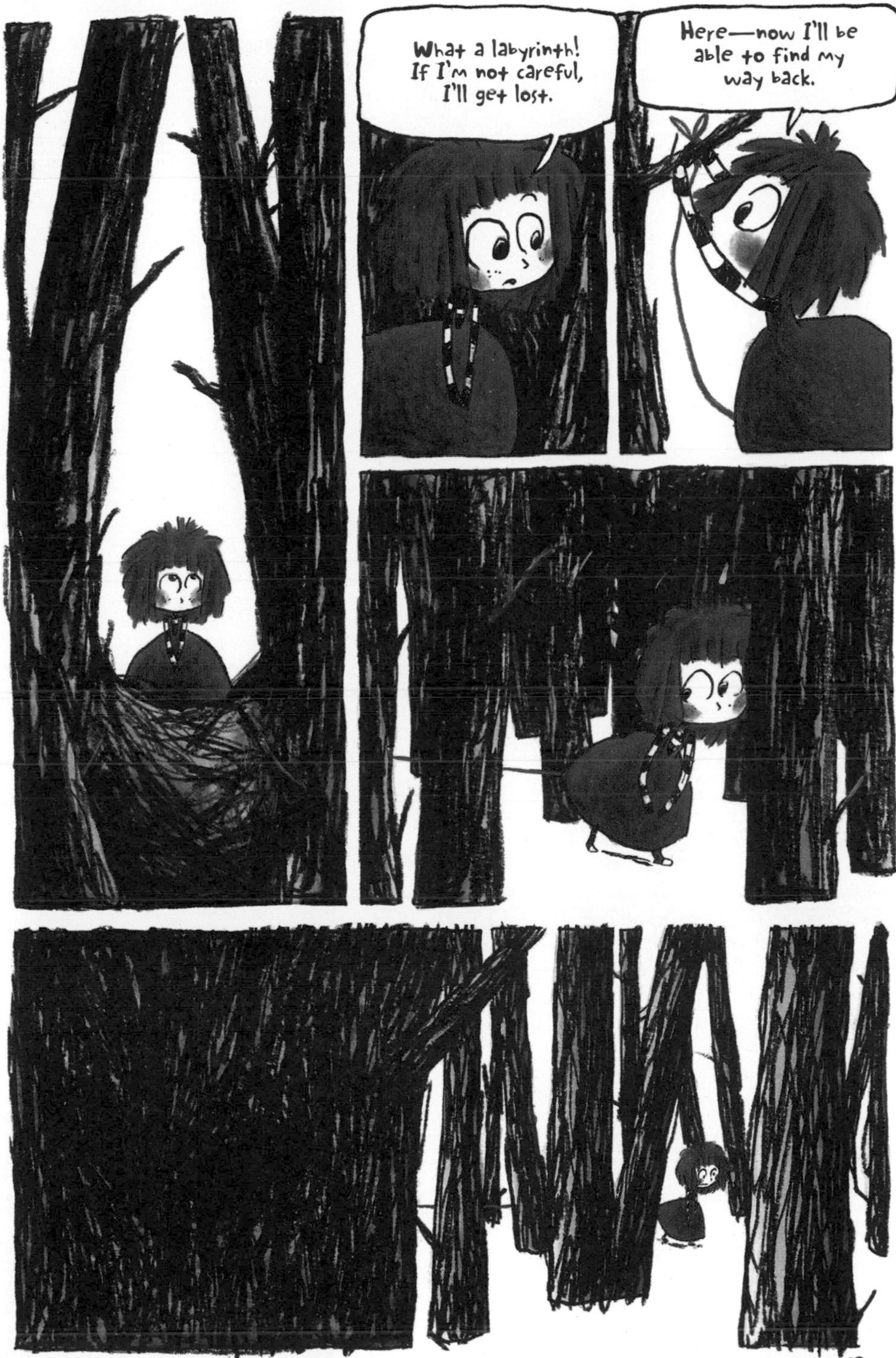
What a labyrinth! If I'm not careful, I'll get lost.
Here—now I'll be able to find my way back.

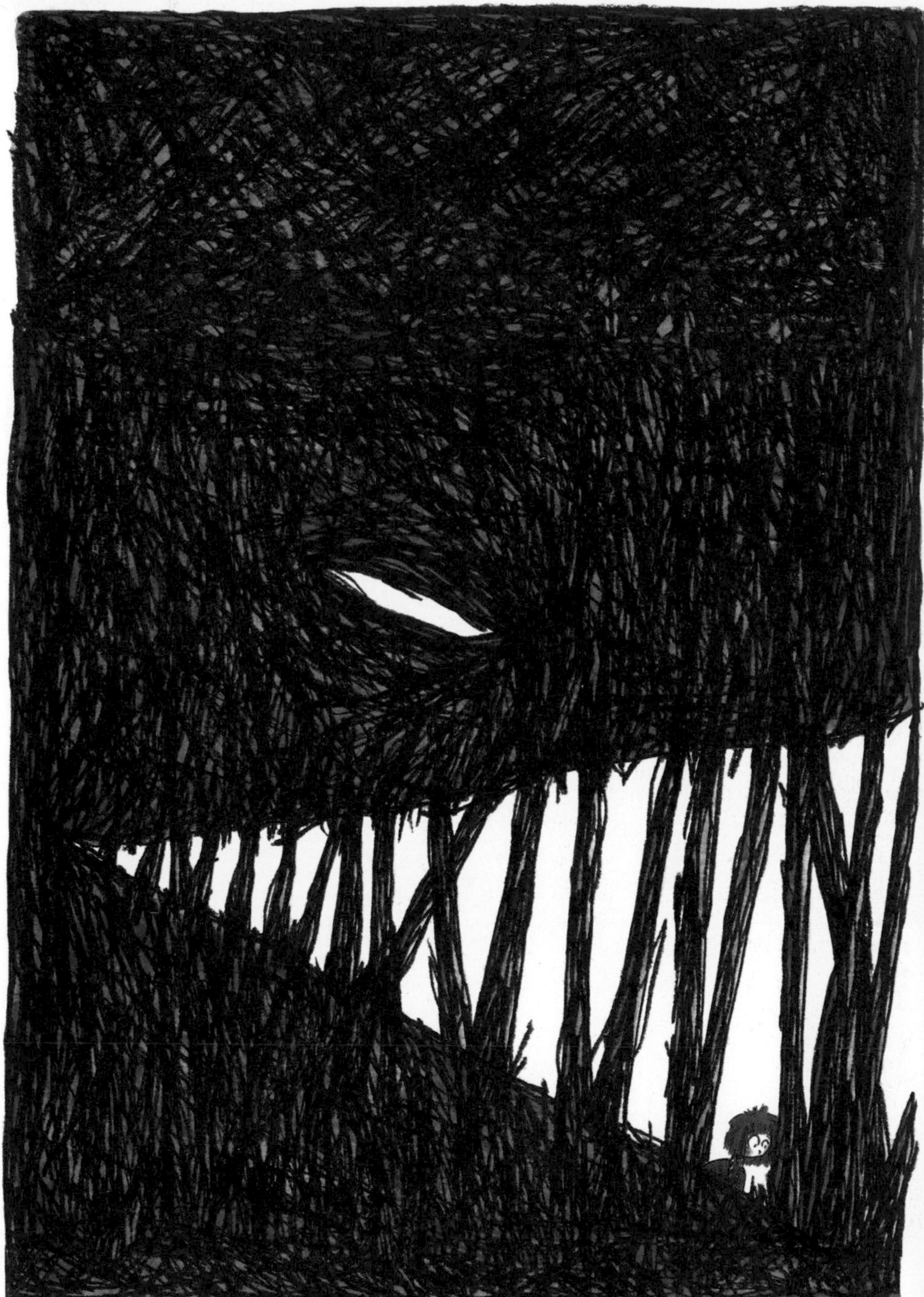

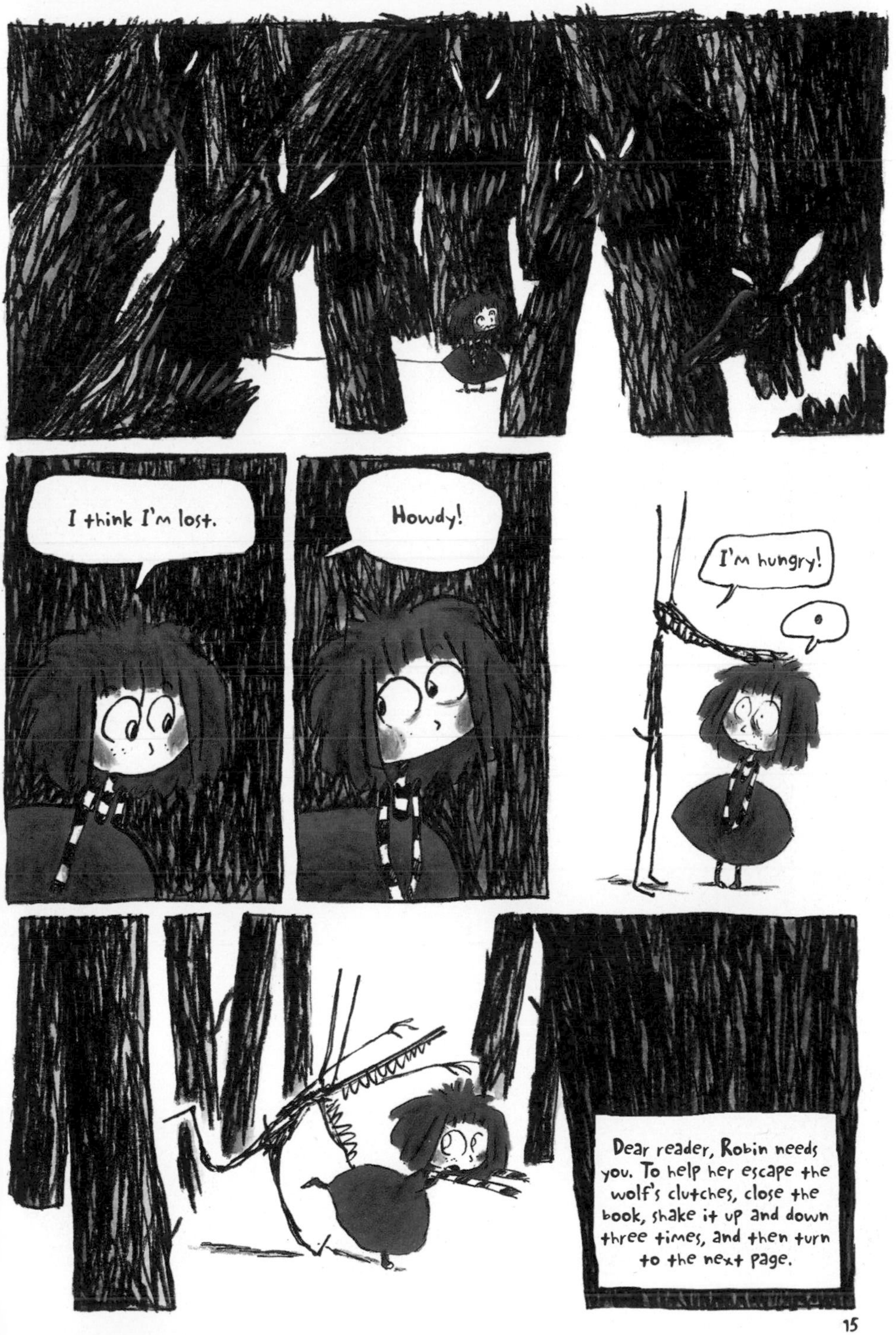

I think I'm lost.
Howdy!
I'm hungry!
?
Dear reader, Robin needs you. To help her escape the wolf's clutches, close the book, shake it up and down three times, and then turn to the next page.

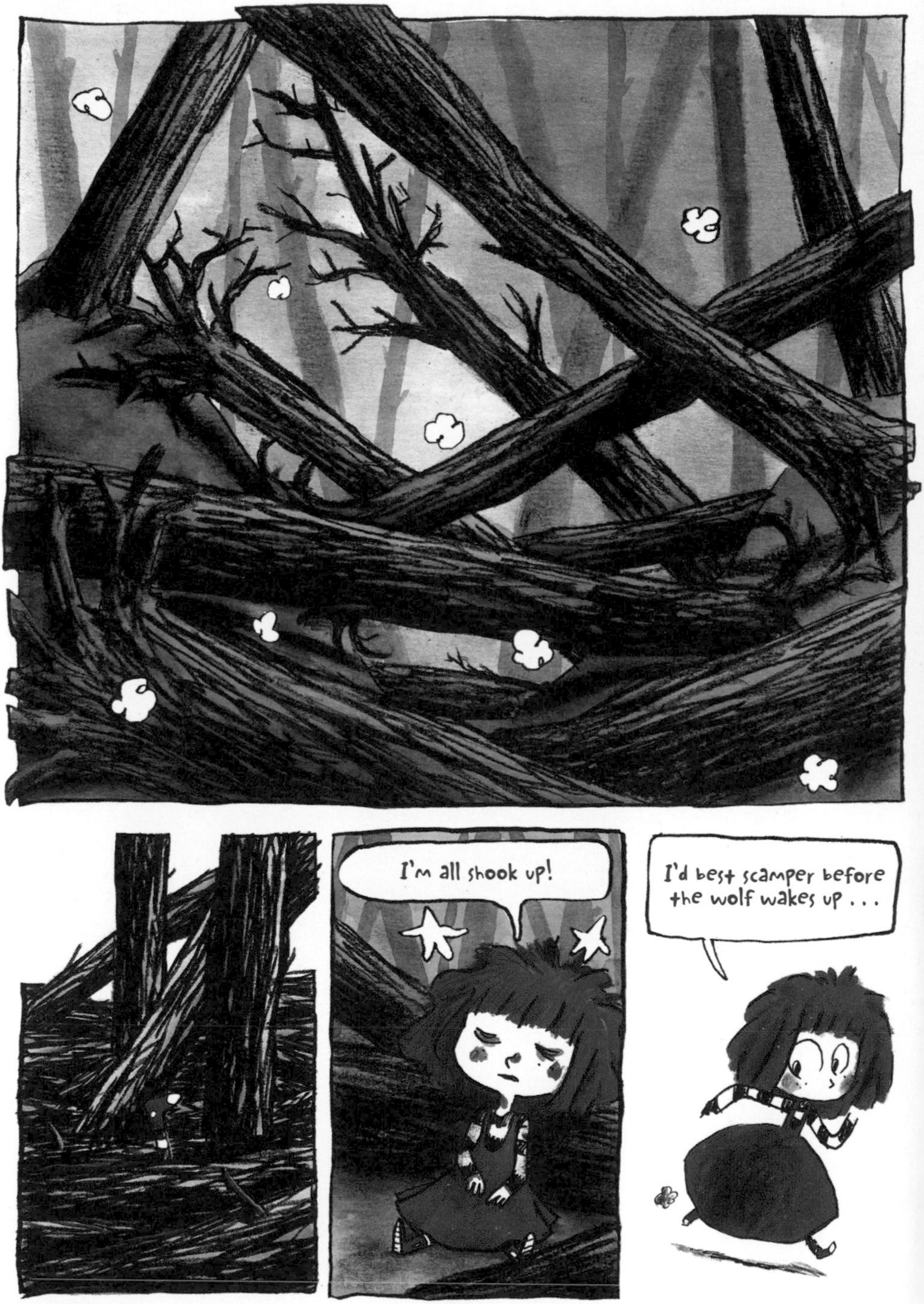
I'm all shook up!
I'd best scamper before the wolf wakes up . . .

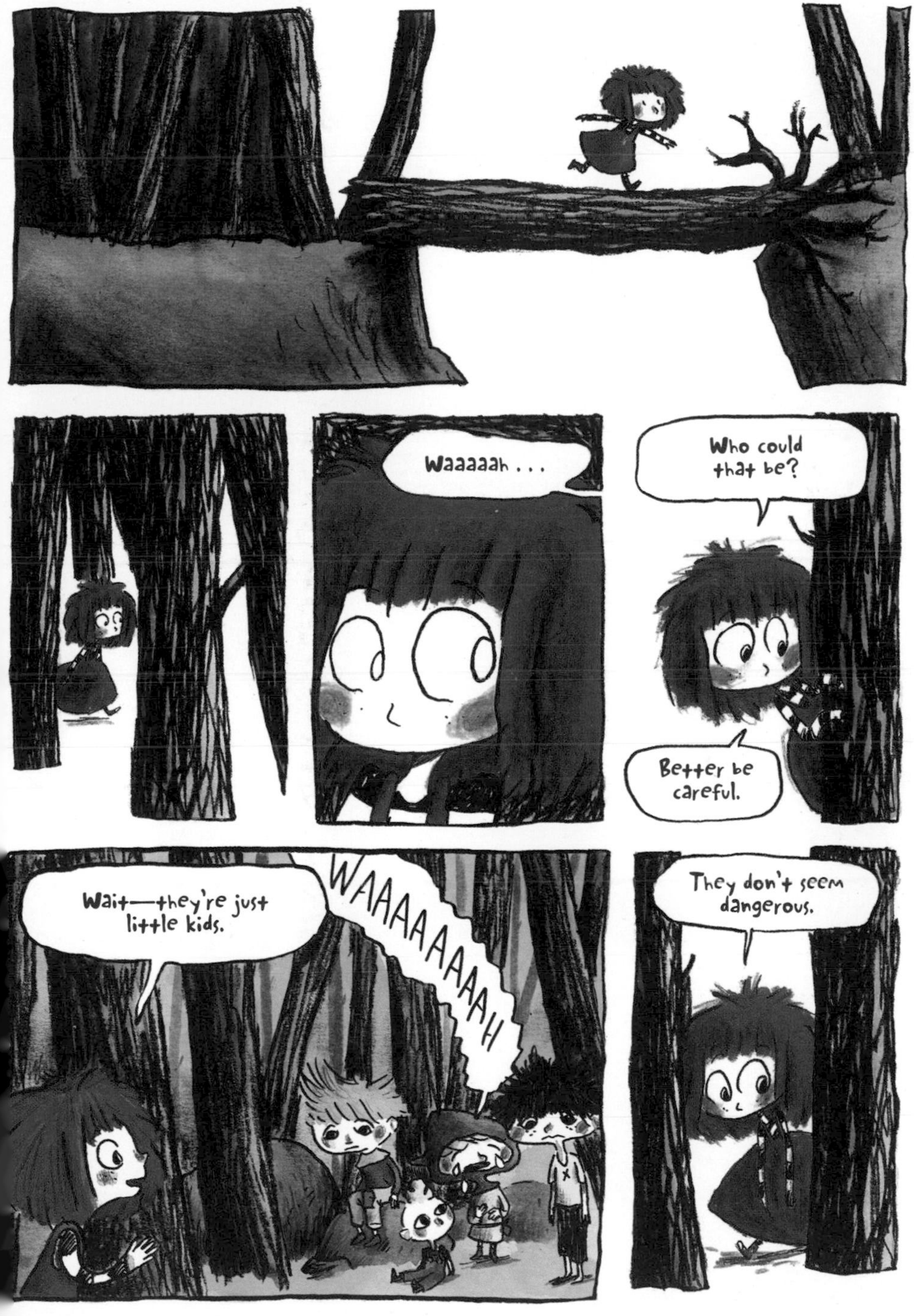
Waaaaah . . .
Who could that be?
Better be careful.
Wait—they're just little kids.
WAAAAAAAAAAH
They don't seem dangerous.

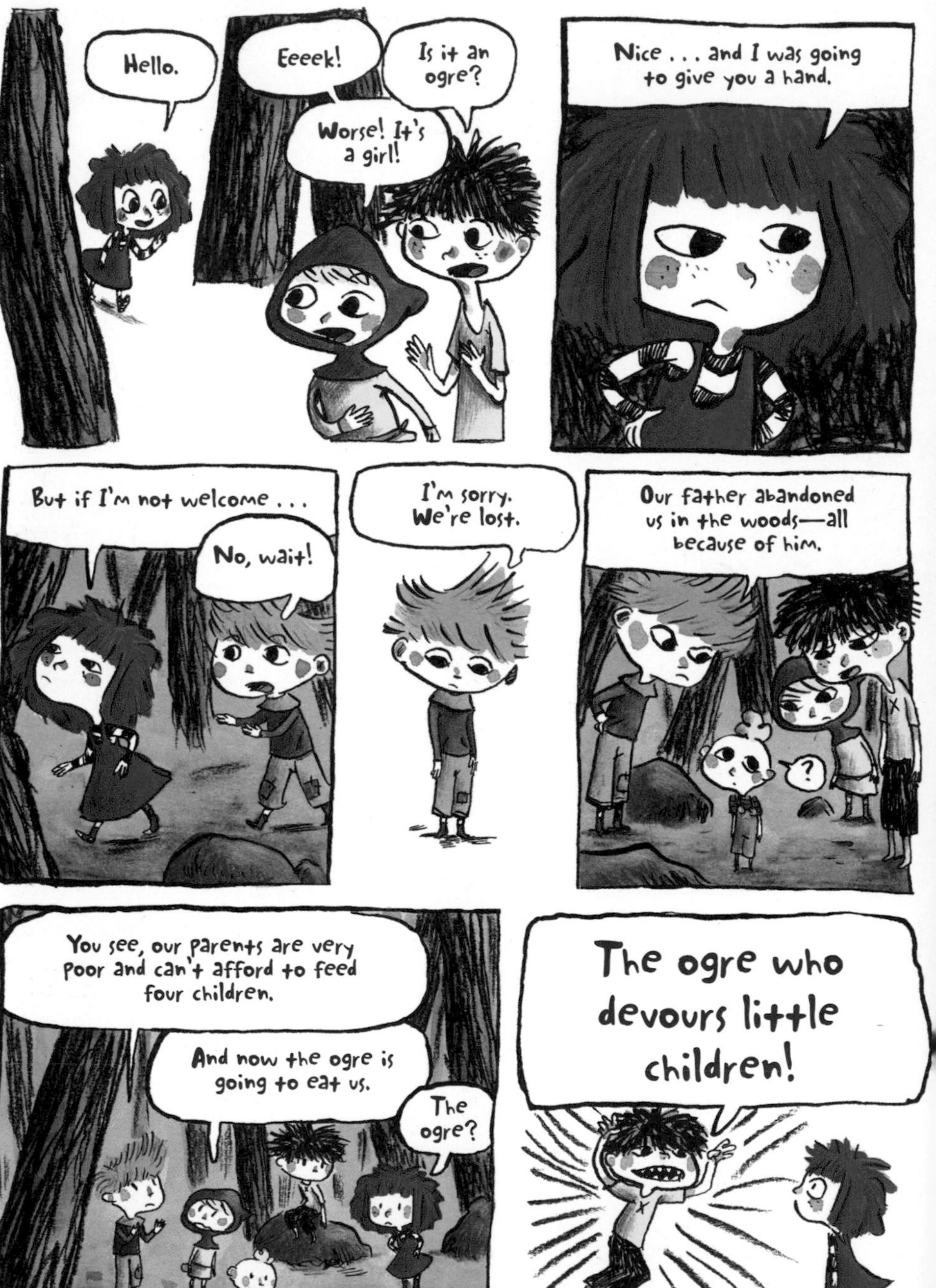

Hello.
Eeeek!
Is it an ogre?
Worse! It's a girl!
Nice . . . and I was going to give you a hand.
But if I'm not welcome . . .
No, wait!
I'm sorry. We're lost.
Our father abandoned us in the woods—all because of him.
?
You see, our parents are very poor and can't afford to feed four children.
And now the ogre is going to eat us.
The ogre?
The ogre who devours little children!

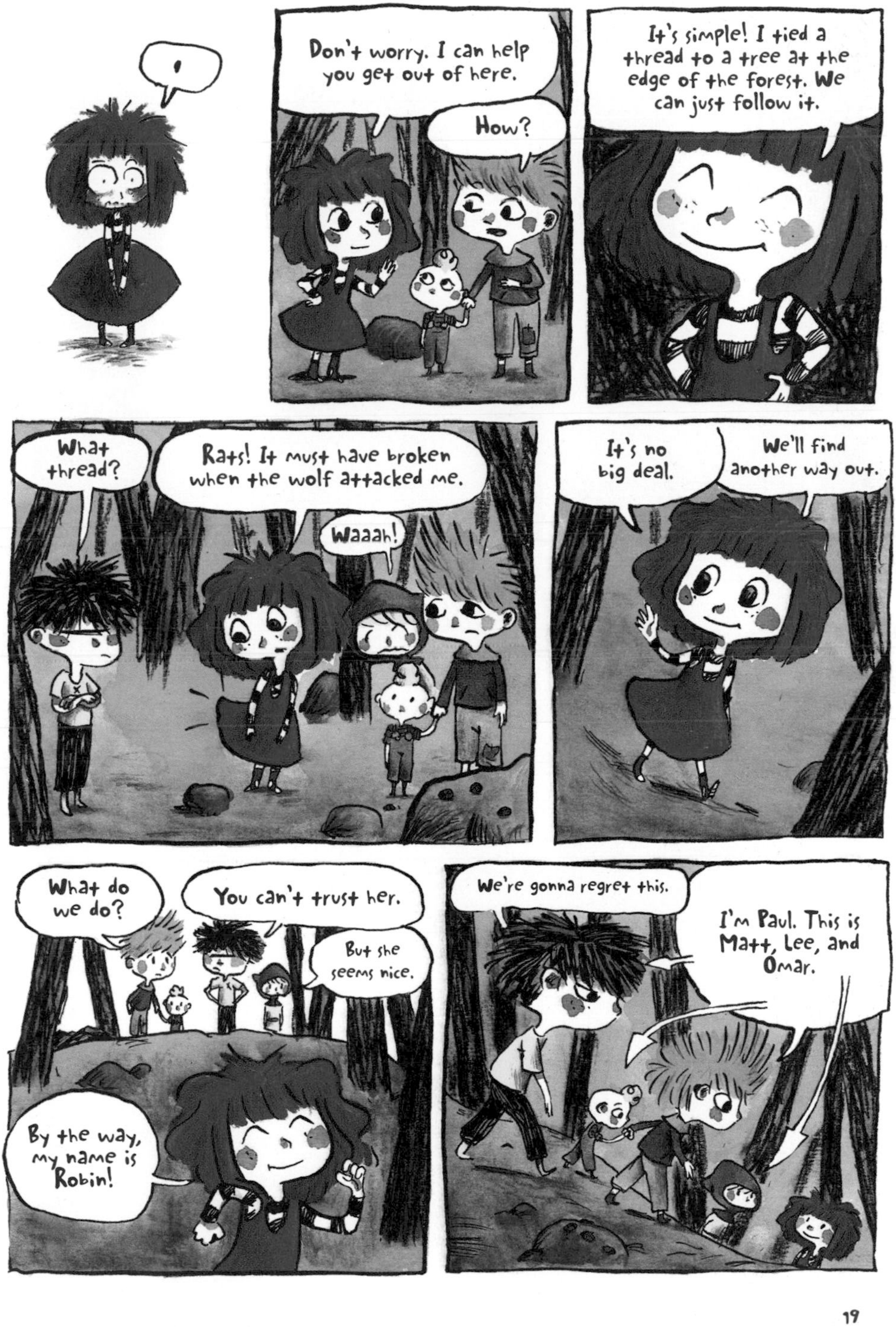
!
Don't worry. I can help you get out of here.
How?
It's simple! I tied a thread to a tree at the edge of the forest. We can just follow it.
What thread?
Rats! It must have broken when the wolf attacked me.
Waaah!
It's no big deal.
We'll find another way out.
What do we do?
You can't trust her.
But she seems nice.
By the way, my name is Robin!
We're gonna regret this.
I'm Paul. This is Matt, Lee, and Omar.

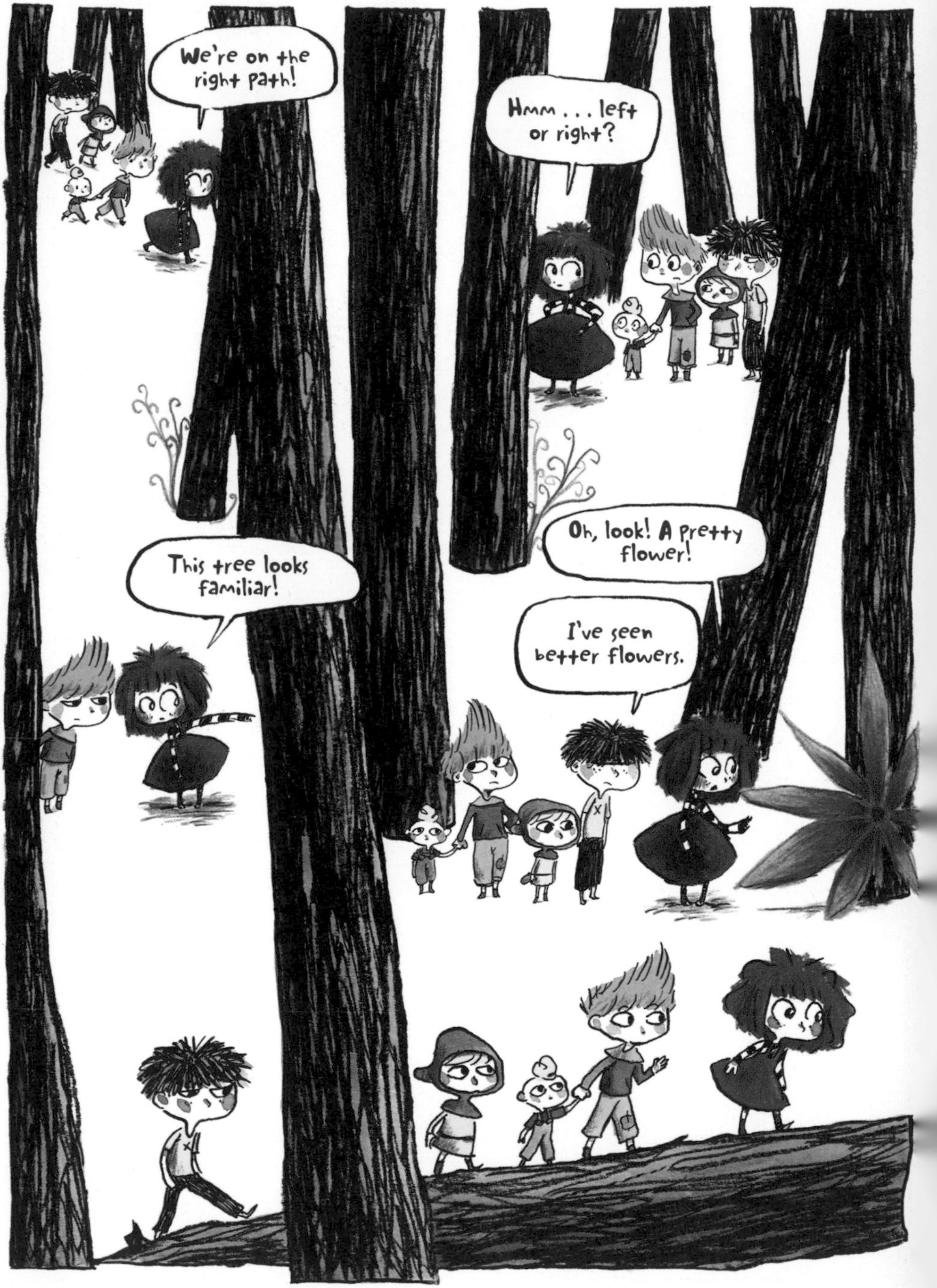
We're on the right path!
Hmm . . . left or right?
This tree looks familiar!
Oh, look! A pretty flower!
I've seen better flowers.

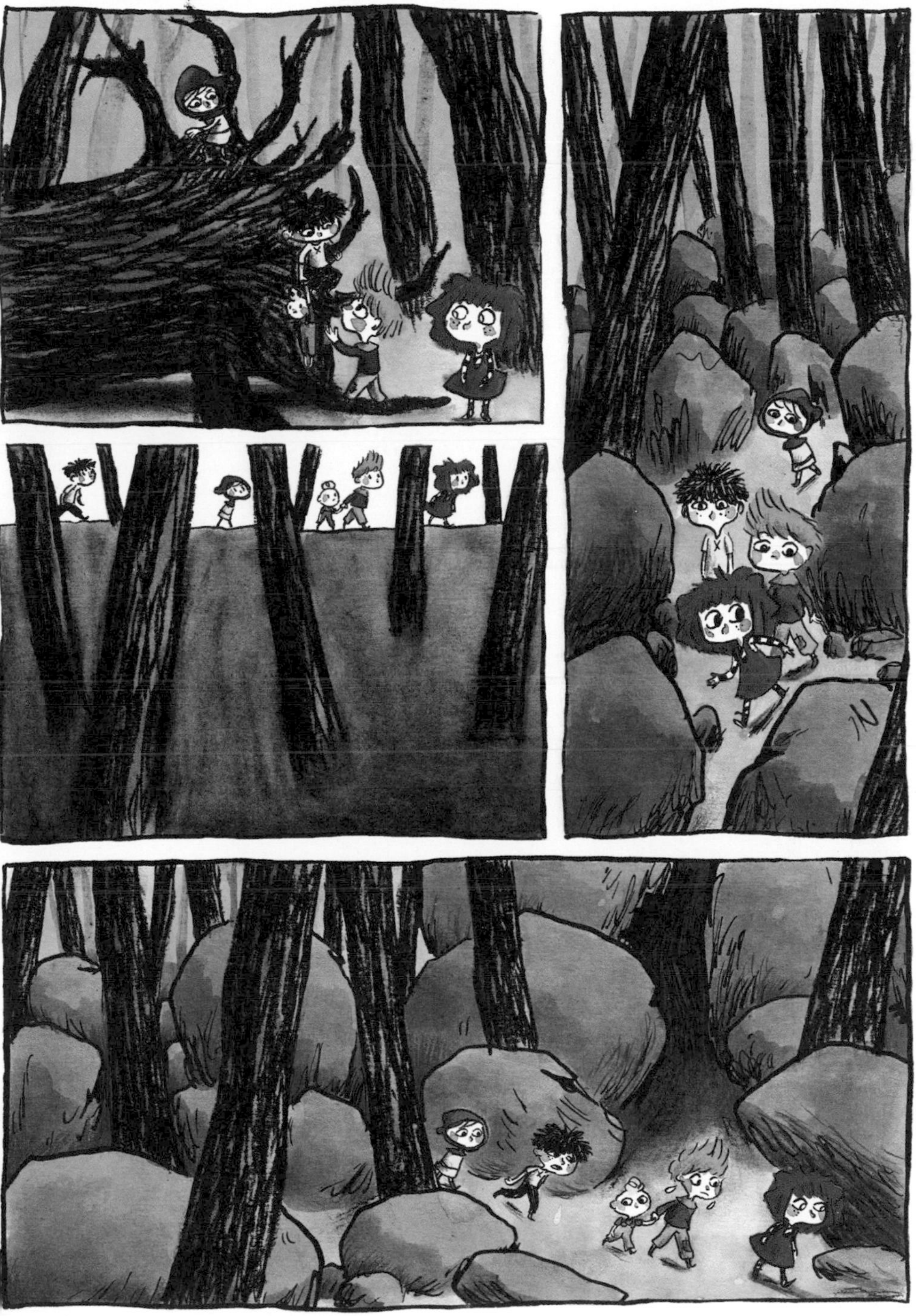

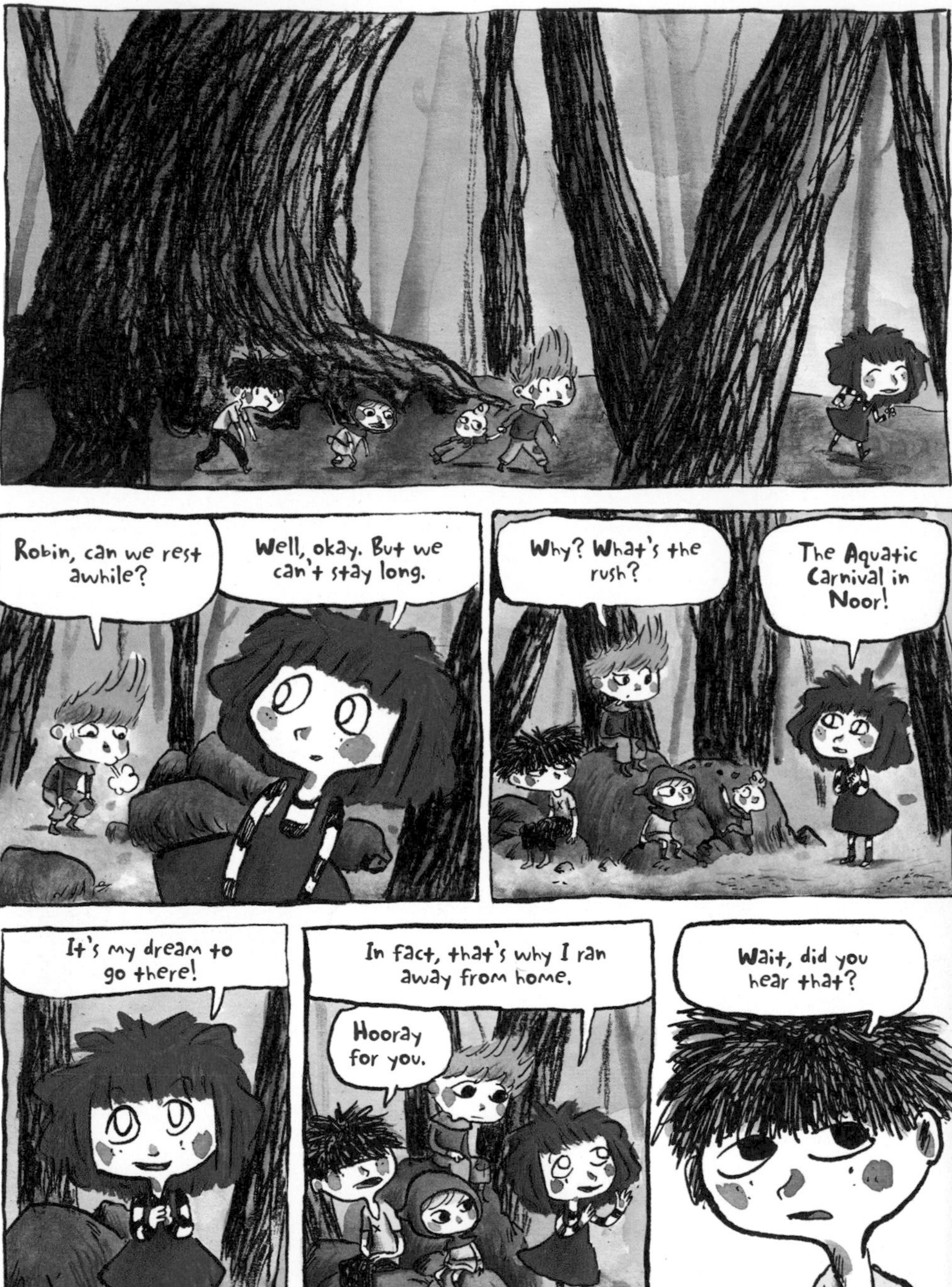
Robin, can we rest awhile?
Well, okay. But we can't stay long.
Why? What's the rush?
The Aquatic Carnival in Noor!
It's my dream to go there!
In fact, that's why I ran away from home.
Hooray for you.
Wait, did you hear that?

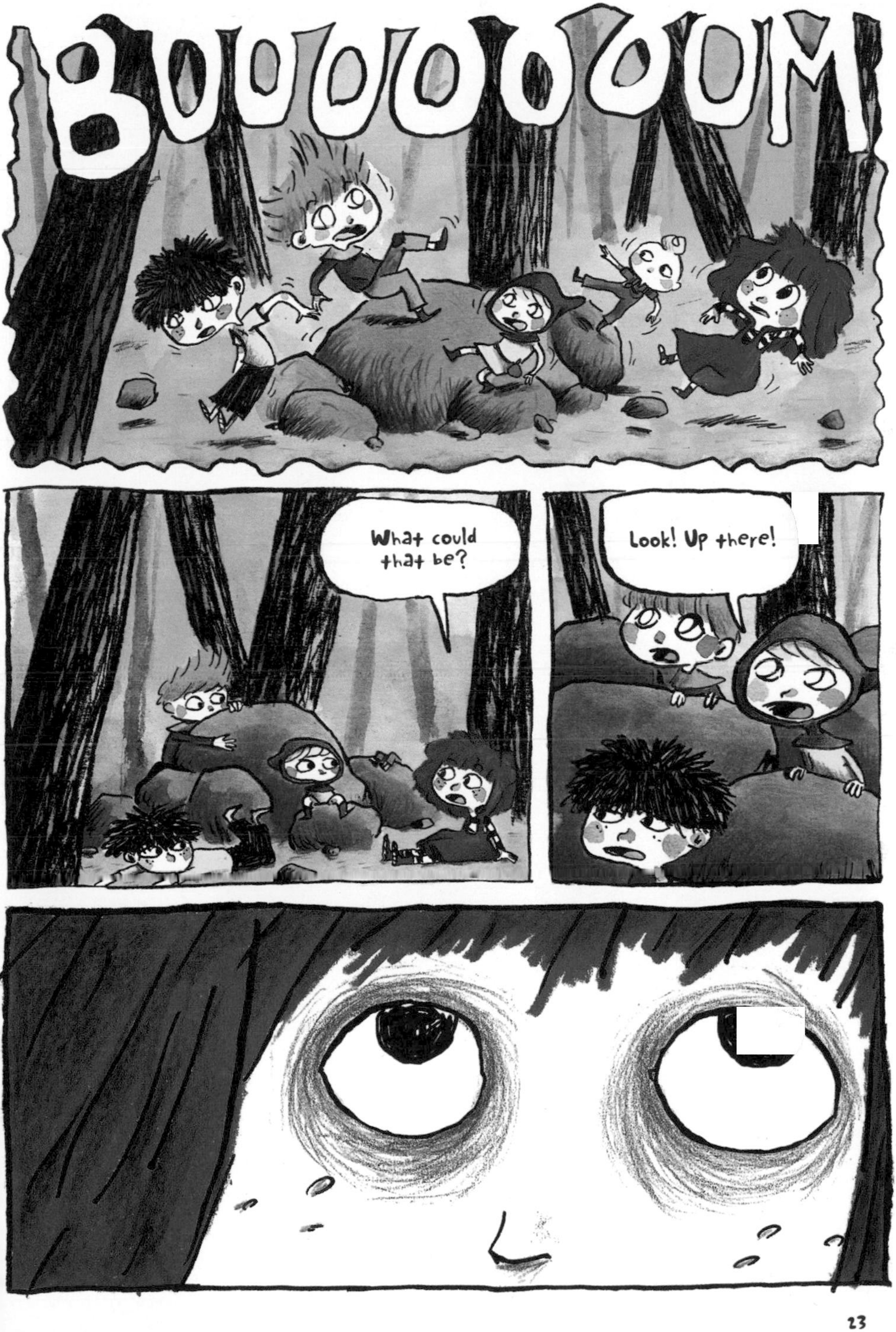
BOOOOOOOOM!
What could that be?
Look! Up there!

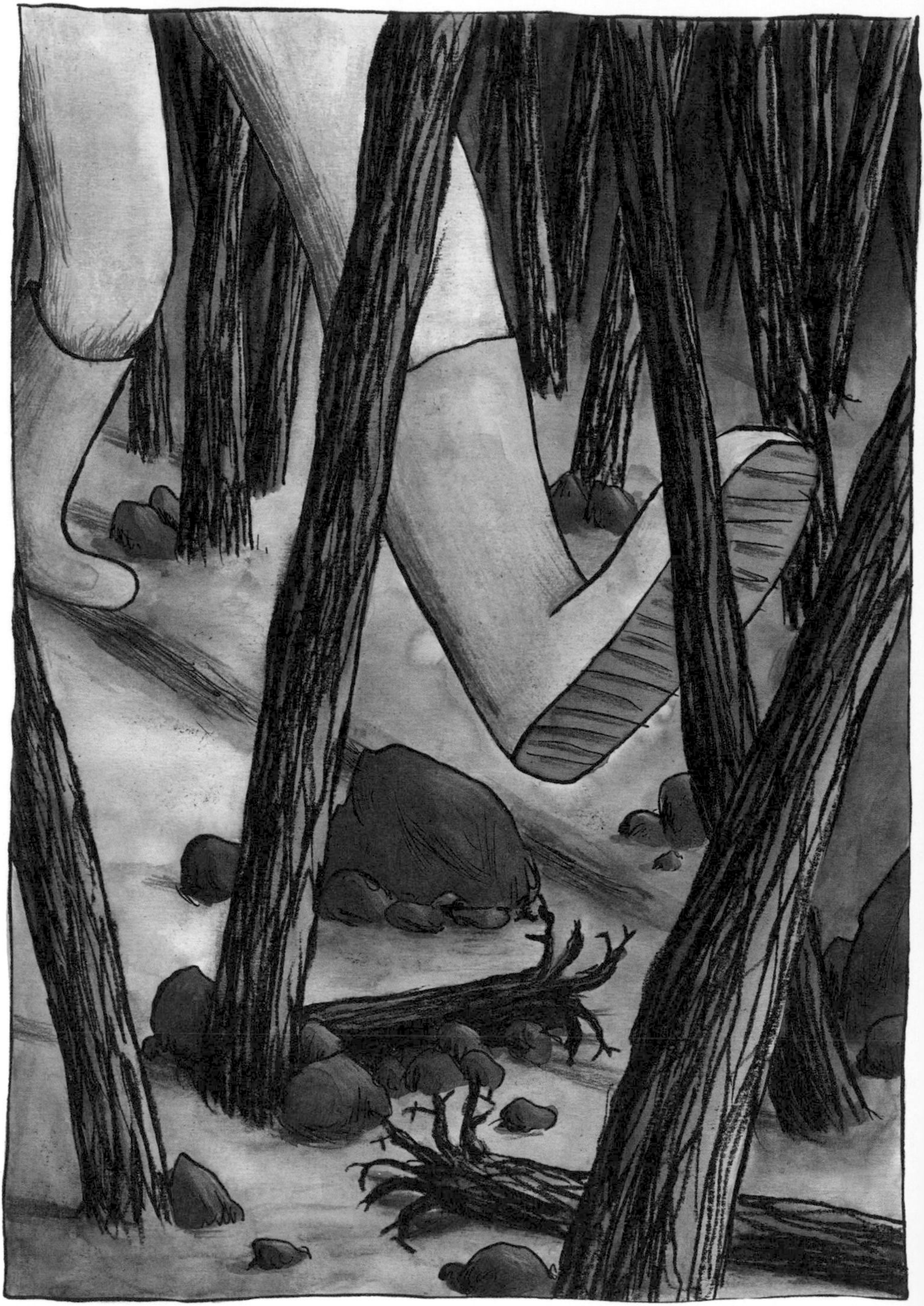

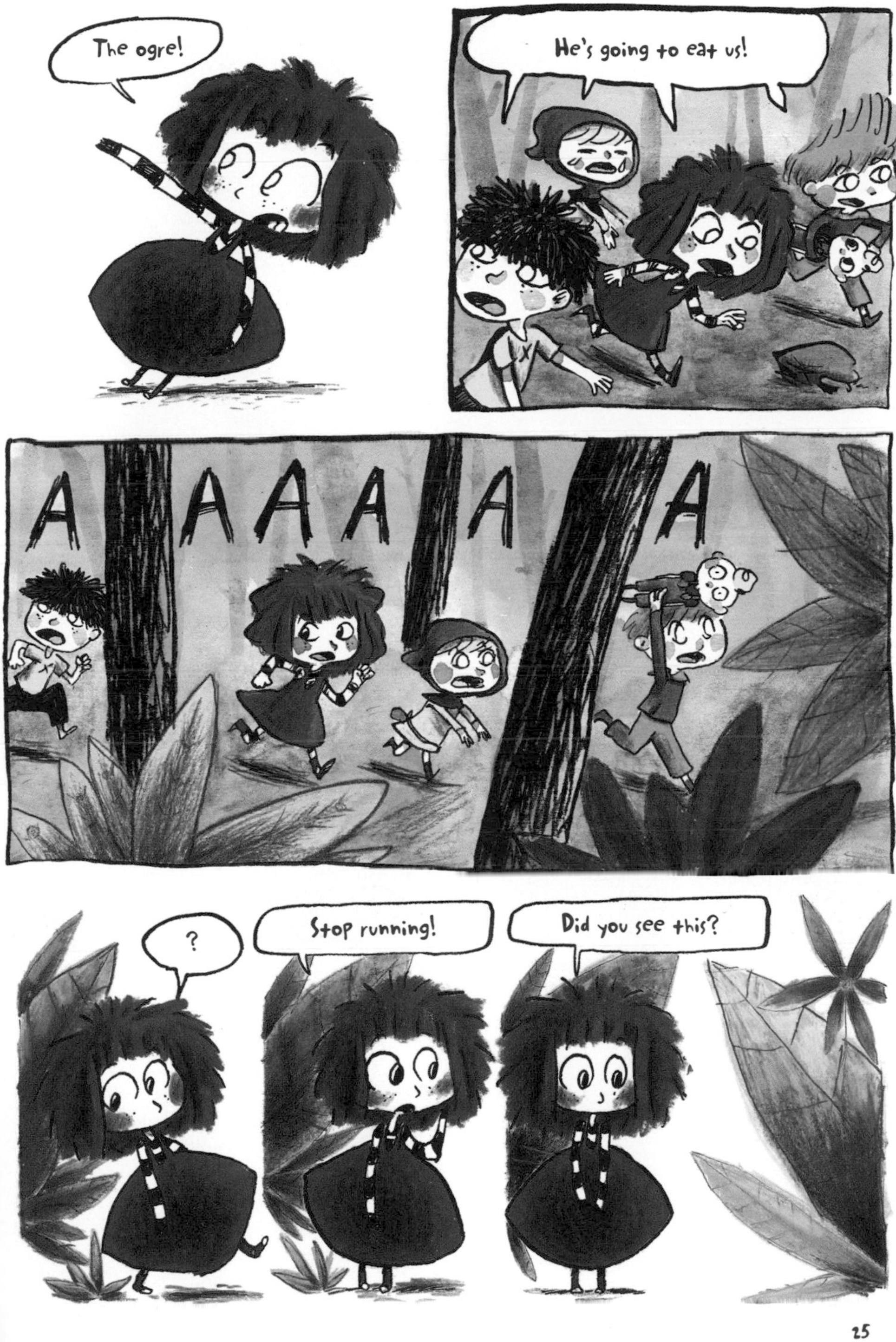
The ogre!
He's going to eat us!
A A A A A A
?
Stop running!
Did you see this?

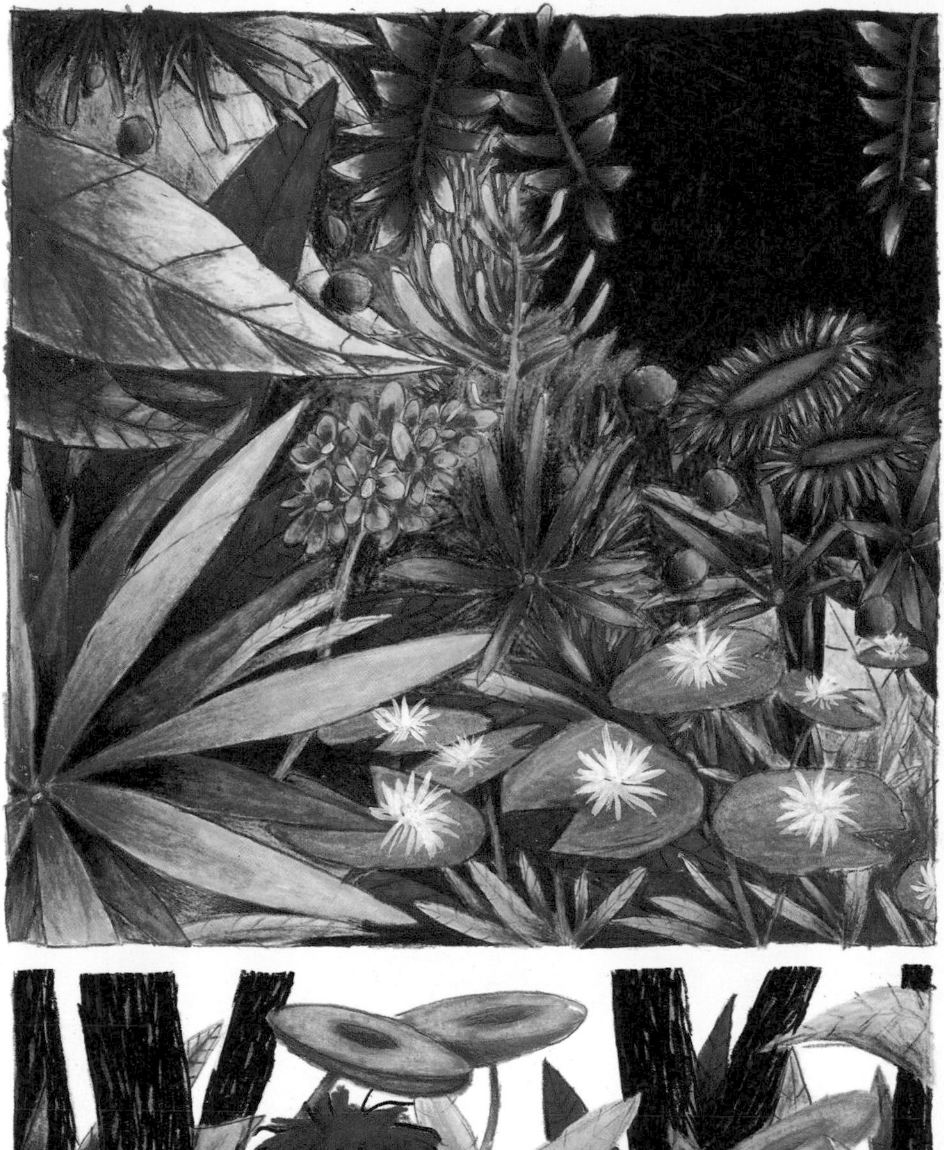

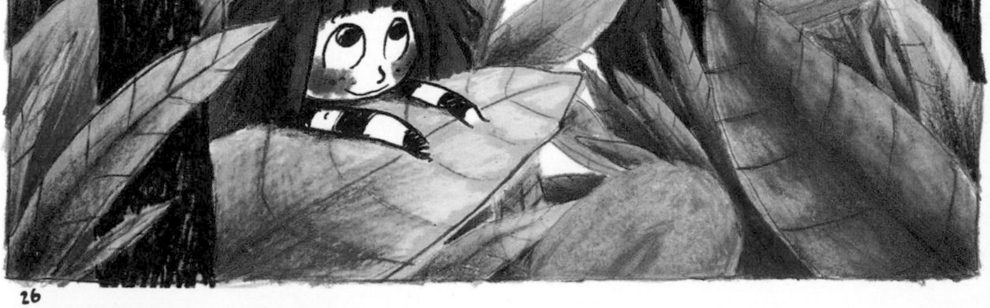

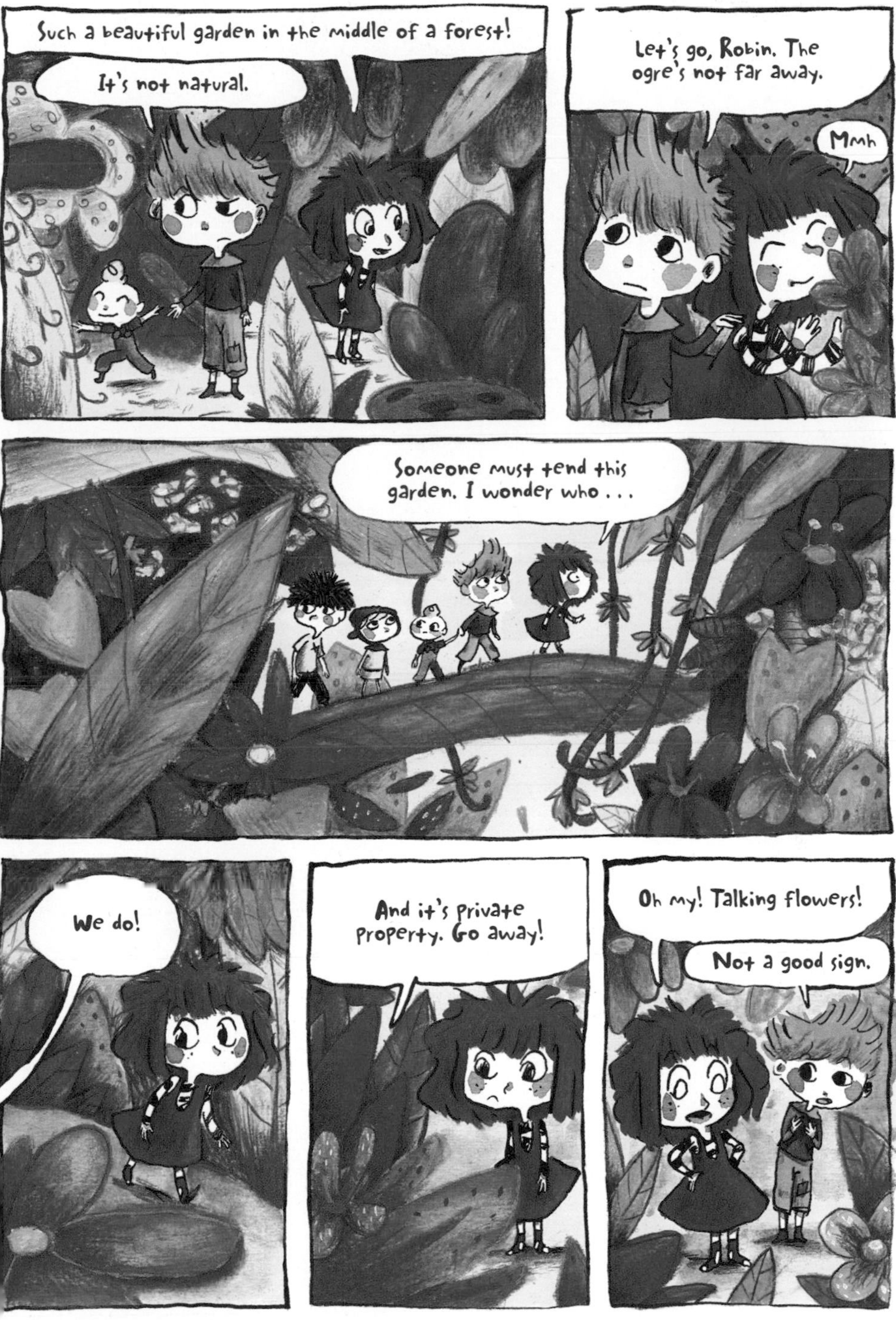

Such a beautiful garden in the middle of a forest!
It's not natural.
Let's go, Robin. The ogre's not far away.
Mmh
Someone must tend this garden. I wonder who . . .
We do!
And it's private property. Go away!
Oh my! Talking flowers!
Not a good sign.

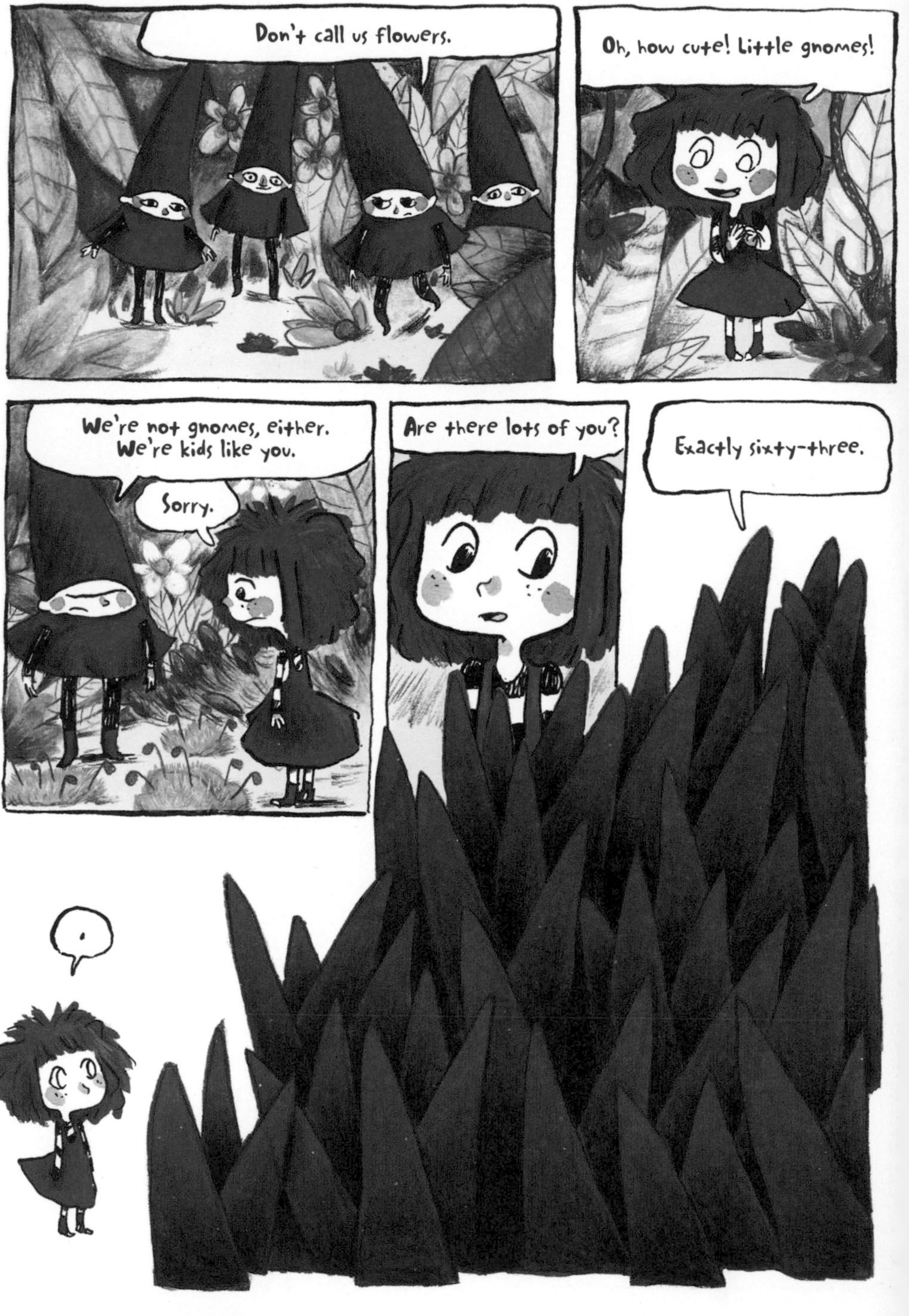

Don't call us flowers.
Oh, how cute! Little gnomes!
We're not gnomes, either. We're kids like you.
Sorry.
Are there lots of you?
Exactly sixty-three.

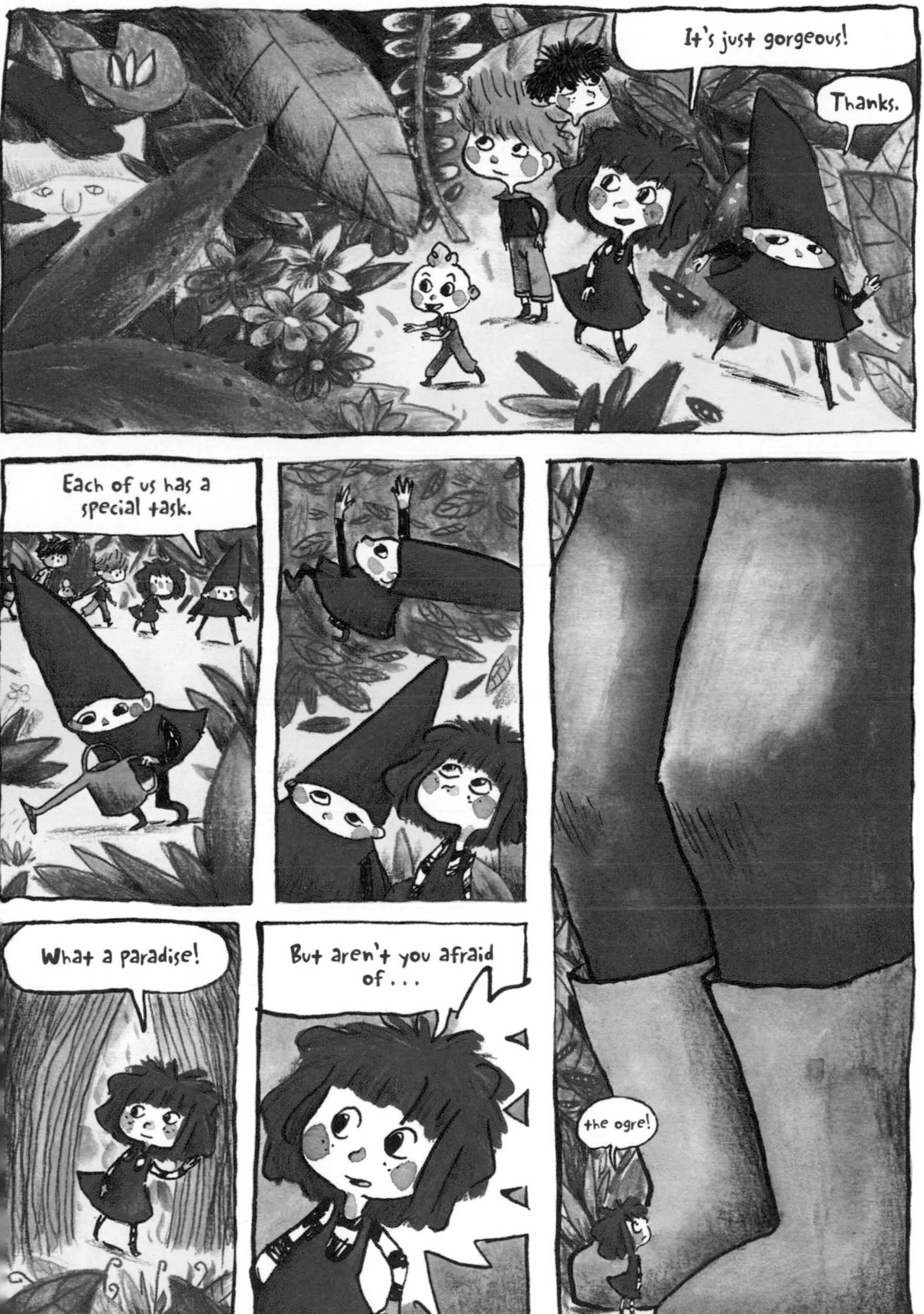
It's just gorgeous!
Thanks.
Each of us has a special task.
What a paradise!
But aren't you afraid of . . .
the ogre!

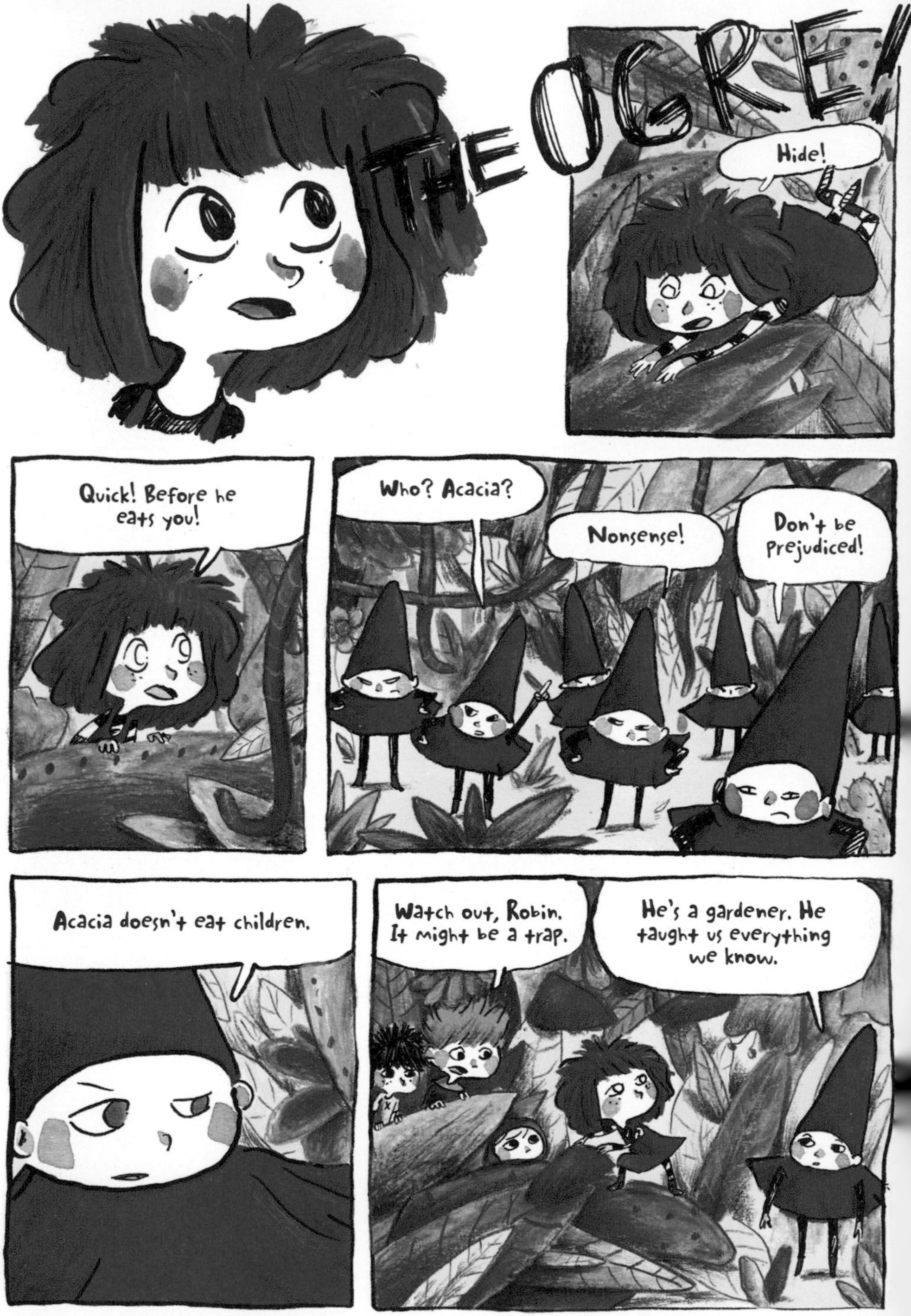
THE OGRE!
Hide!
Quick! Before he eats you!
Who? Acacia?
Nonsense!
Don't be prejudiced!
Acacia doesn't eat children.
Watch out, Robin. It might be a trap.
He's a gardener. He taught us everything we know.

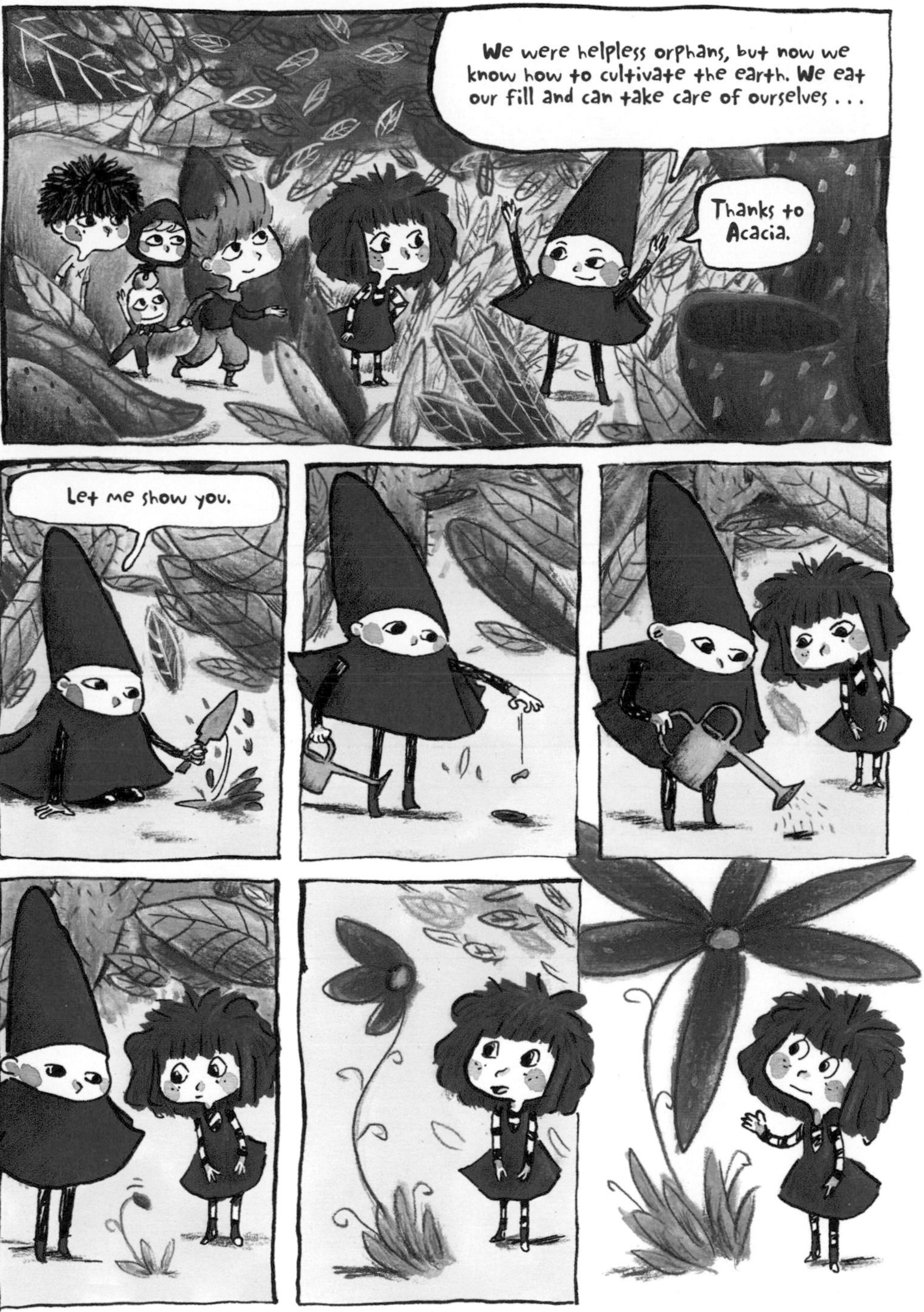
We were helpless orphans, but now we know how to cultivate the earth. We eat our fill and can take care of ourselves . . .
Thanks to Acacia.
Let me show you.

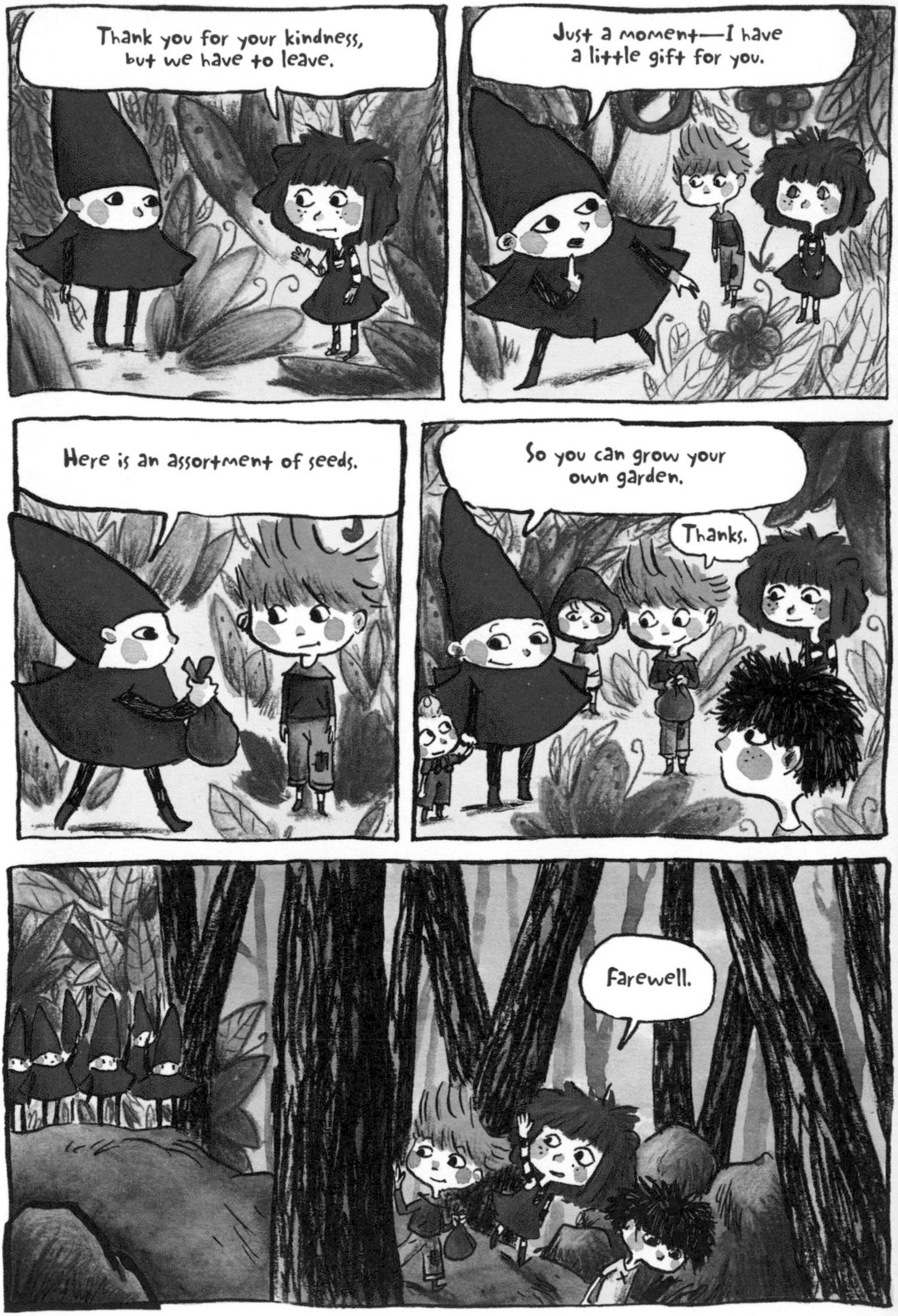
Thank you for your kindness, but we have to leave.
Just a moment—I have a little gift for you.
Here is an assortment of seeds.
So you can grow your own garden.
Thanks.
Farewell.

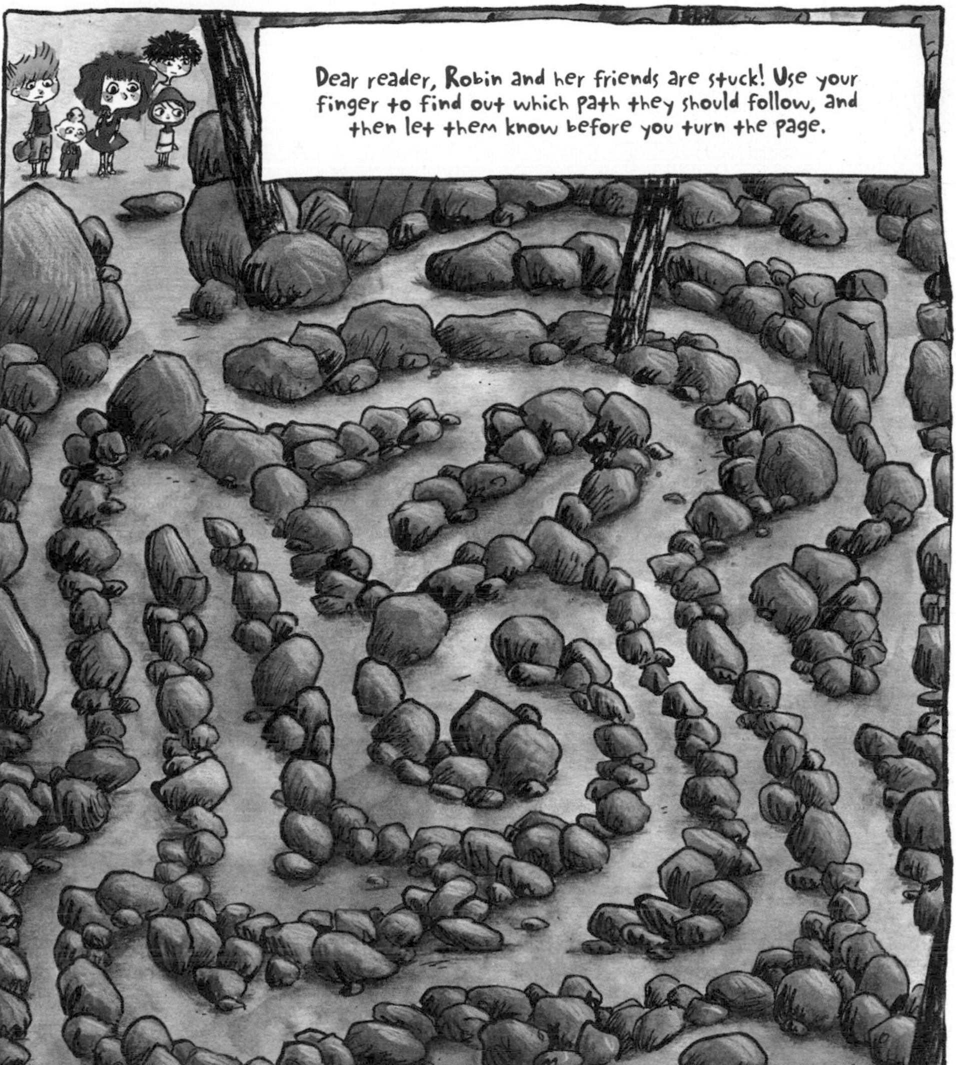
Dear reader, Robin and her friends are stuck! Use your finger to find out which path they should follow, and then let them know before you turn the page.
NOOR

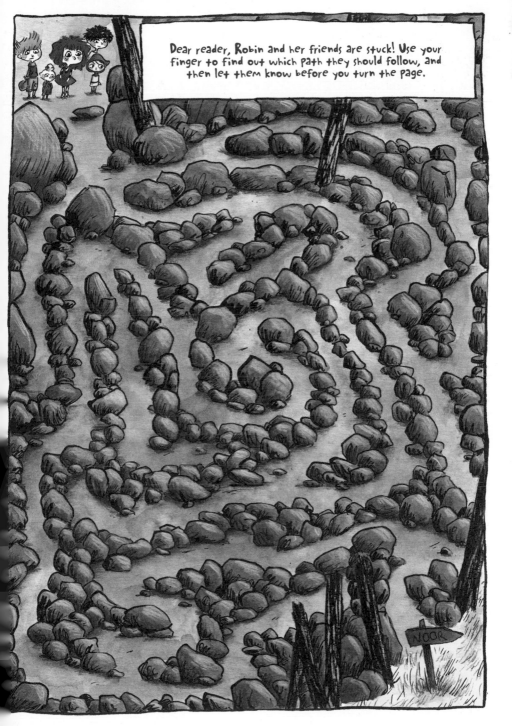

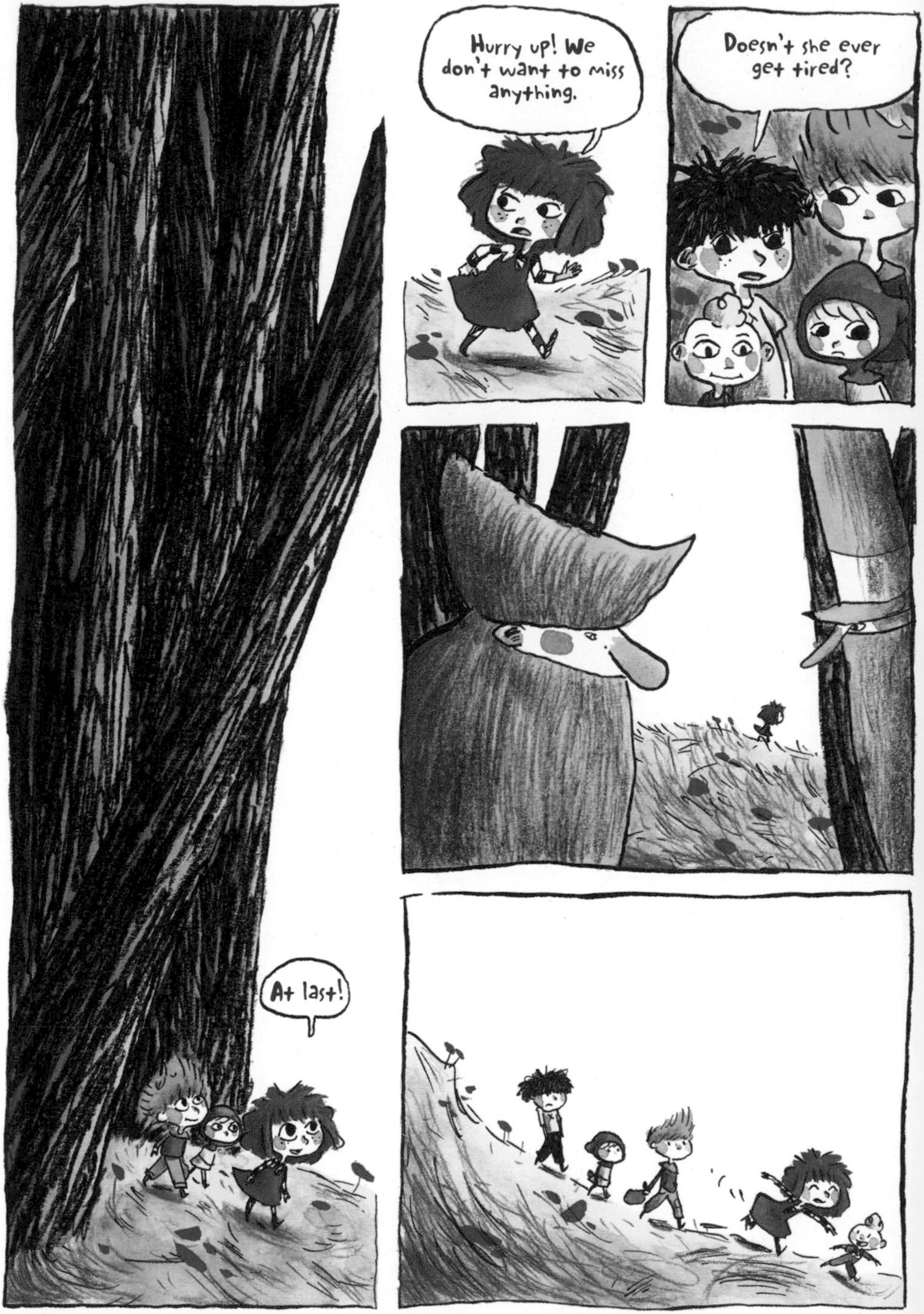

Hurry up! We don't want to miss anything.
Doesn't she ever get tired?
At last!

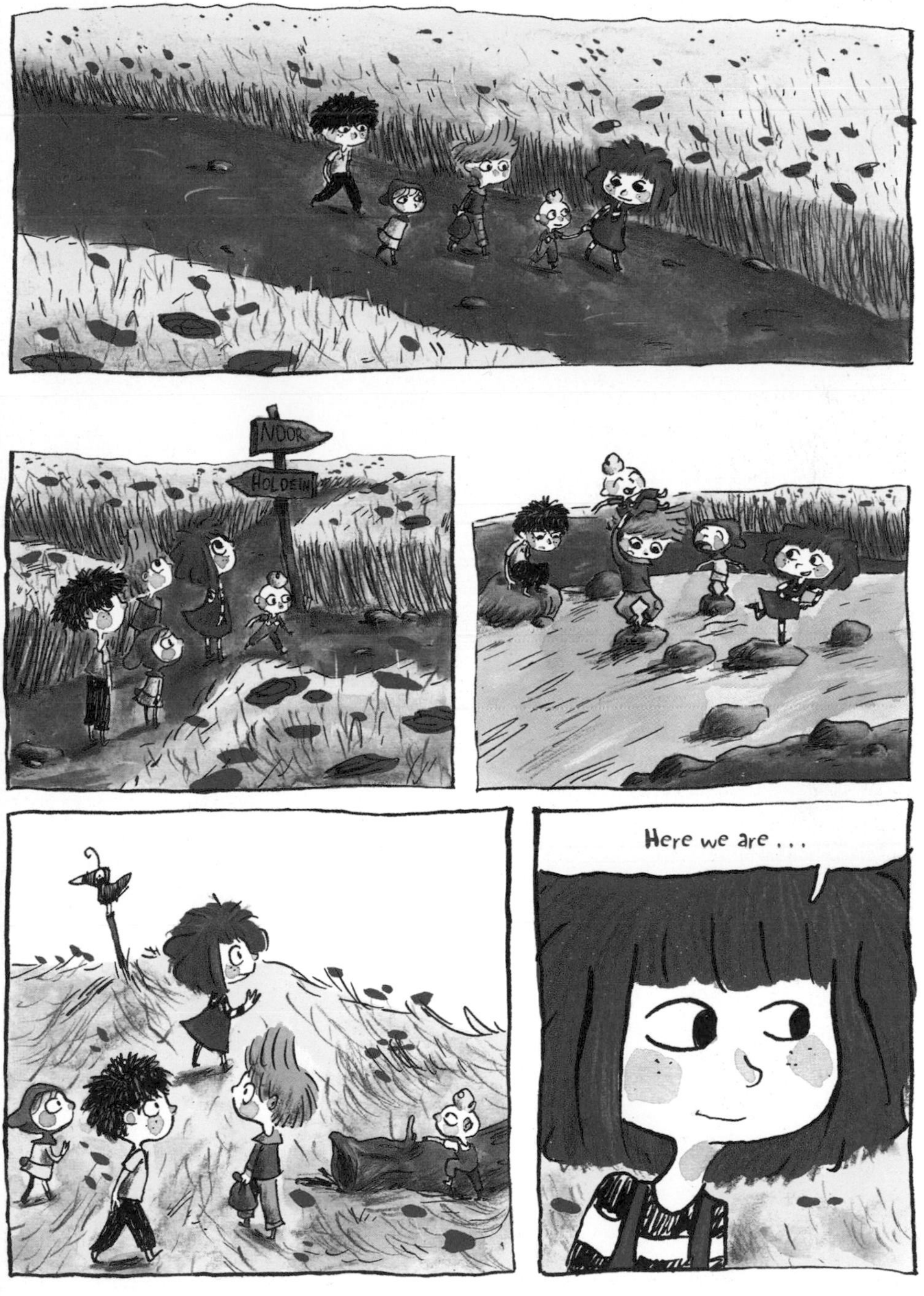
NOOR
HOLDEIN
Here we are . . .

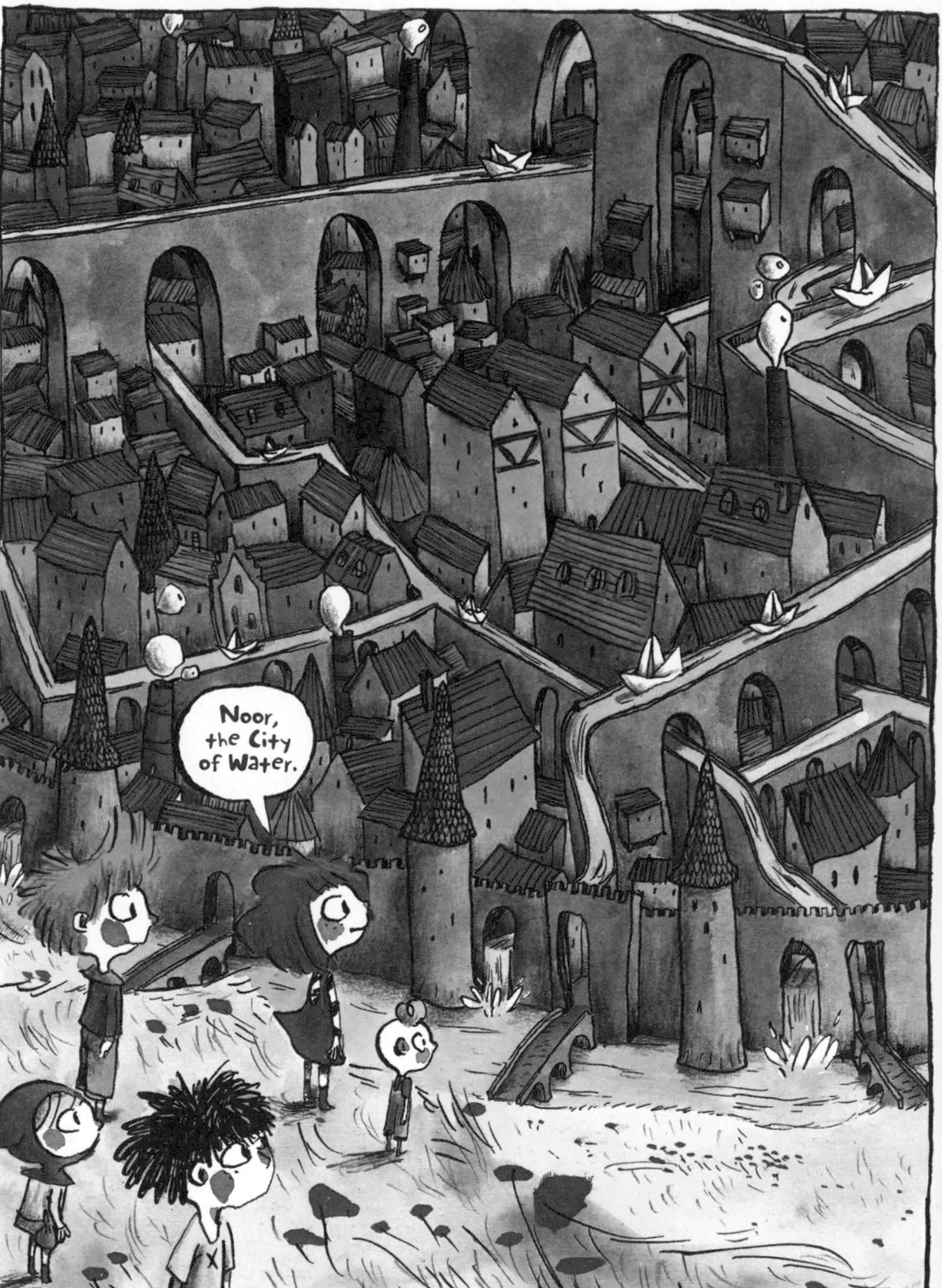
Noor, the City of Water.

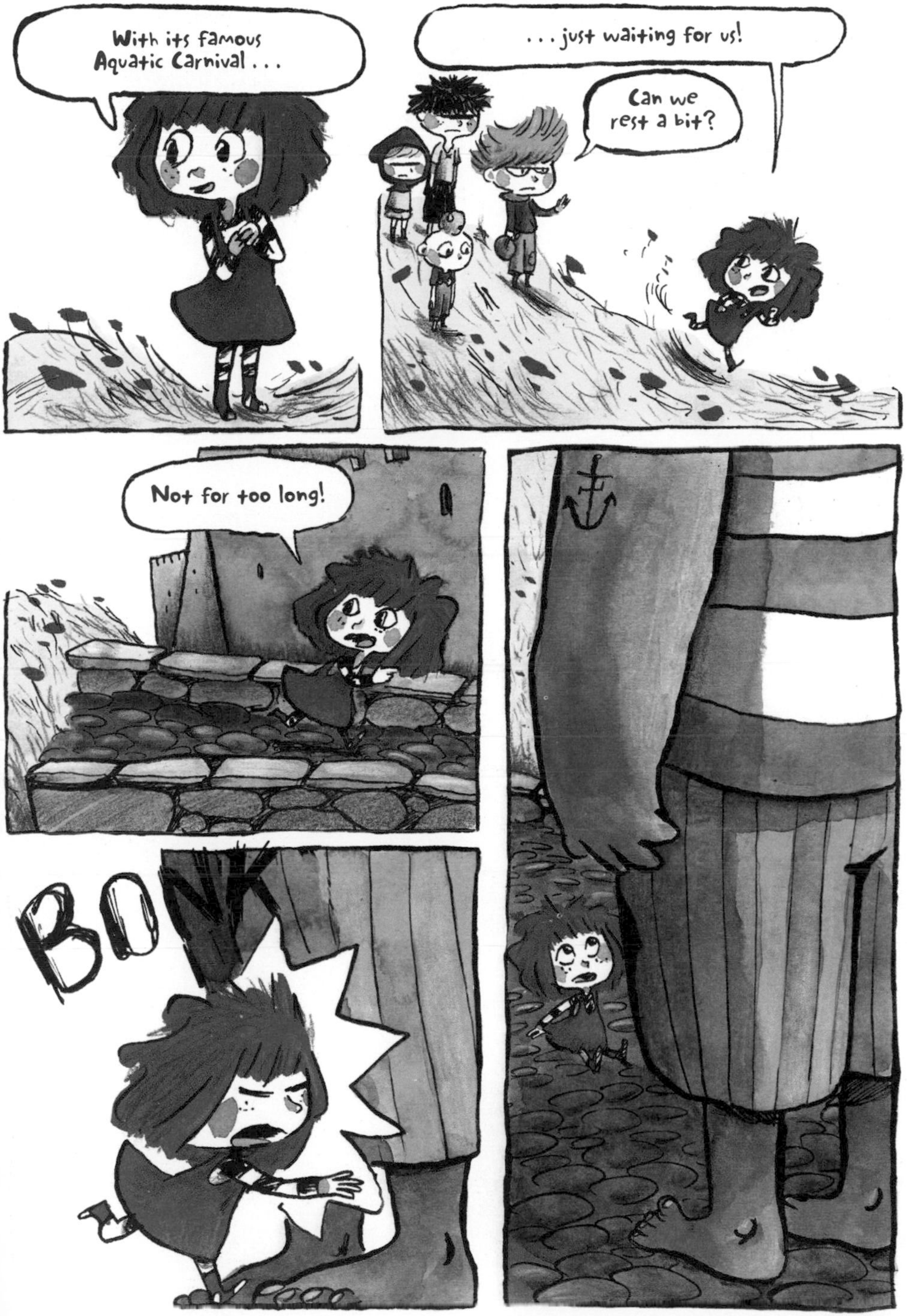
With its famous Aquatic Carnival . . .
. . . just waiting for us!
Can we rest a bit?
Not for too long!
BONK

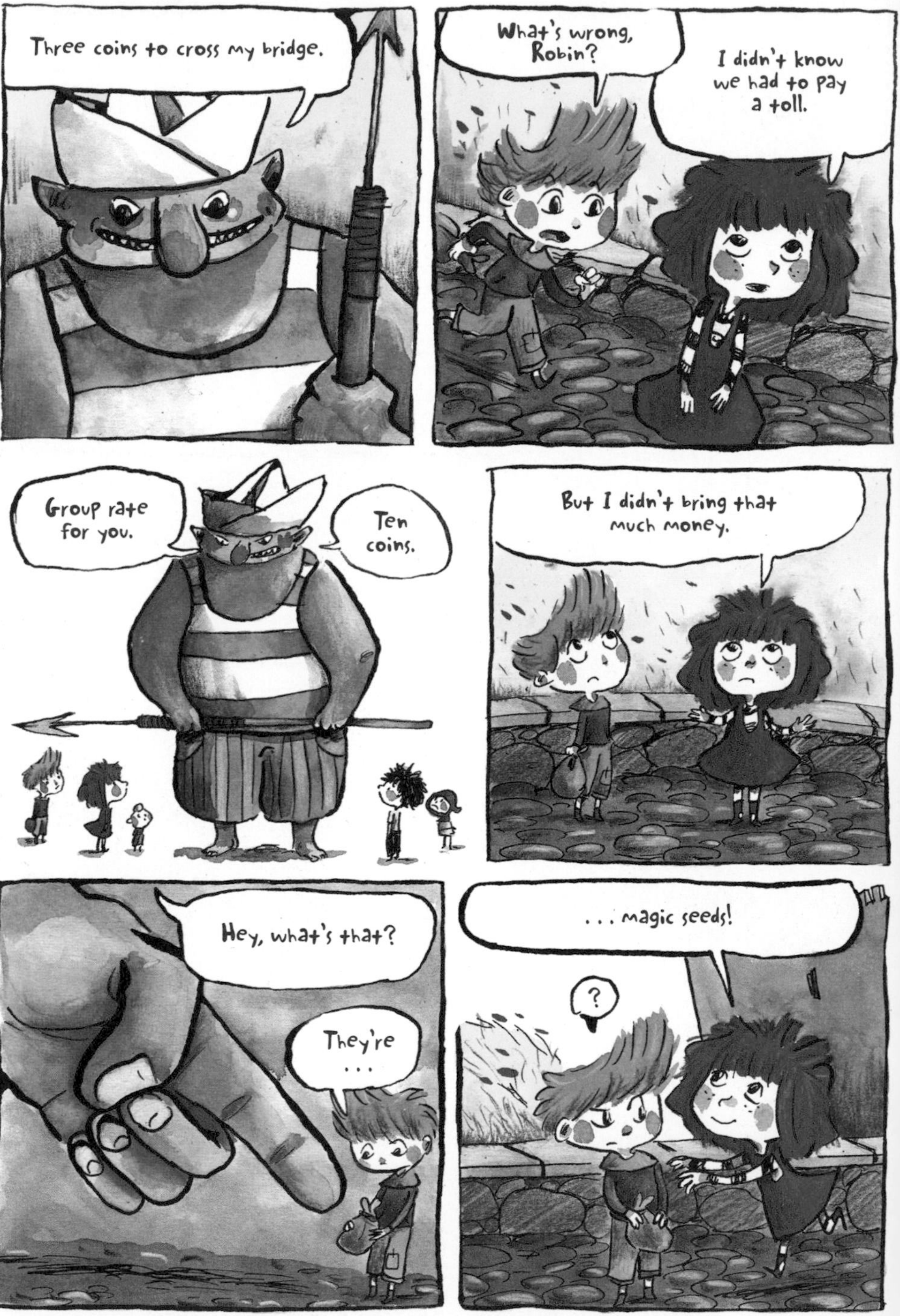
Three coins to cross my bridge.
What's wrong, Robin?
I didn't know we had to pay a toll.
Group rate for you.
Ten coins.
But I didn't bring that much money.
Hey, what's that?
They're . . .
?
. . . magic seeds!

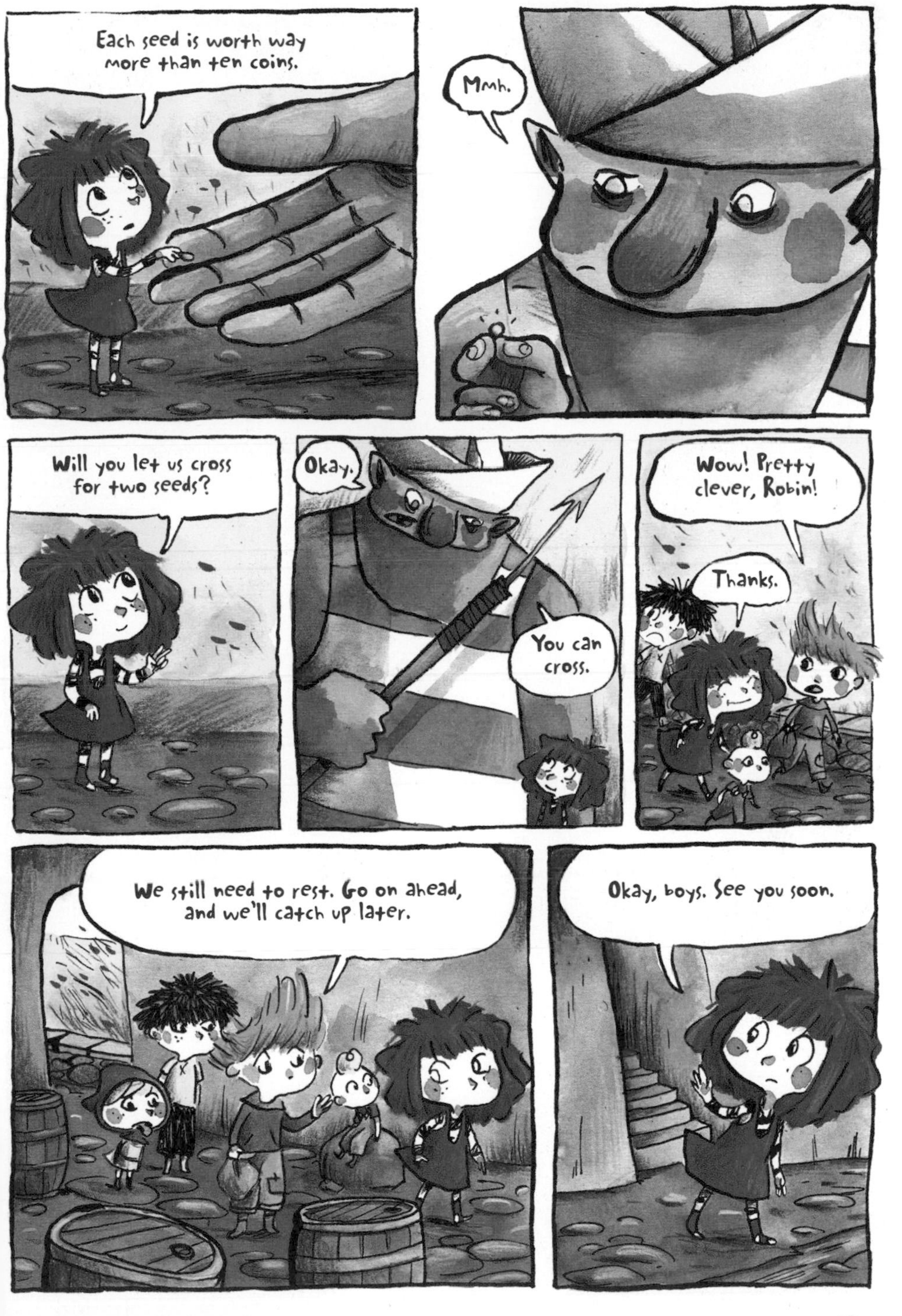

Each seed is worth way more than ten coins.
Mmh.
Will you let us cross for two seeds?
Okay.
You can cross.
Wow! Pretty clever, Robin!
Thanks.
We still need to rest. Go on ahead, and we'll catch up later.
Okay, boys. See you soon.

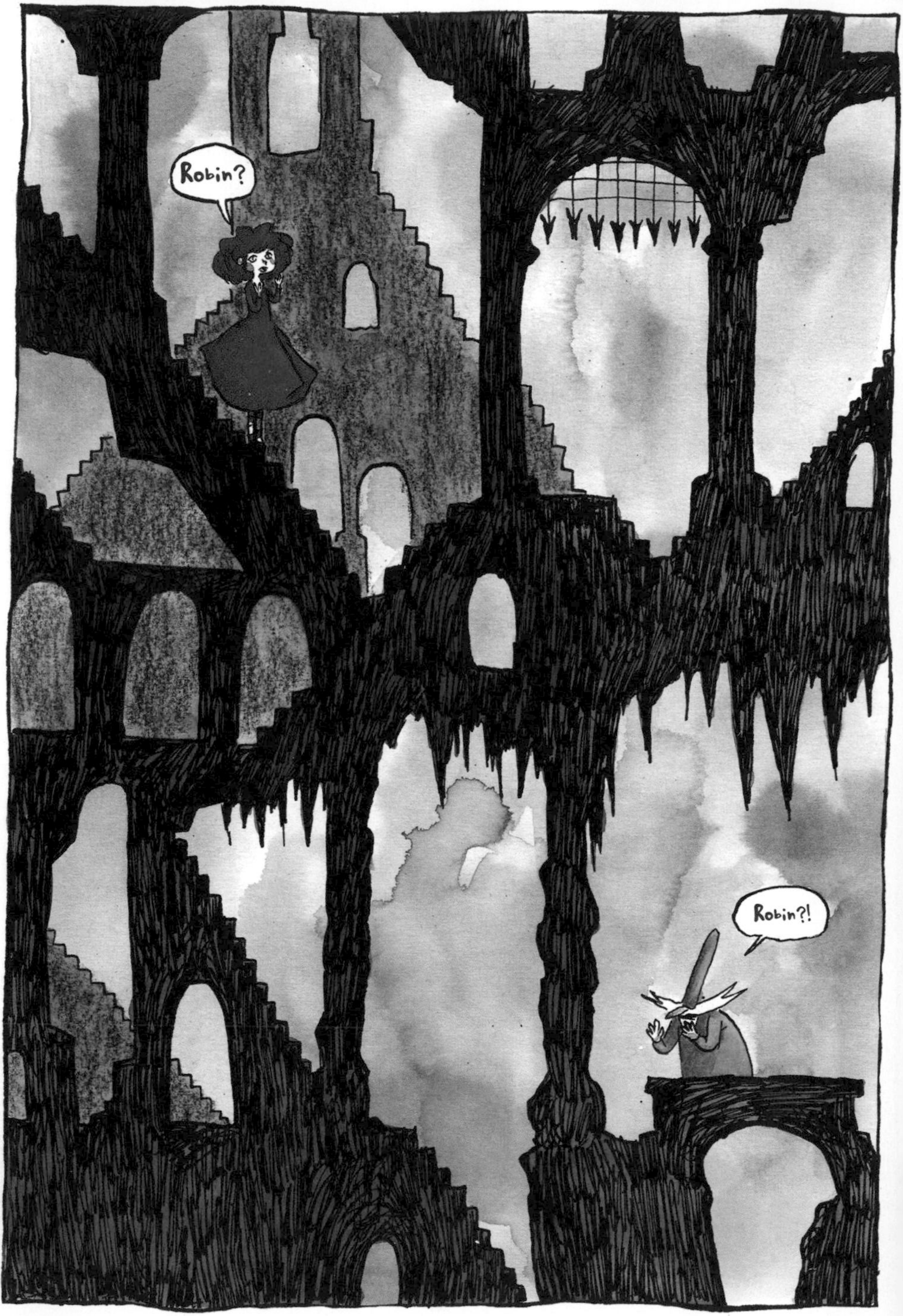
Robin?
Robin?!

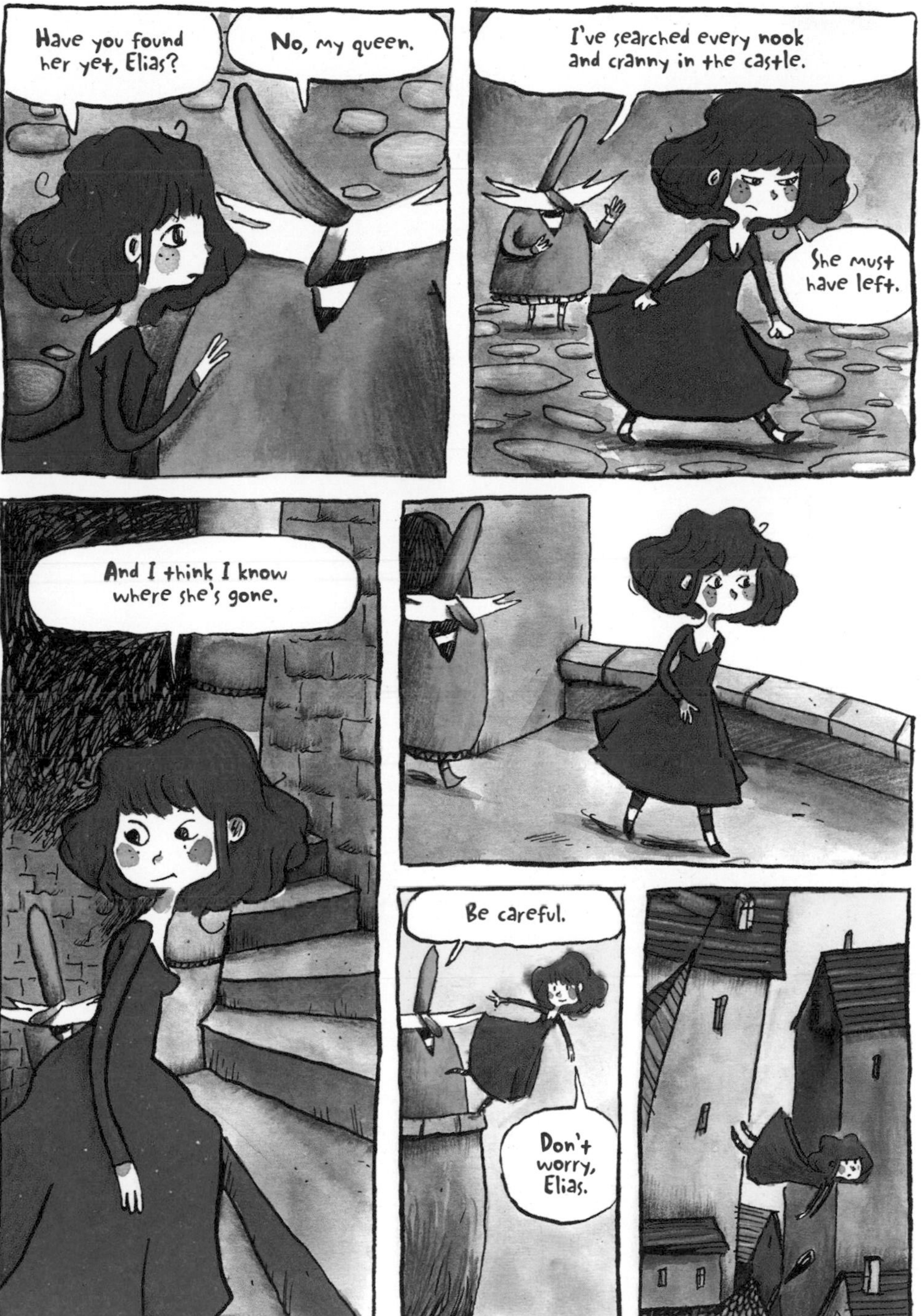
Have you found her yet, Elias?
No, my queen.
I've searched every nook and cranny in the castle.
She must have left.
And I think I know where she's gone.
Be careful.
Don't worry, Elias.

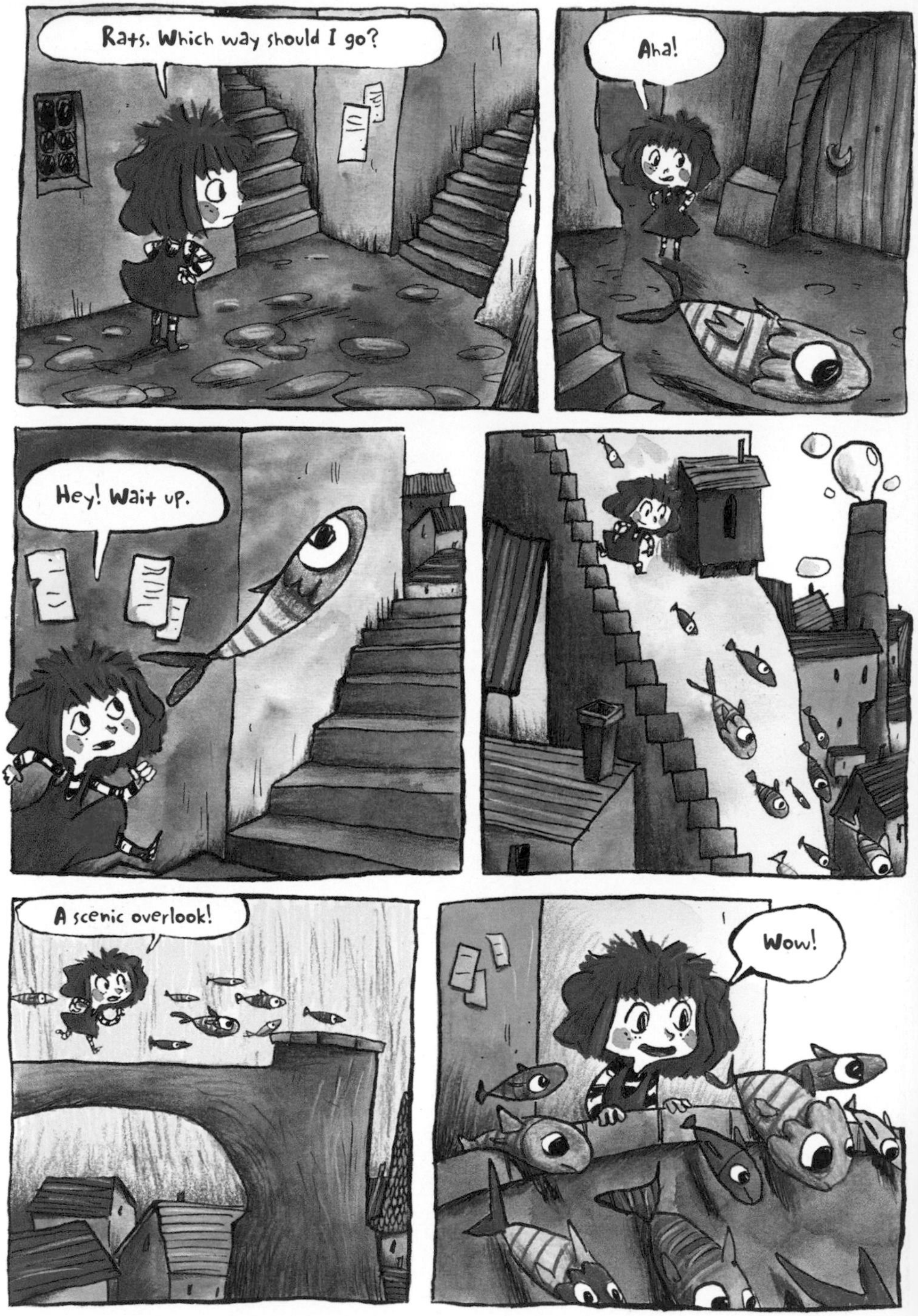
Rats. Which way should I go?
Aha!
Hey! Wait up.
A scenic overlook!
Wow!

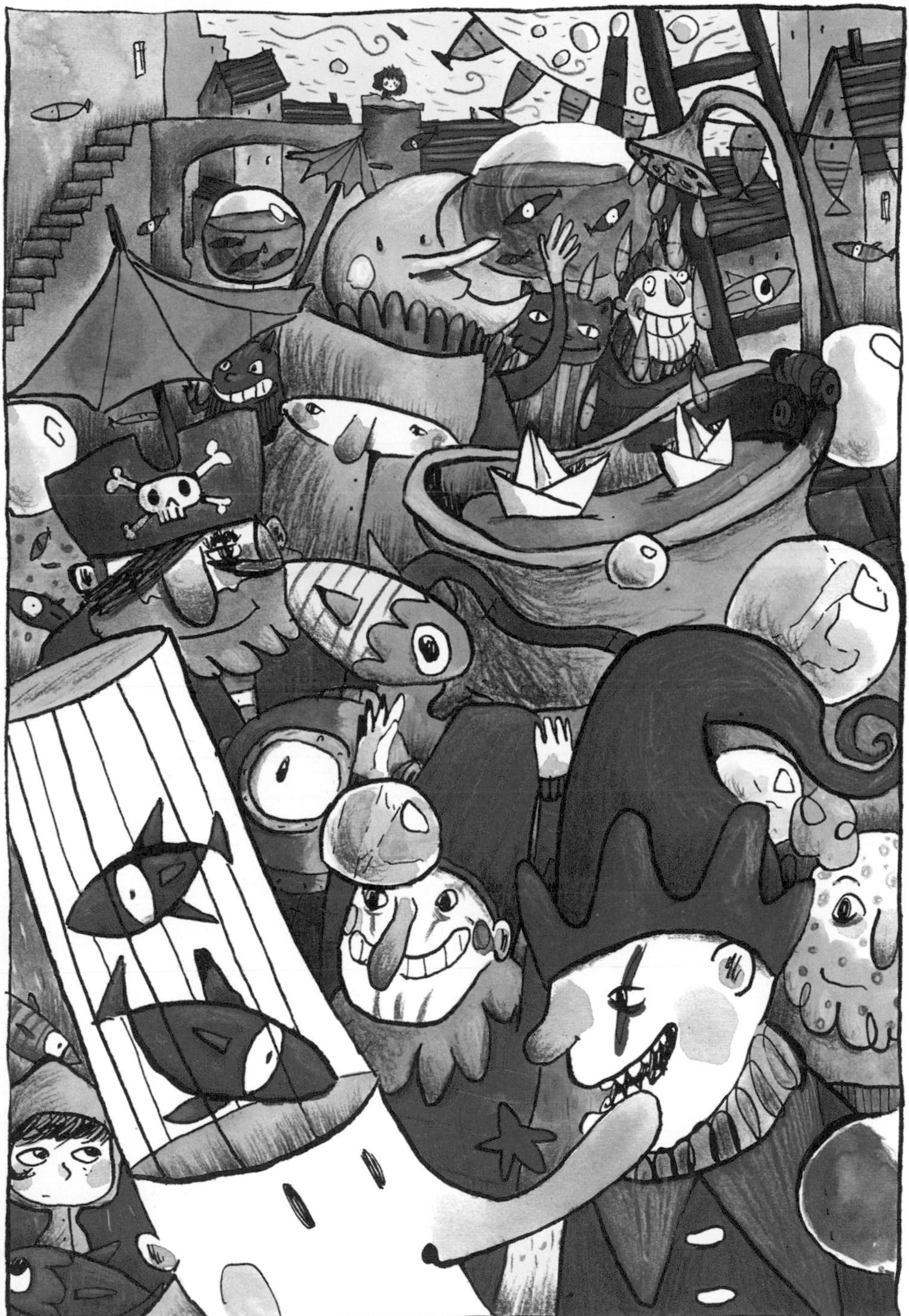

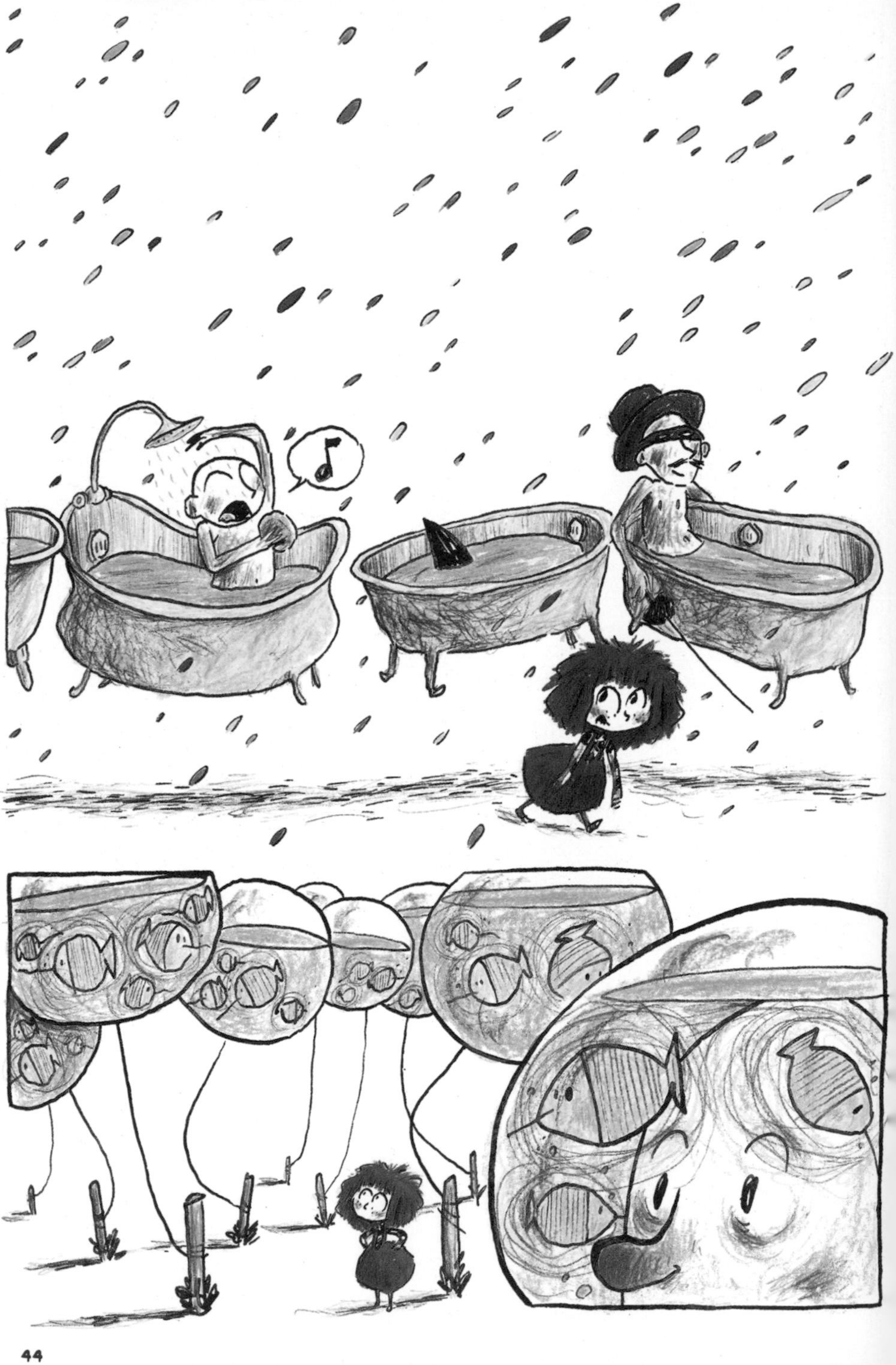

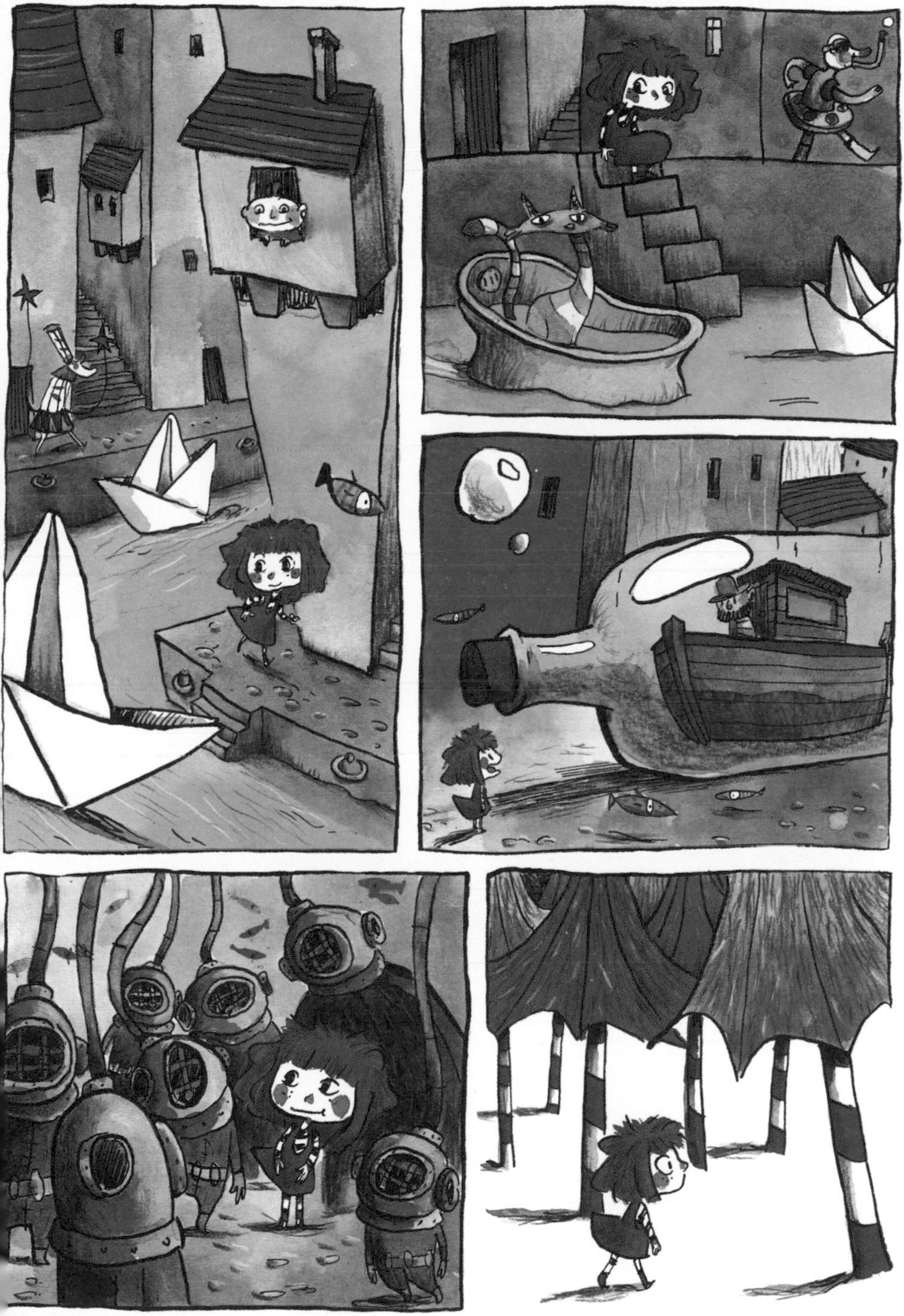

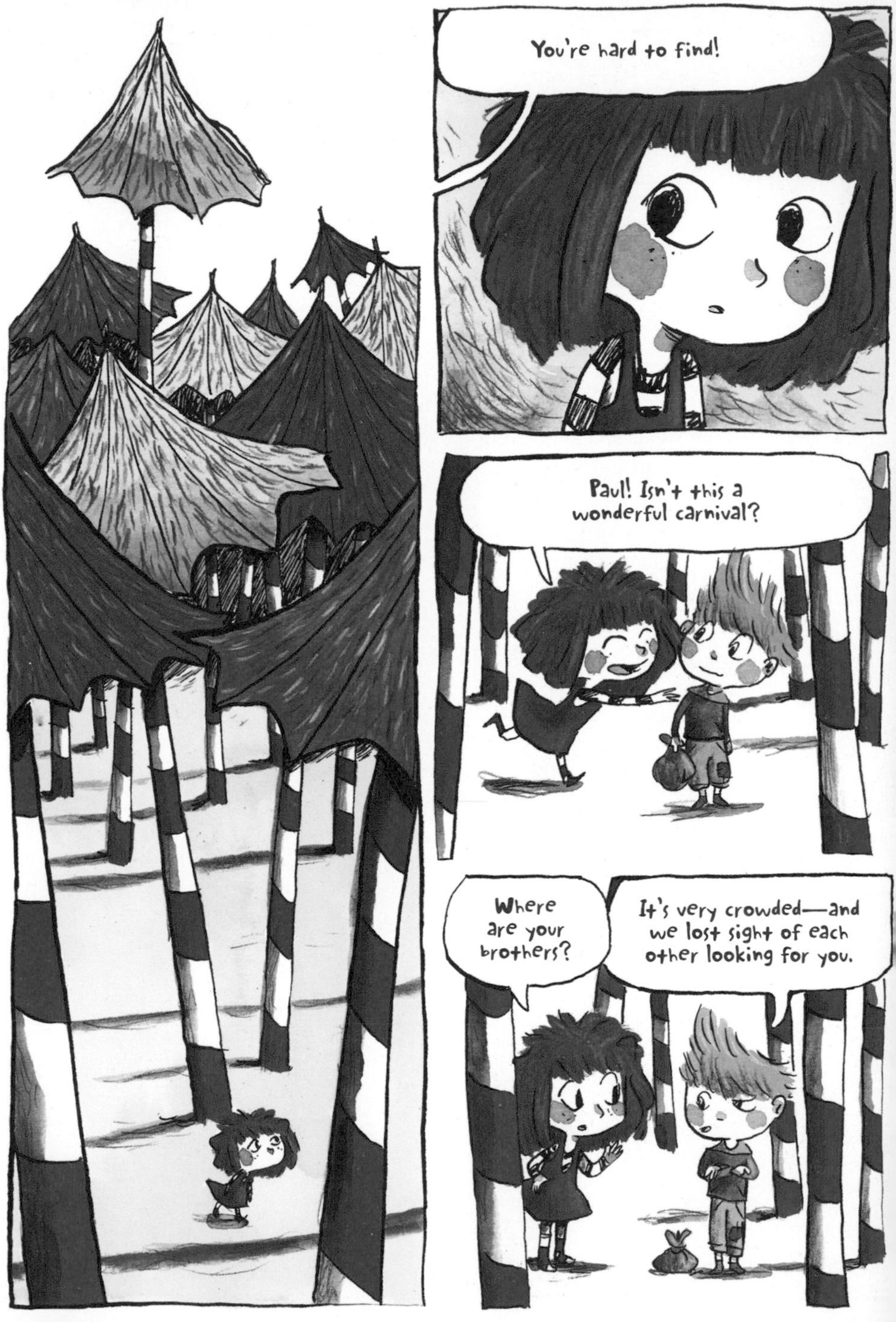
You're hard to find!
Paul! Isn't this a wonderful carnival?
Where are your brothers?
It's very crowded—and we lost sight of each other looking for you.

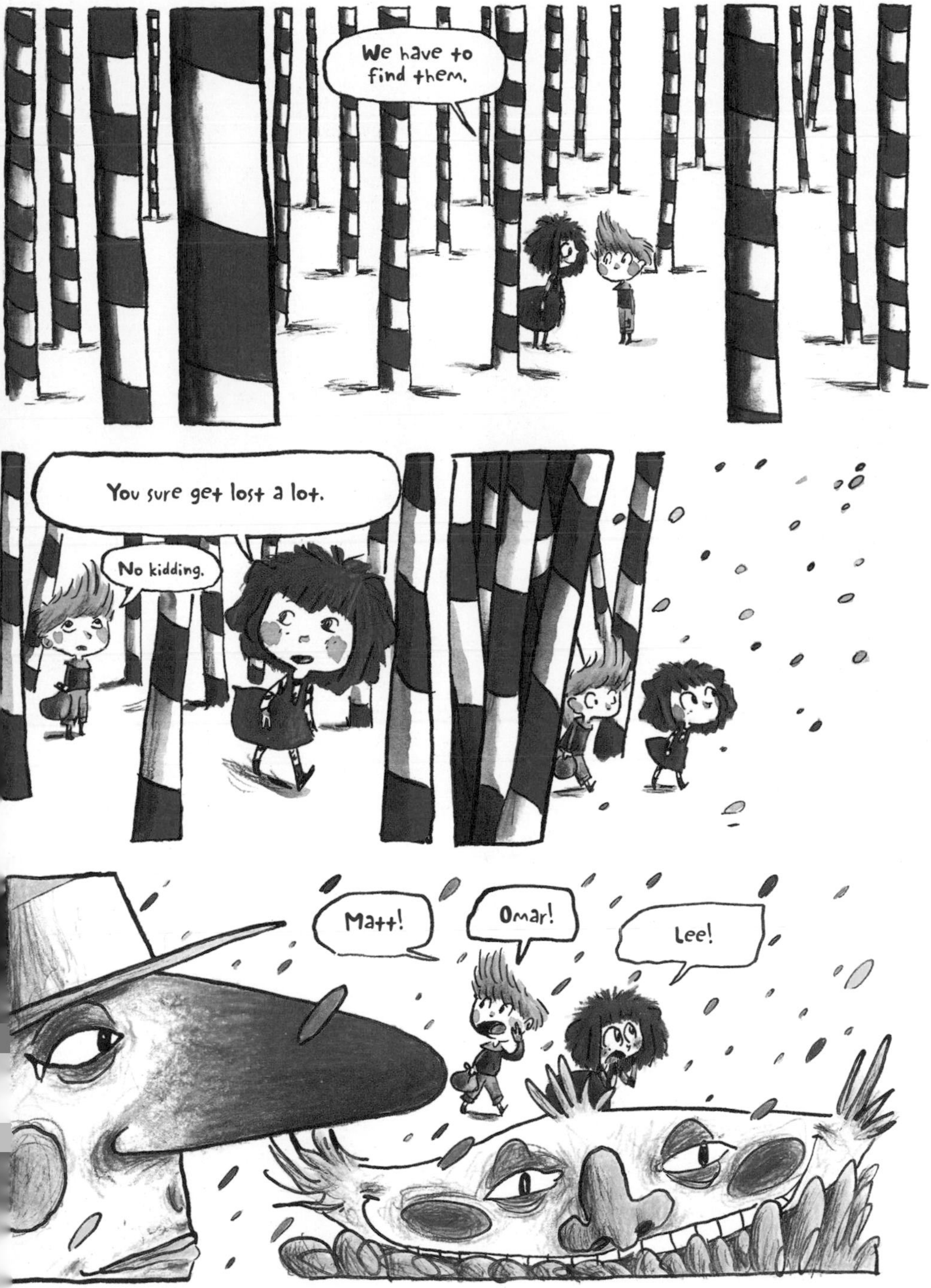
We have to find them.
You sure get lost a lot.
No kidding.
Matt!
Omar!
Lee!

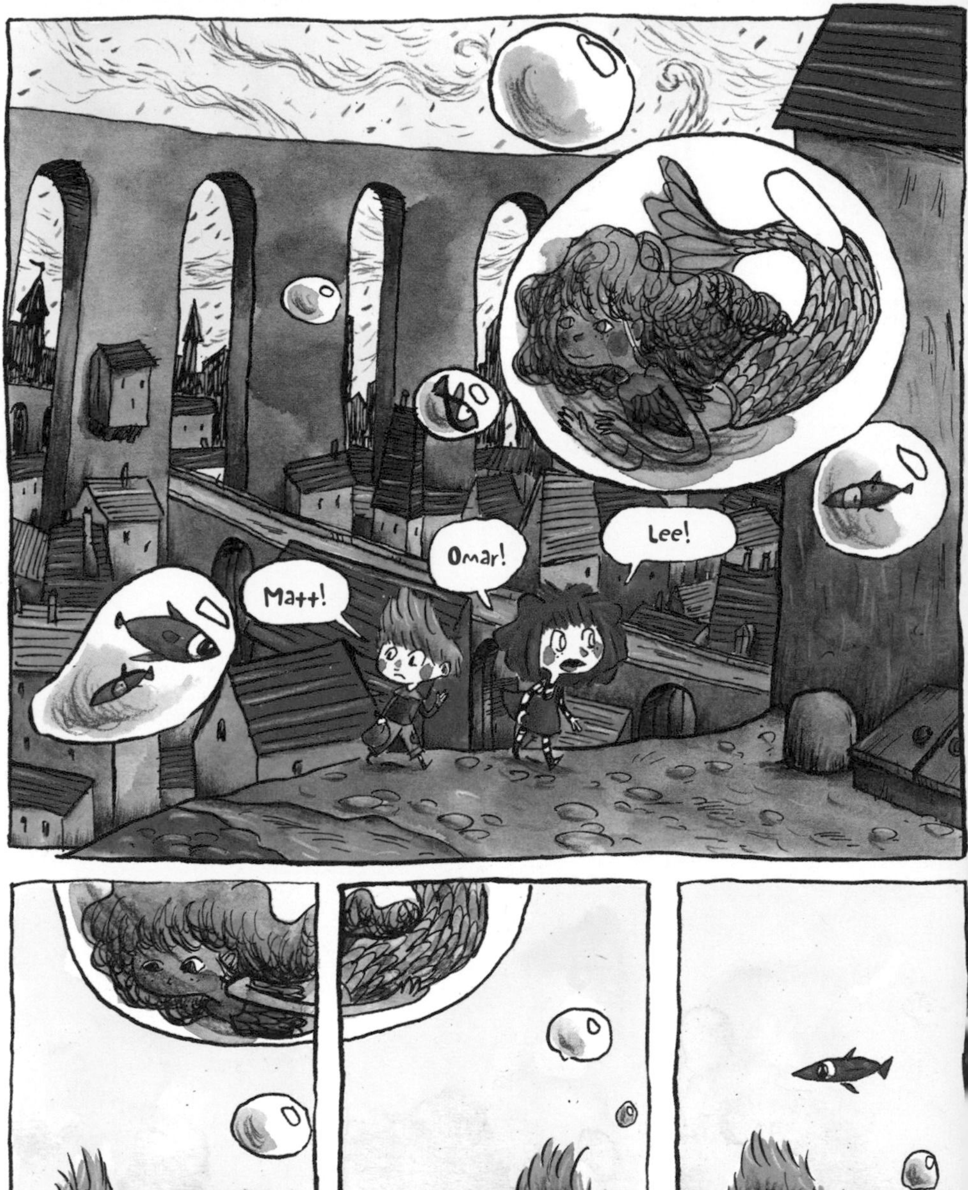
Matt!
Omar!
Lee!

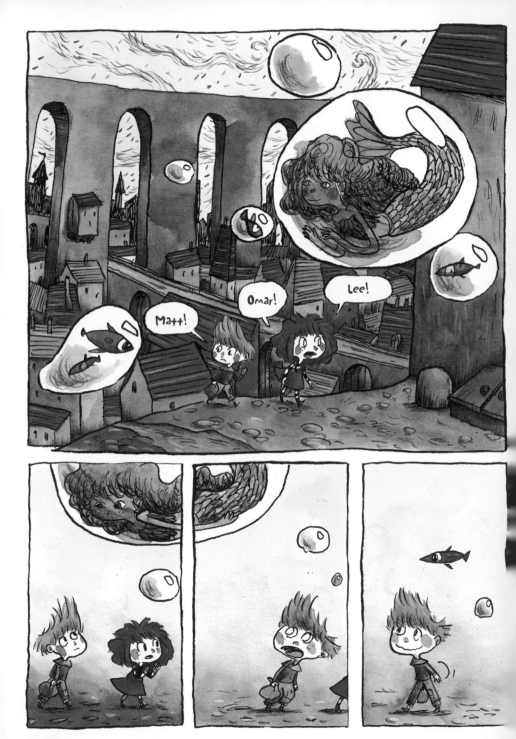

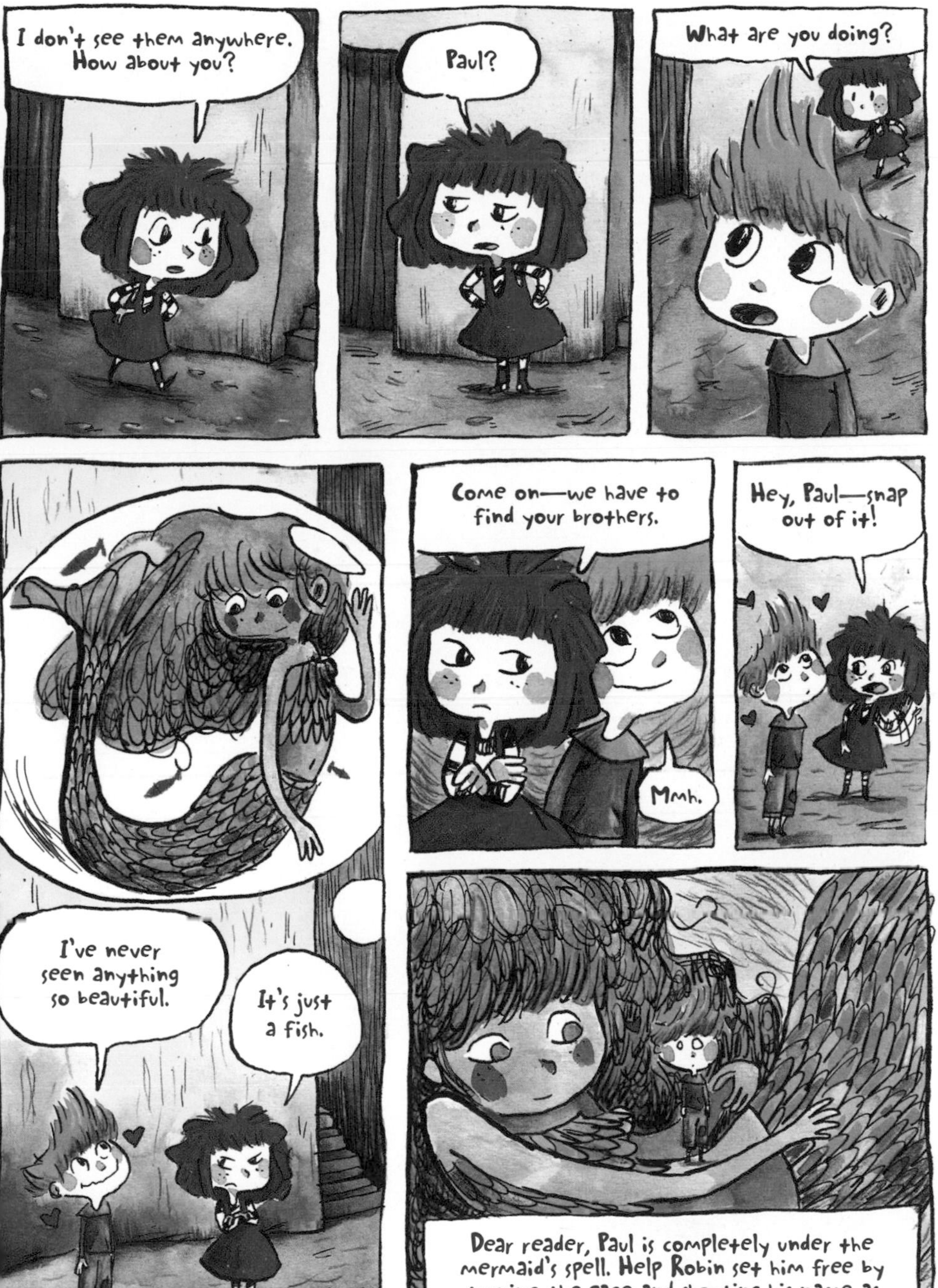
I don't see them anywhere. How about you?
Paul?
What are you doing?
I've never seen anything so beautiful.
It's just a fish.
Come on—we have to find your brothers.
Mmh.
Hey, Paul—snap out of it!
Dear reader, Paul is completely under the mermaid's spell. Help Robin set him free by turning the page and shouting his name as loudly as possible.

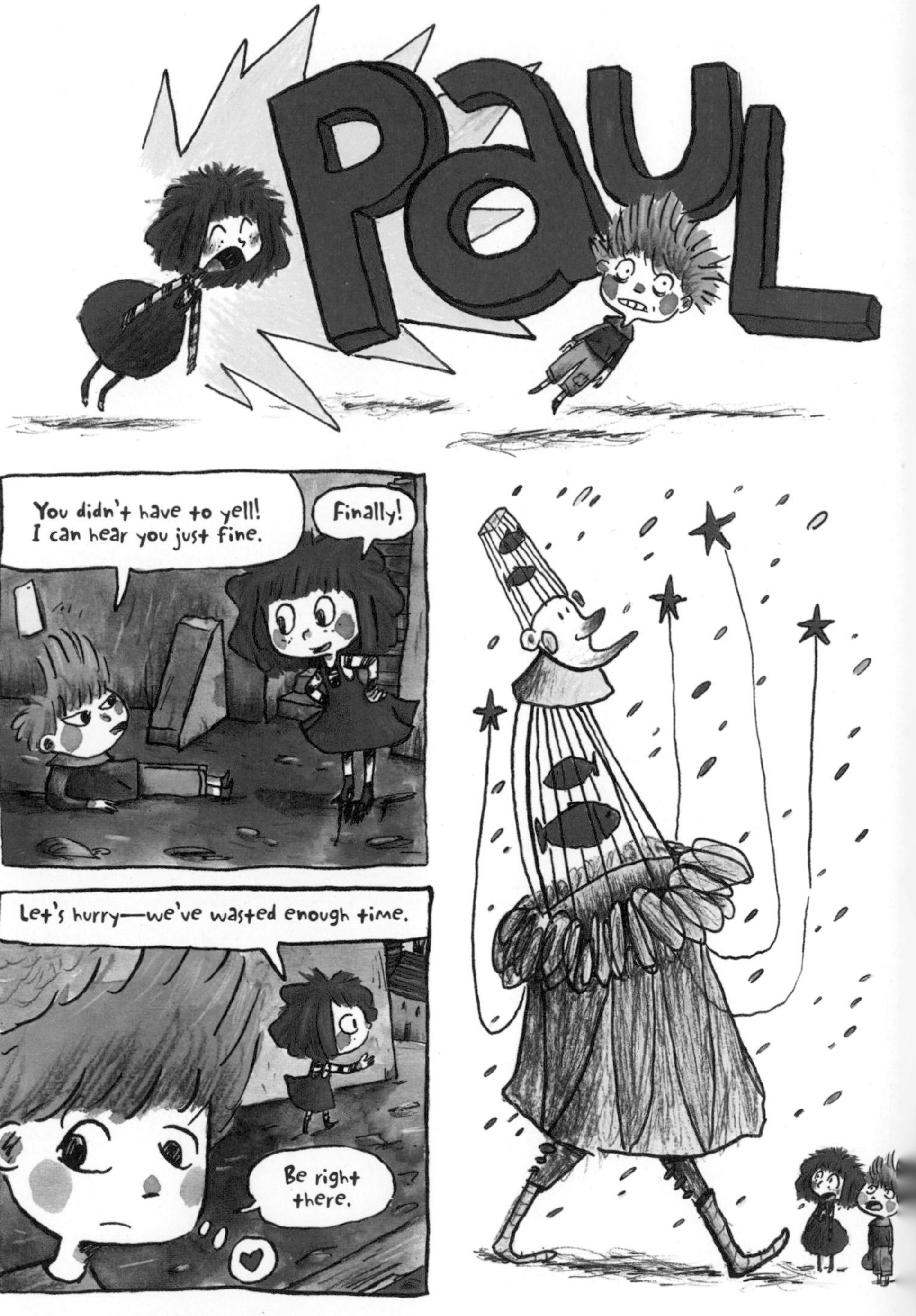
PAUL
You didn't have to yell! I can hear you just fine.
Finally!
Let's hurry—we've wasted enough time.
Be right there.

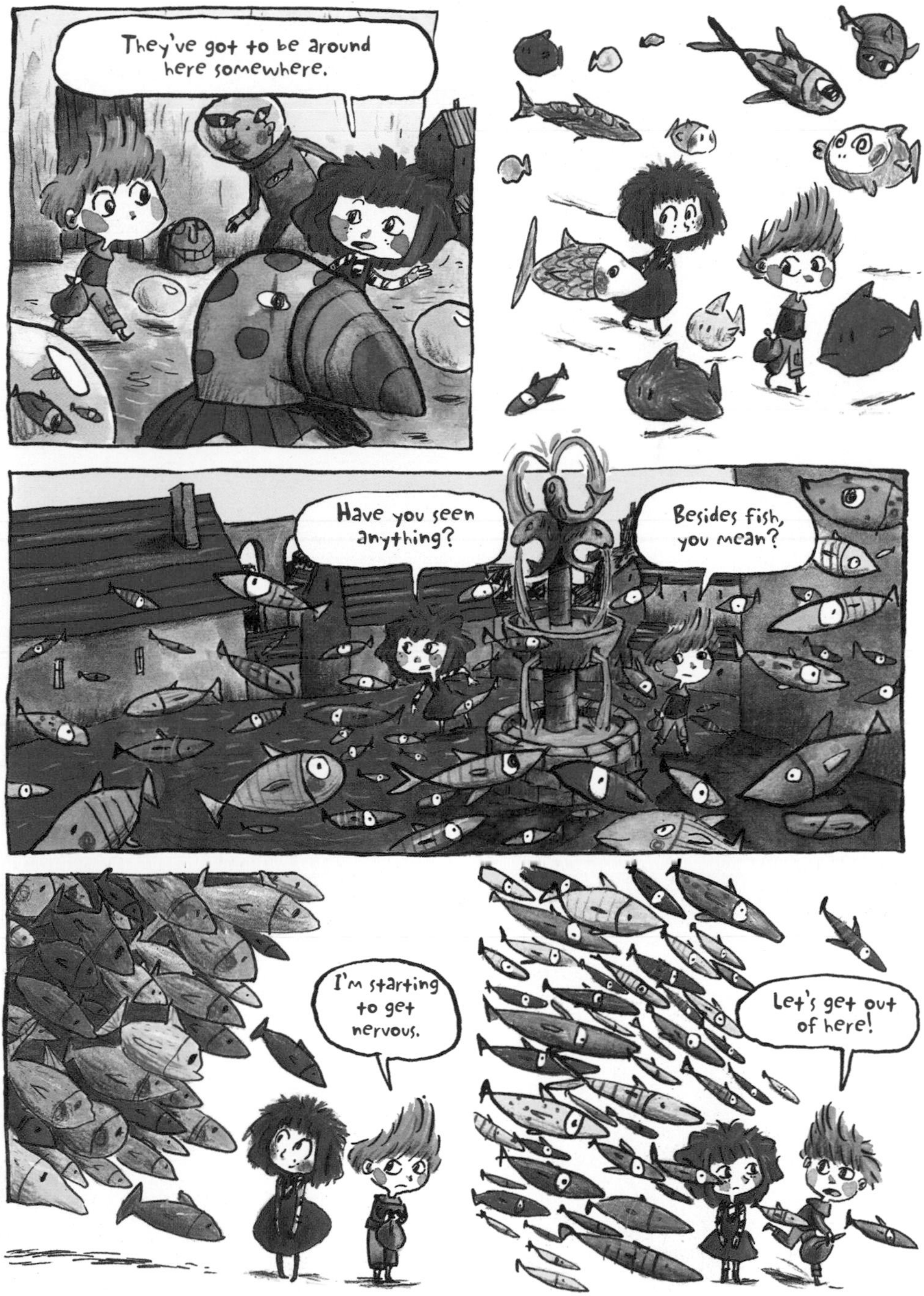
They've got to be around here somewhere.
Have you seen anything?
Besides fish, you mean?
I'm starting to get nervous.
Let's get out of here!

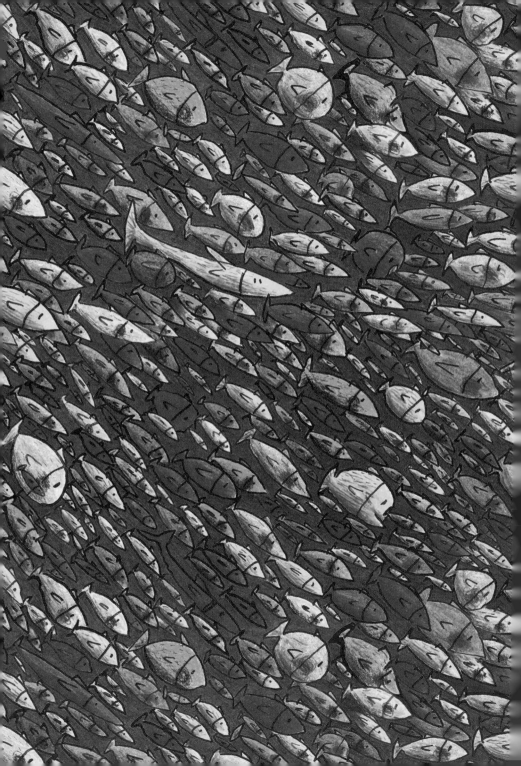

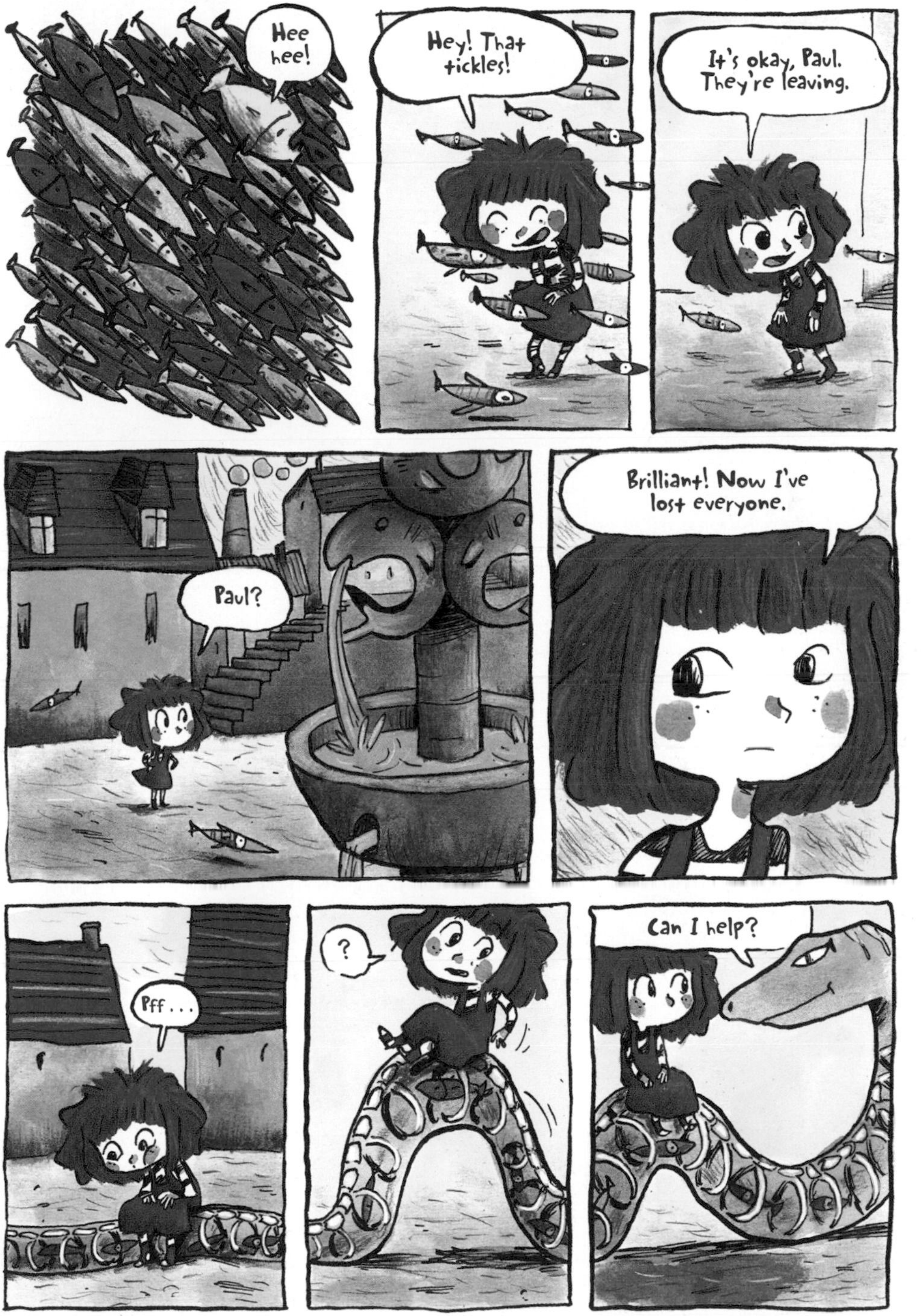

Hee hee!
Hey! That tickles!
It's okay, Paul. They're leaving.
Paul?
Brilliant! Now I've lost everyone.
Pff . . .
?
Can I help?

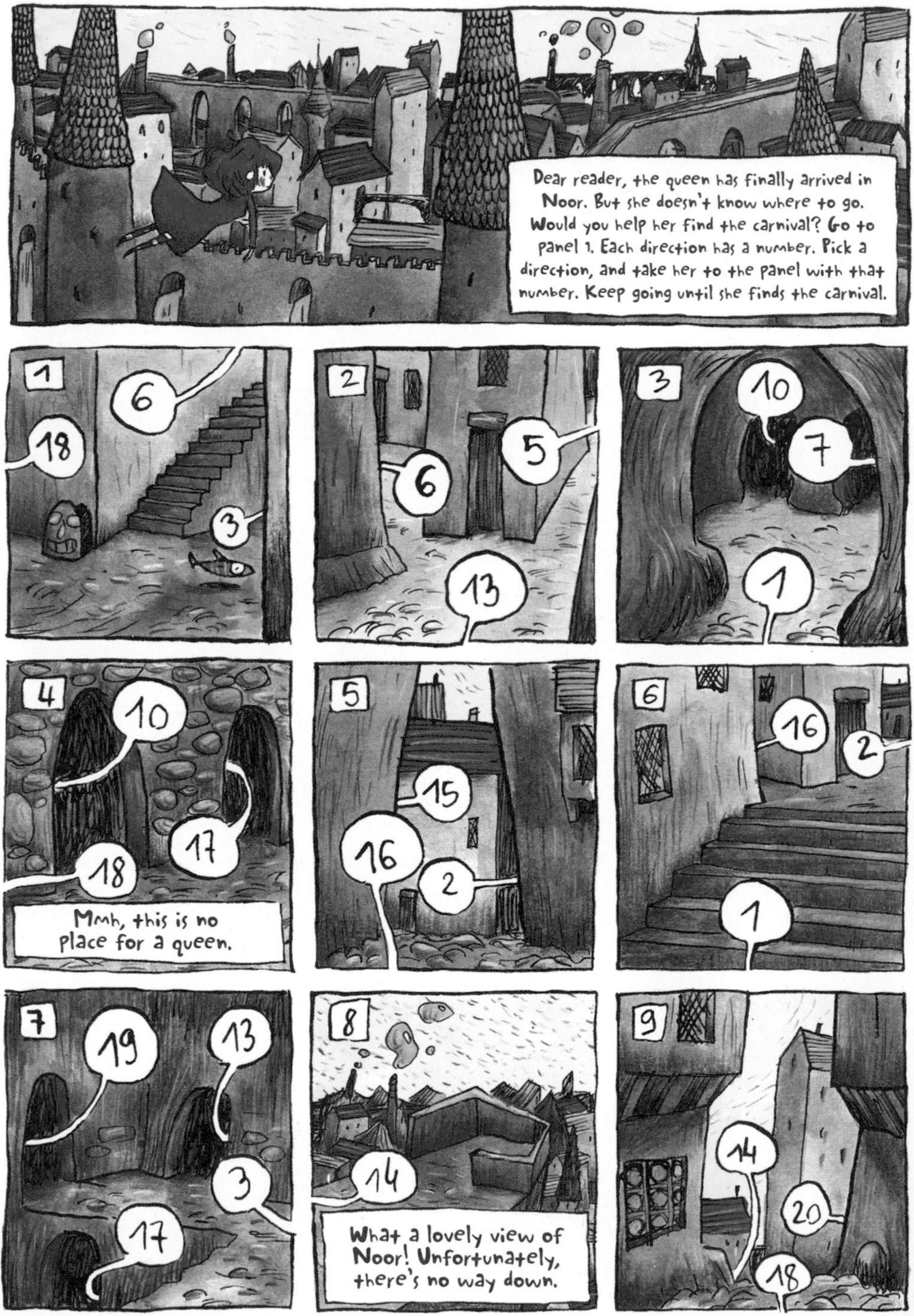
Dear reader, the queen has finally arrived in Noor. But she doesn't know where to go. Would you help her find the carnival? Go to panel 1. Each direction has a number. Pick a direction, and take her to the panel with that number. Keep going until she finds the carnival.
1
6
18
3
2
6
5
13
3
10
7
1
4
10
17
18
Mmh, this is no place for a queen.
5
15
16
2
6
16
2
1
7
19
13
3
17
8
14
What a lovely view of Noor! Unfortunately, there's no way down.
9
14
20
18

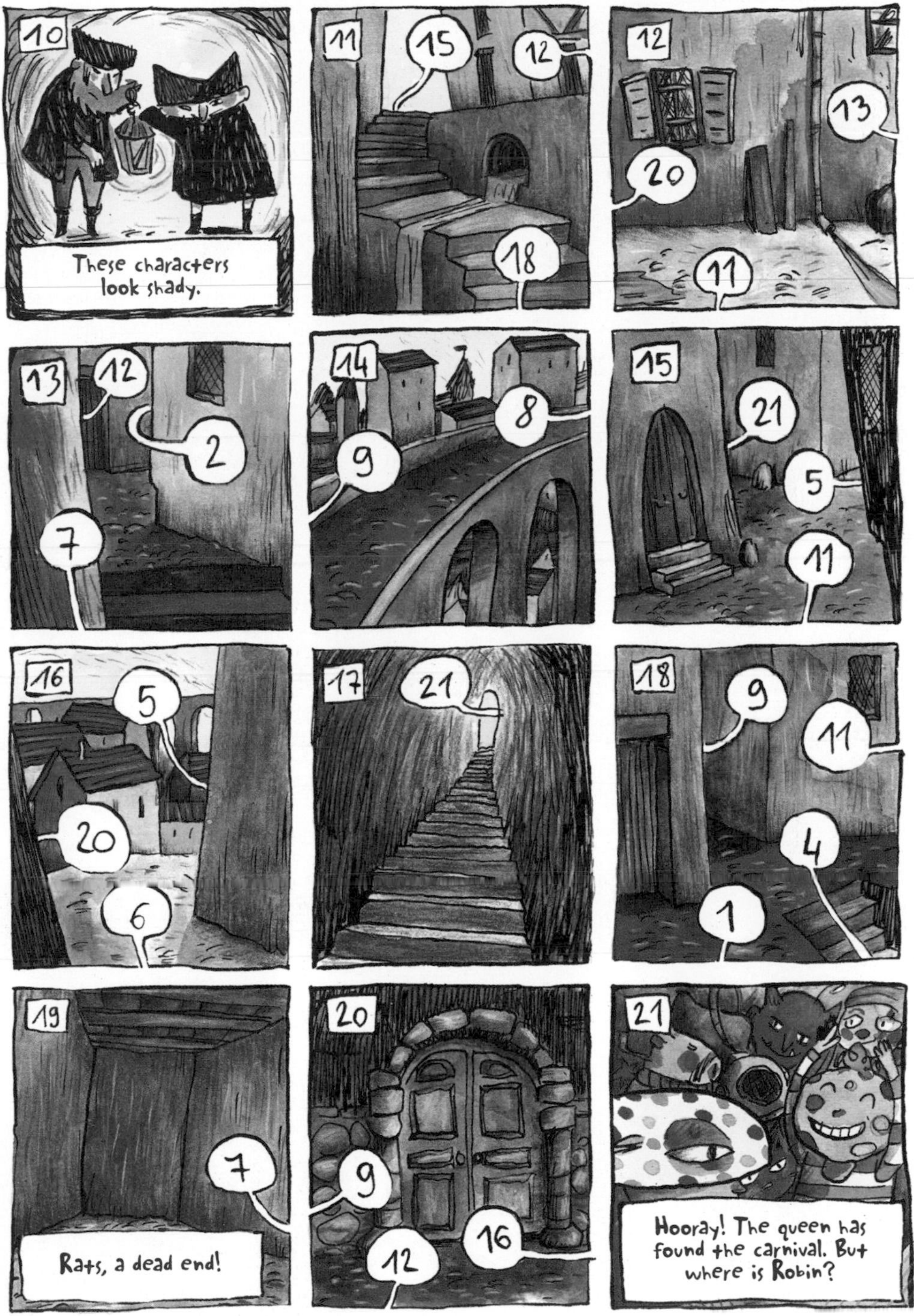
10
These characters look shady.
11
15
12
18
12
13
20
11
13
12
2
7
14
8
9
15
21
5
11
16
5
20
6
17
21
18
9
11
4
1
19
7
Rats, a dead end!
20
9
16
12
21
Hooray! The queen has found the carnival. But where is Robin?

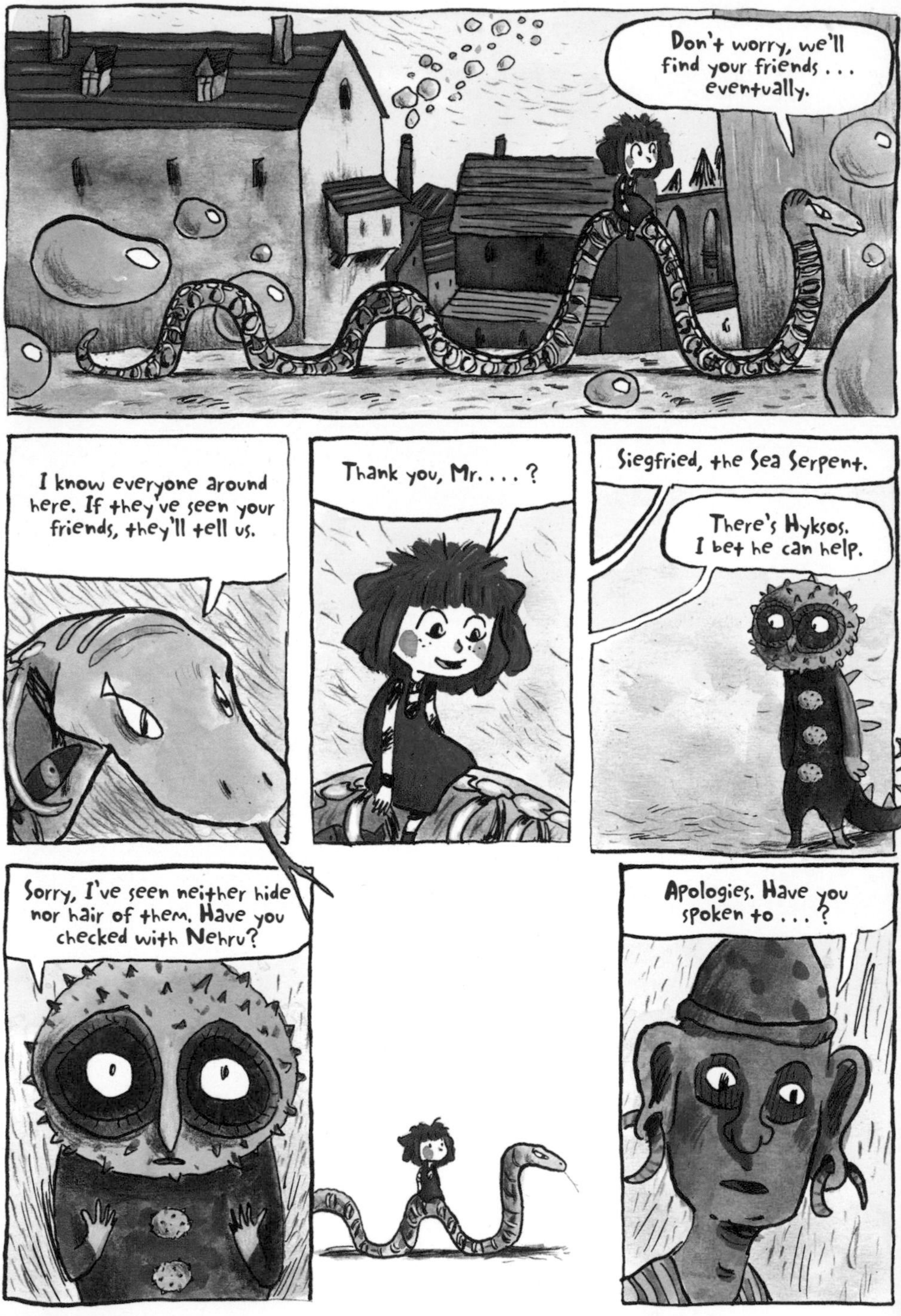
Don't worry, we'll find your friends . . . eventually.
I know everyone around here. If they've seen your friends, they'll tell us.
Thank you, Mr. . . . ?
Siegfried, the Sea Serpent.
There's Hyksos. I bet he can help.
Sorry, I've seen neither hide nor hair of them. Have you checked with Nehru?
Apologies. Have you spoken to . . . ?

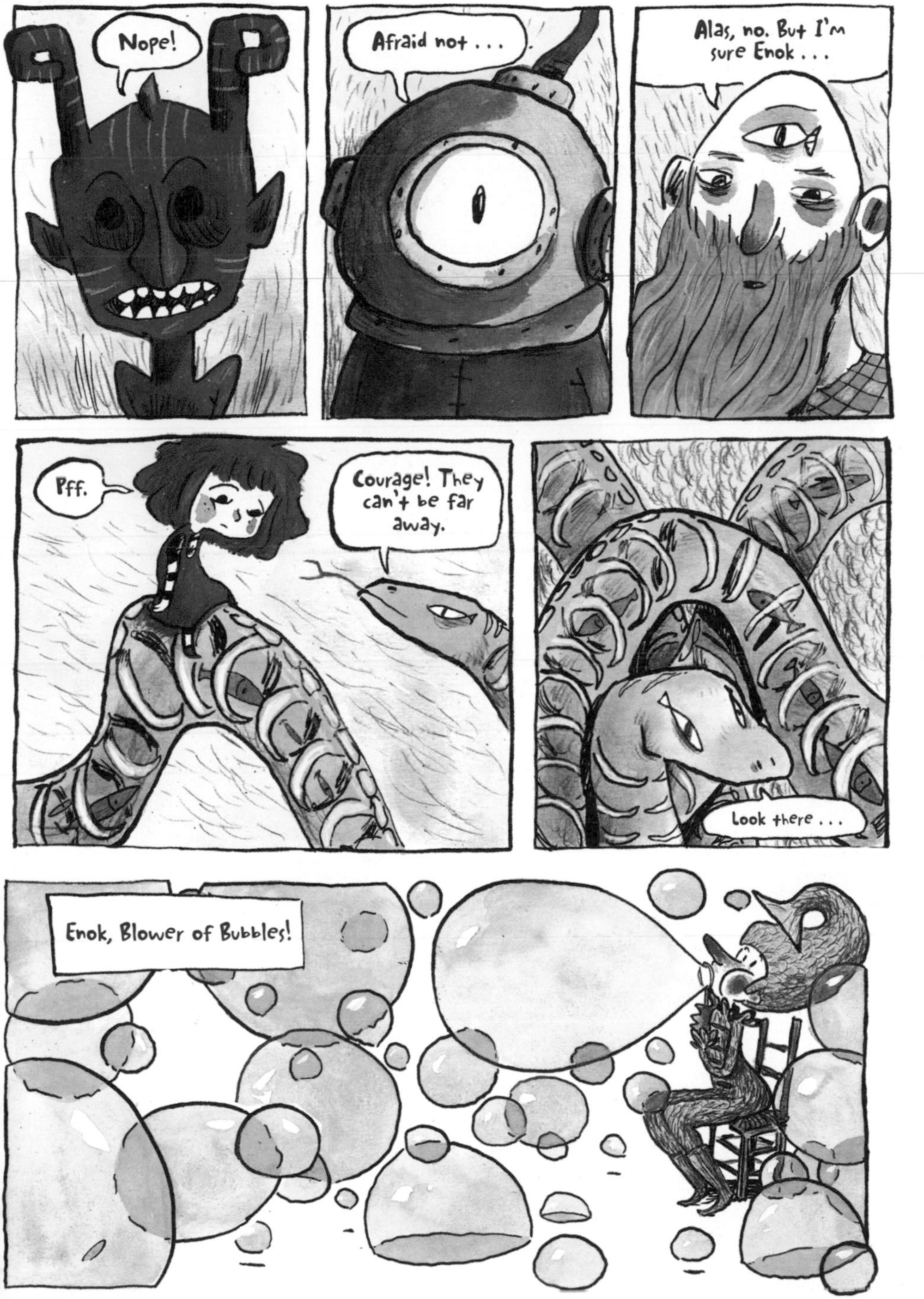
Nope!
Afraid not . . .
Alas, no. But I'm sure Enok . . .
Pff.
Courage! They can't be far away.
Look there . . .
Enok, Blower of Bubbles!

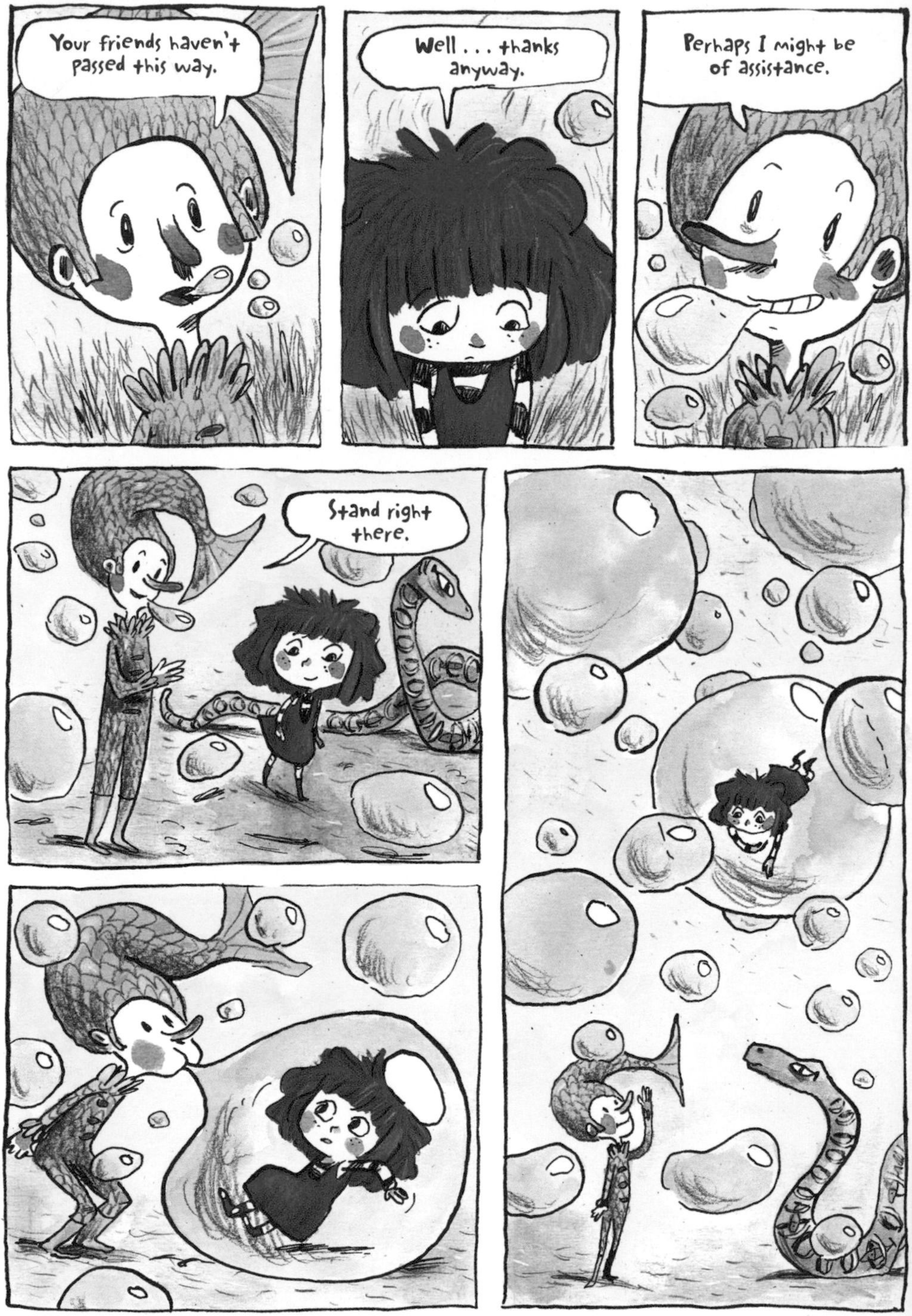
Your friends haven't passed this way.
Well . . . thanks anyway.
Perhaps I might be of assistance.
Stand right there.

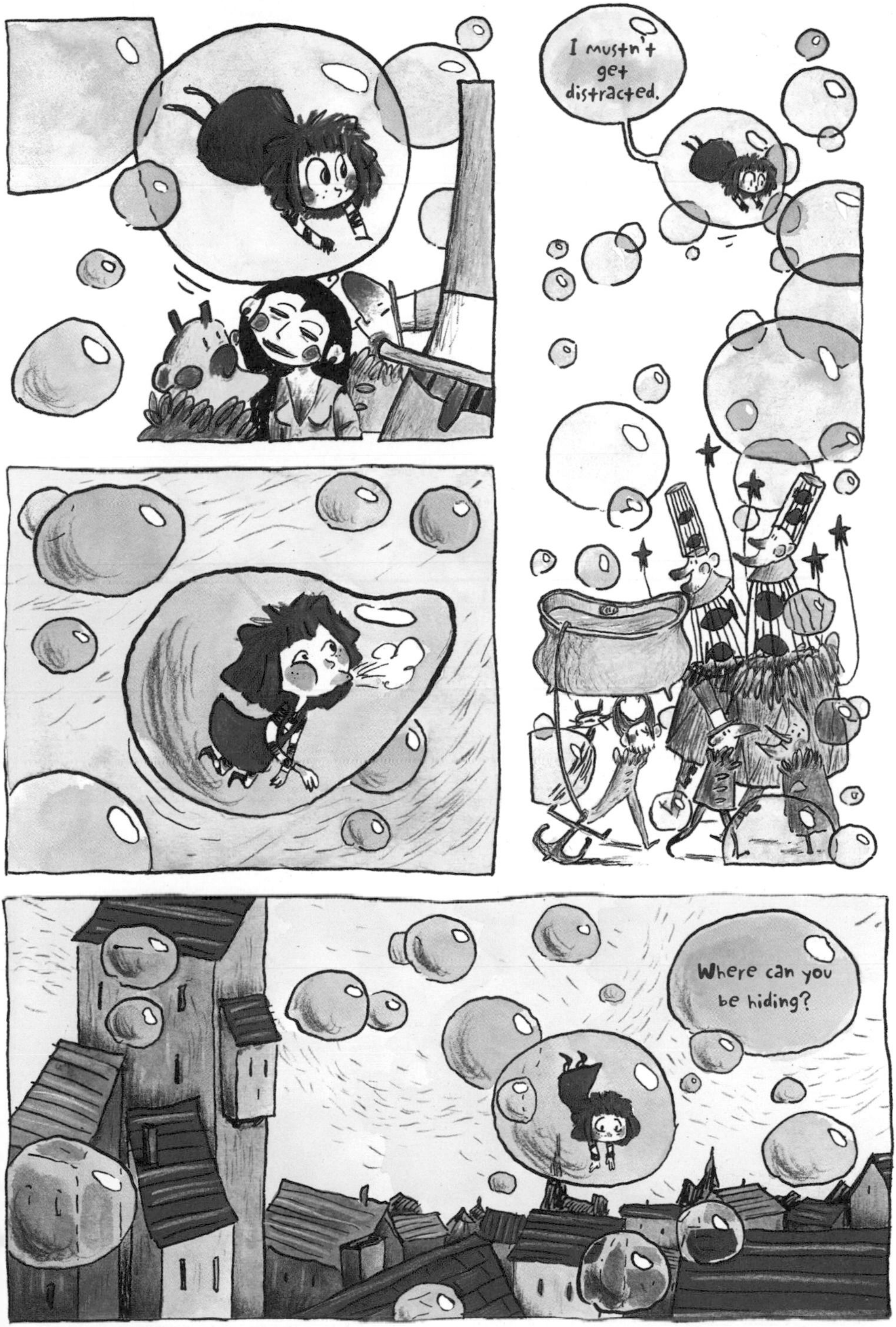
I mustn't get distracted.
Where can you be hiding?

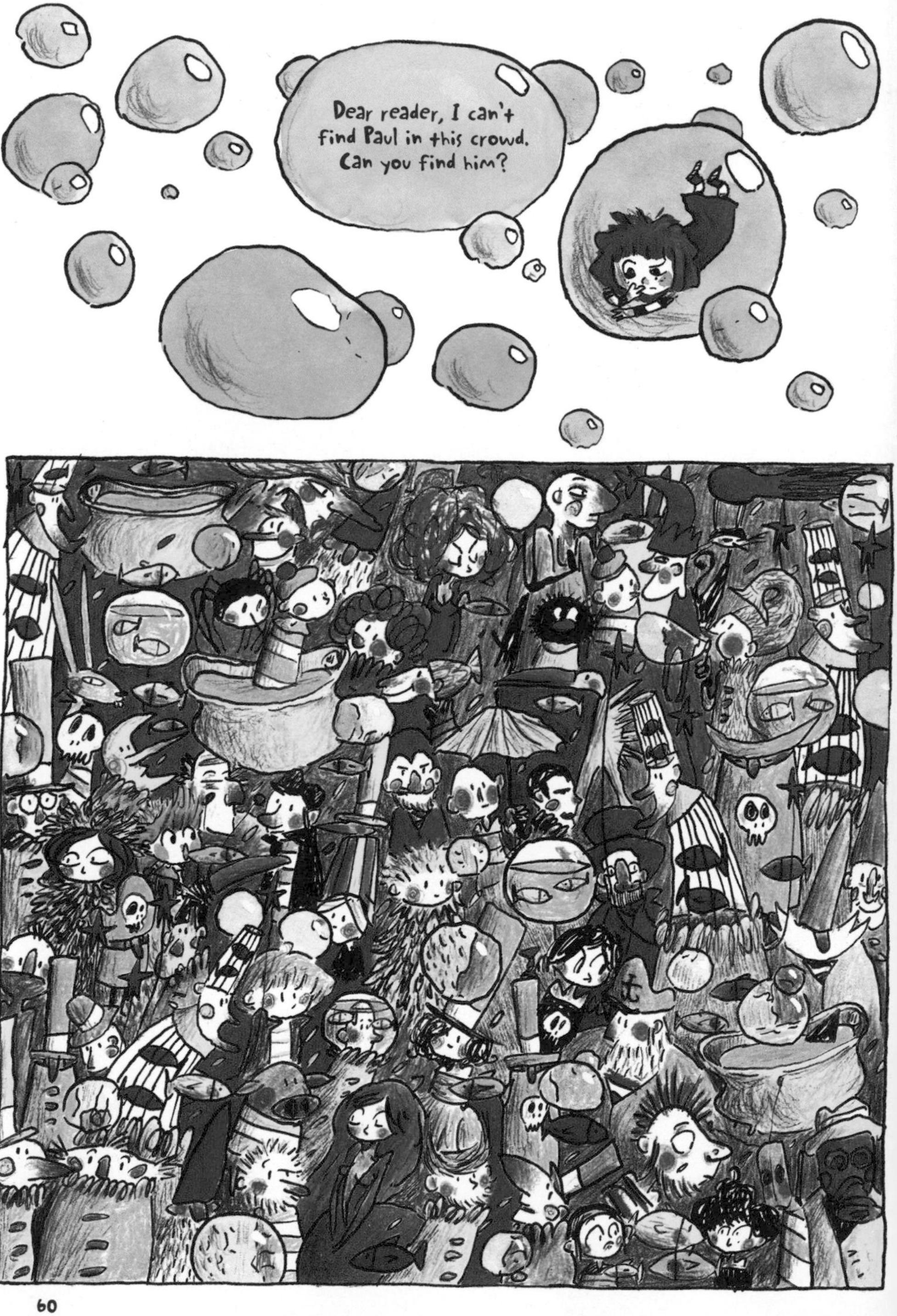
Dear reader, I can't find Paul in this crowd. Can you find him?

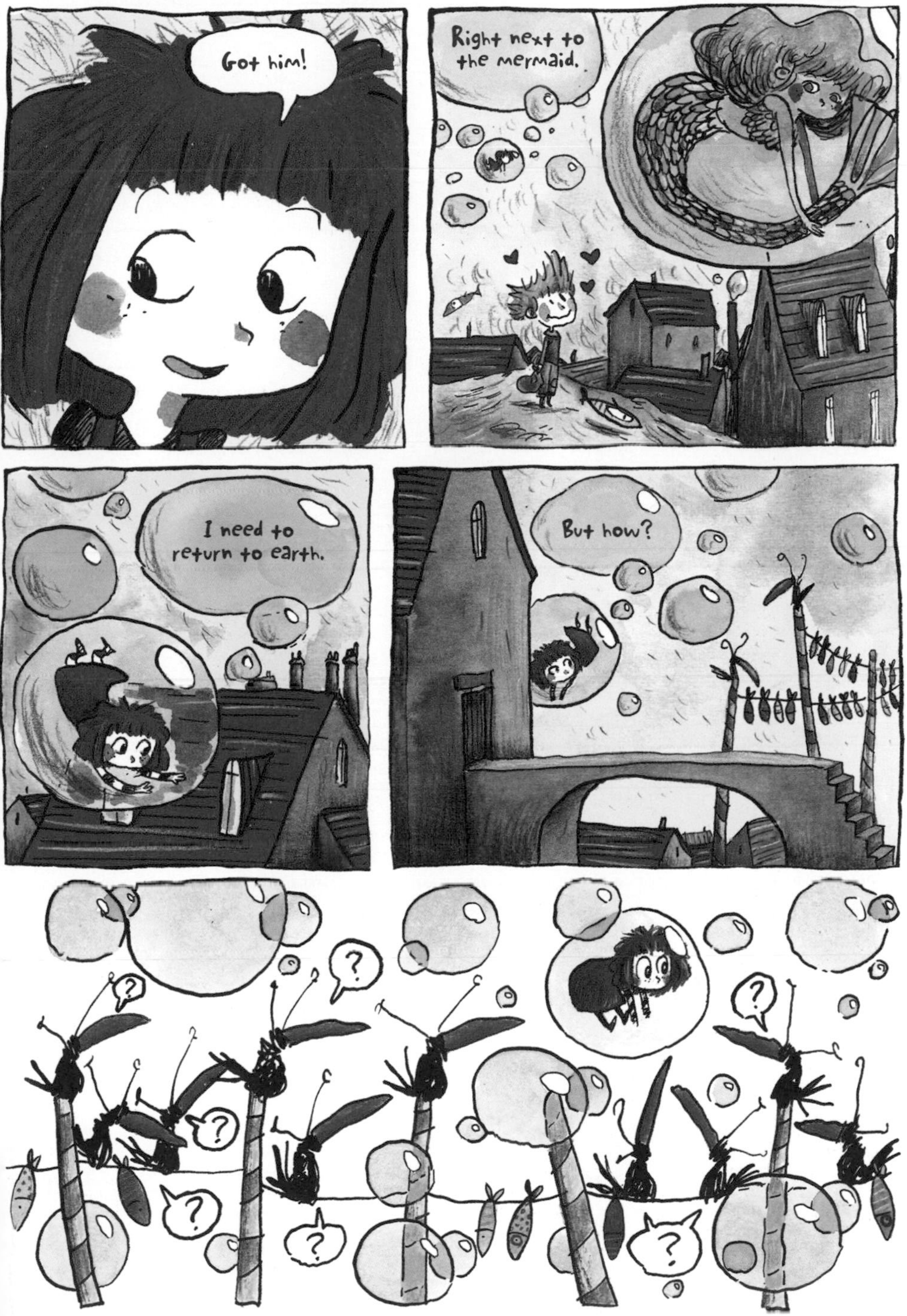
Got him!
Right next to the mermaid.
I need to return to earth.
But how?
?
?
?
?
?
?
?

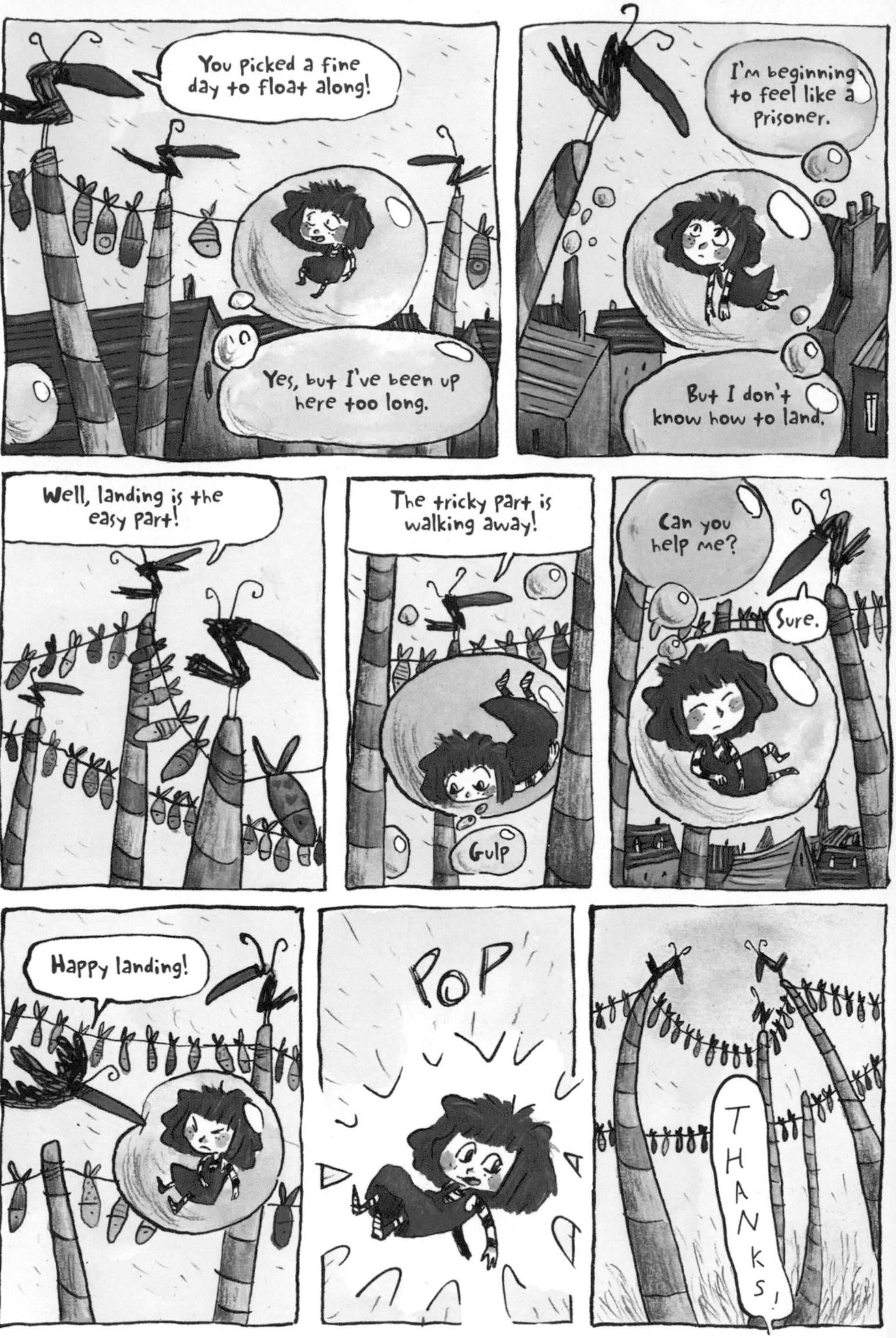
You picked a fine day to float along!
Yes, but I've been up here too long.
I'm beginning to feel like a prisoner.
But I don't know how to land.
Well, landing is the easy part!
The tricky part is walking away!
Gulp
Can you help me?
Sure.
Happy landing!
POP
THANKS!

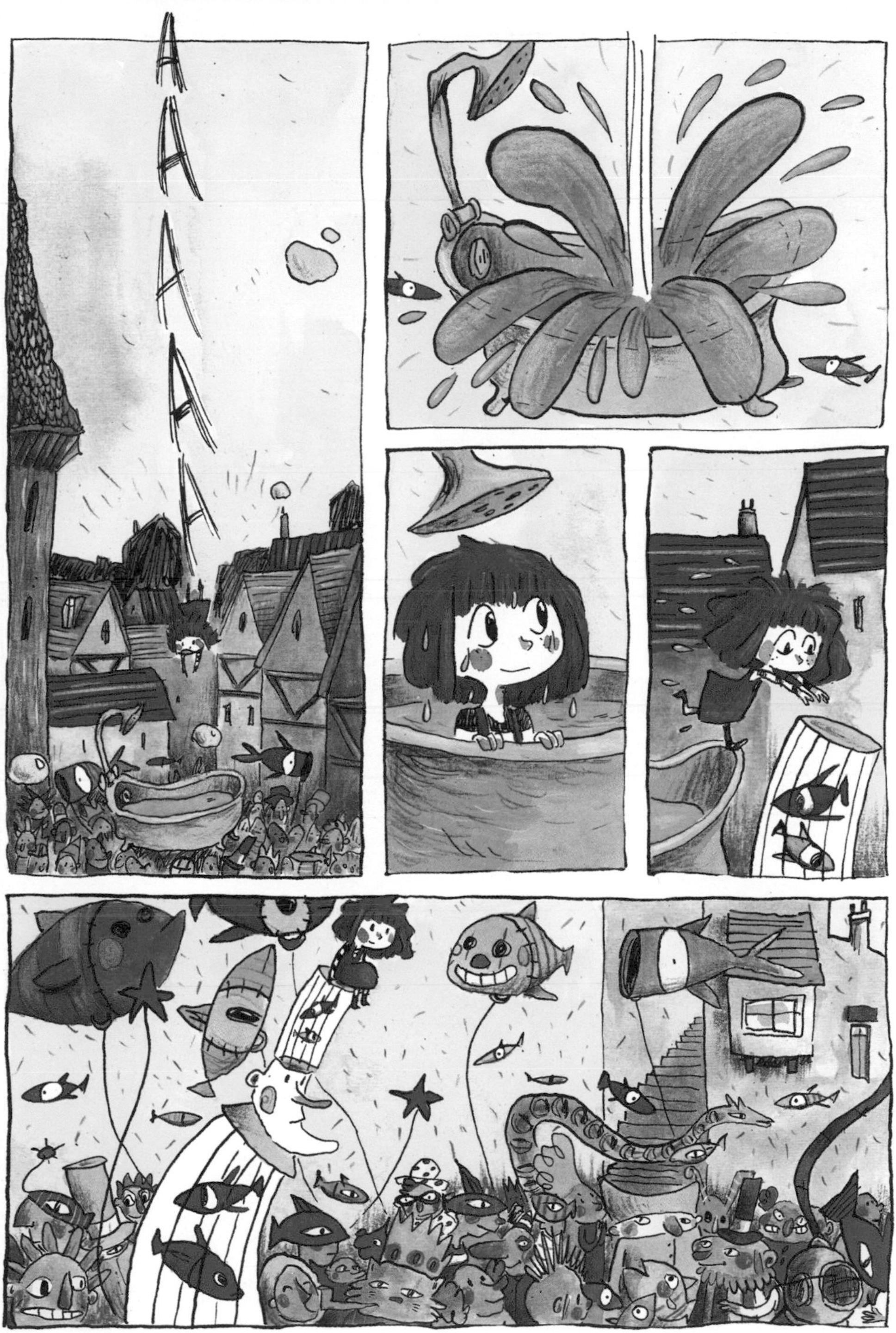
AAAAAAA

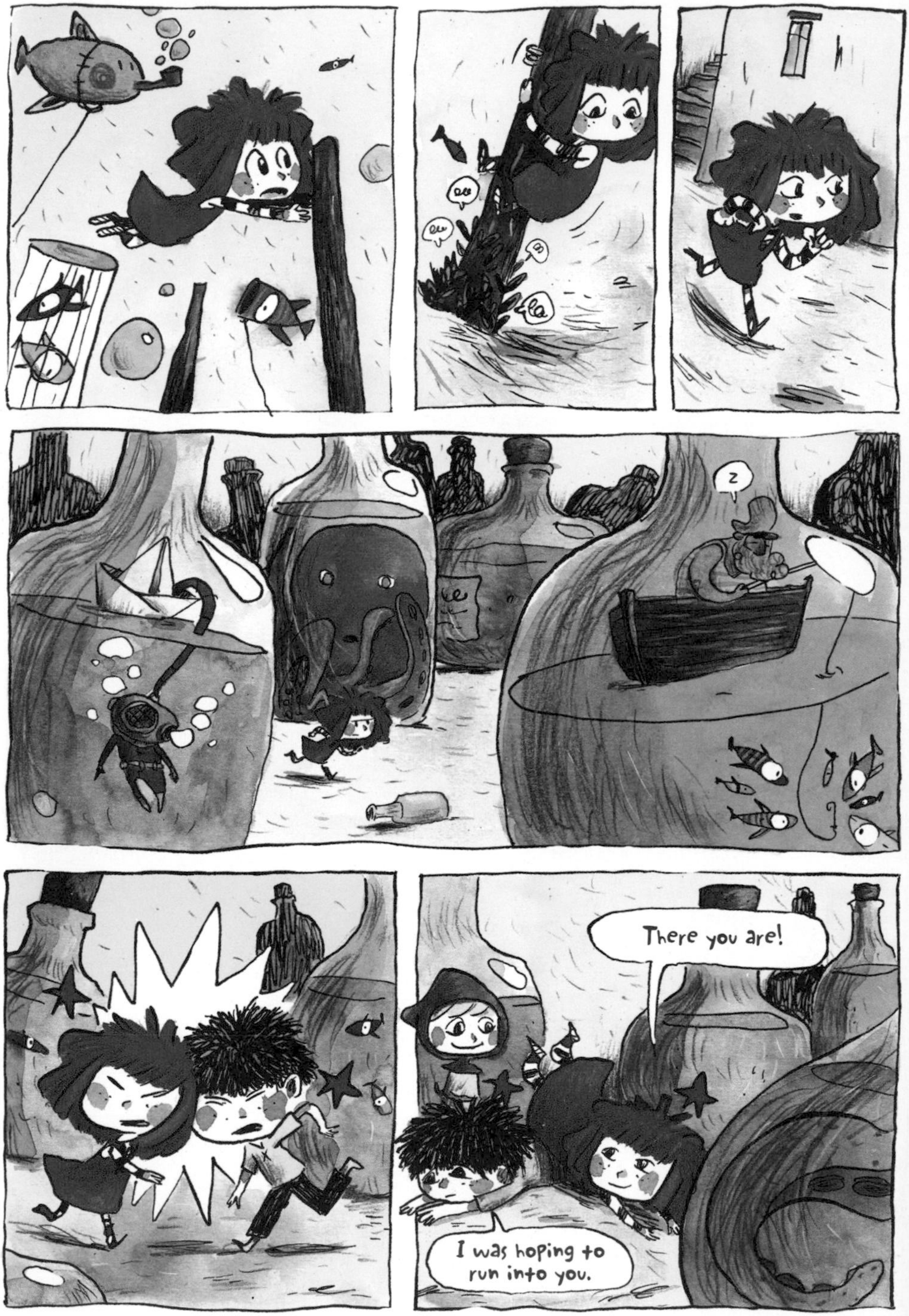
There you are!
I was hoping to run into you.

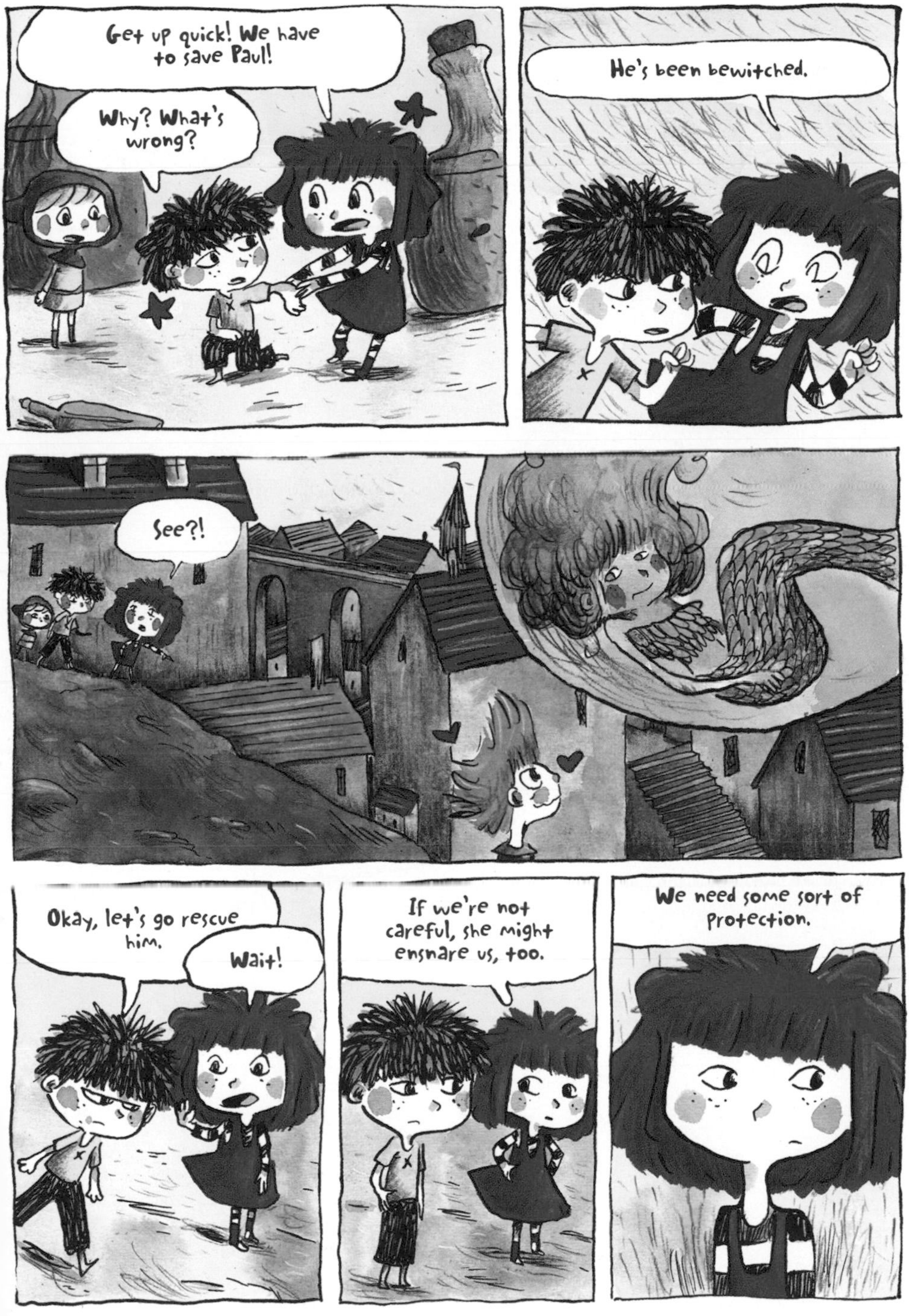
Get up quick! We have to save Paul!
Why? What's wrong?
He's been bewitched.
See?!
Okay, let's go rescue him.
Wait!
If we're not careful, she might ensnare us, too.
We need some sort of protection.

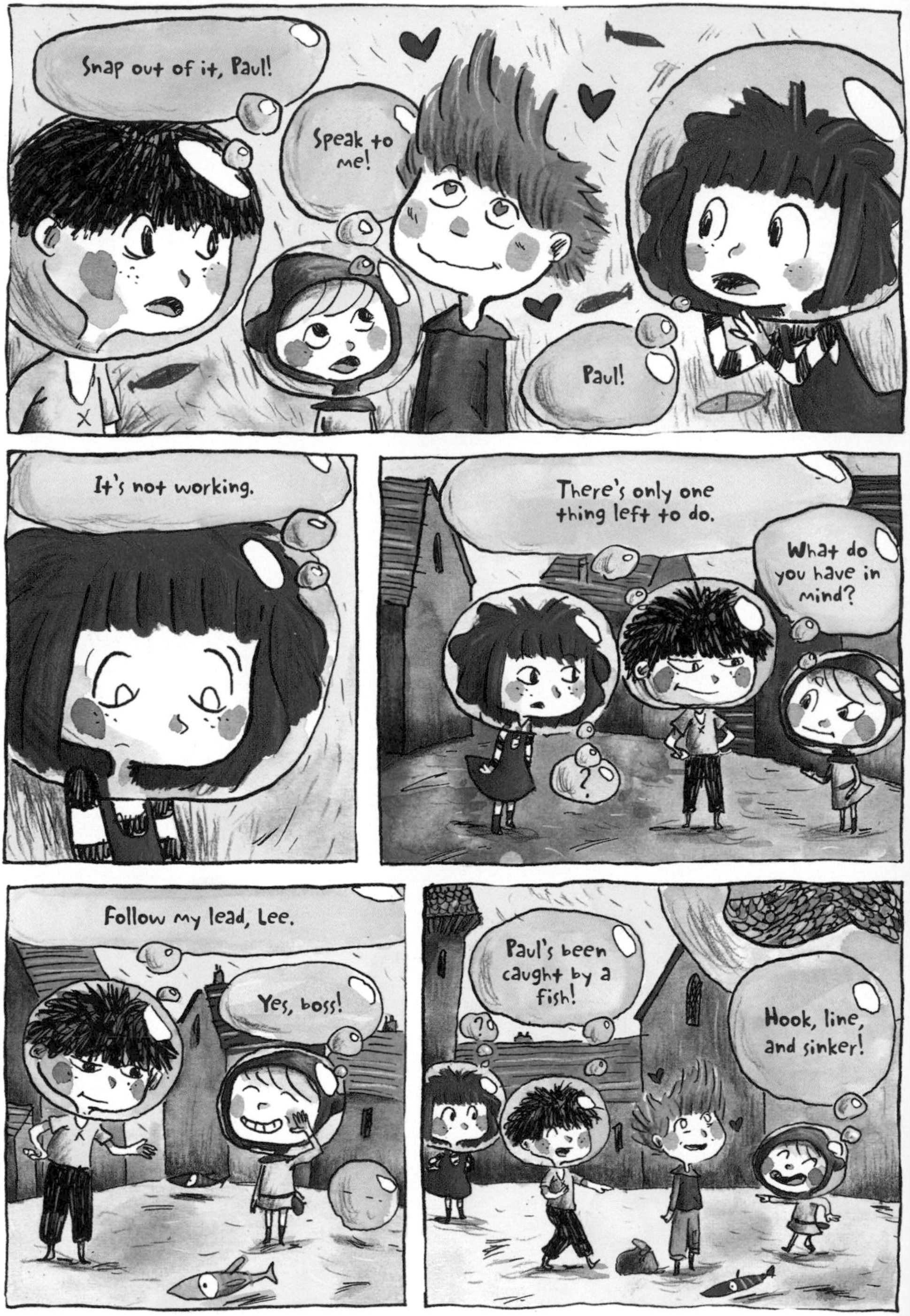
Snap out of it, Paul!
Speak to me!
Paul!
It's not working.
There's only one thing left to do.
What do you have in mind?
?
Follow my lead, Lee.
Yes, boss!
Paul's been caught by a fish!
?
Hook, line, and sinker!

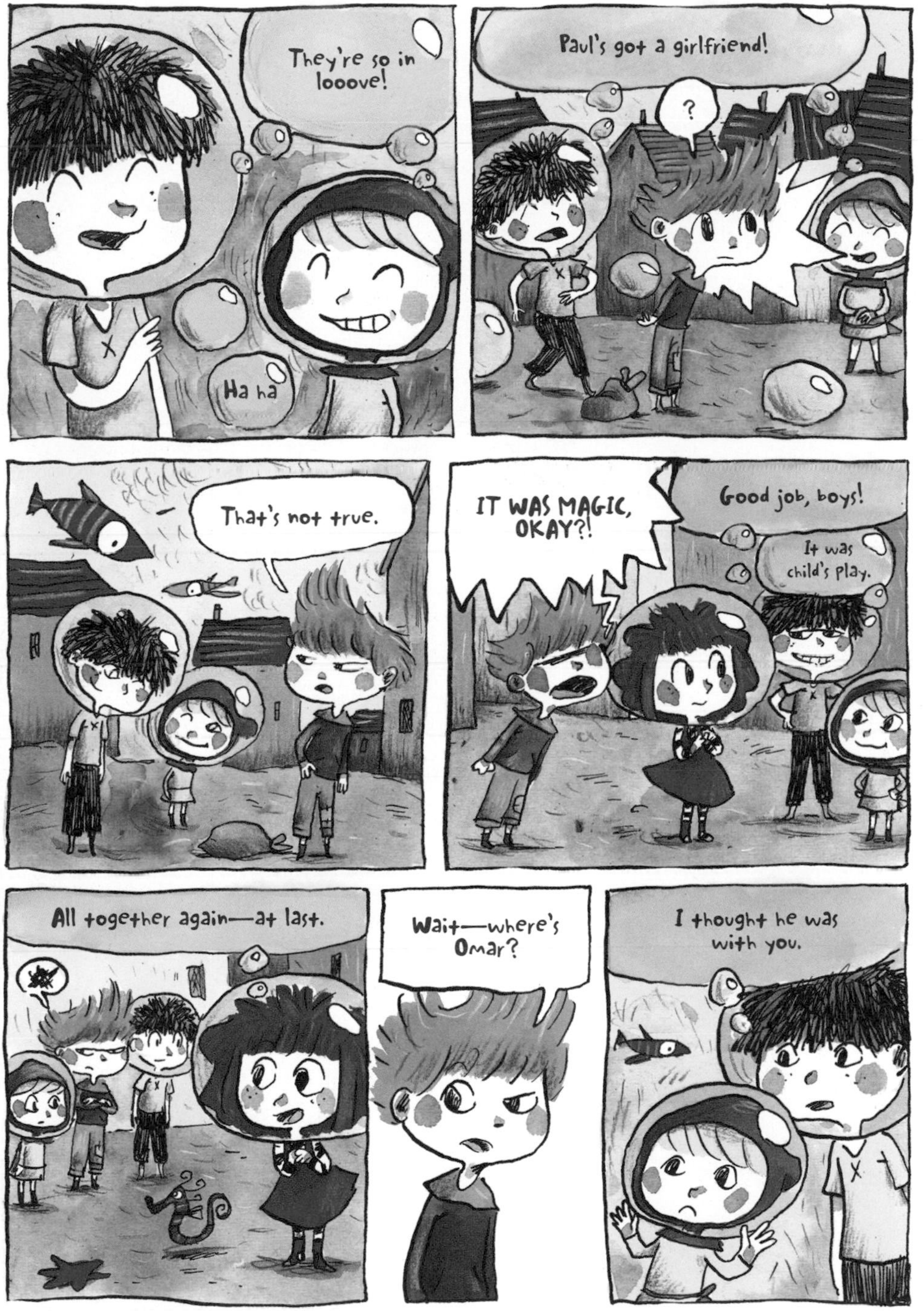

They're so in looove!
Ha ha
Paul's got a girlfriend!
?
That's not true.
IT WAS MAGIC, OKAY?!
Good job, boys!
It was child's play.
All together again—at last.
Wait—where's Omar?
I thought he was with you.

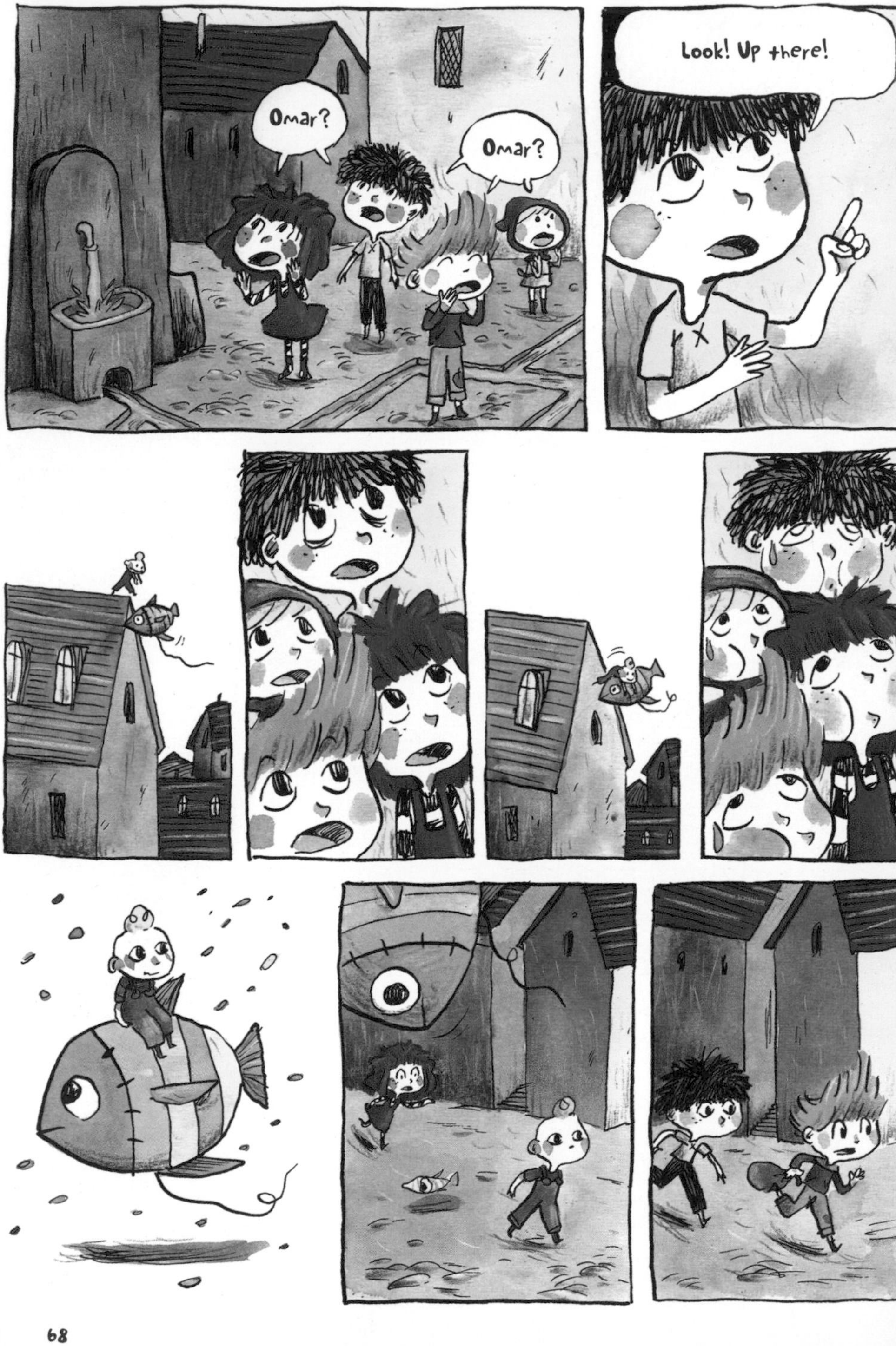
Omar?
Omar?
Look! Up there!

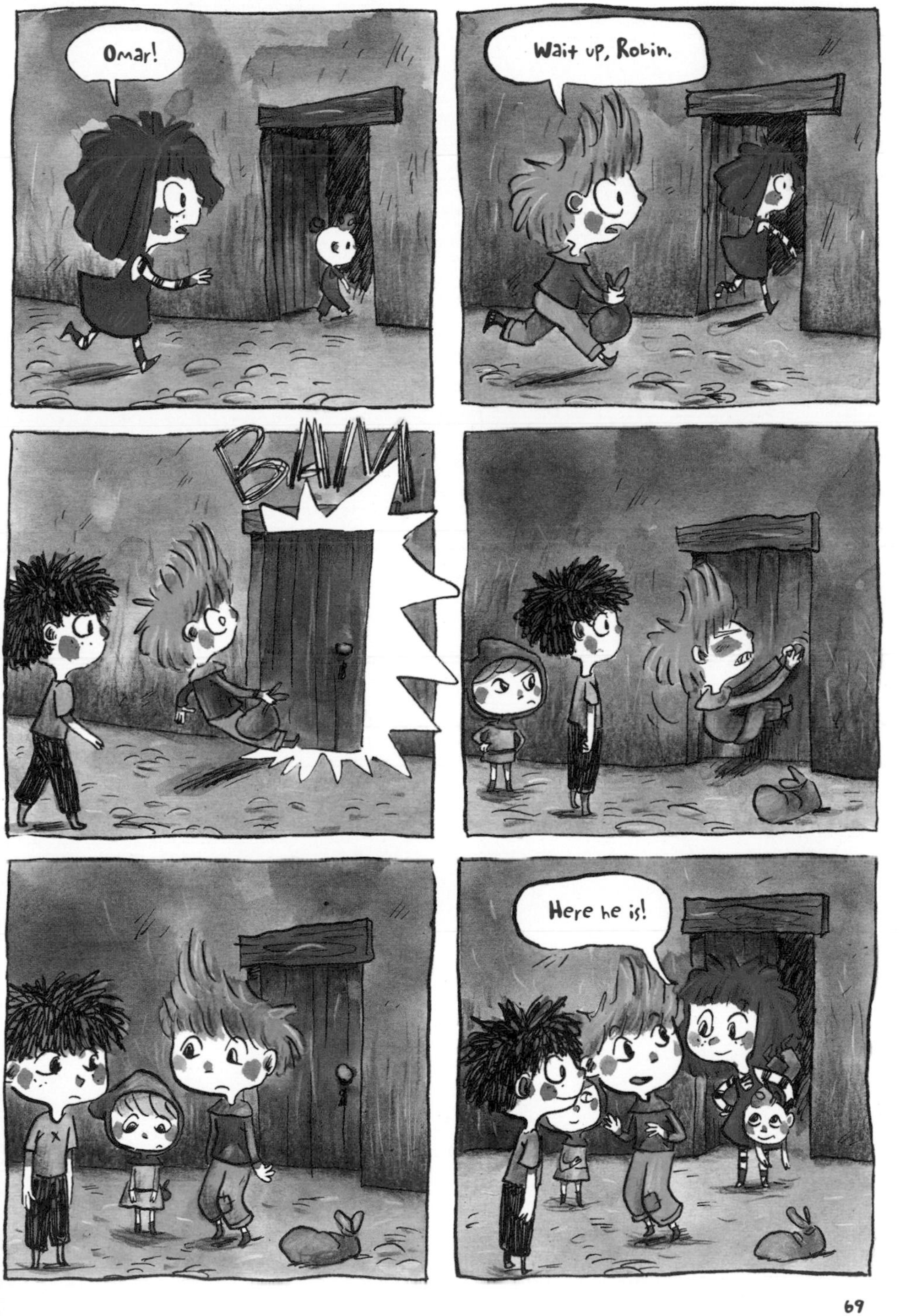
Omar!
Wait up, Robin.
BAM
Here he is!

To find out what happened on the other side of the door . . .

. . . read from right to left.

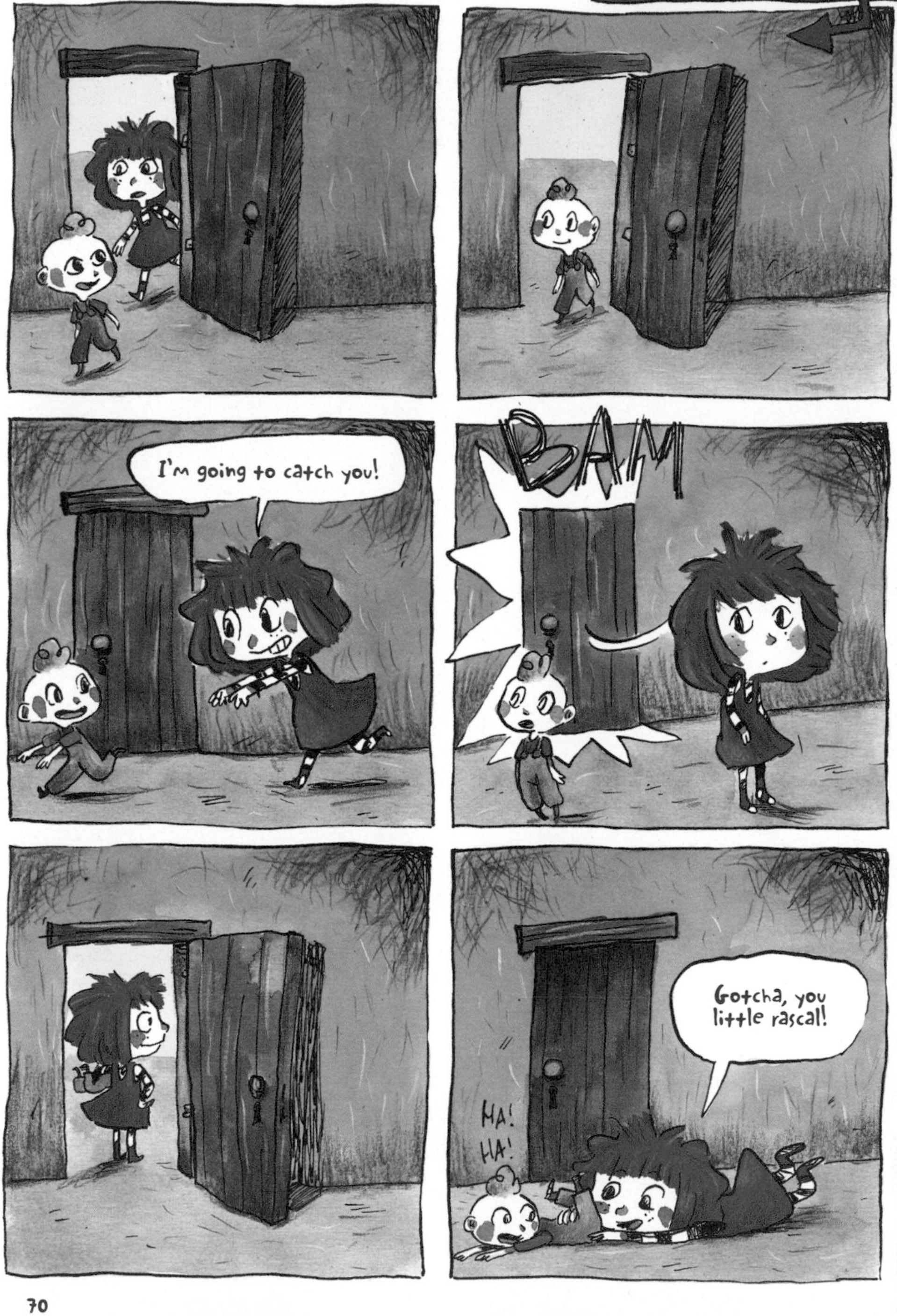
BAM
I'm going to catch you!
HA! HA!
Gotcha, you little rascal!

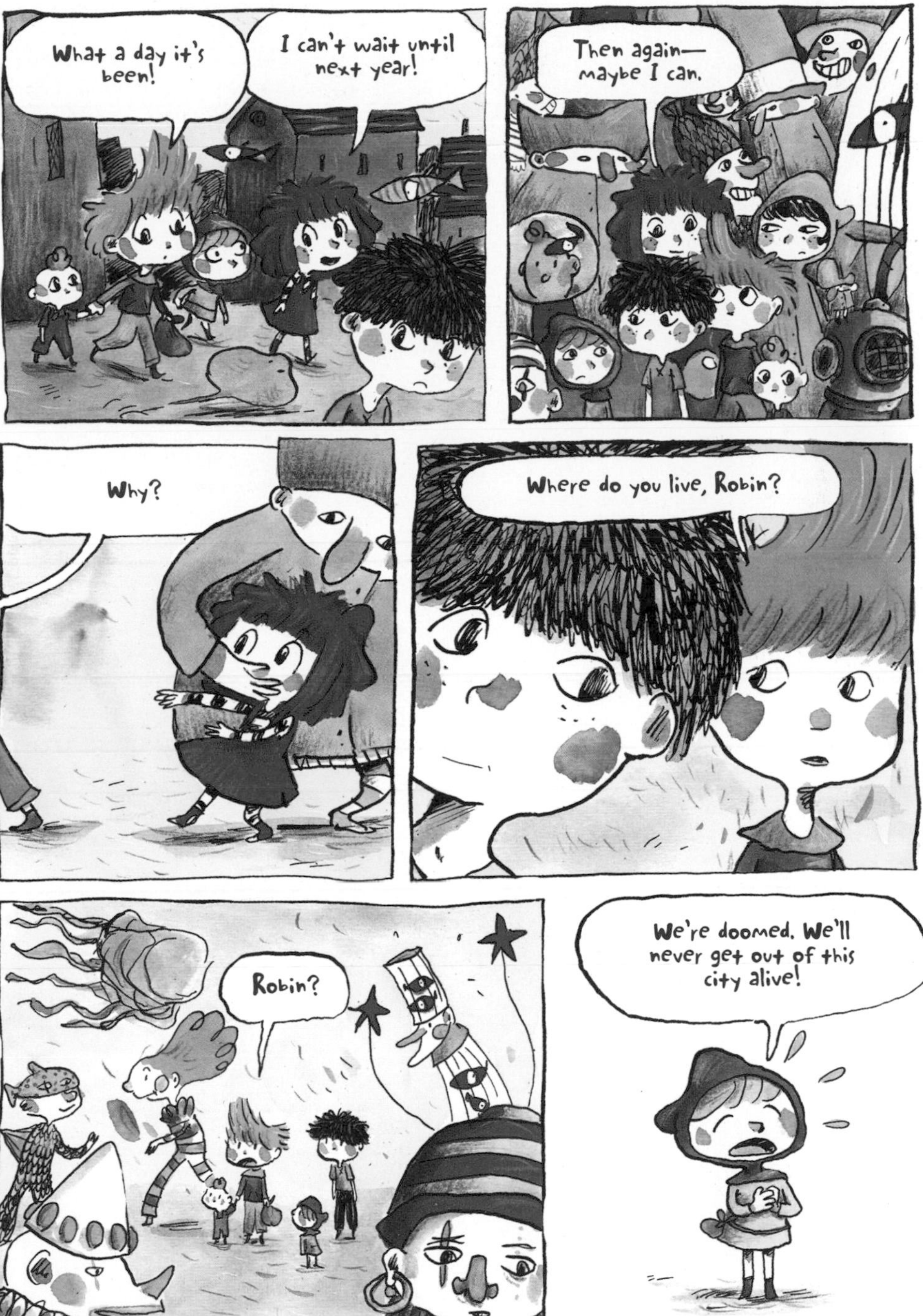
What a day it's been!
I can't wait until next year!
Then again— maybe I can.
Why?
Where do you live, Robin?
Robin?
We're doomed. We'll never get out of this city alive!

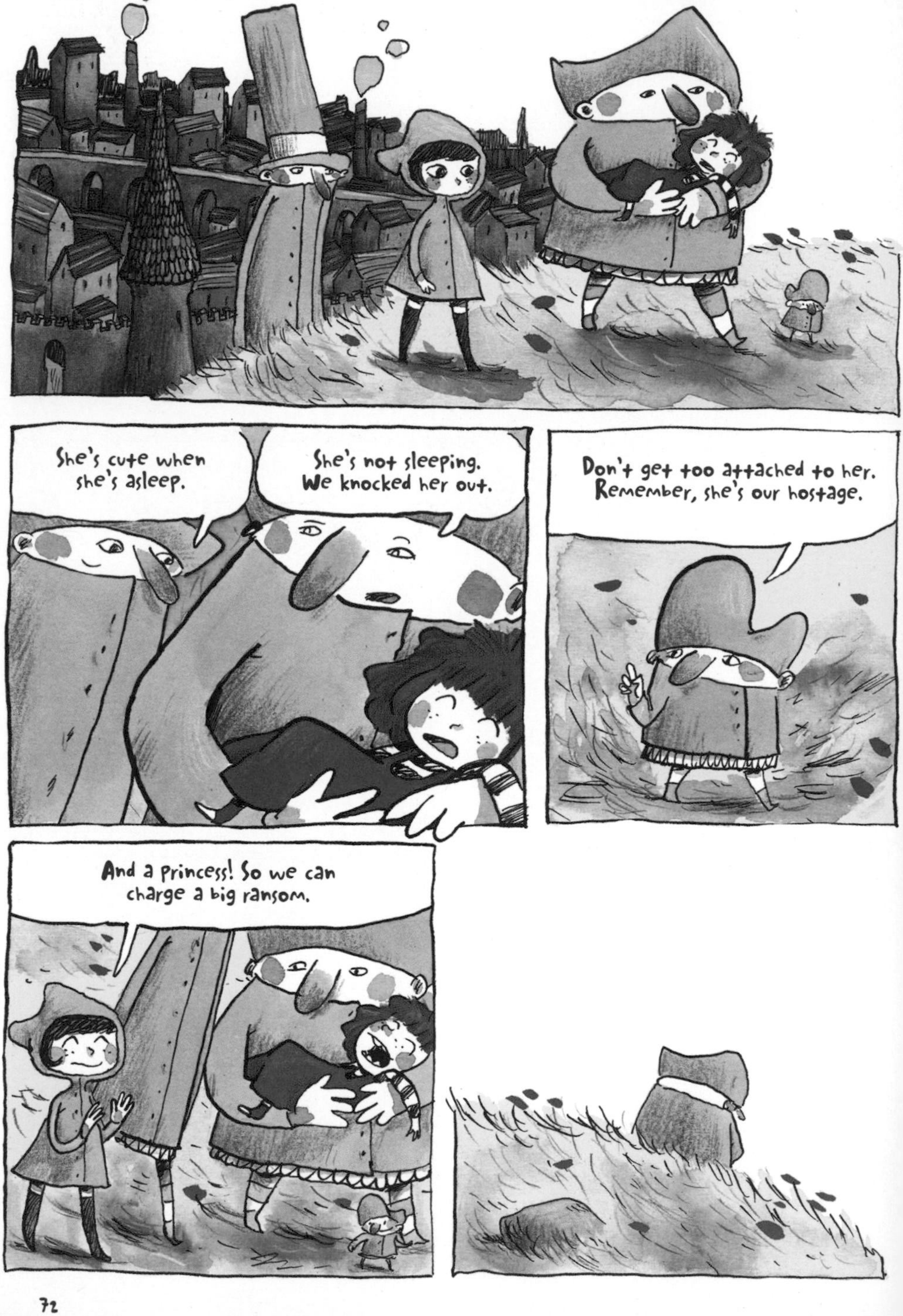

She's cute when she's asleep.
She's not sleeping. We knocked her out.
Don't get too attached to her. Remember, she's our hostage.
And a princess! So we can charge a big ransom.

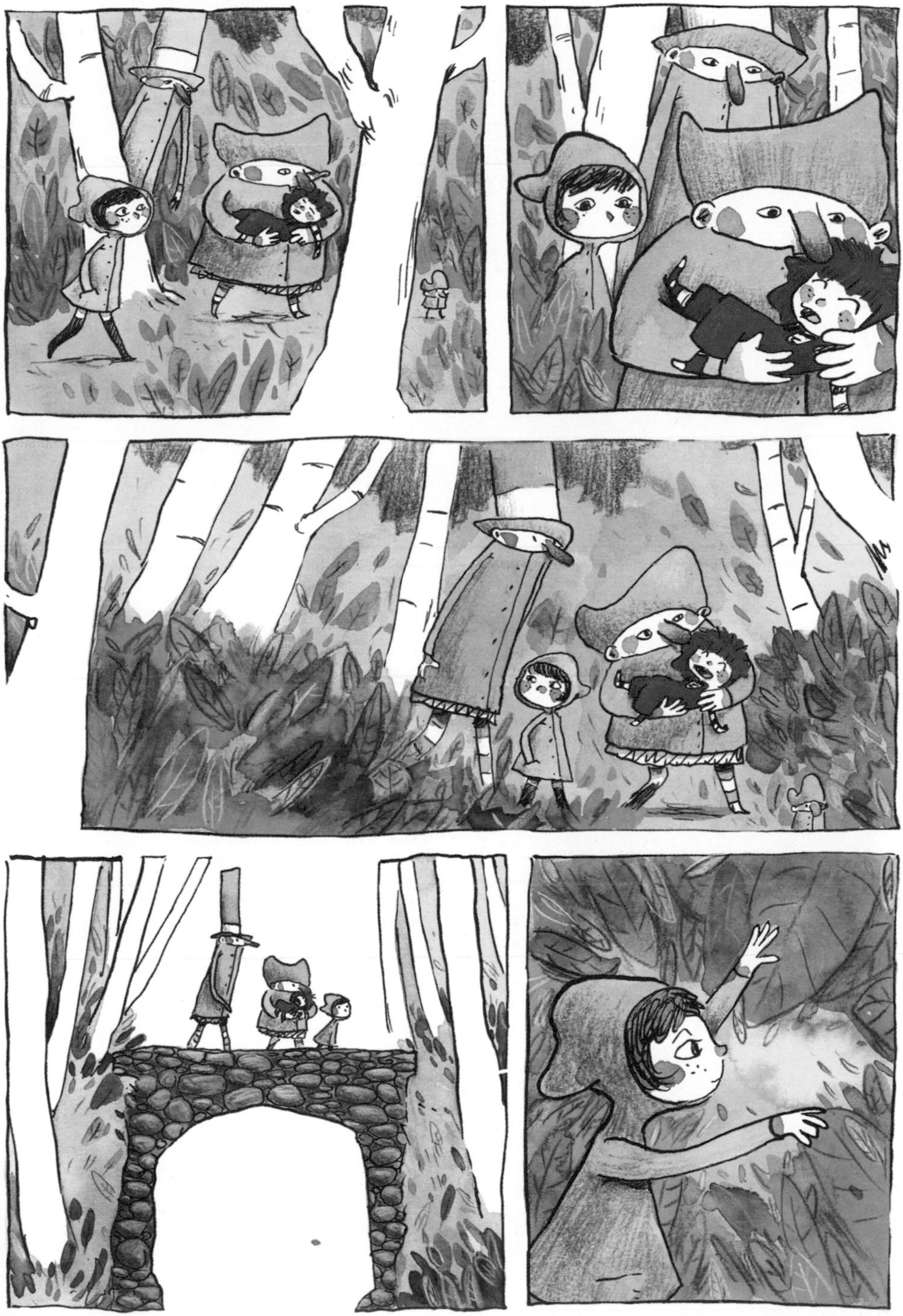

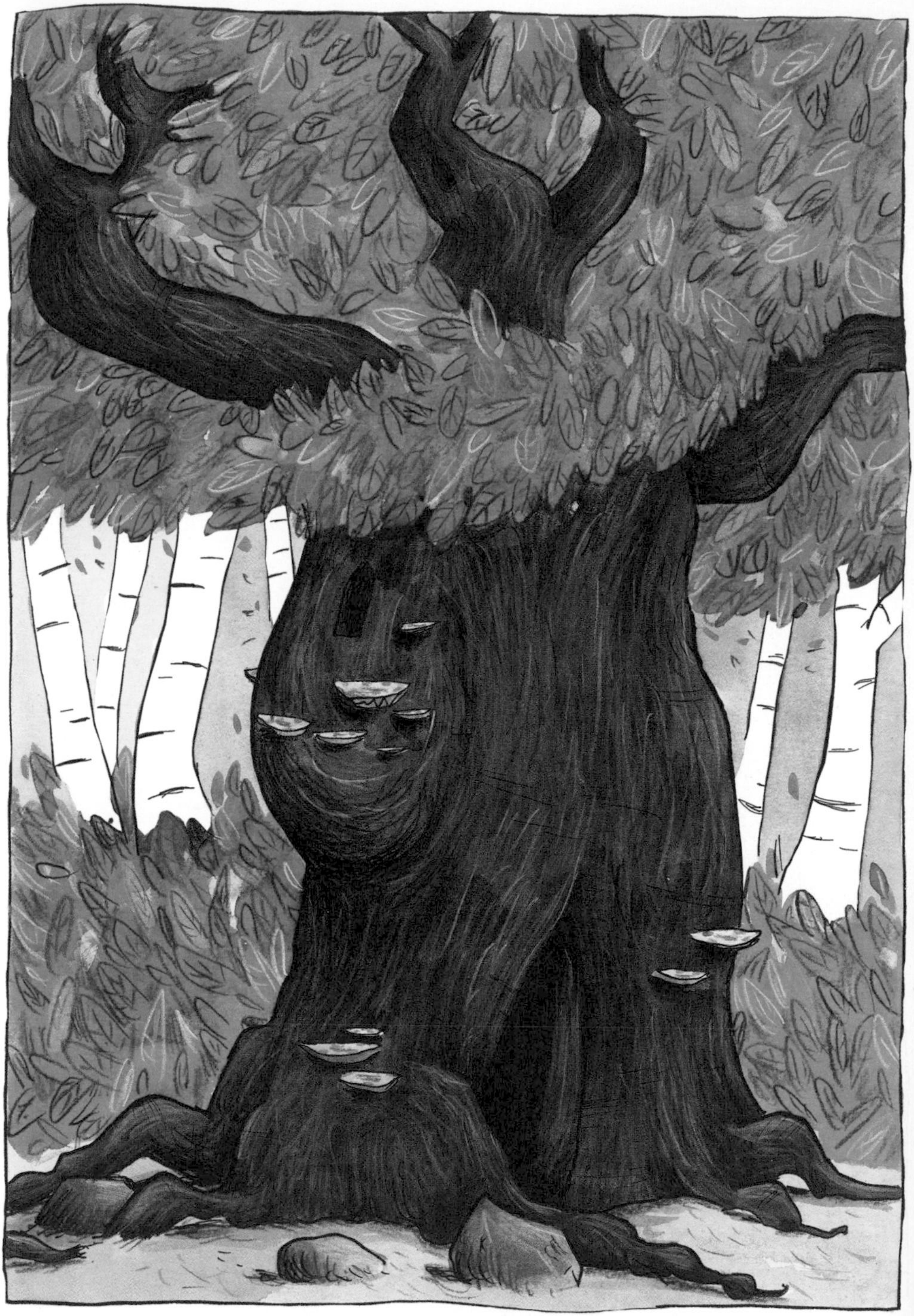

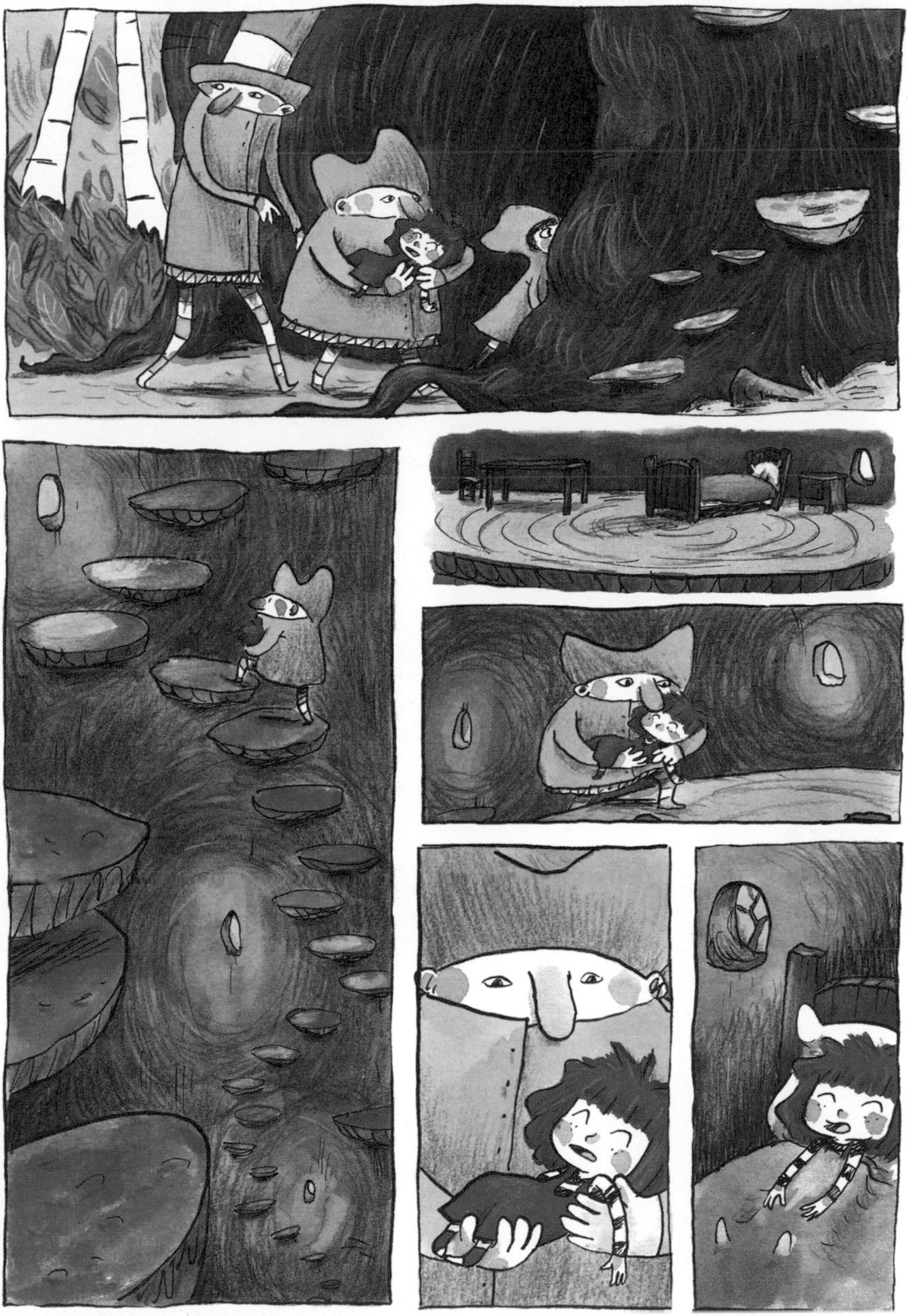

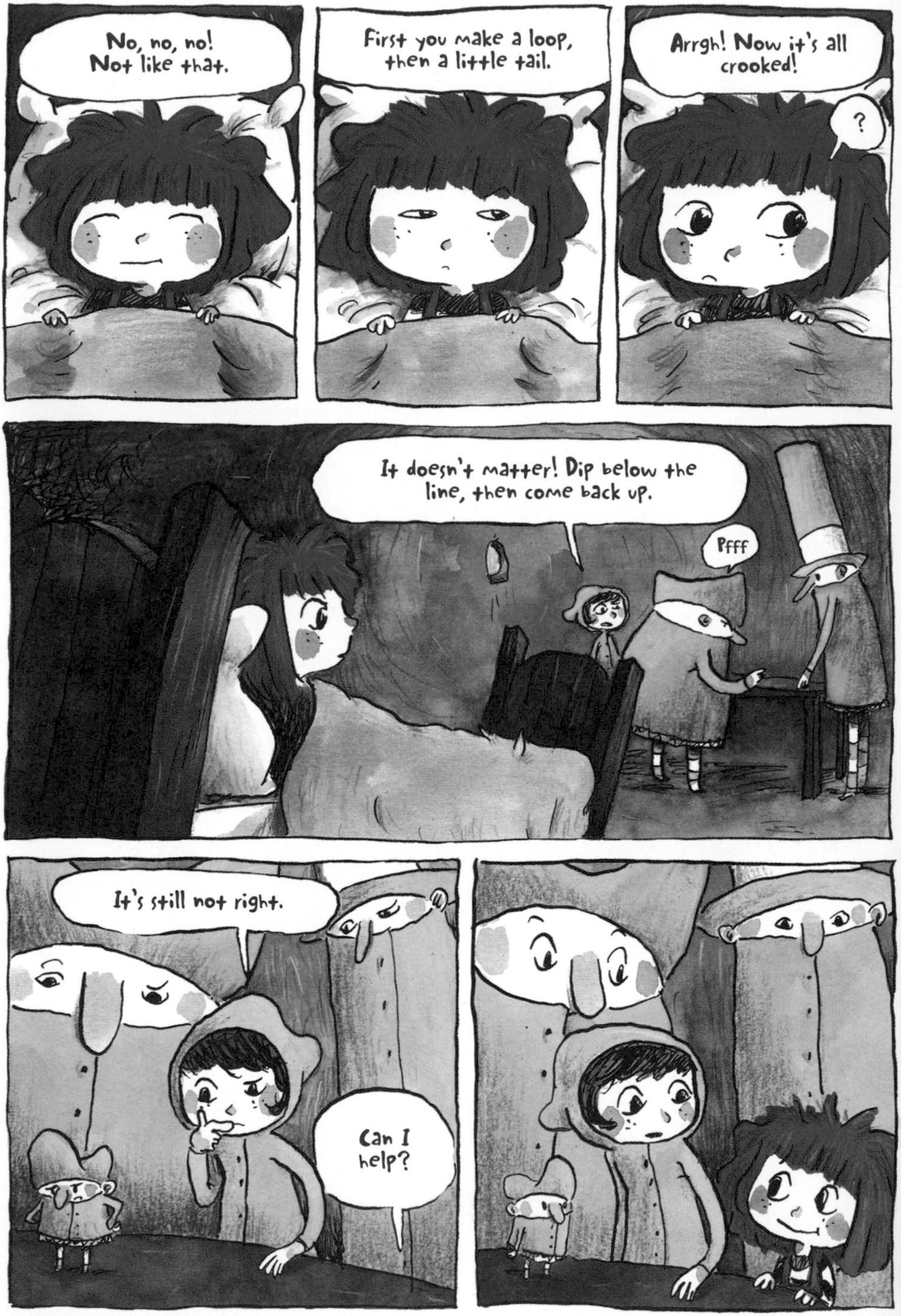
No, no, no!
Not like that.
First you make a loop,
then a little tail.
Arrgh! Now it's all
crooked!
?
It doesn't matter! Dip below the
line, then come back up.
Pfff
It's still not right.
Can I
help?

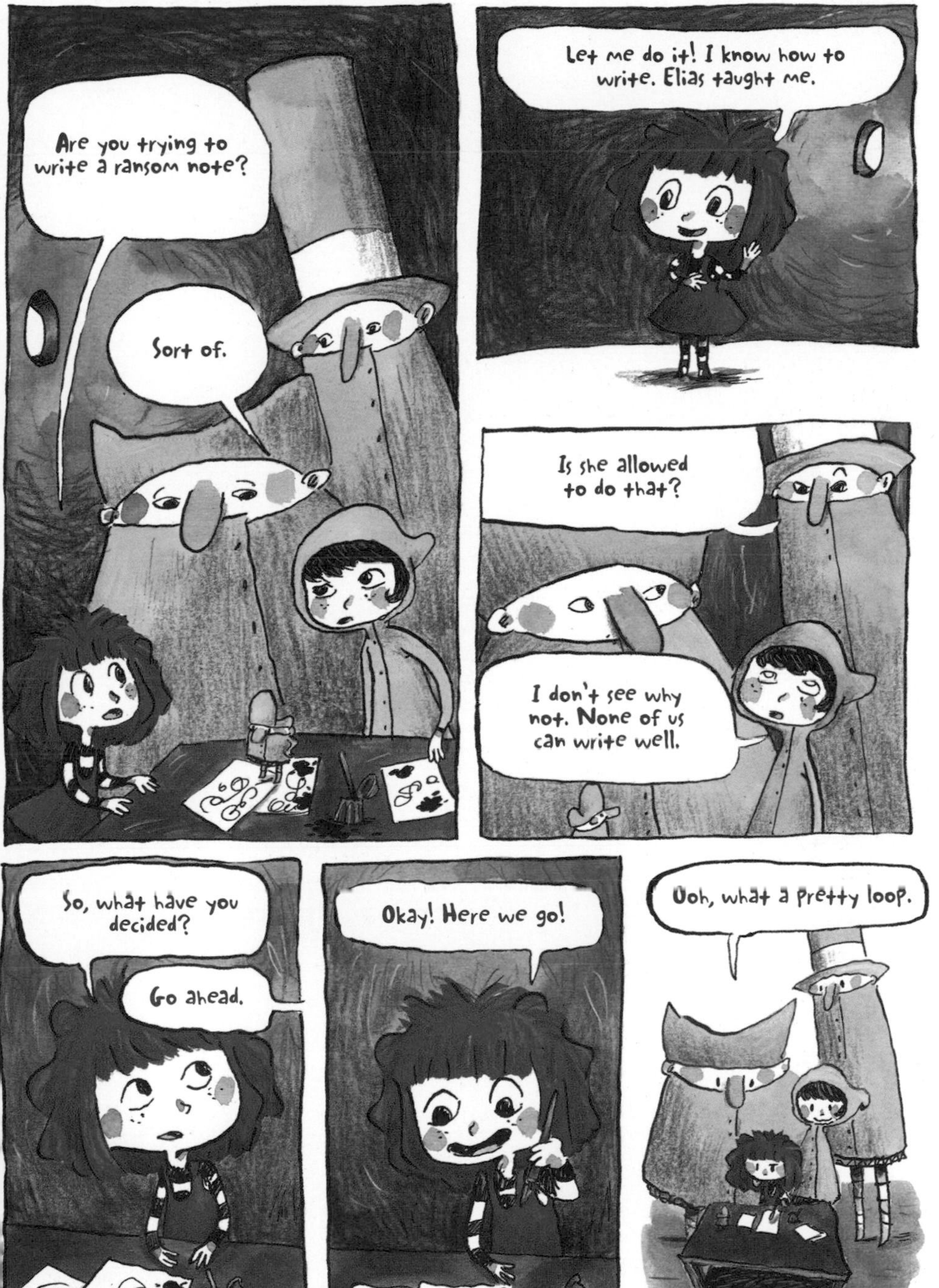

Are you trying to write a ransom note?
Sort of.
Let me do it! I know how to write. Elias taught me.
Is she allowed to do that?
I don't see why not. None of us can write well.
So, what have you decided?
Go ahead.
Okay! Here we go!
Ooh, what a pretty loop.

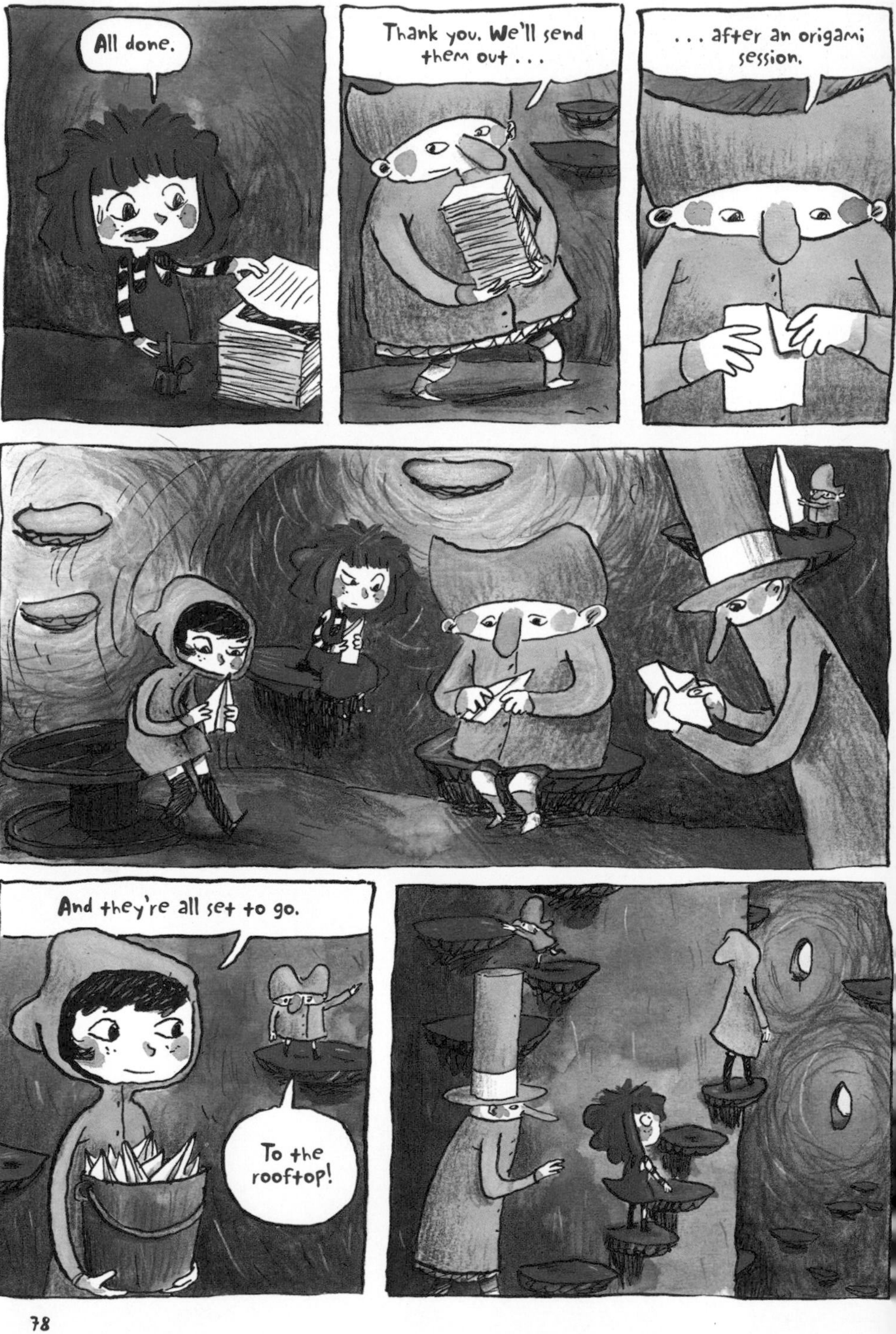
All done.
Thank you. We'll send them out . . .
. . . after an origami session.
And they're all set to go.
To the rooftop!

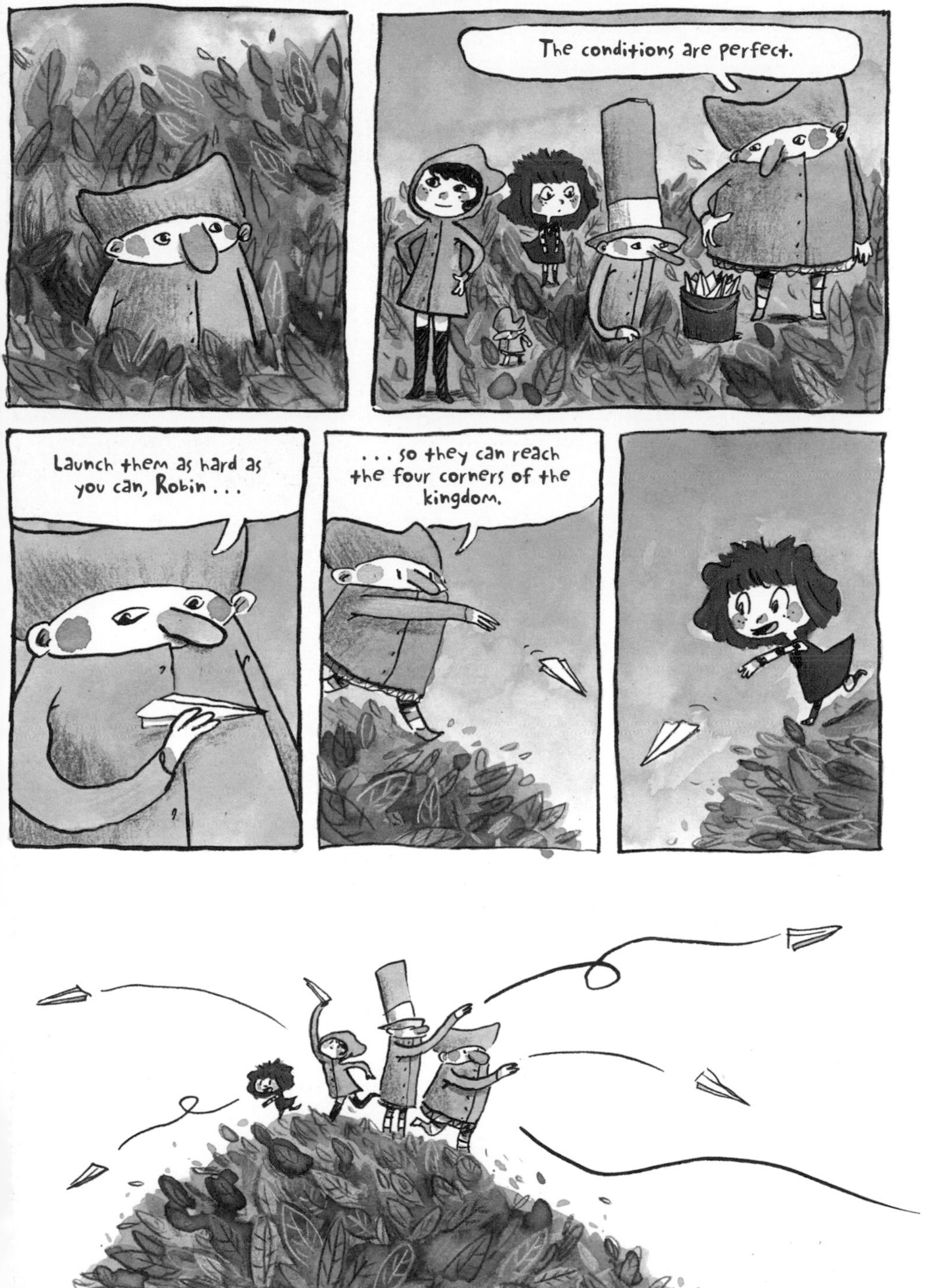
The conditions are perfect.
Launch them as hard as you can, Robin . . .
. . . so they can reach the four corners of the kingdom.

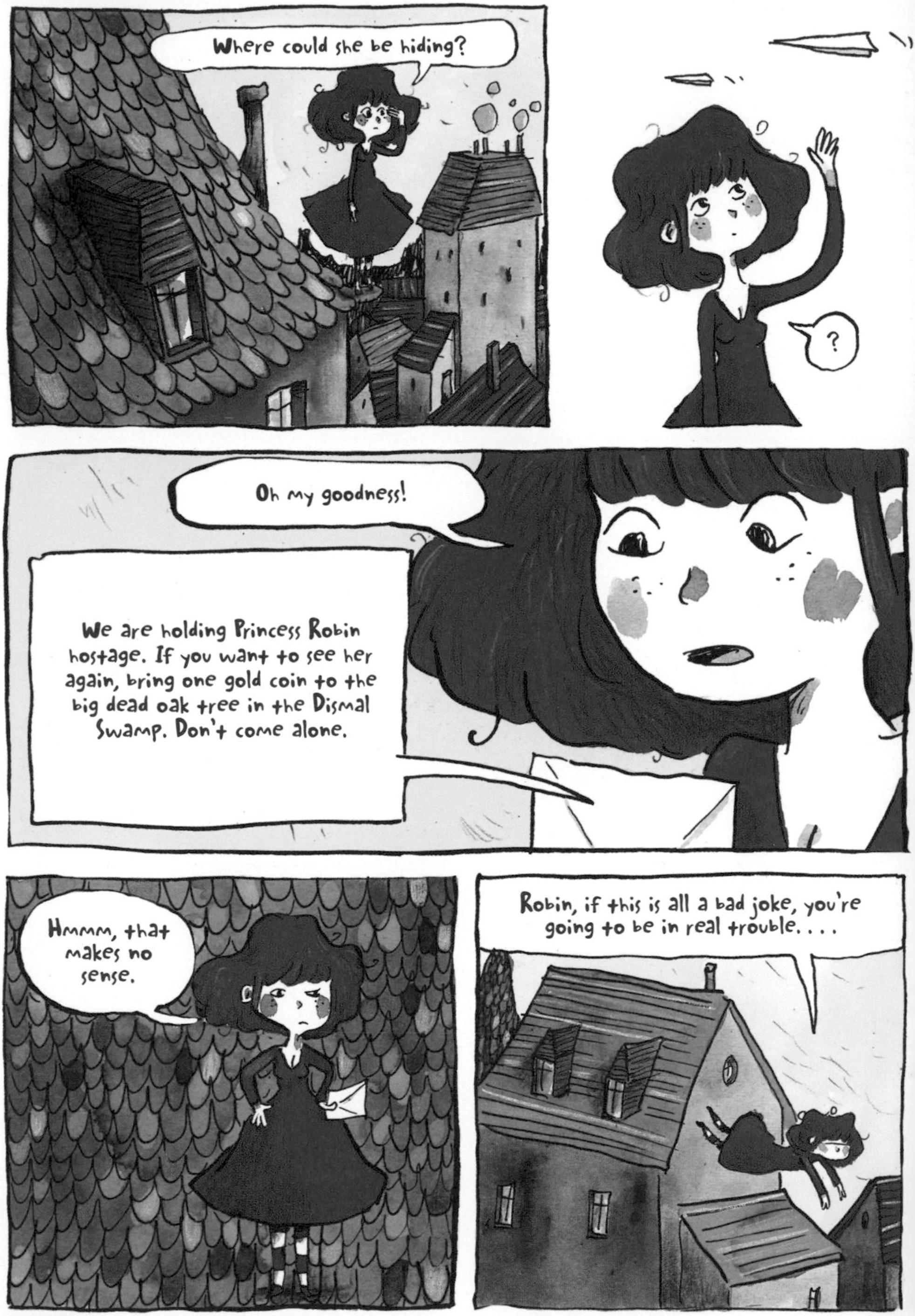
Where could she be hiding?
?
Oh my goodness!
We are holding Princess Robin hostage. If you want to see her again, bring one gold coin to the big dead oak tree in the Dismal Swamp. Don't come alone.
Hmmm, that makes no sense.
Robin, if this is all a bad joke, you're going to be in real trouble. . . .

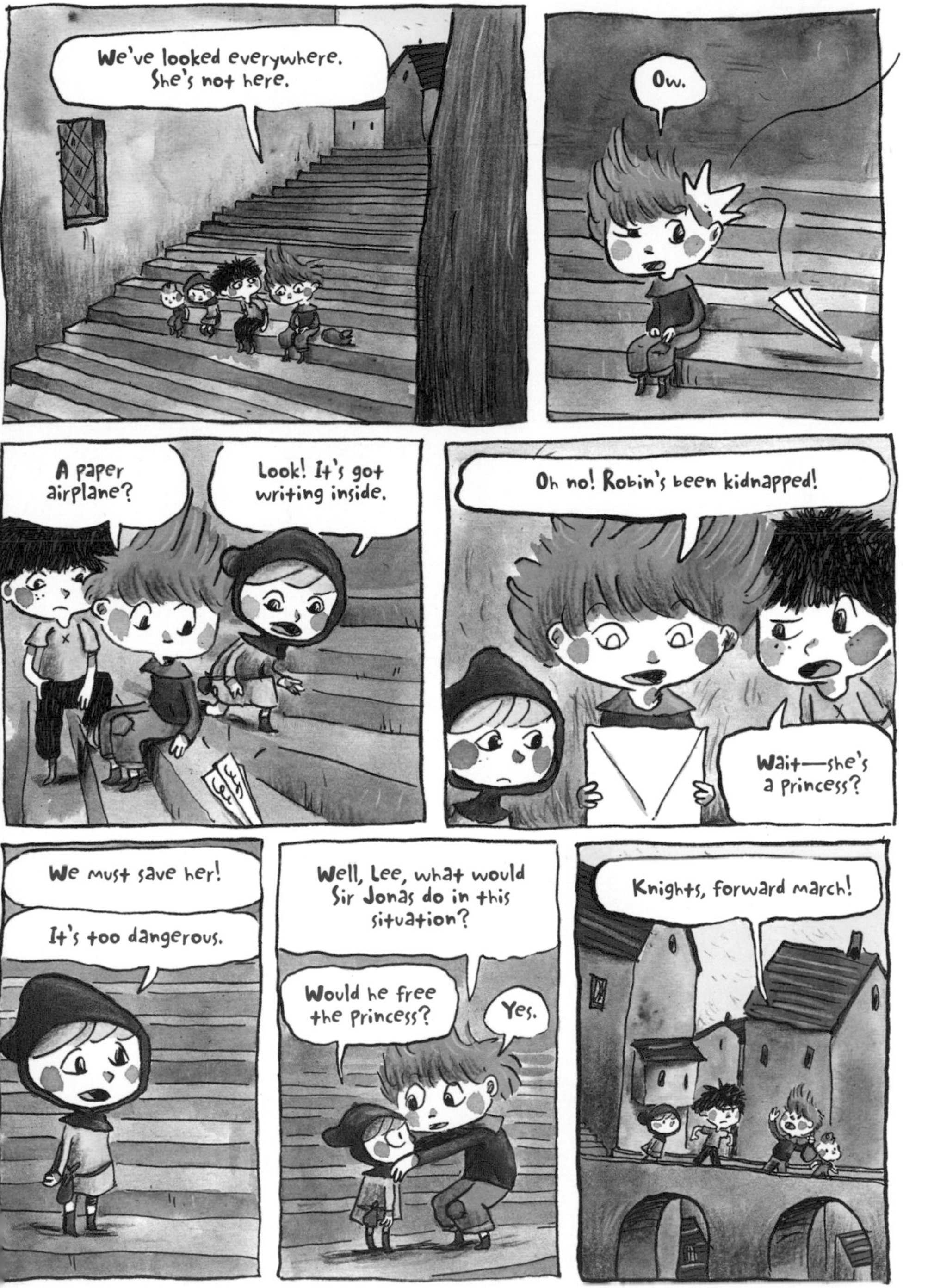
We've looked everywhere. She's not here.
Ow.
A paper airplane?
Look! It's got writing inside.
Oh no! Robin's been kidnapped!
Wait—she's a princess?
We must save her!
It's too dangerous.
Well, Lee, what would Sir Jonas do in this situation?
Would he free the princess?
Yes.
Knights, forward march!

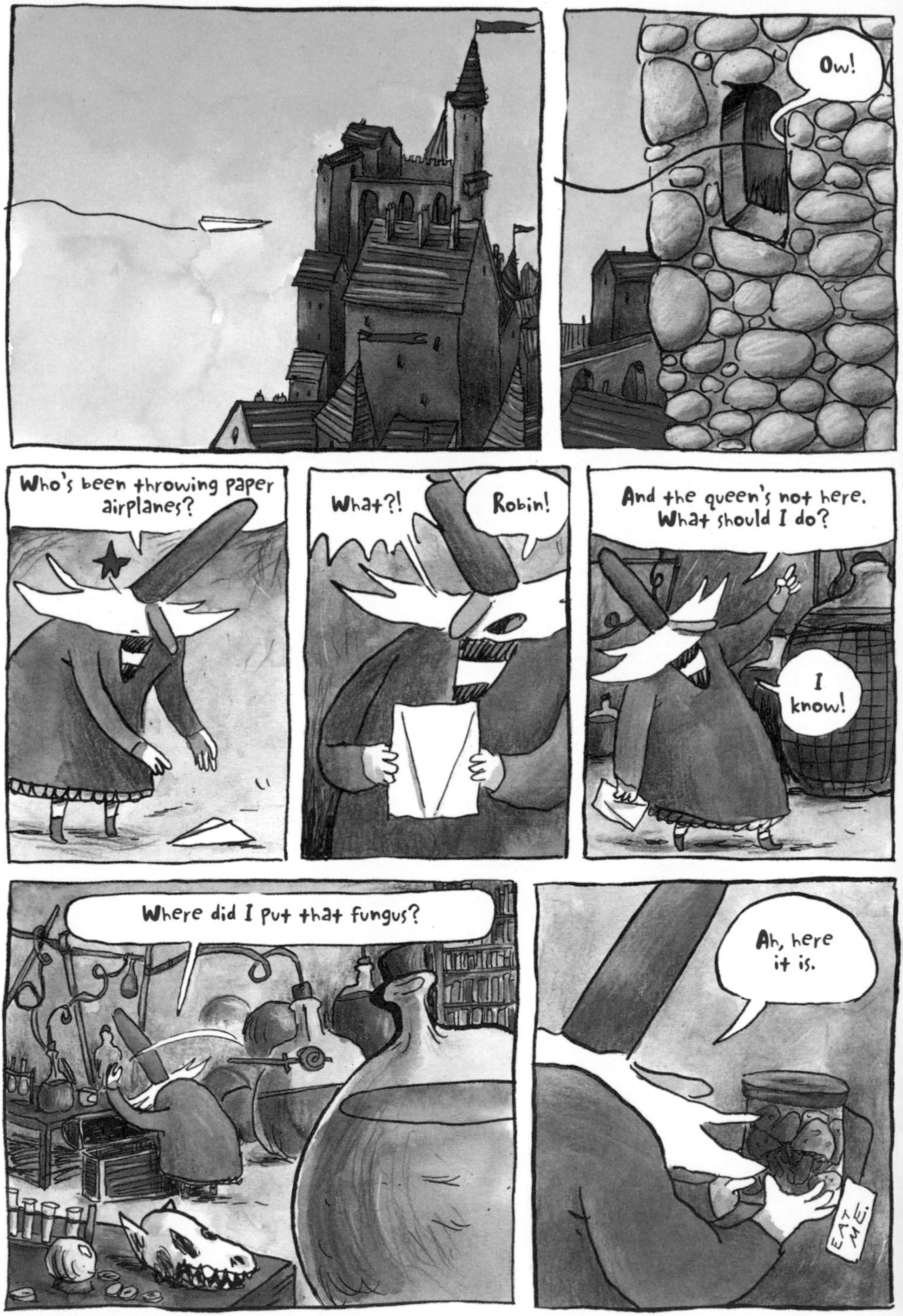
Ow!
Who's been throwing paper airplanes?
What?!
Robin!
And the queen's not here. What should I do?
I know!
Where did I put that fungus?
Ah, here it is.
EAT ME.

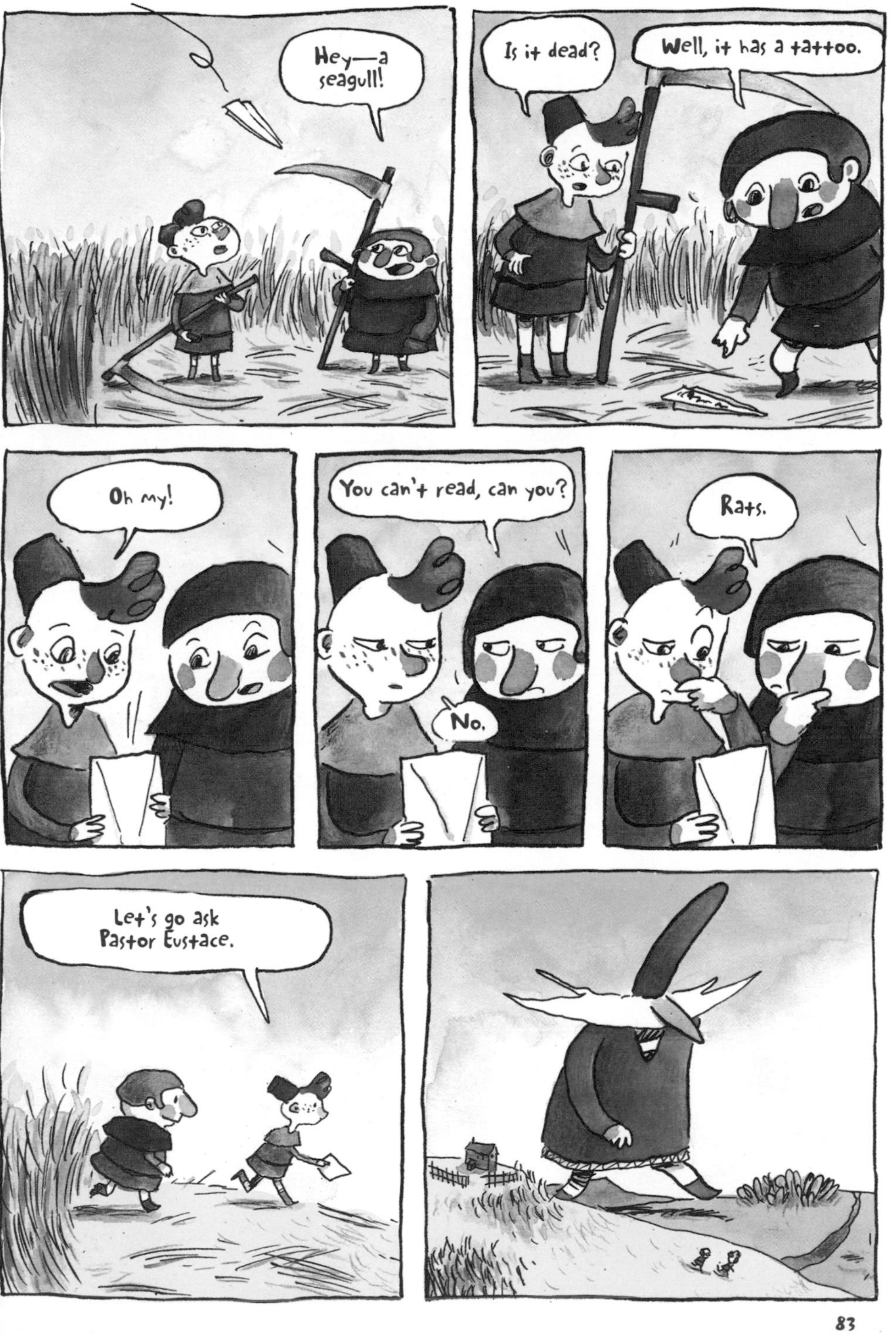
Hey—a seagull!
Is it dead?
Well, it has a tattoo.
Oh my!
You can't read, can you?
No.
Rats.
Let's go ask Pastor Eustace.

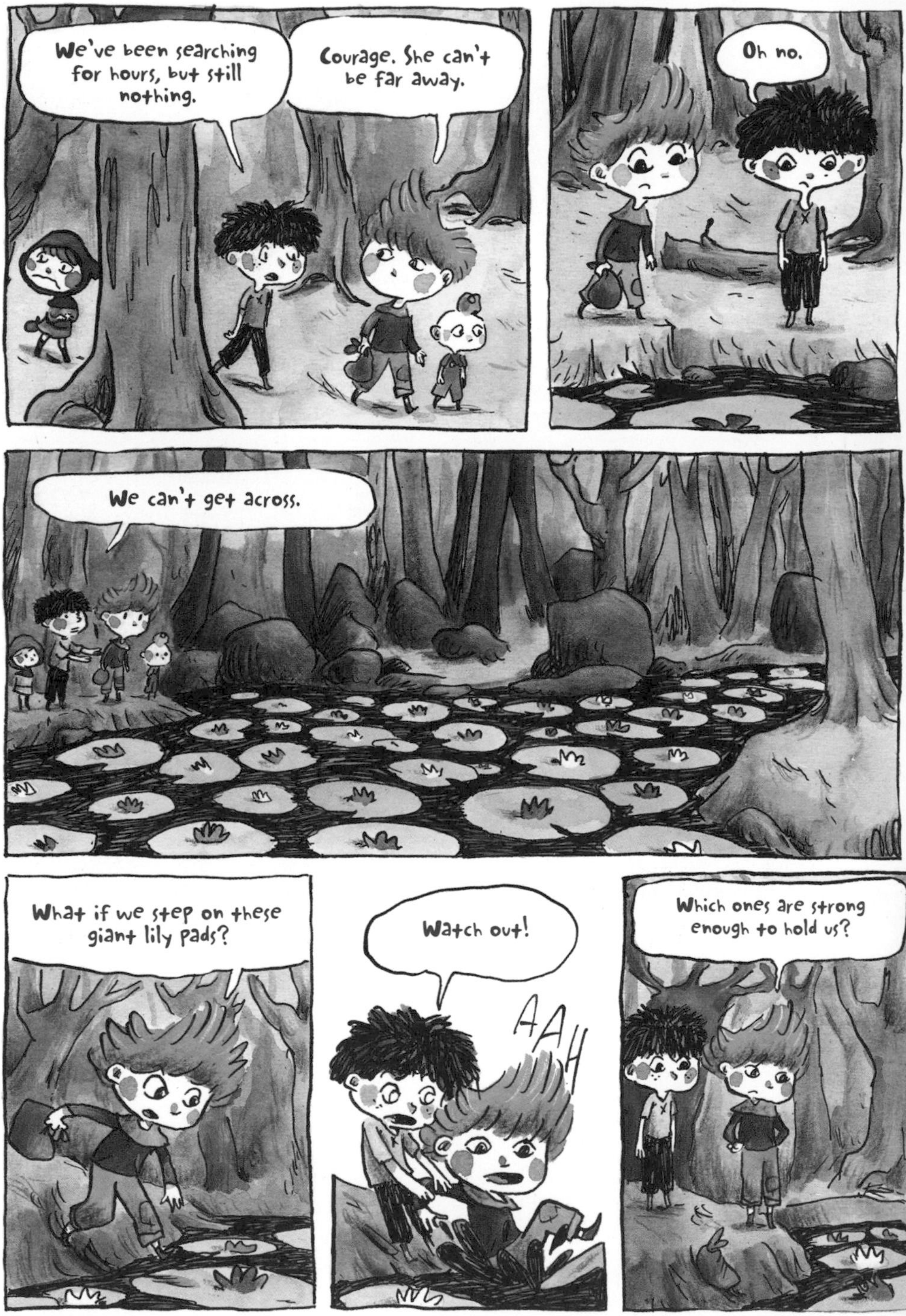
We've been searching for hours, but still nothing.
Courage. She can't be far away.
Oh no.
We can't get across.
What if we step on these giant lily pads?
Watch out!
AAH
Which ones are strong enough to hold us?

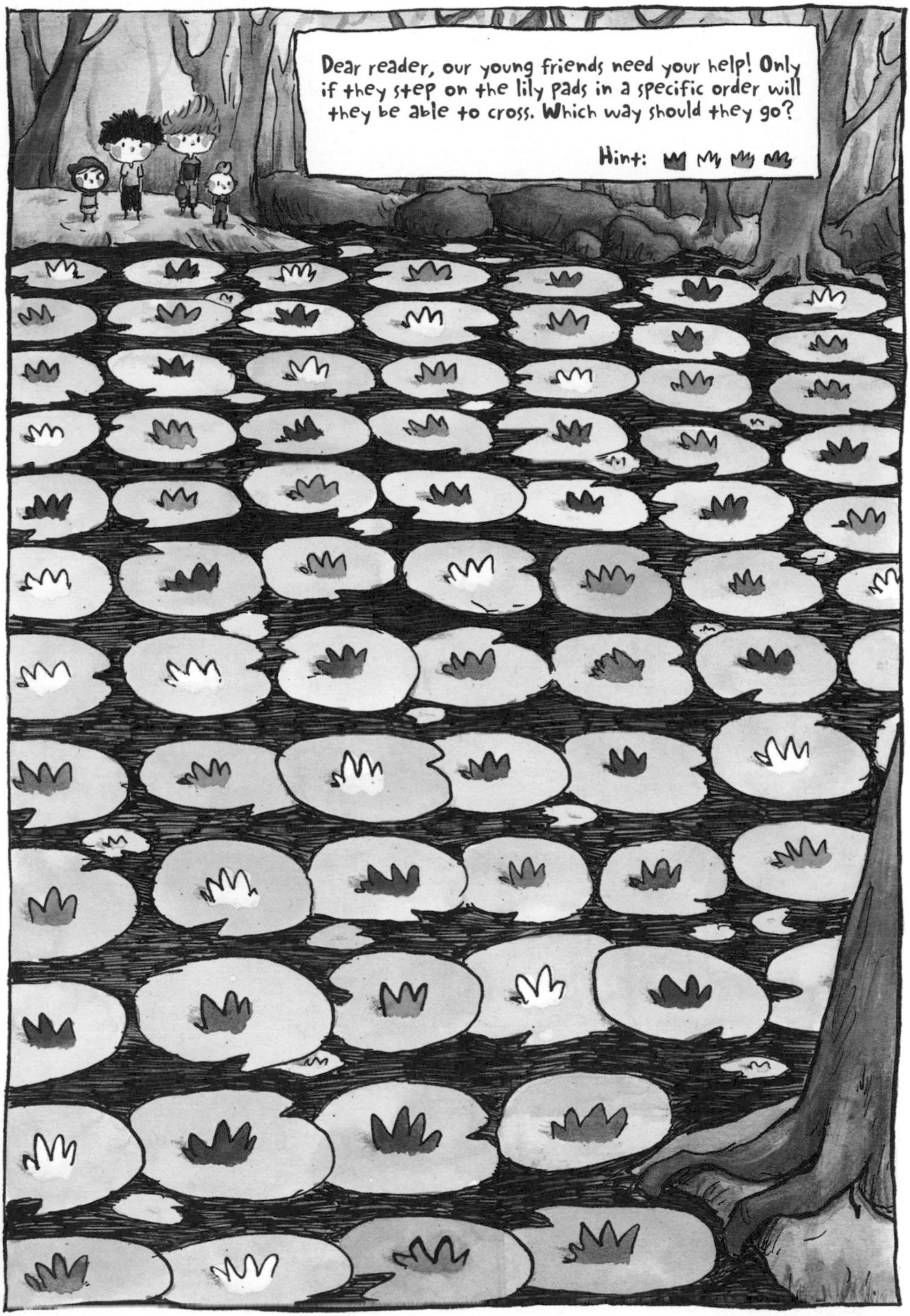
Dear reader, our young friends need your help! Only if they step on the lily pads in a specific order will they be able to cross. Which way should they go?
Hint:

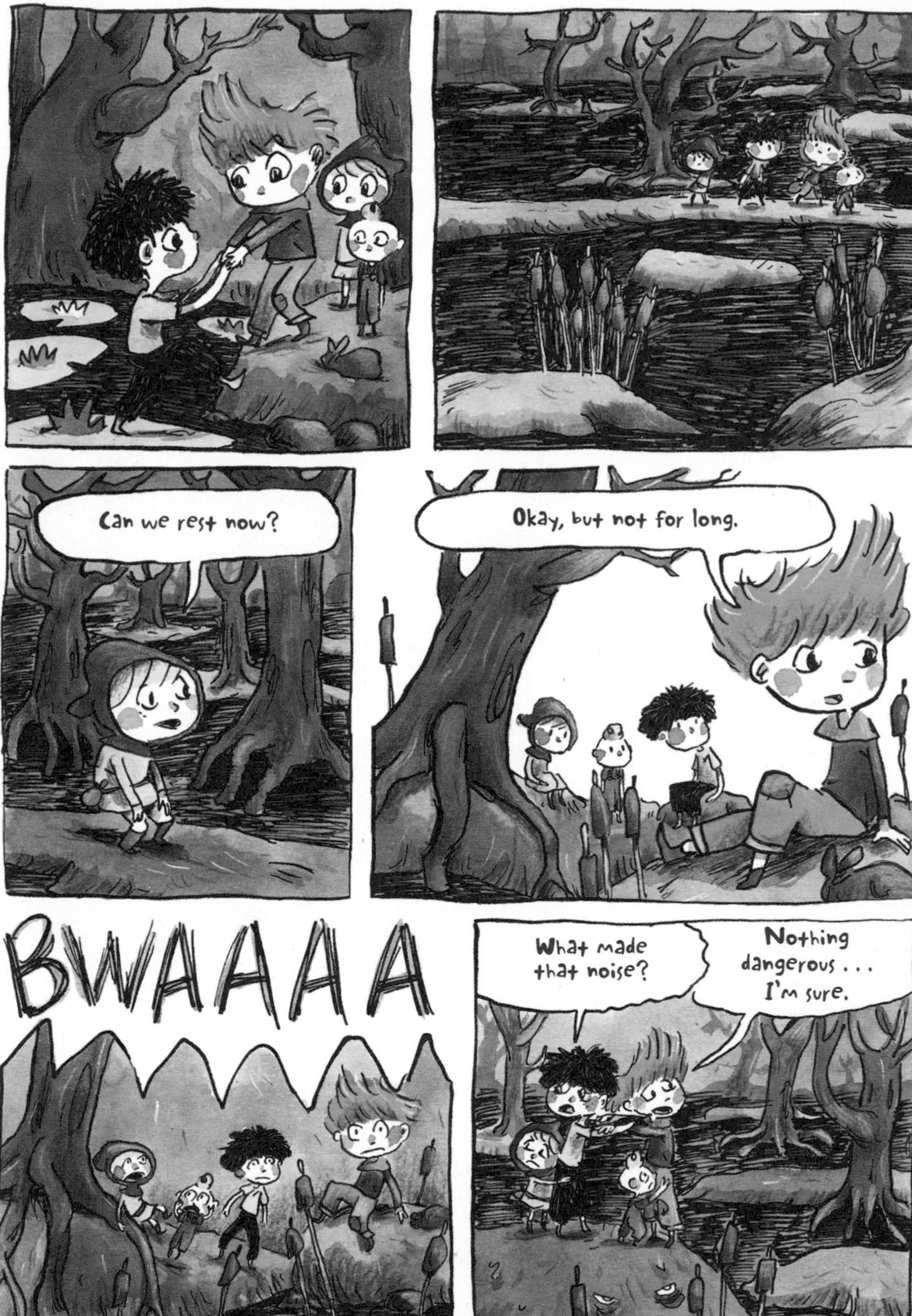
Can we rest now?
Okay, but not for long.
BWAAAA
What made that noise?
Nothing dangerous . . . I'm sure.

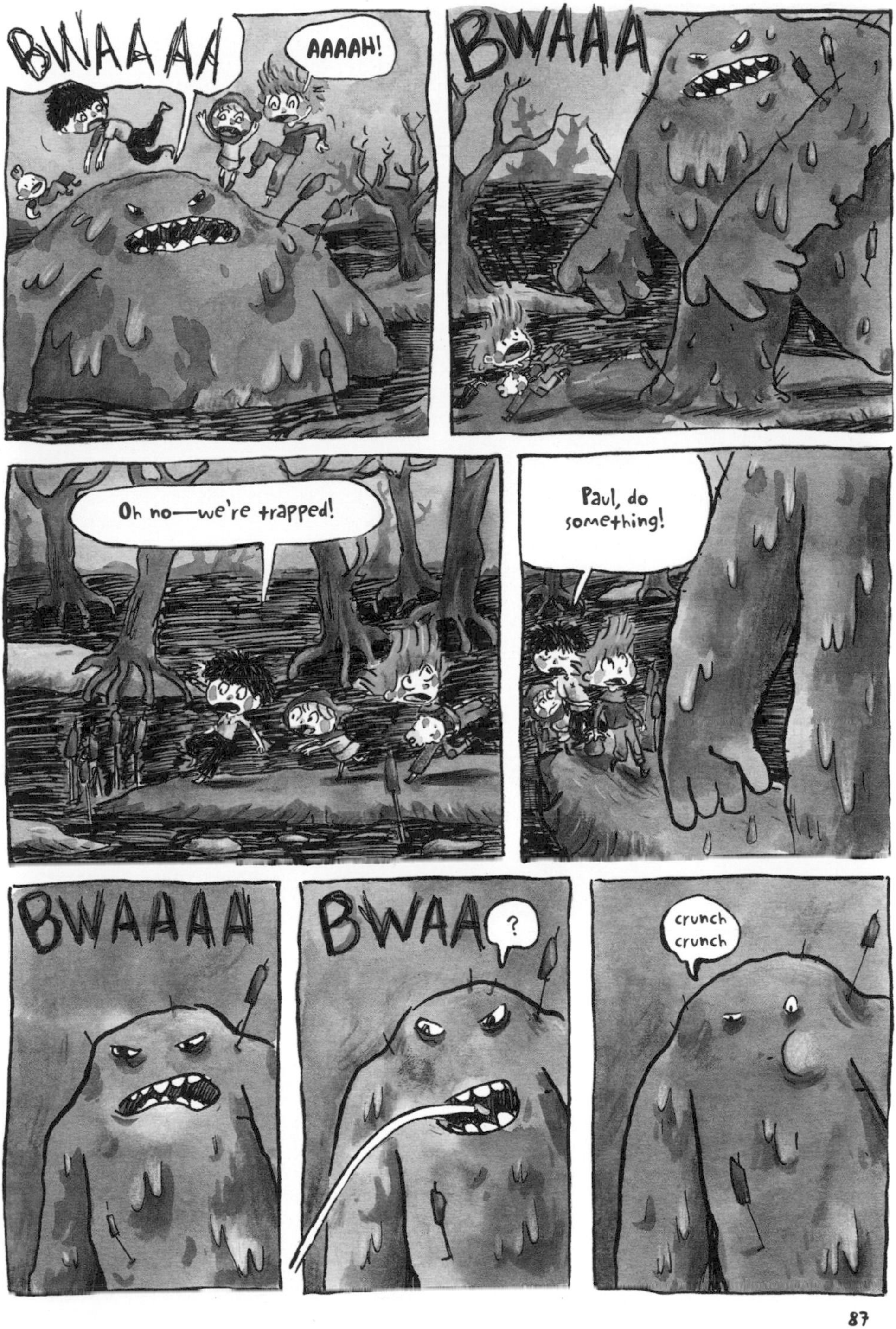
BWAAAA
AAAAH!
BWAAA
Oh no—we're trapped!
Paul, do something!
BWAAAA
BWAA
?
crunch crunch

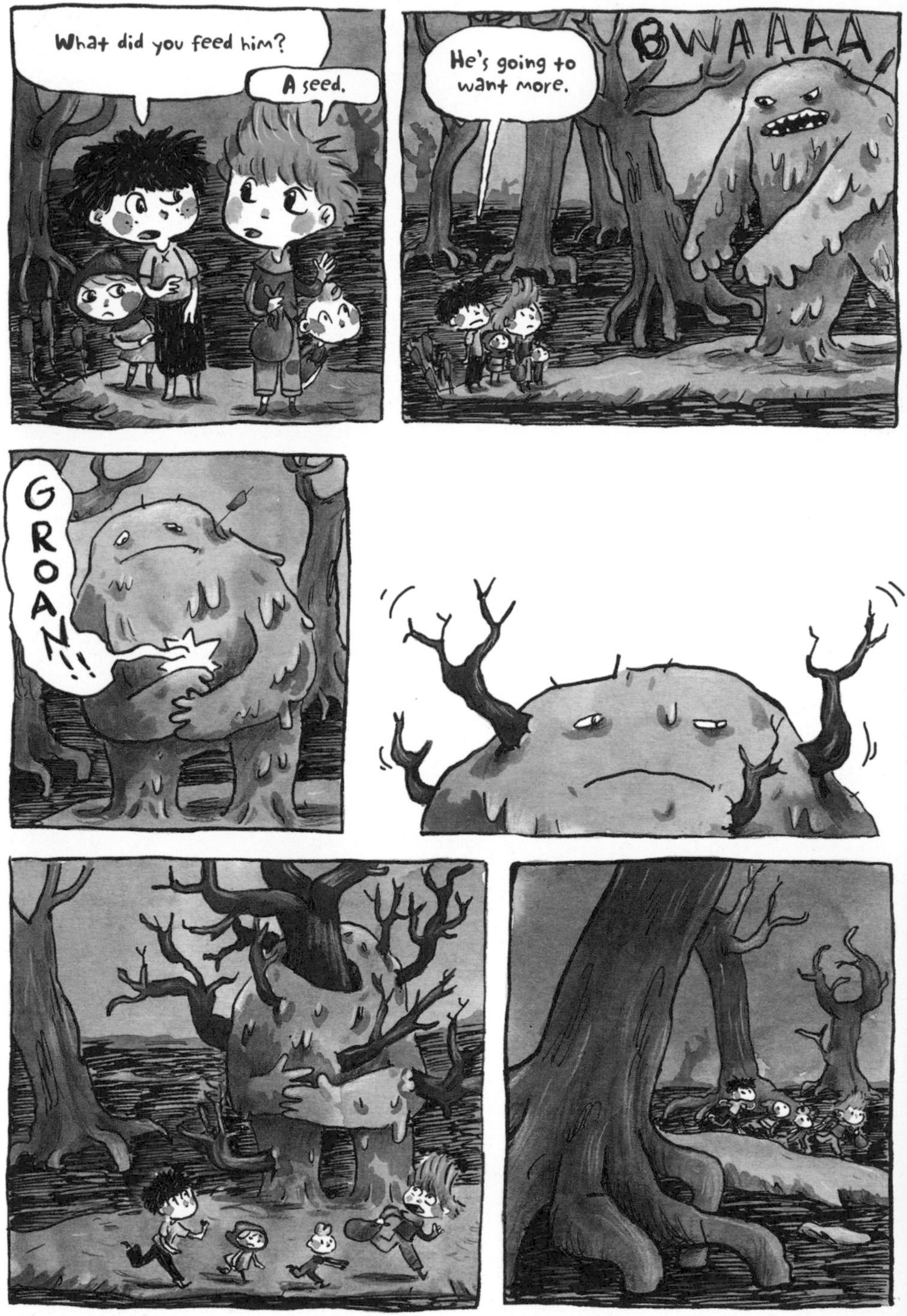

What did you feed him?
A seed.
He's going to want more.
BWAAAA
GROAN!!

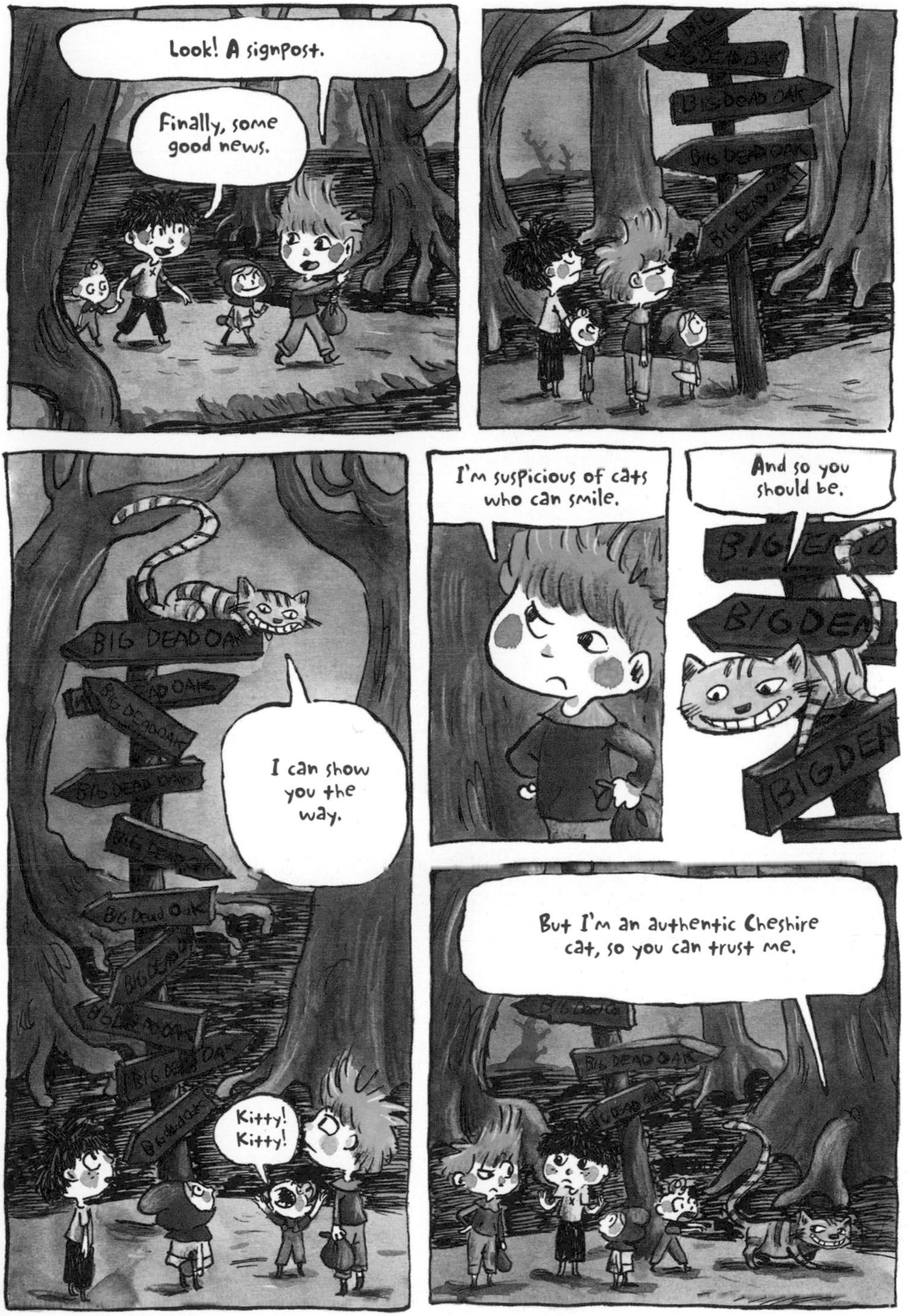
Look! A signpost.
Finally, some good news.
BIG DEAD OAK
BIG DEAD OAK
BIG DEAD OAK
I can show you the way.
Kitty! Kitty!
I'm suspicious of cats who can smile.
And so you should be.
But I'm an authentic Cheshire cat, so you can trust me.
BIG DEAD OAK

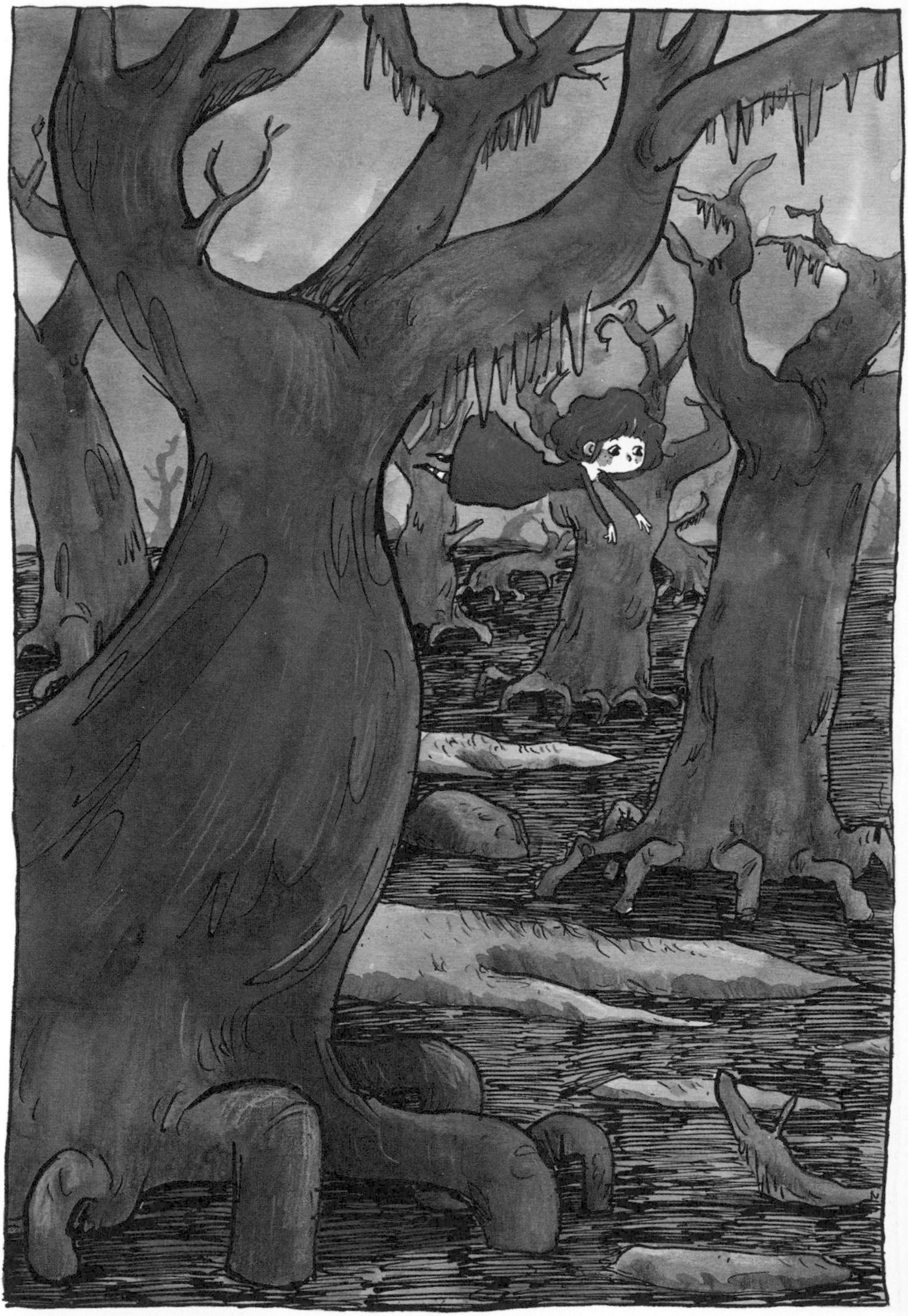

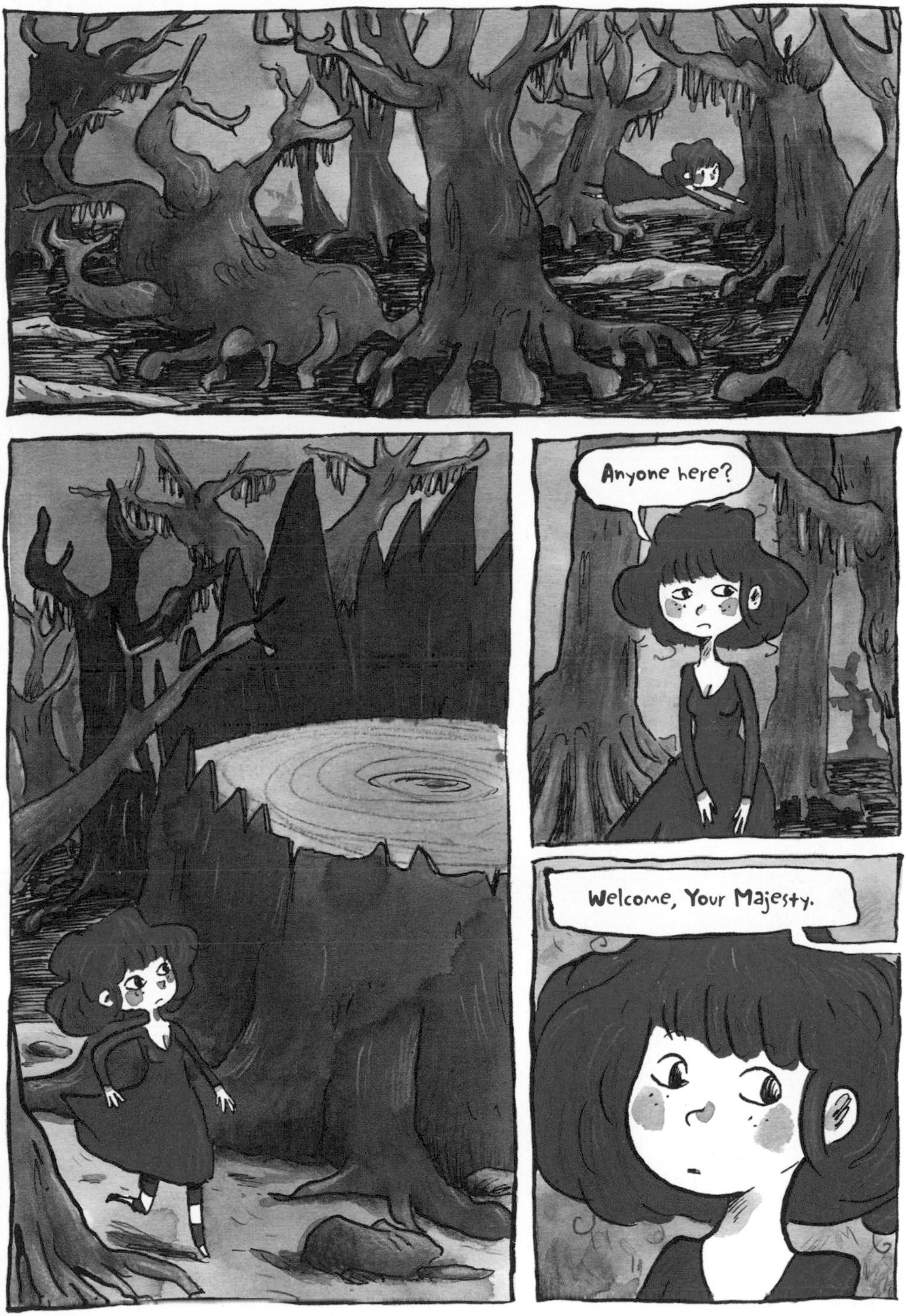
Anyone here?
Welcome, Your Majesty.

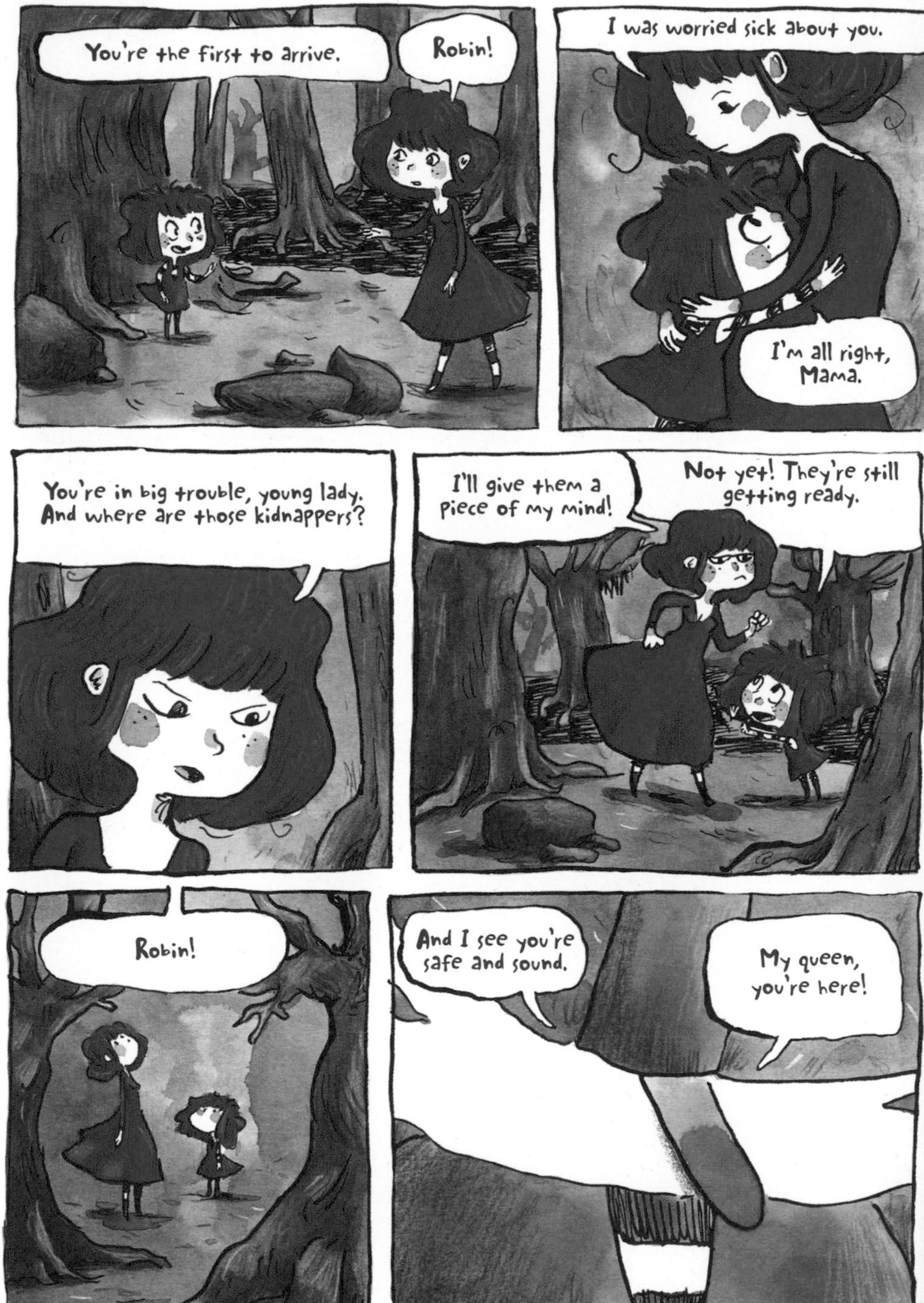

You're the first to arrive.
Robin!
I was worried sick about you.
I'm all right, Mama.
You're in big trouble, young lady. And where are those kidnappers?
I'll give them a piece of my mind!
Not yet! They're still getting ready.
Robin!
And I see you're safe and sound.
My queen, you're here!

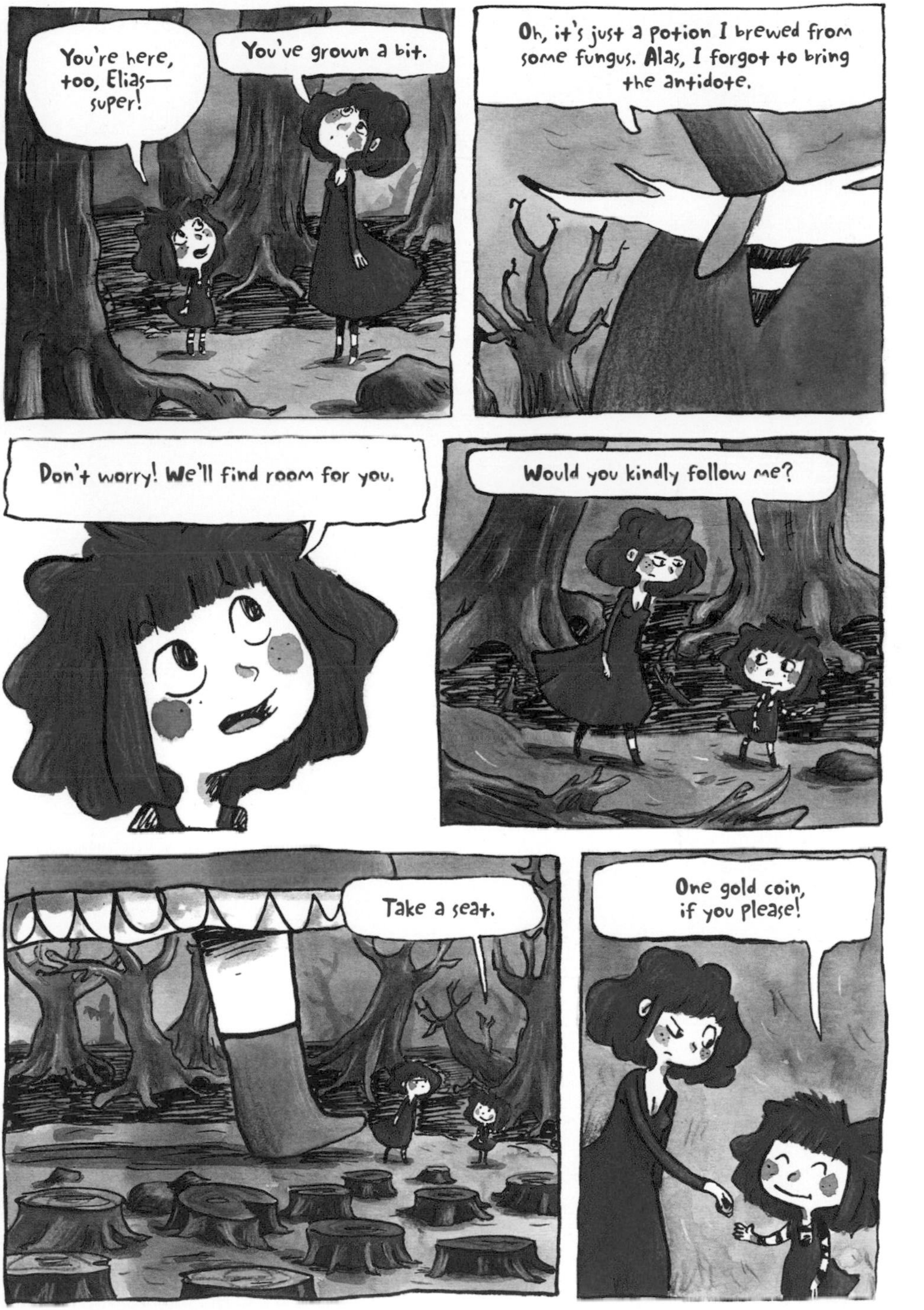
You're here, too, Elias—super!
You've grown a bit.
Oh, it's just a potion I brewed from some fungus. Alas, I forgot to bring the antidote.
Don't worry! We'll find room for you.
Would you kindly follow me?
Take a seat.
One gold coin, if you please!

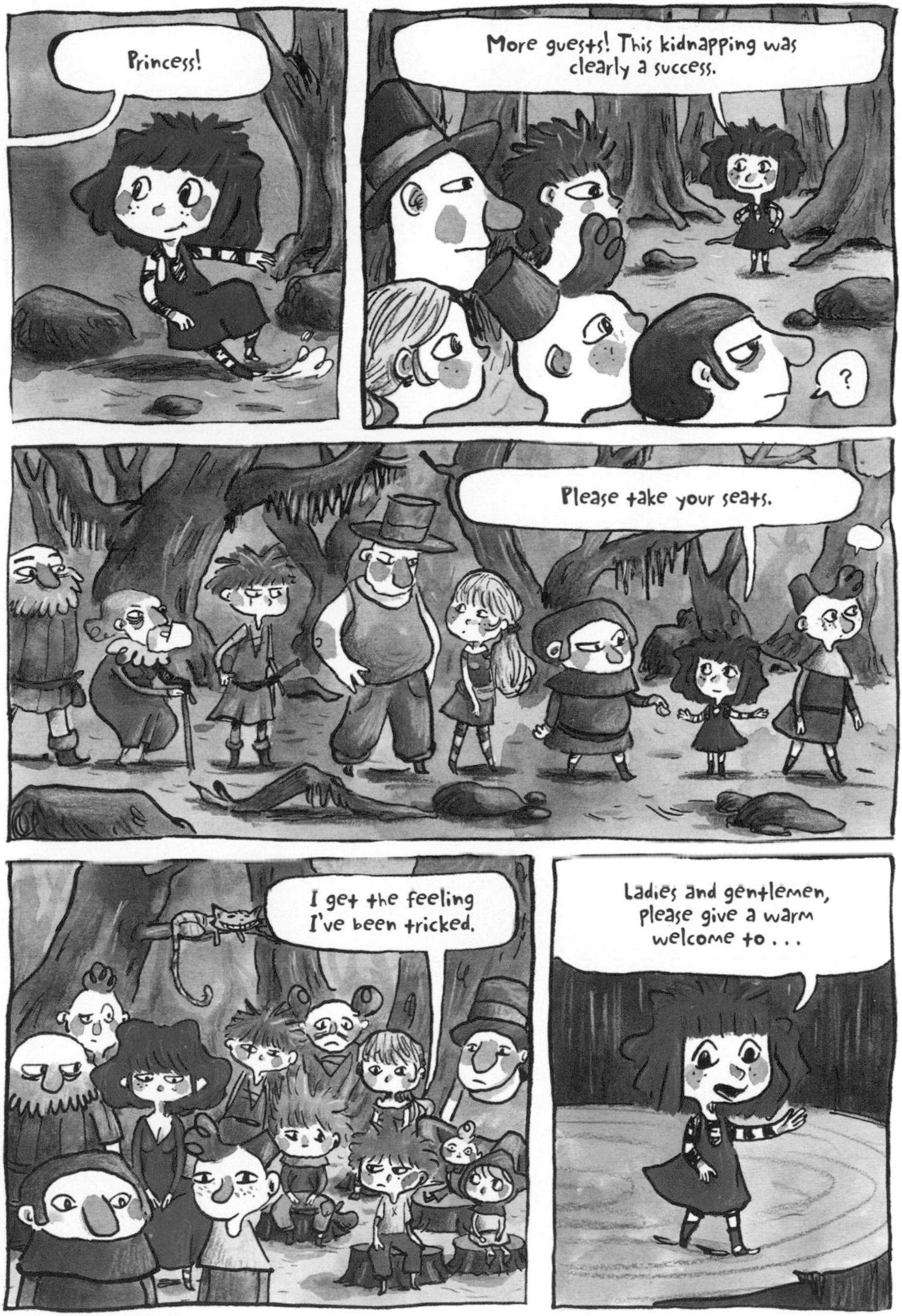
Princess!
More guests! This kidnapping was clearly a success.
?
Please take your seats.
I get the feeling I've been tricked.
Ladies and gentlemen, please give a warm welcome to . . .

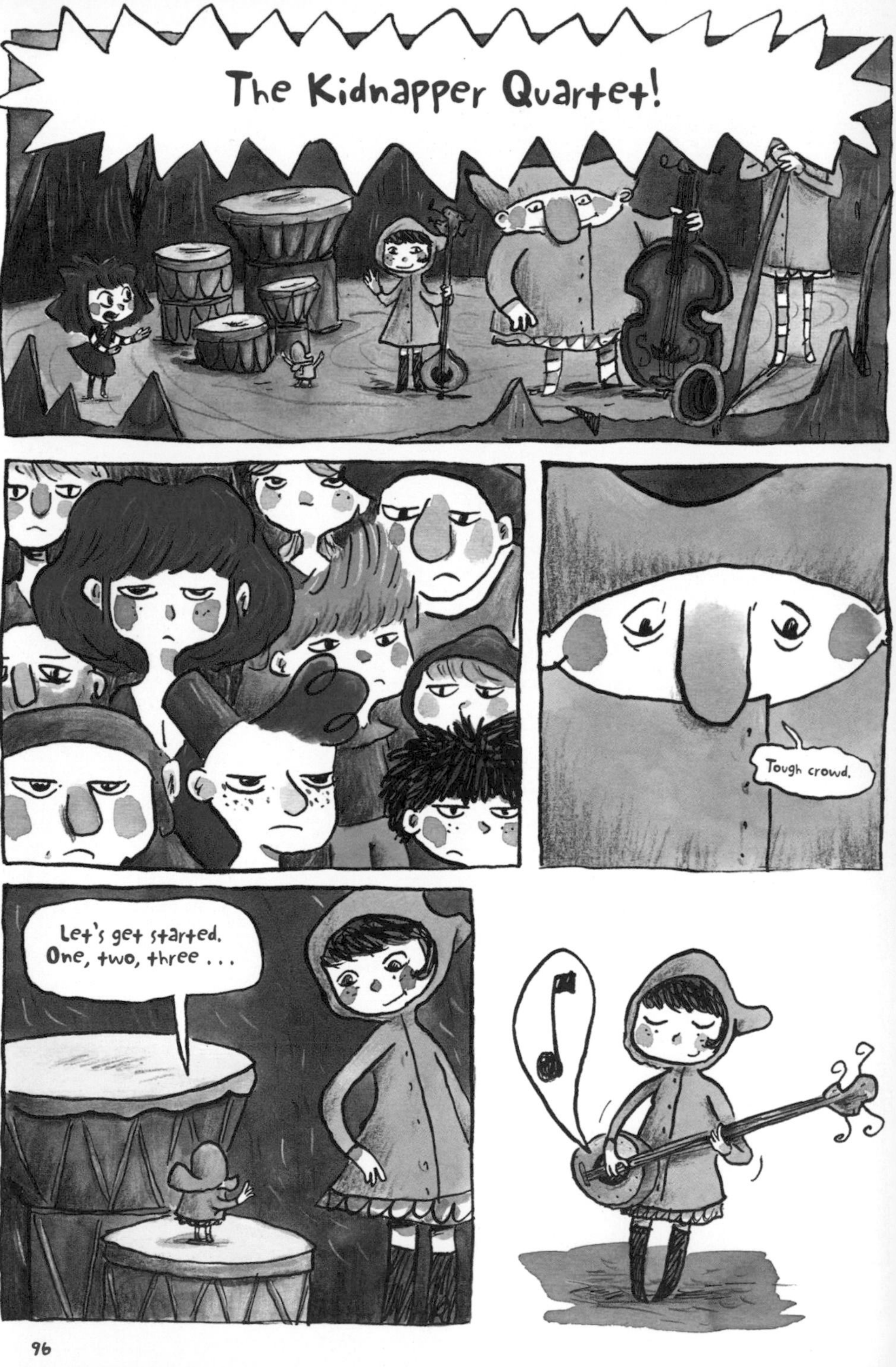
The Kidnapper Quartet!
Tough crowd.
Let's get started. One, two, three . . .

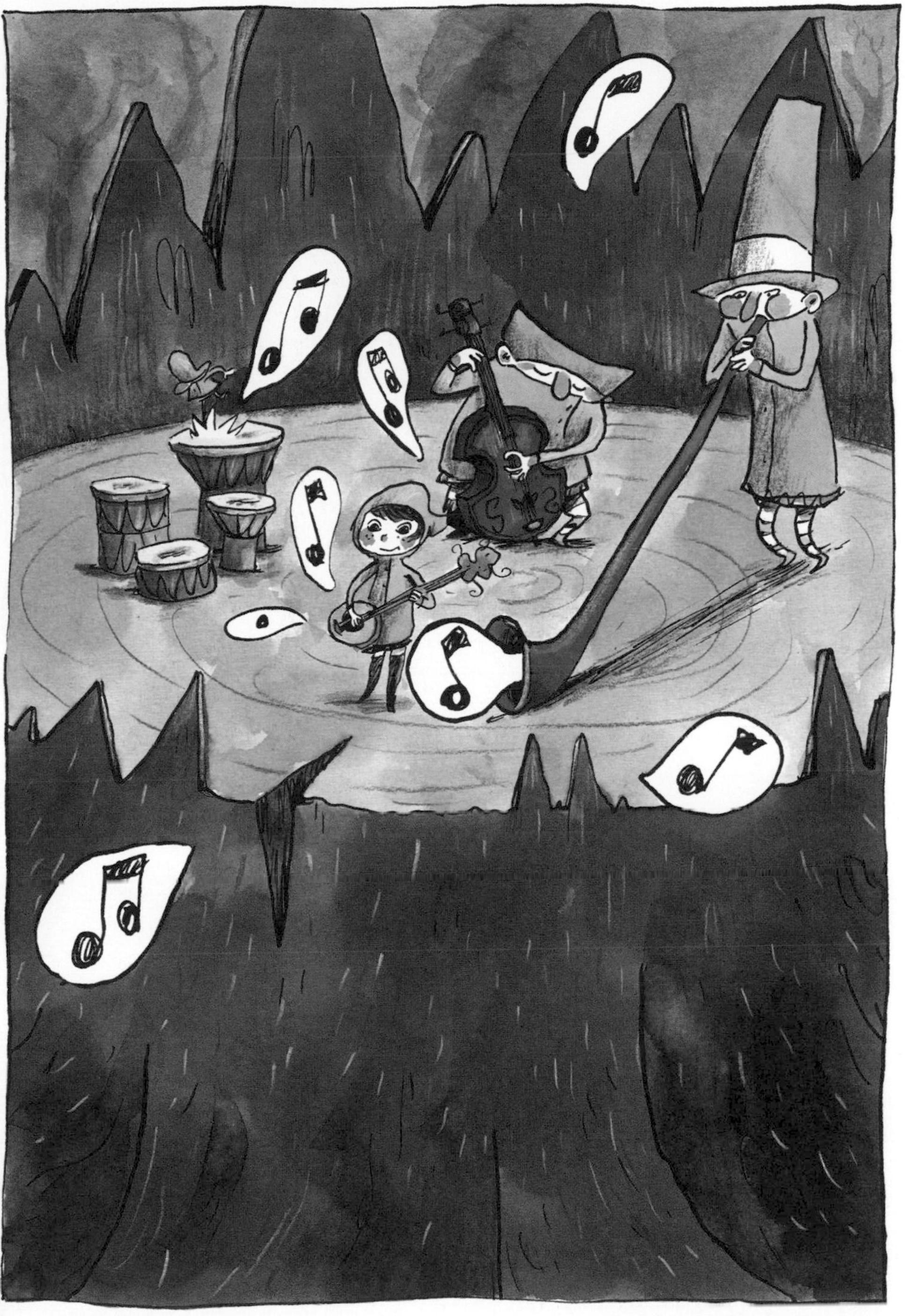

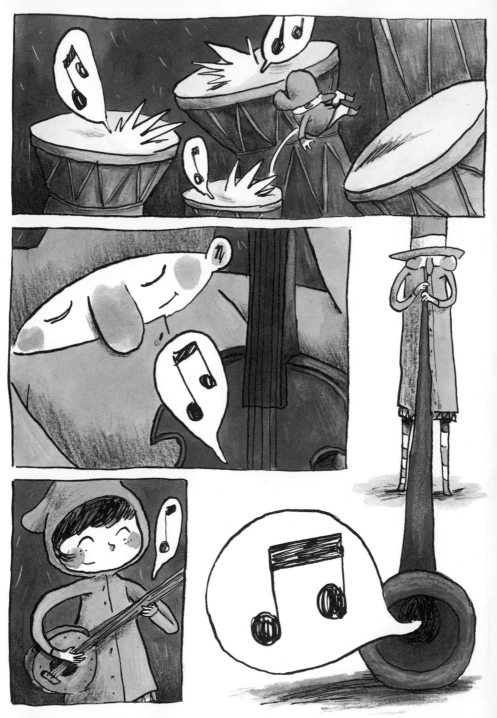

99

Paul, Matt, Lee, and Omar went home and showed their parents the bag of seeds. Immediately, the boys began to plant a garden and were soon able to feed the whole family.

TROIA1SNOWSKI

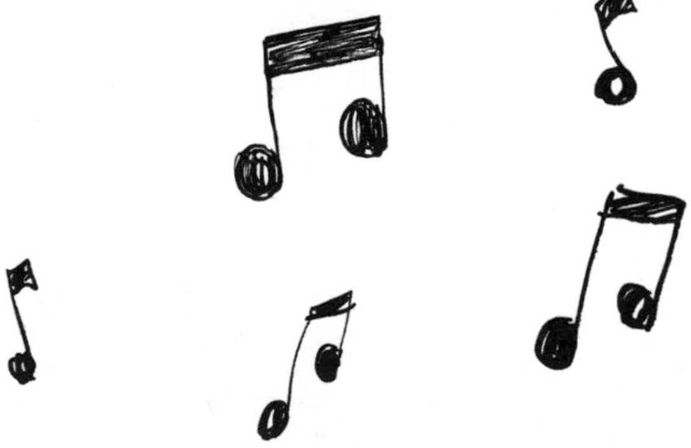

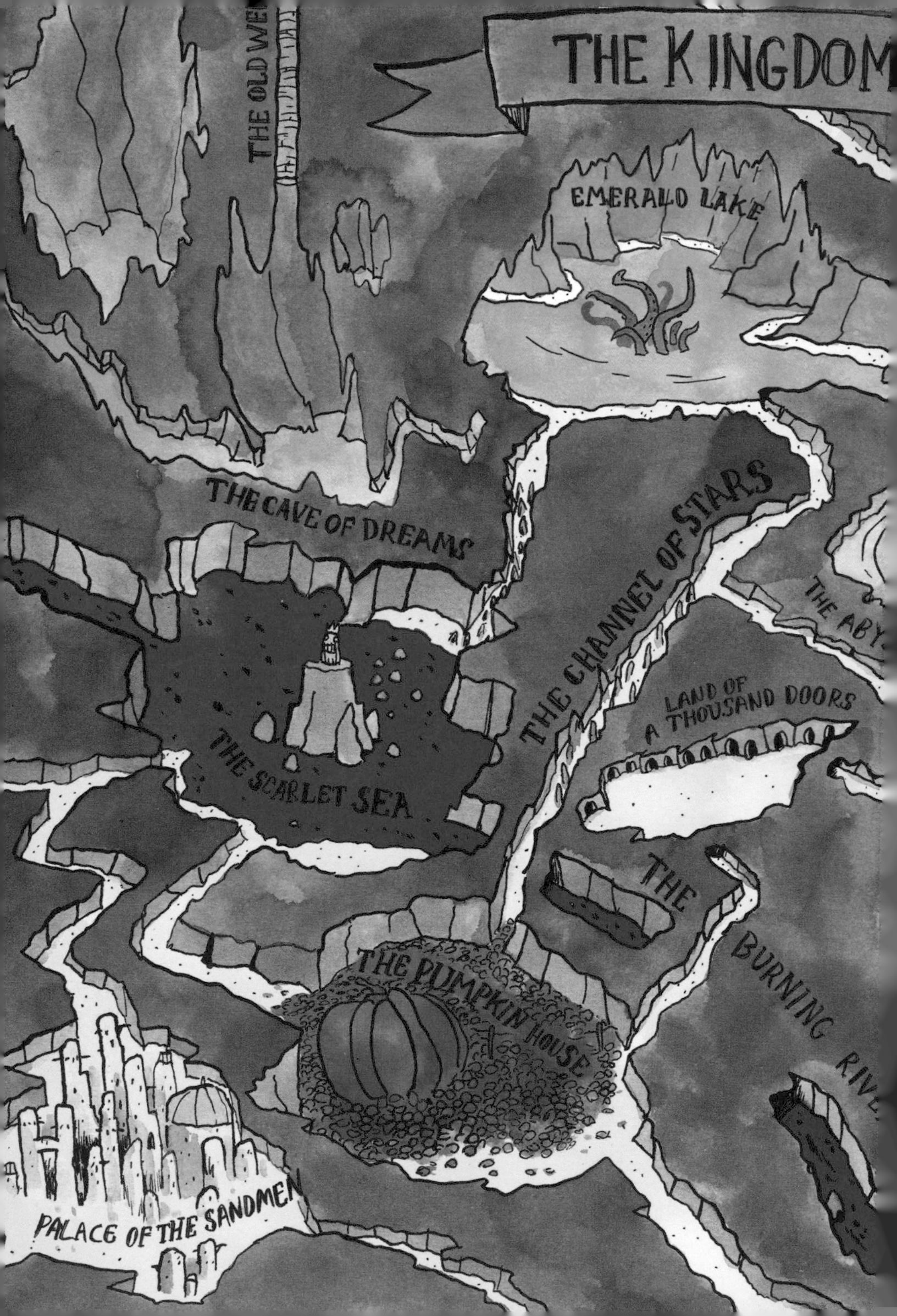

THE KINGDOM
THE OLD WE
EMERALD LAKE
THE CAVE OF DREAMS
THE CHANNEL OF STARS
THE ABY
LAND OF A THOUSAND DOORS
THE SCARLET SEA
THE BURNING RIVE
THE PUMPKIN HOUSE
PALACE OF THE SANDMEN

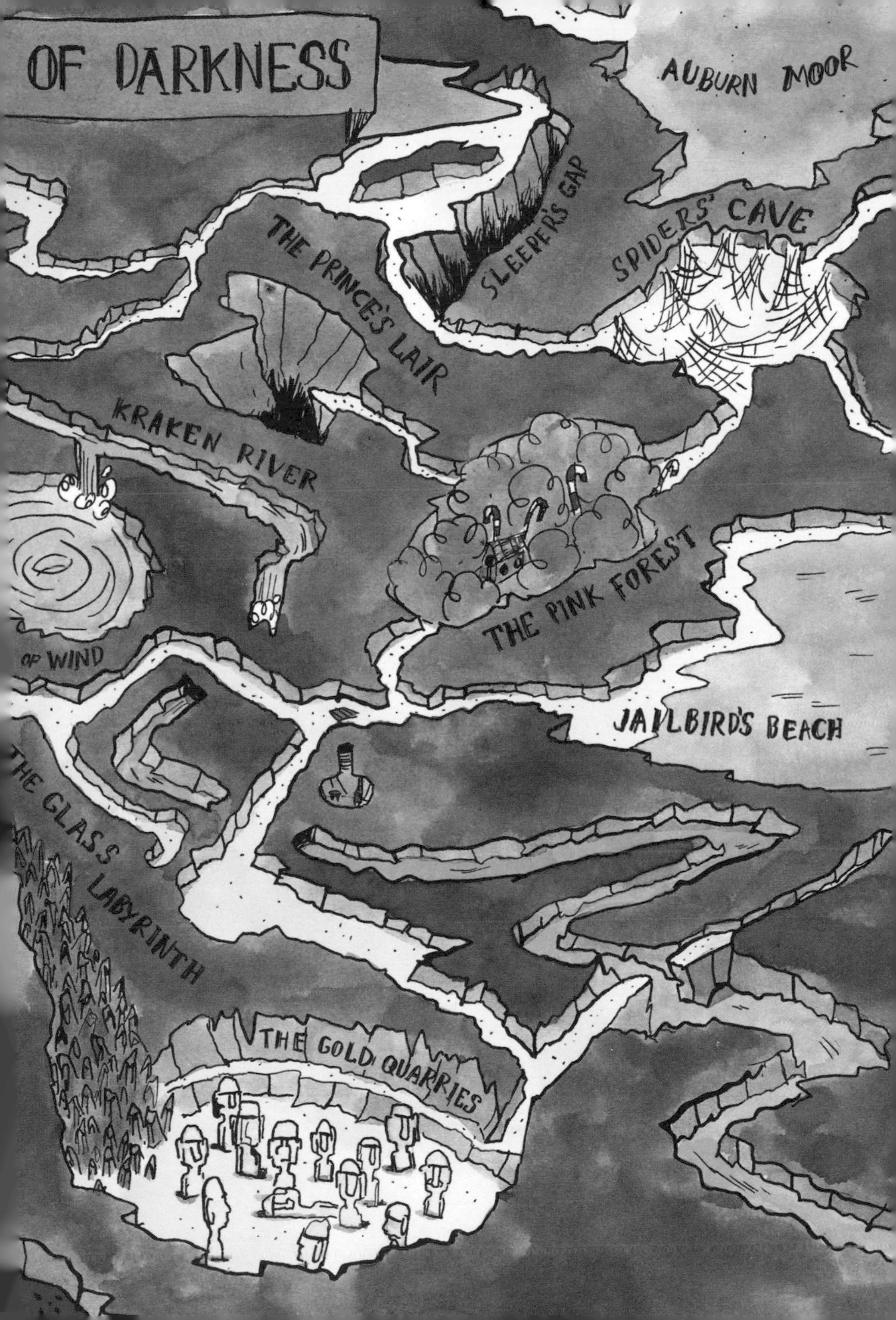
OF DARKNESS
AUBURN MOOR
SLEEPER'S GAP
THE PRINCE'S LAIR
SPIDERS' CAVE
KRAKEN RIVER
THE PINK FOREST
OF WIND
JAILBIRD'S BEACH
THE GLASS LABYRINTH
THE GOLD QUARRIES

THE PRINCESS RUNS AWAY AGAIN

(BY ACCIDENT THIS TIME)

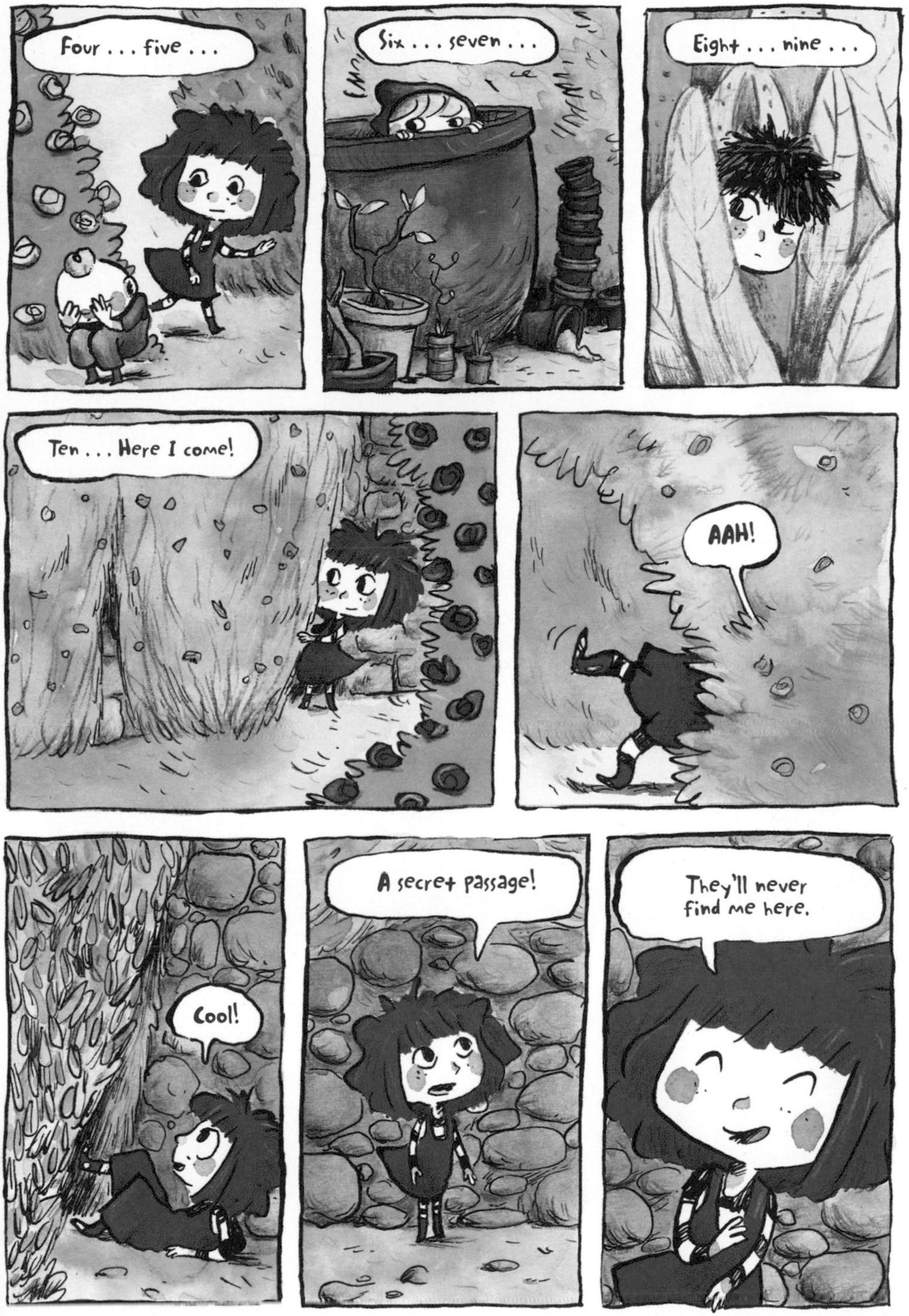
Four . . . five . . .
Six . . . seven . . .
Eight . . . nine . . .
Ten . . . Here I come!
AAH!
Cool!
A secret passage!
They'll never find me here.

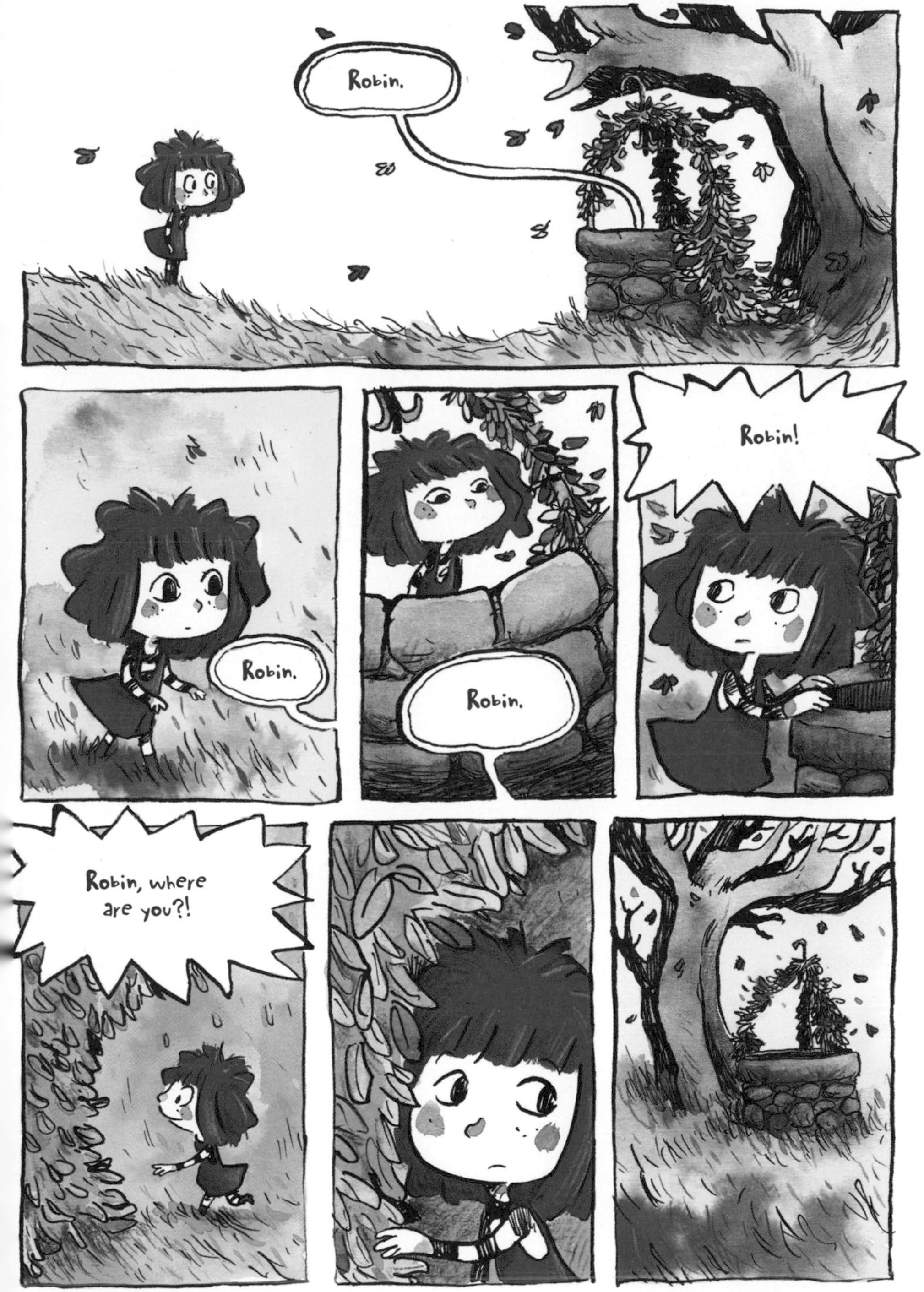
Robin.
Robin.
Robin.
Robin!
Robin, where are you?!

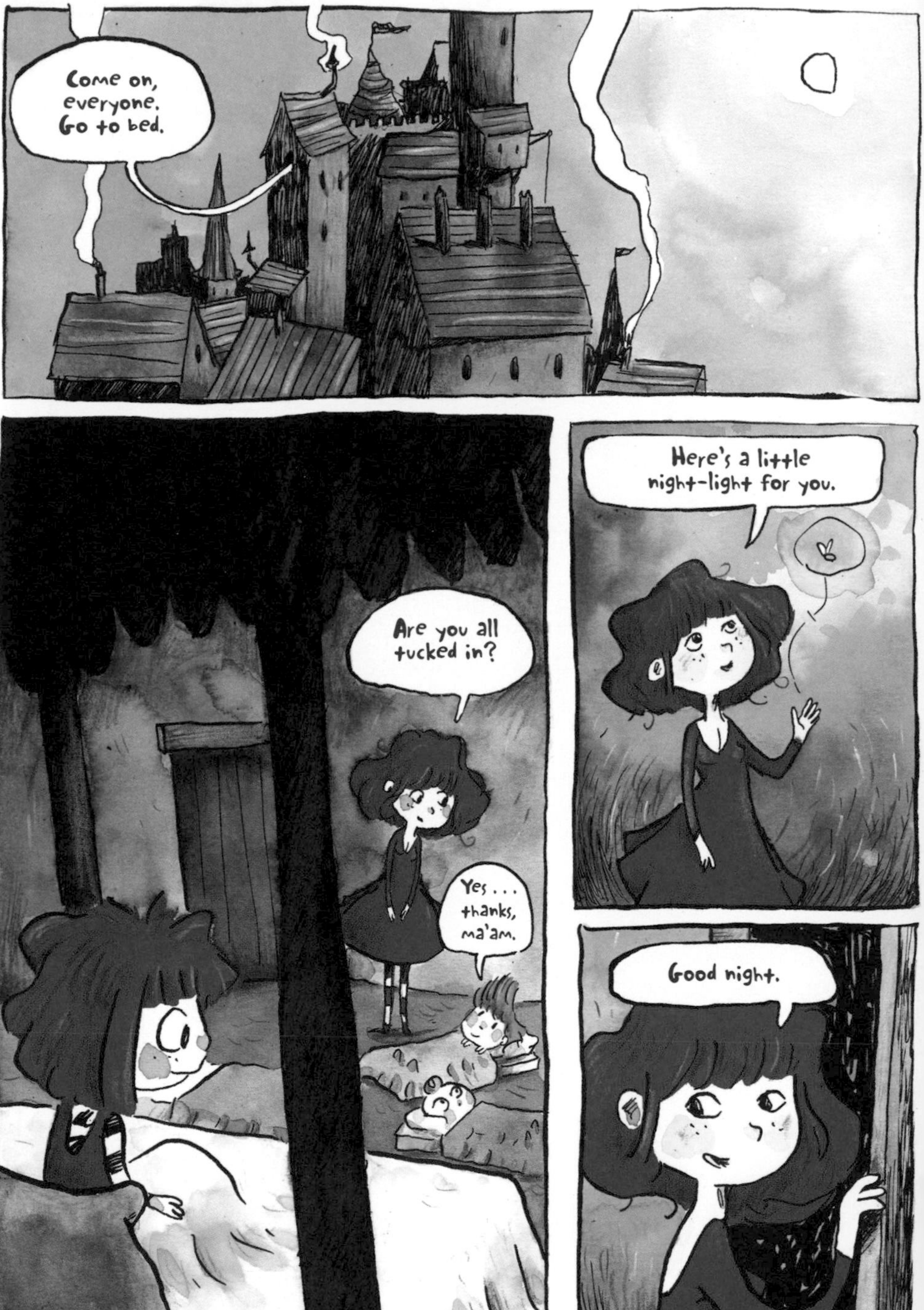
Come on, everyone. Go to bed.
Are you all tucked in?
Yes . . . thanks, ma'am.
Here's a little night-light for you.
Good night.

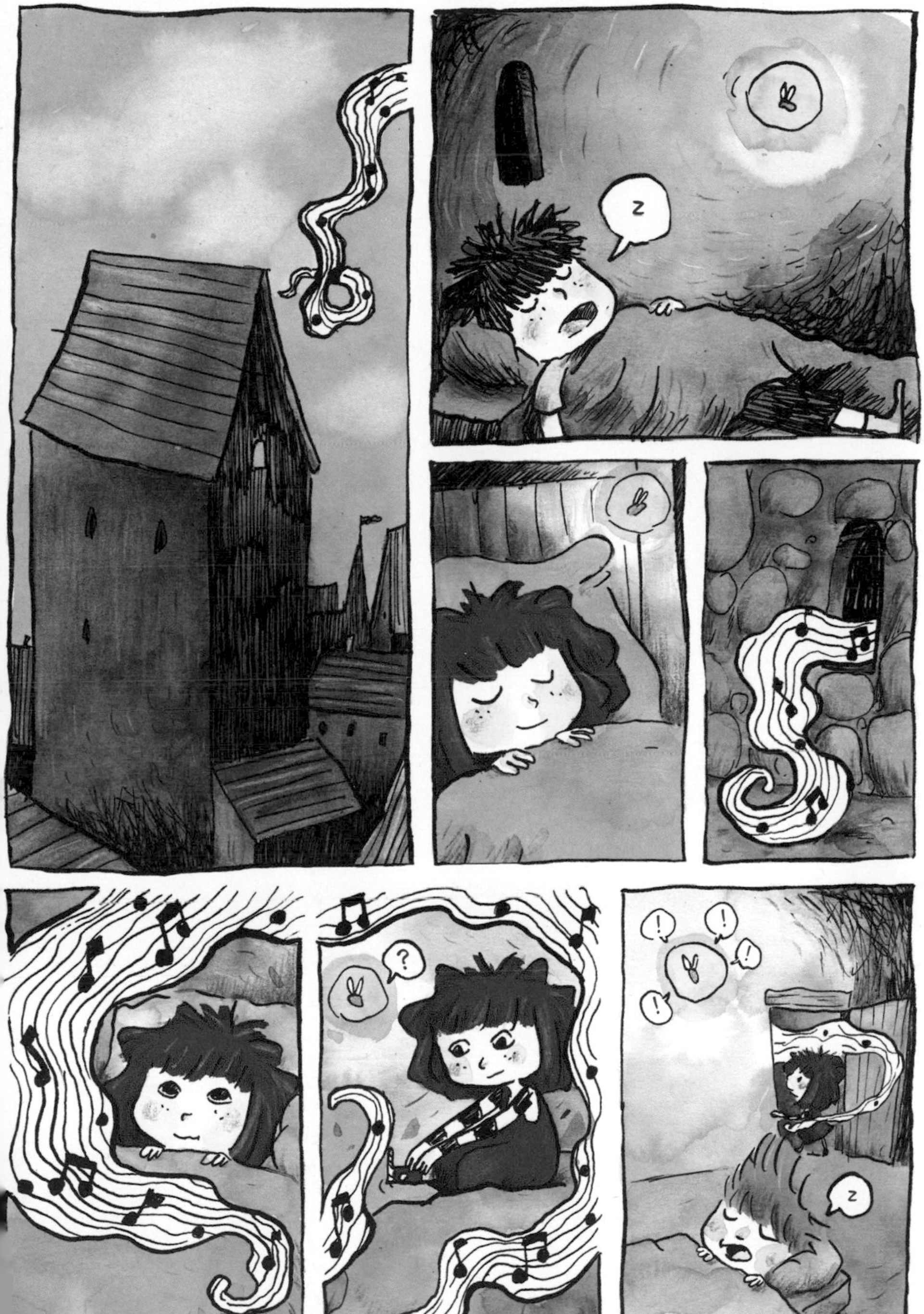

z
?
!
!
!
!
z

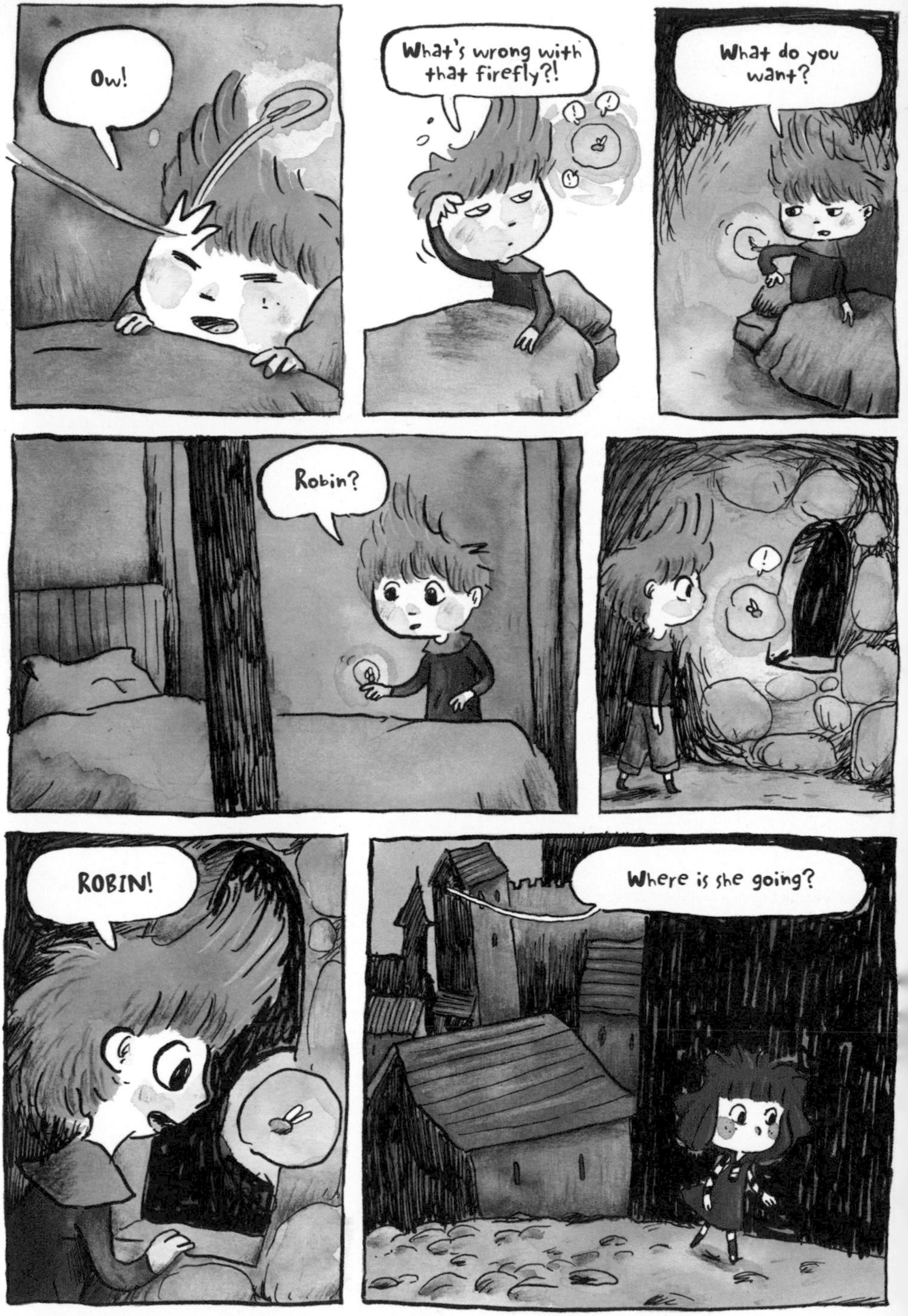
Ow!
What's wrong with that firefly?!
What do you want?
Robin?
ROBIN!
Where is she going?

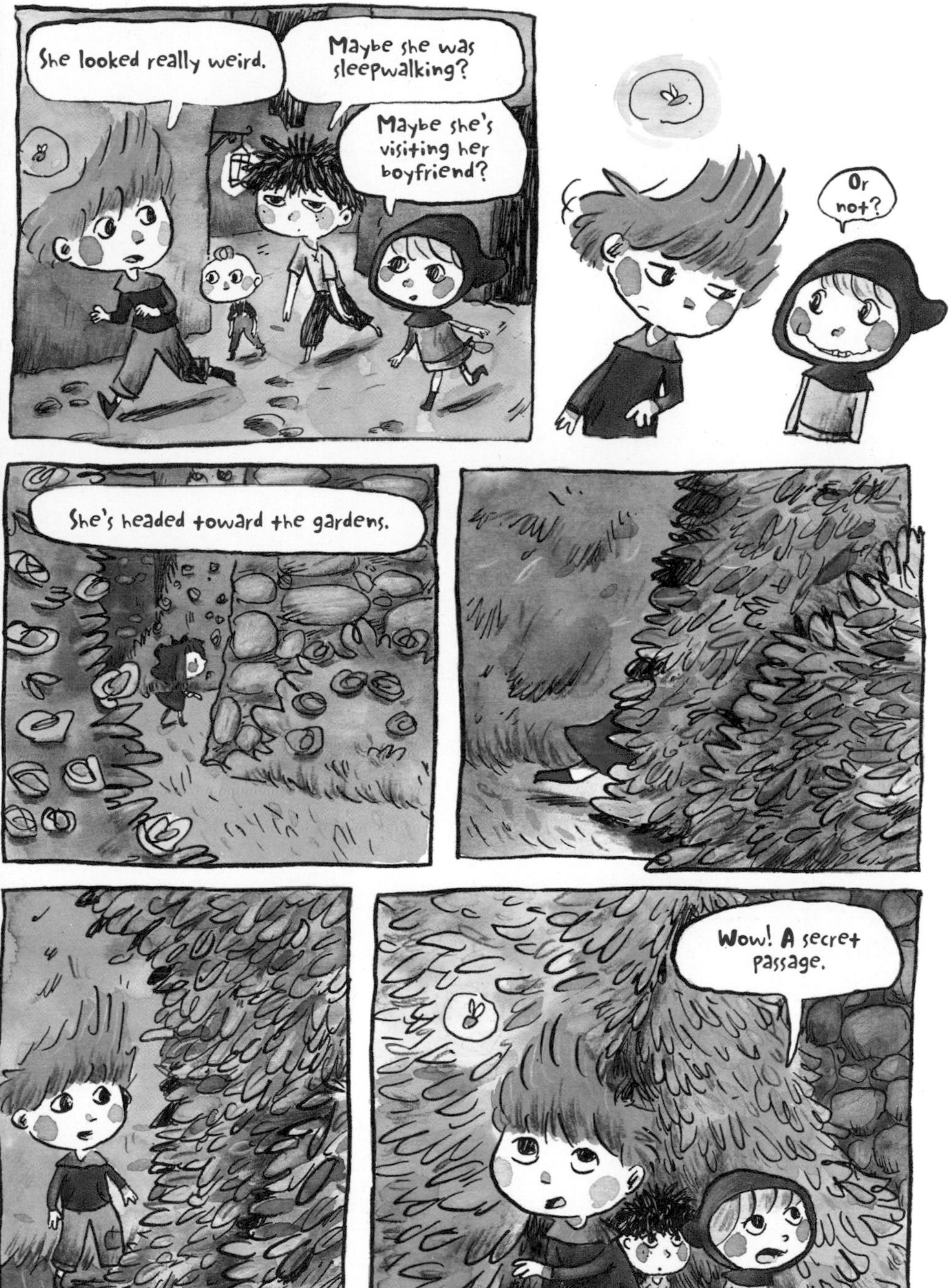
She looked really weird.
Maybe she was sleepwalking?
Maybe she's visiting her boyfriend?
Or not?
She's headed toward the gardens.
Wow! A secret passage.

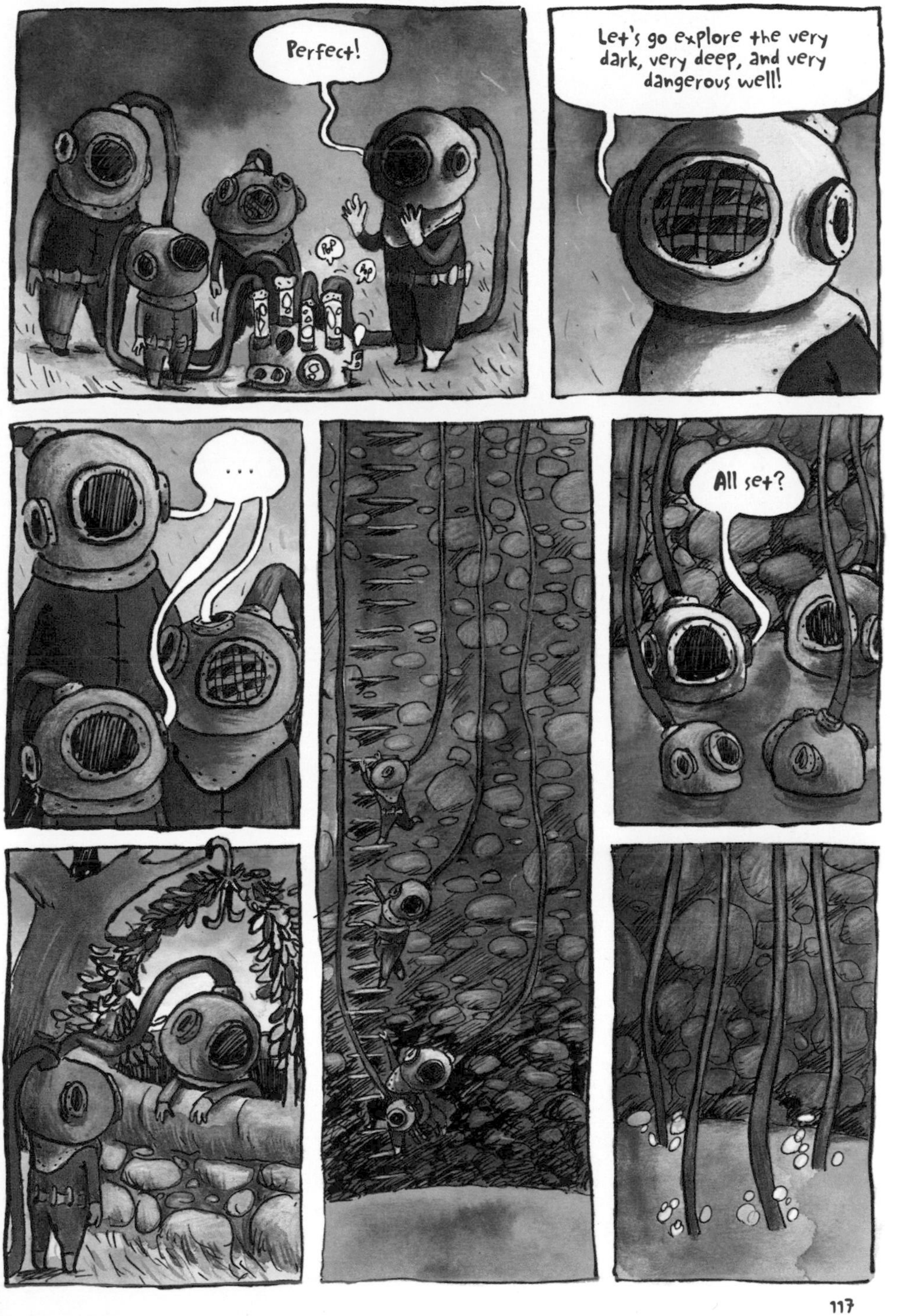

Perfect!
Let's go explore the very dark, very deep, and very dangerous well!
...
All set?

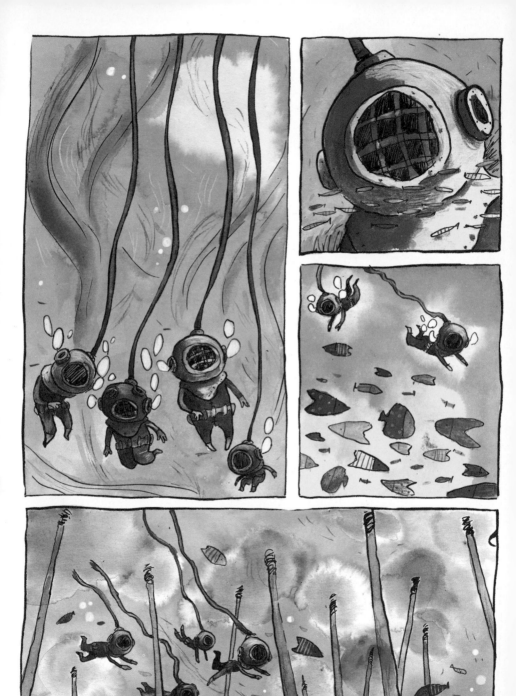

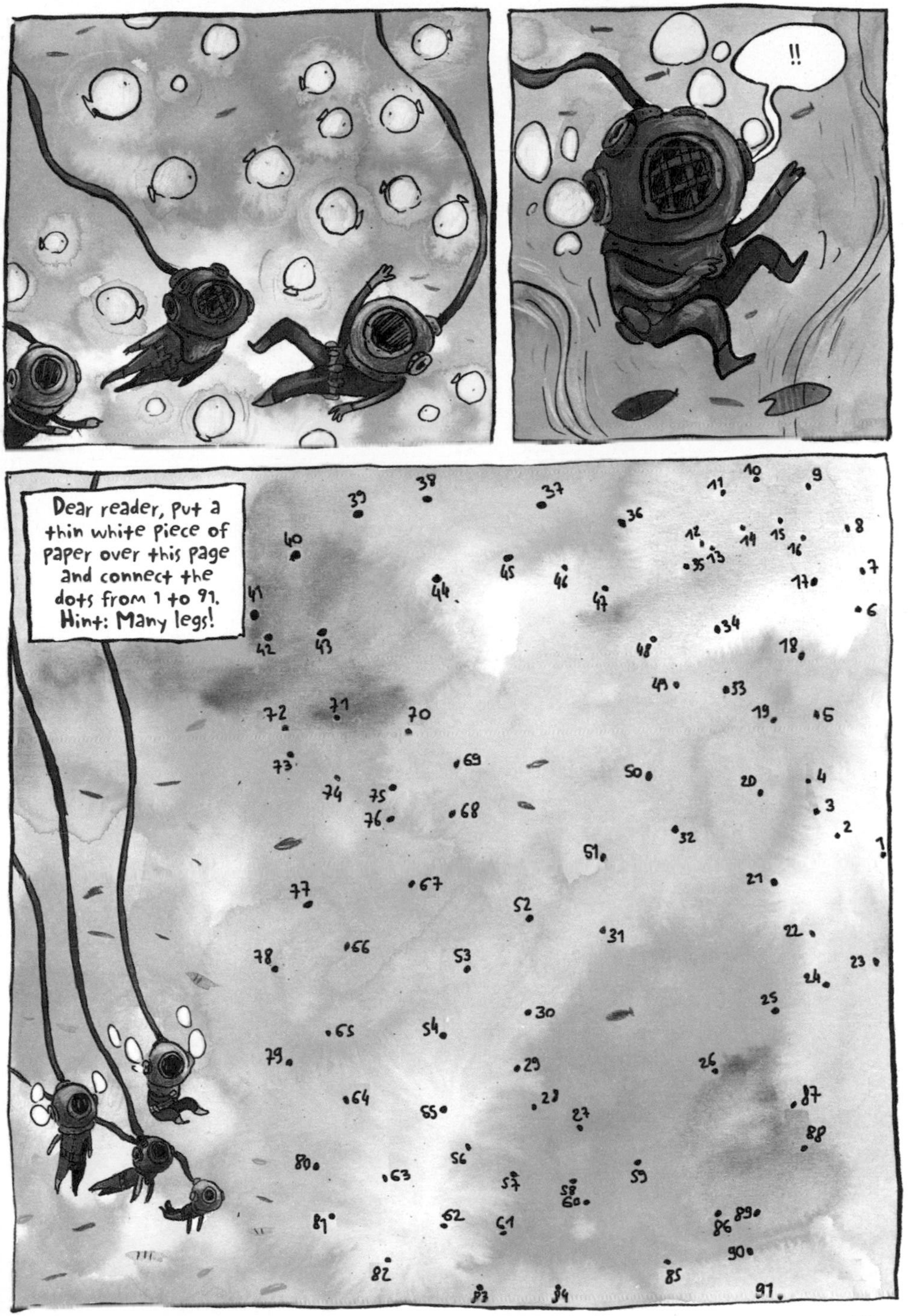
!!
Dear reader, put a thin white piece of paper over this page and connect the dots from 1 to 91. Hint: Many legs!

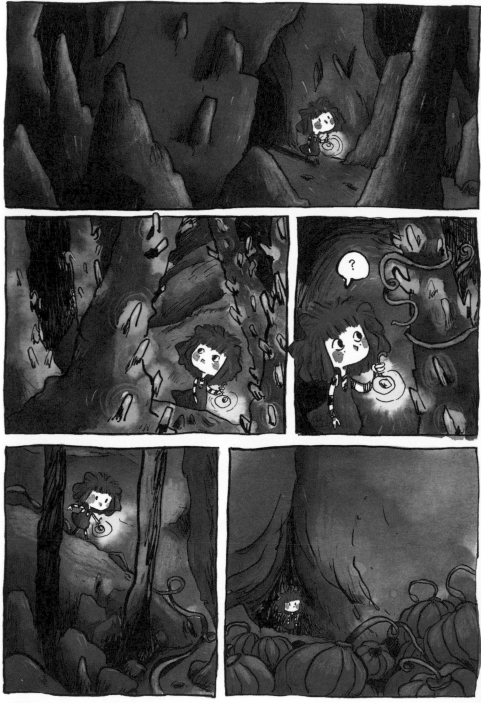

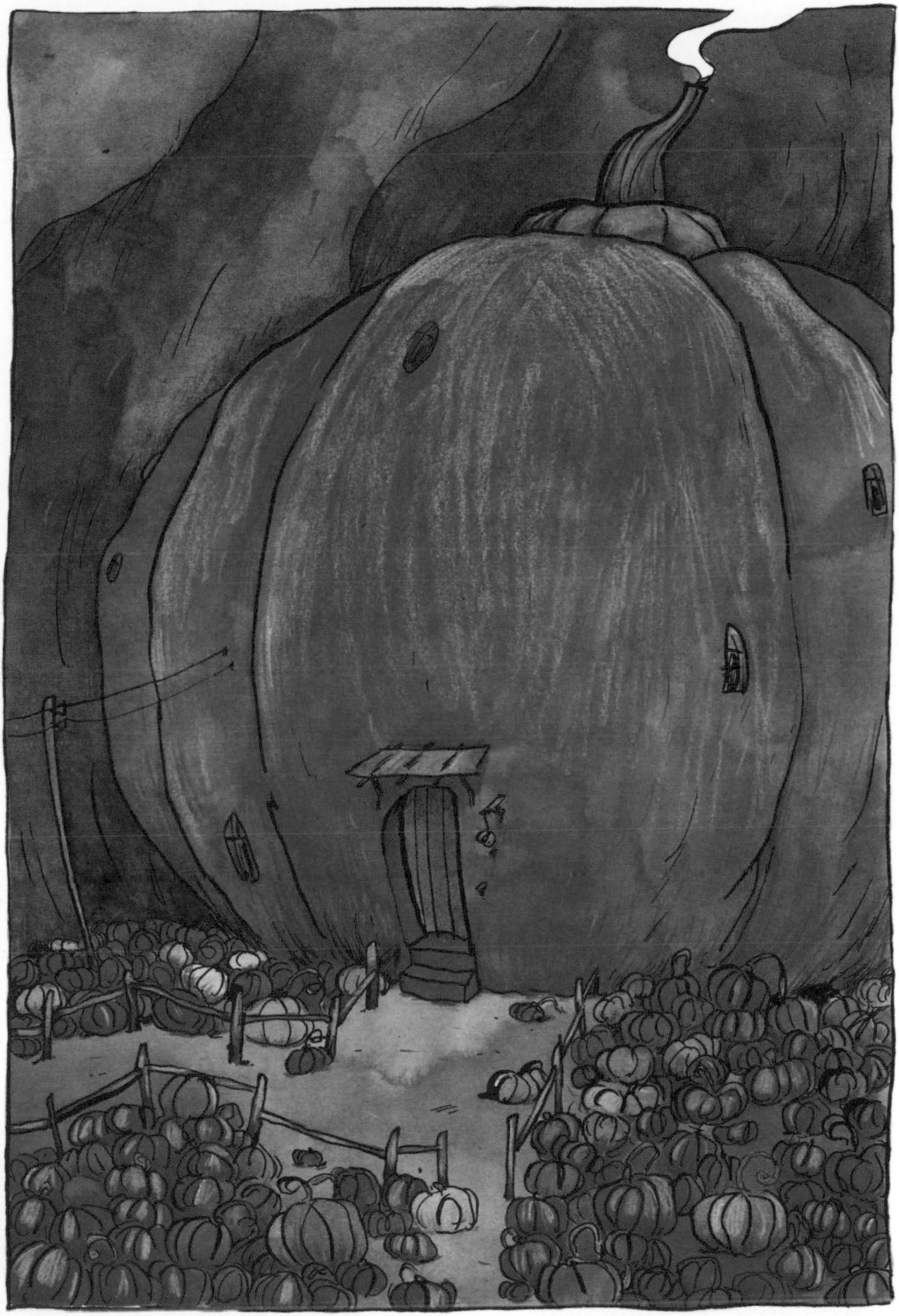

123

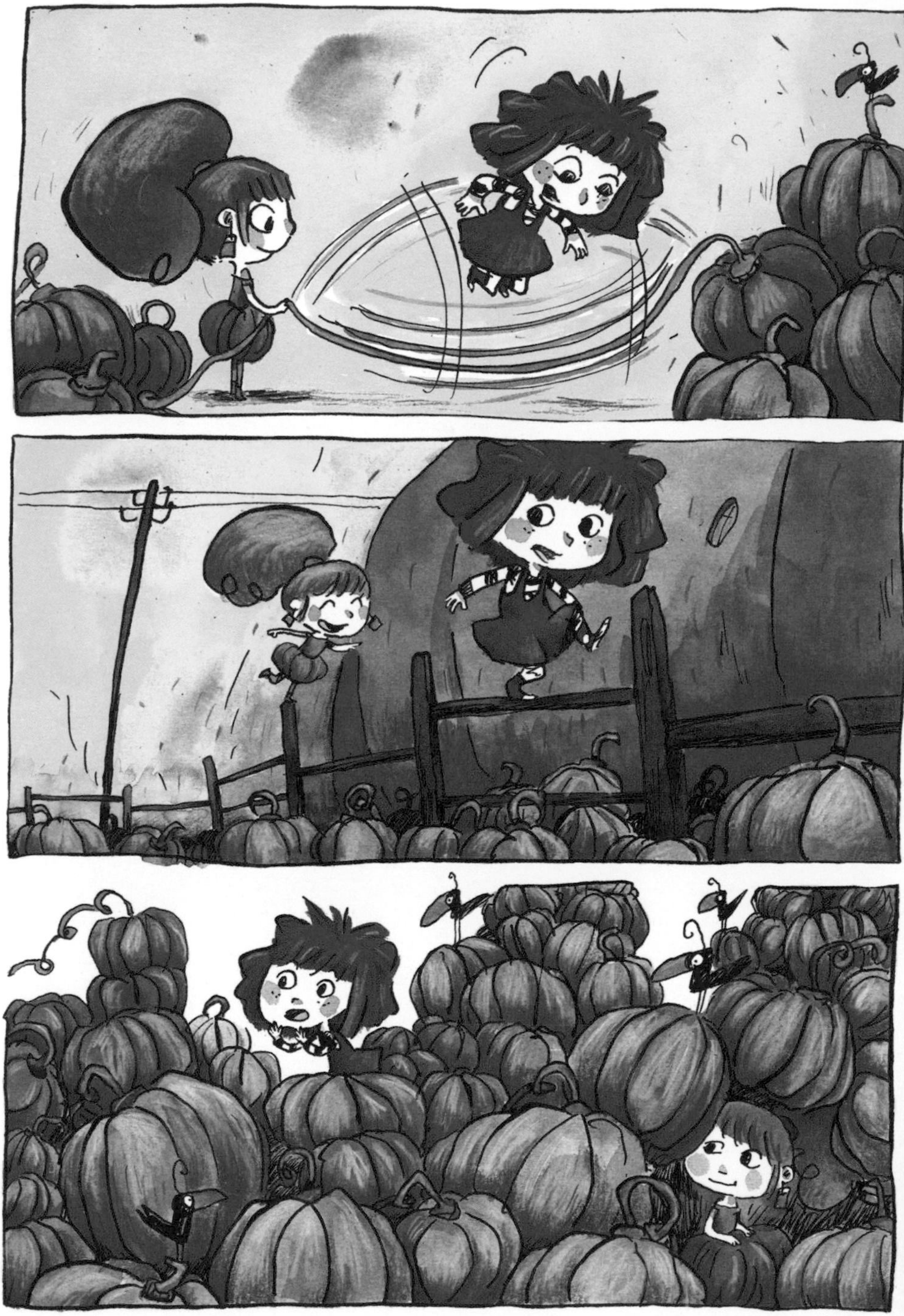

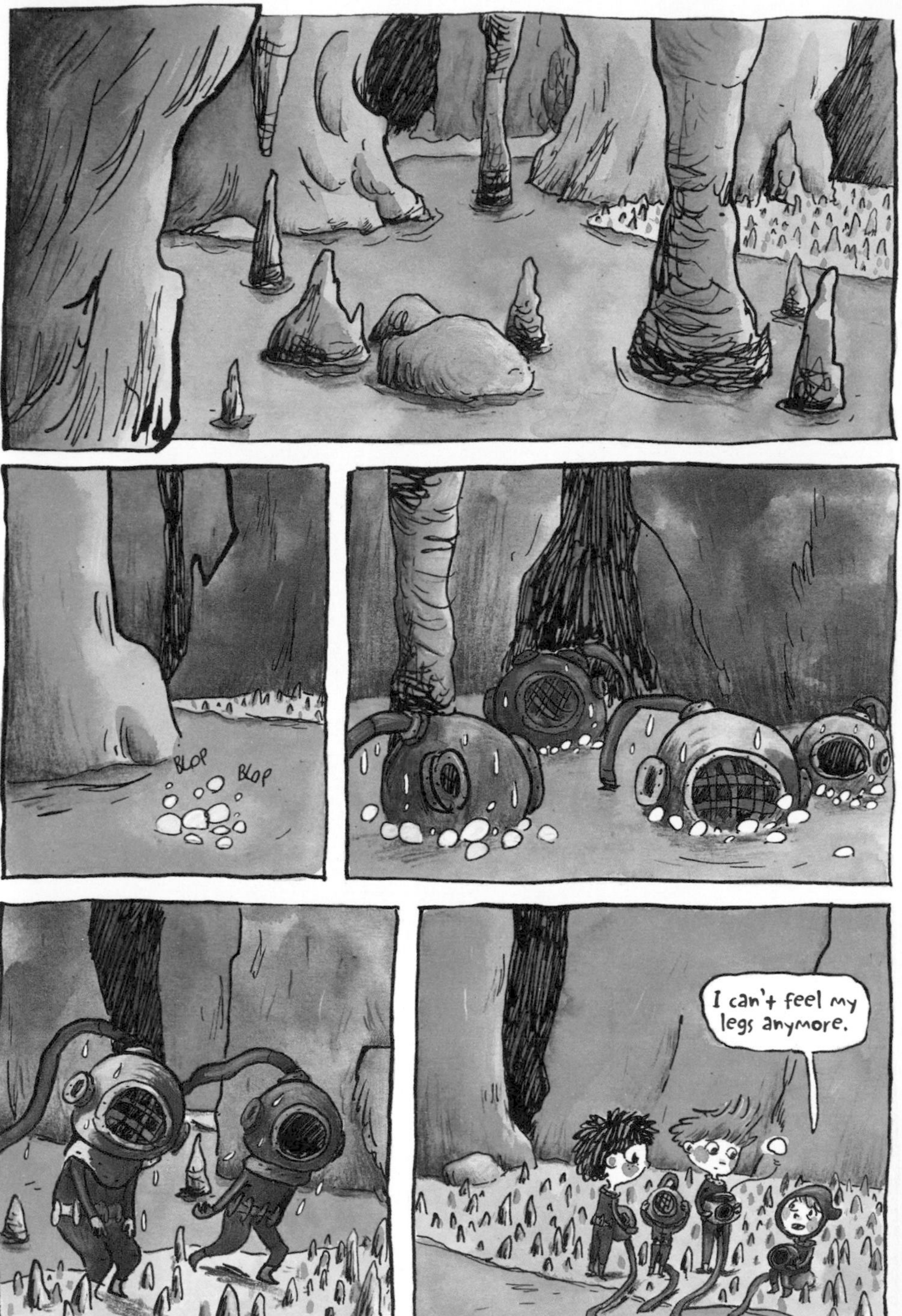
BLOP
BLOP
I can't feel my legs anymore.

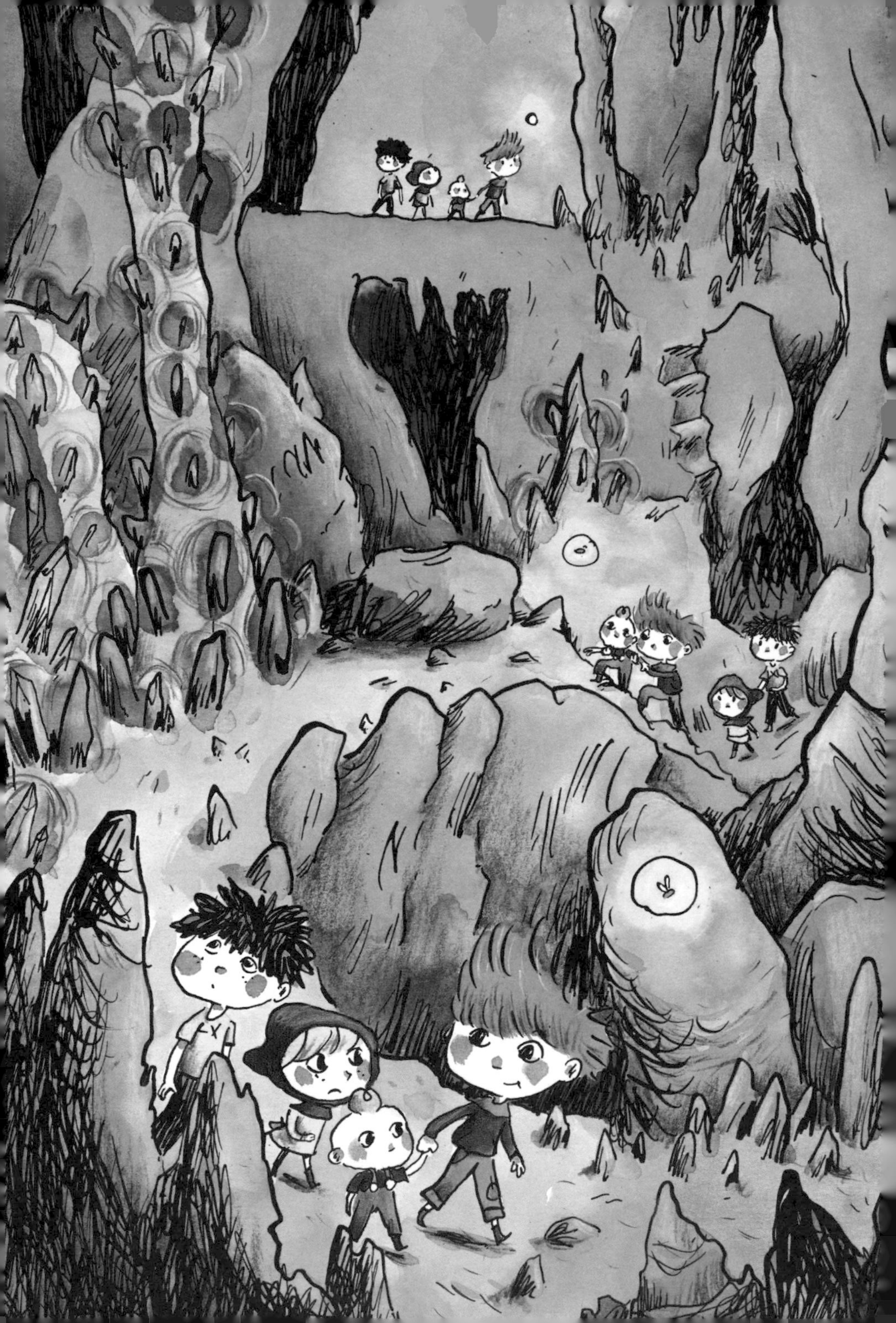

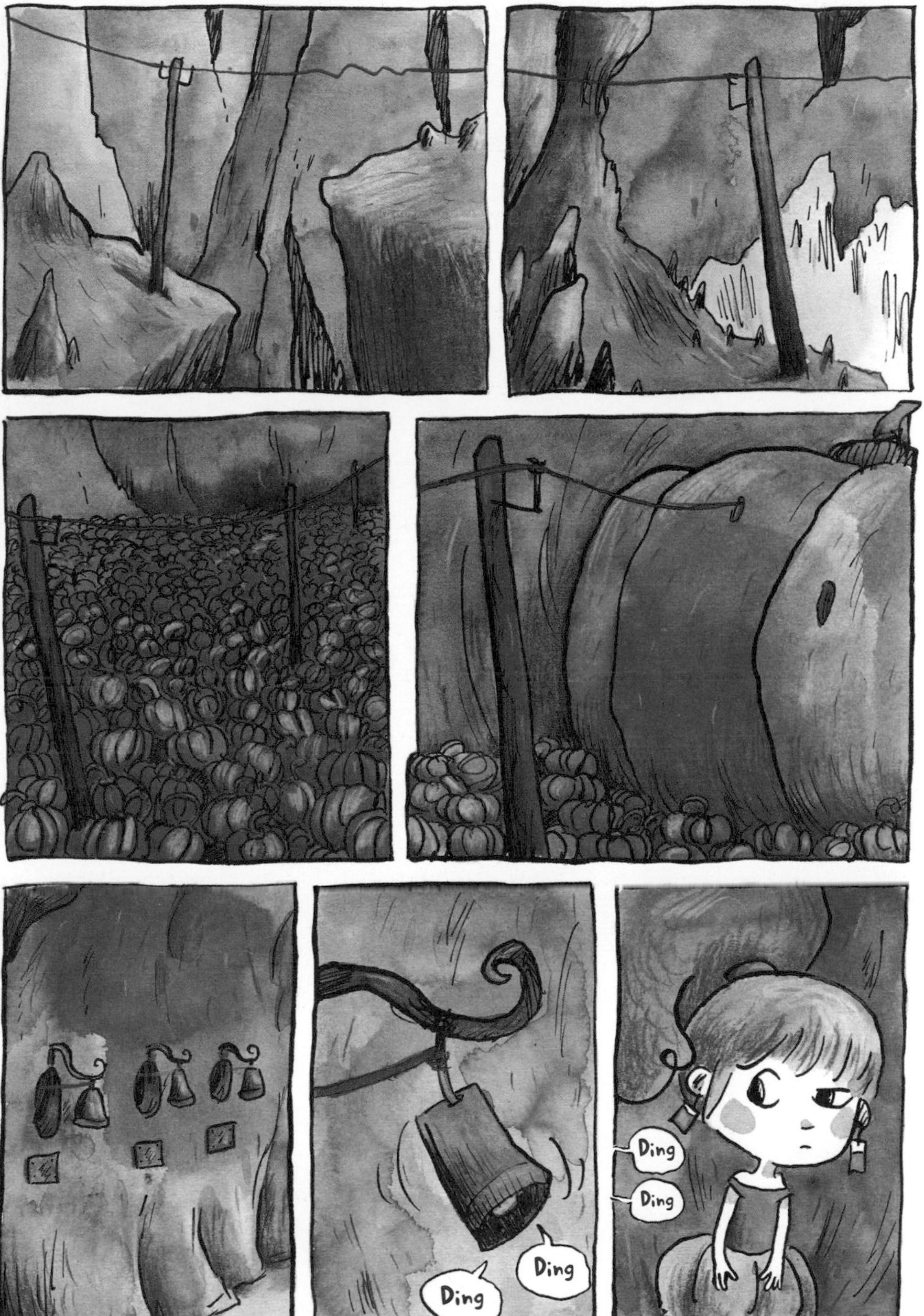
Ding
Ding
Ding
Ding

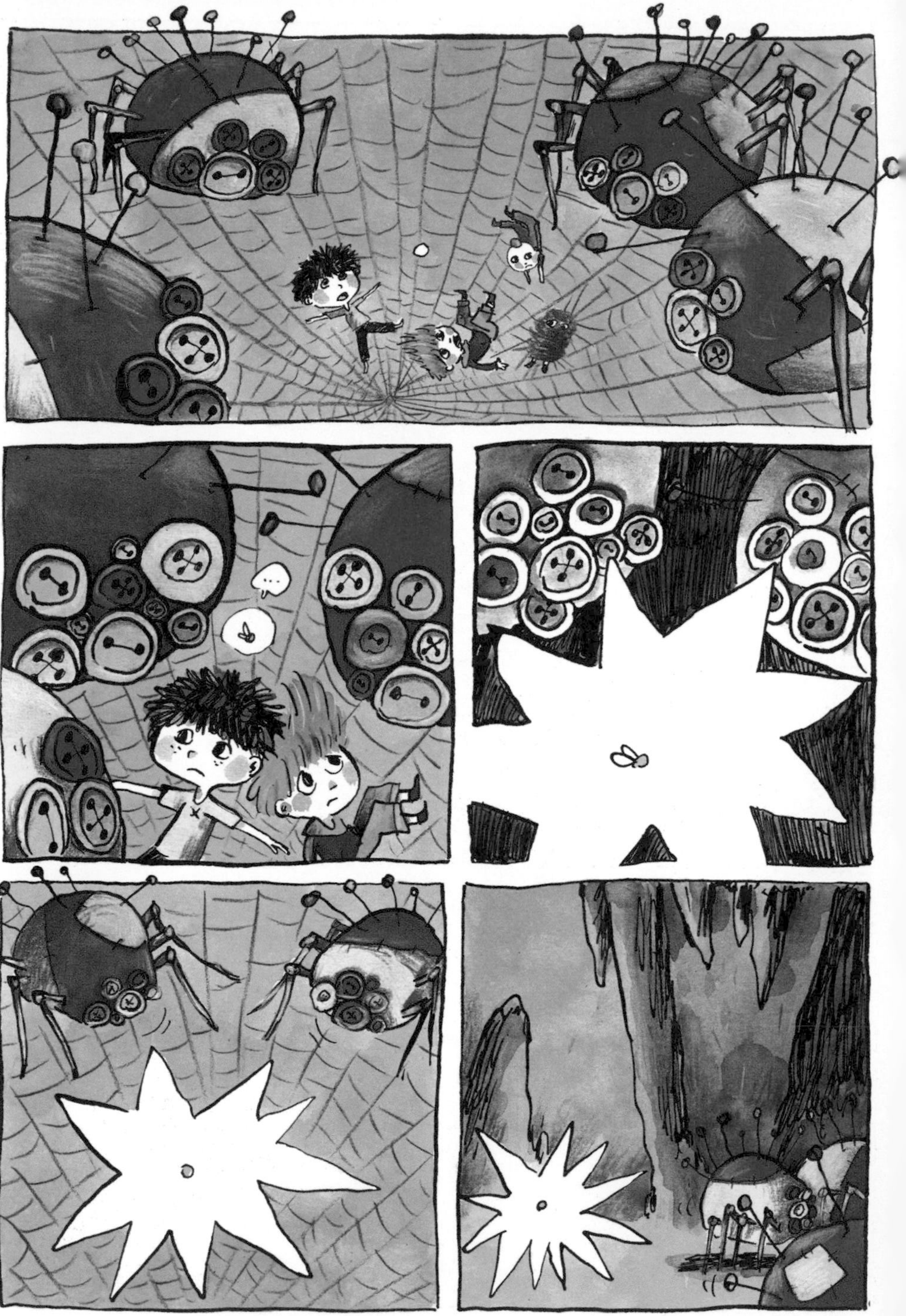
...

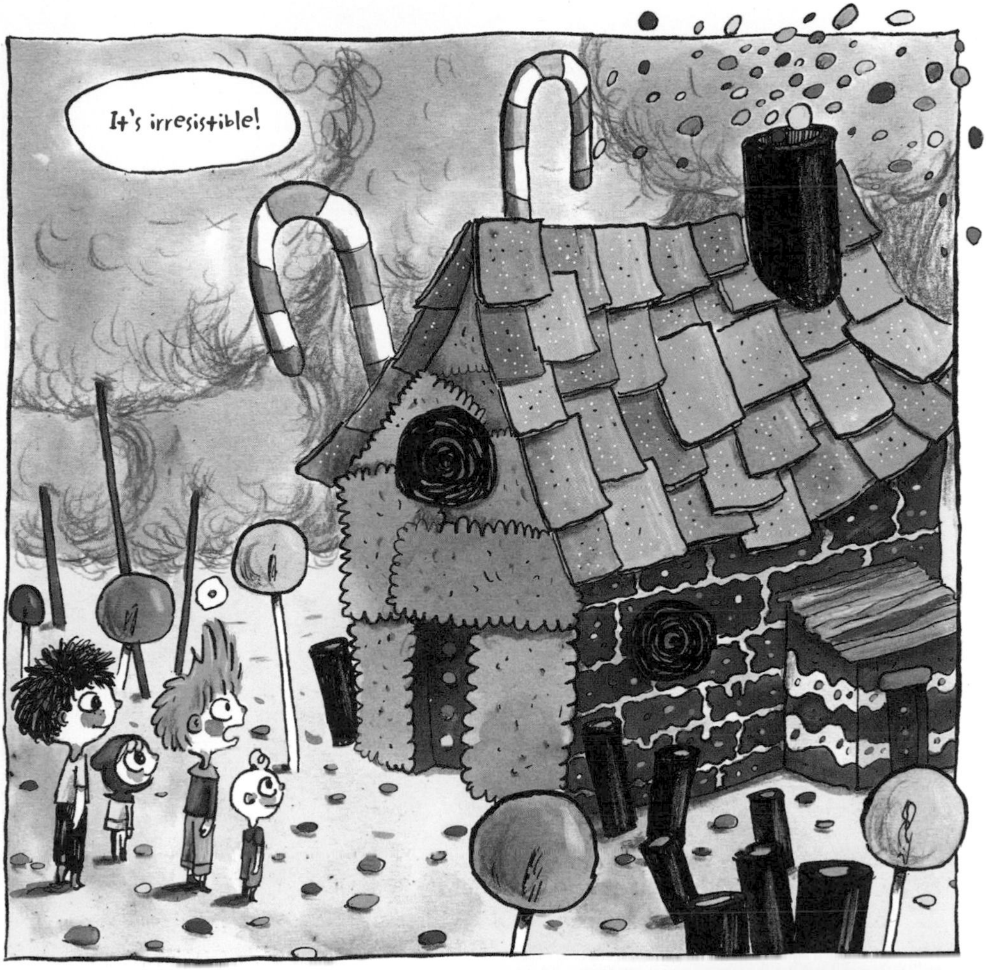
It's irresistible!

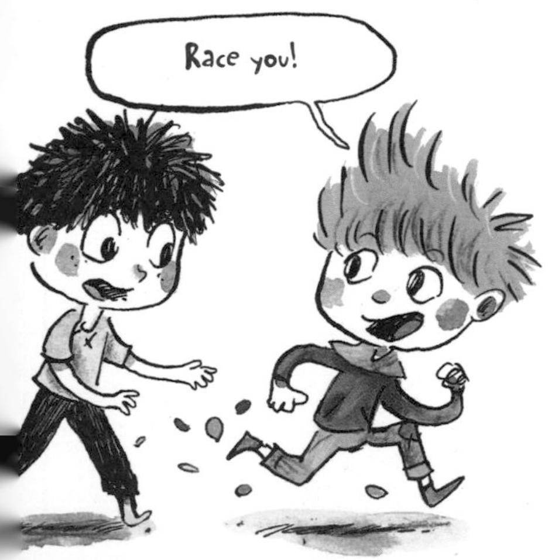
Race you!

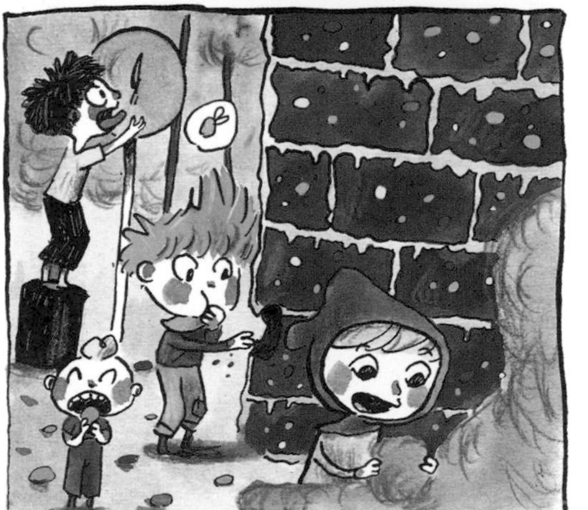

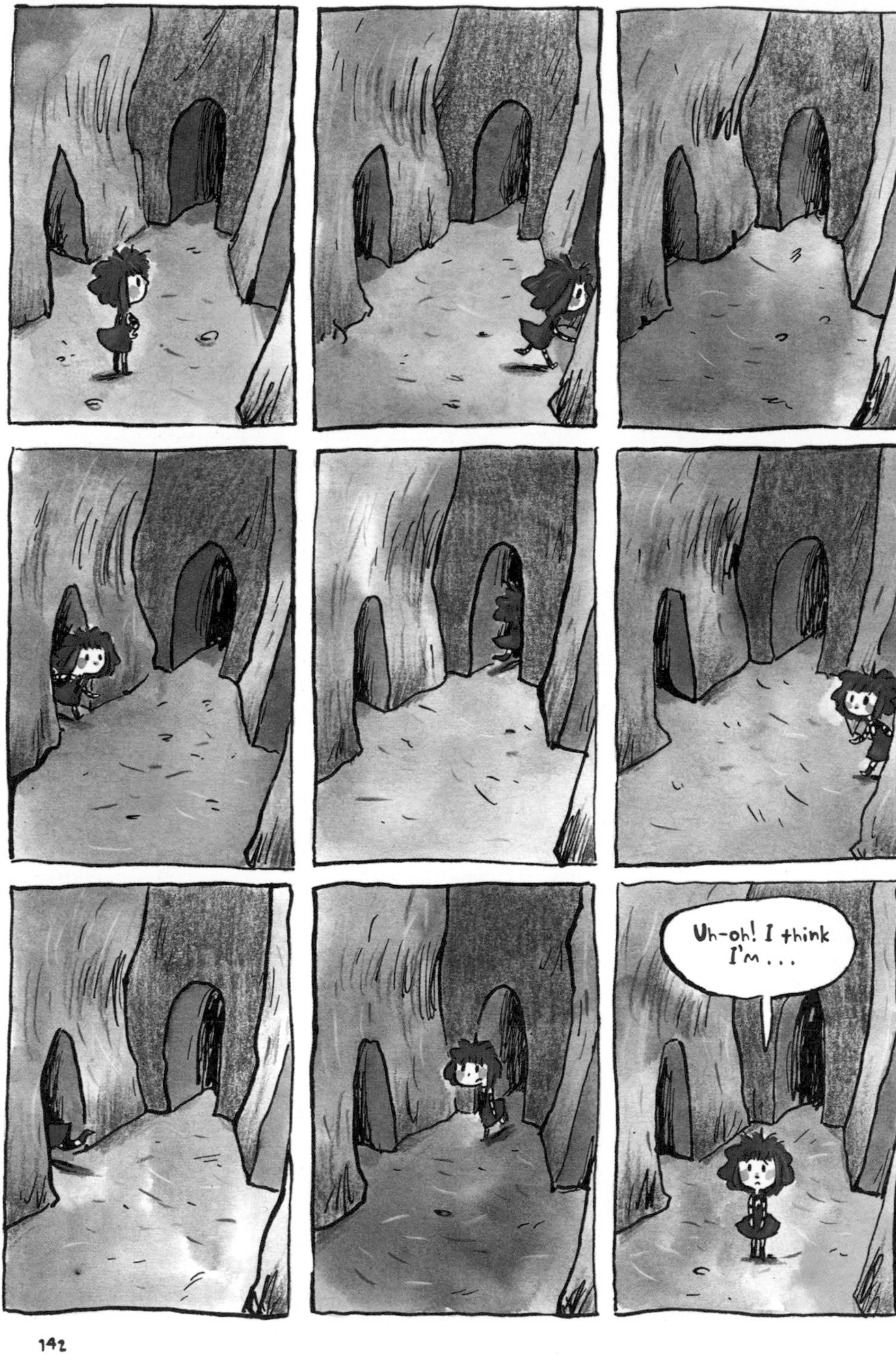
Uh-oh! I think
I'm . . .

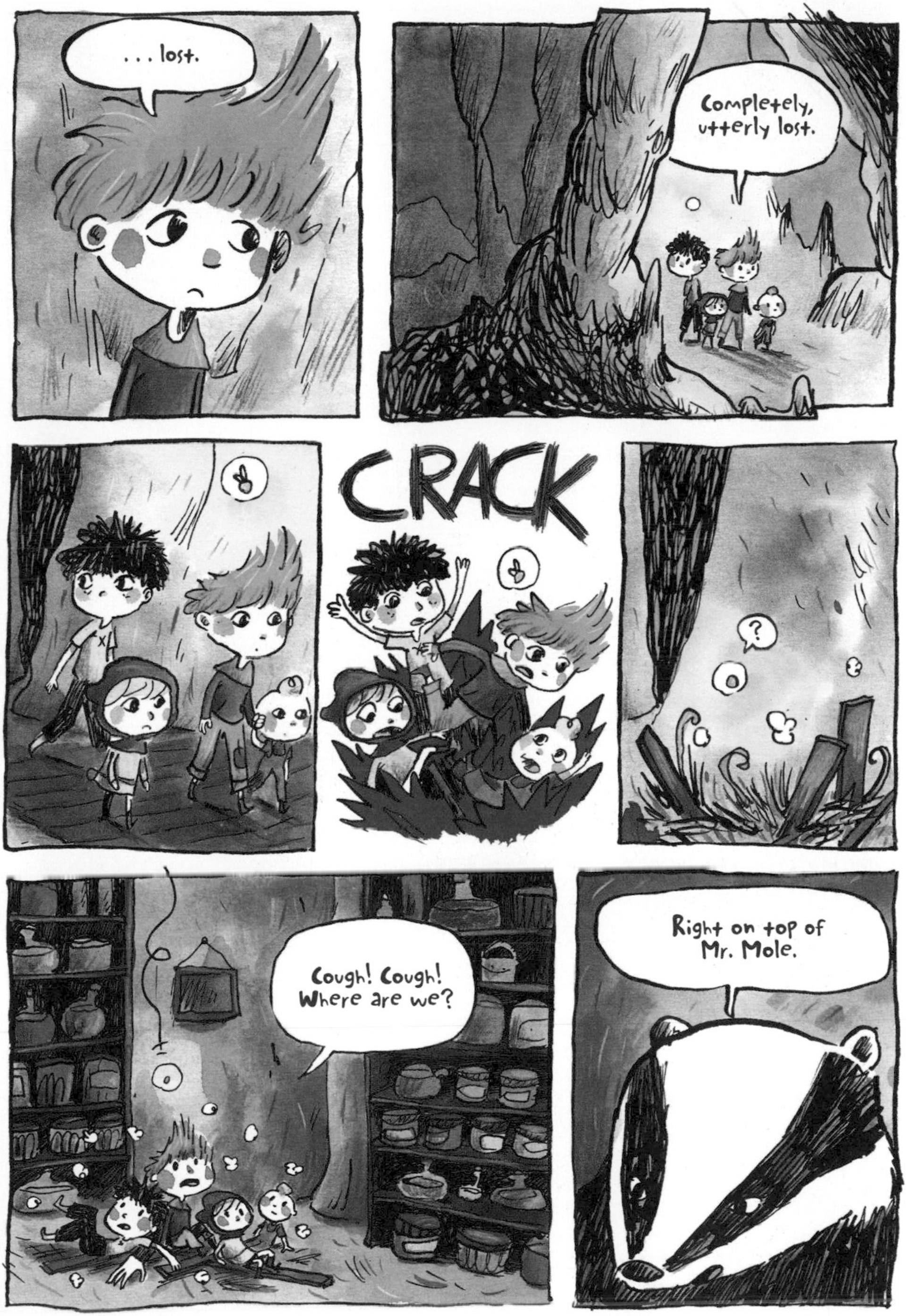
. . . lost.
Completely, utterly lost.
?
CRACK
?
Cough! Cough! Where are we?
Right on top of Mr. Mole.

144

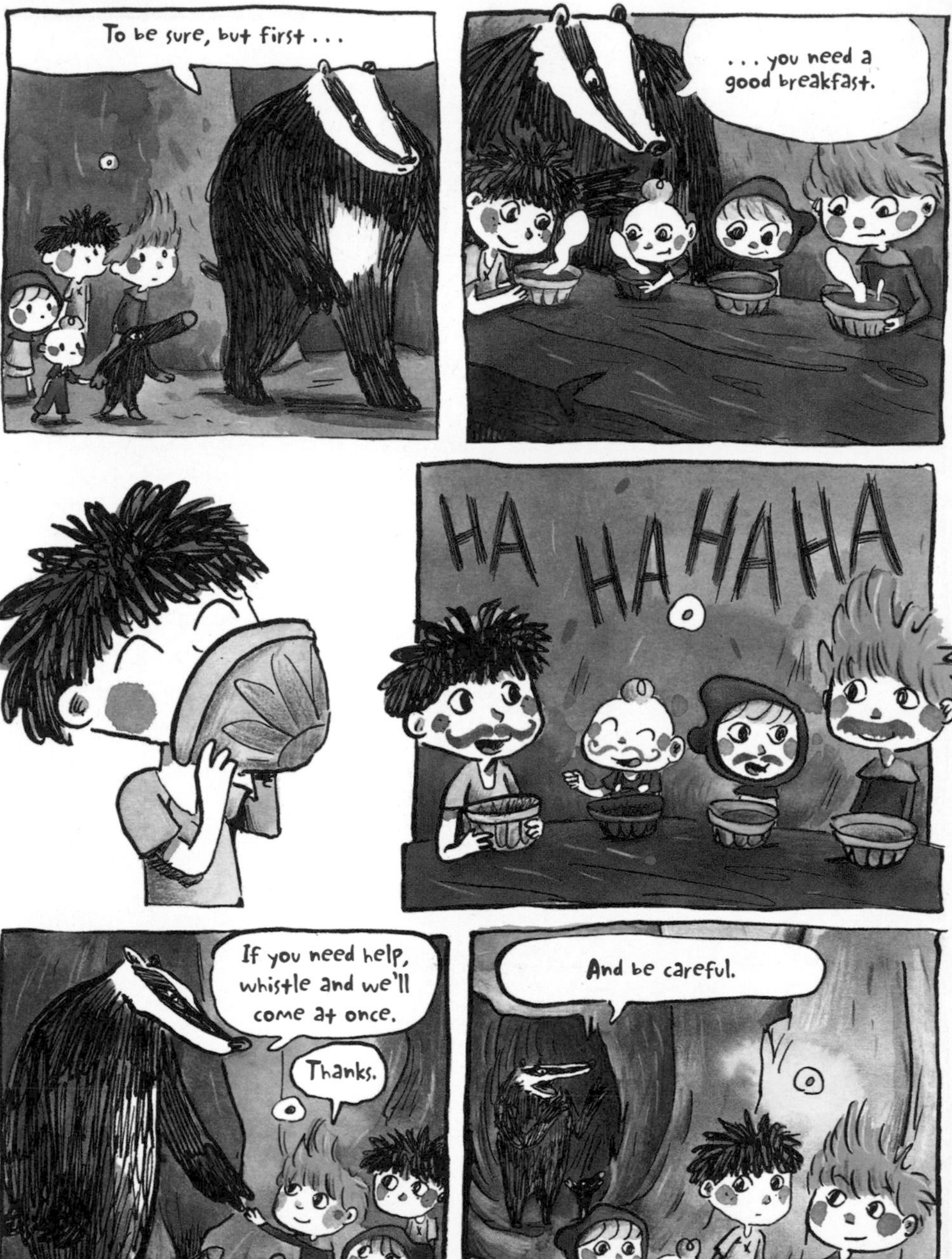
To be sure, but first . . .
. . . you need a good breakfast.
HA HA HA HA HA
If you need help, whistle and we'll come at once.
Thanks.
And be careful.

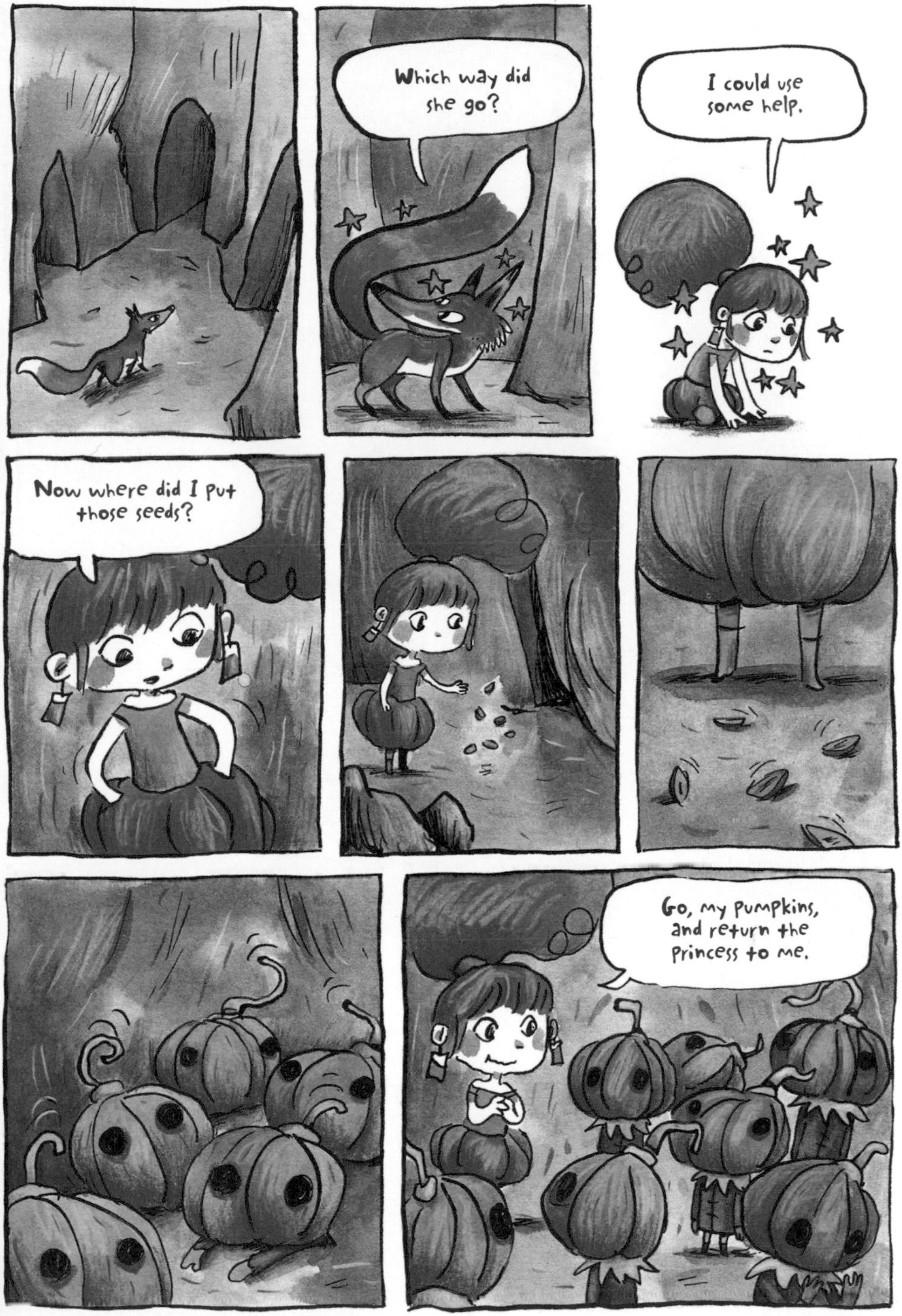
Which way did she go?
I could use some help.
Now where did I put those seeds?
Go, my pumpkins, and return the Princess to me.

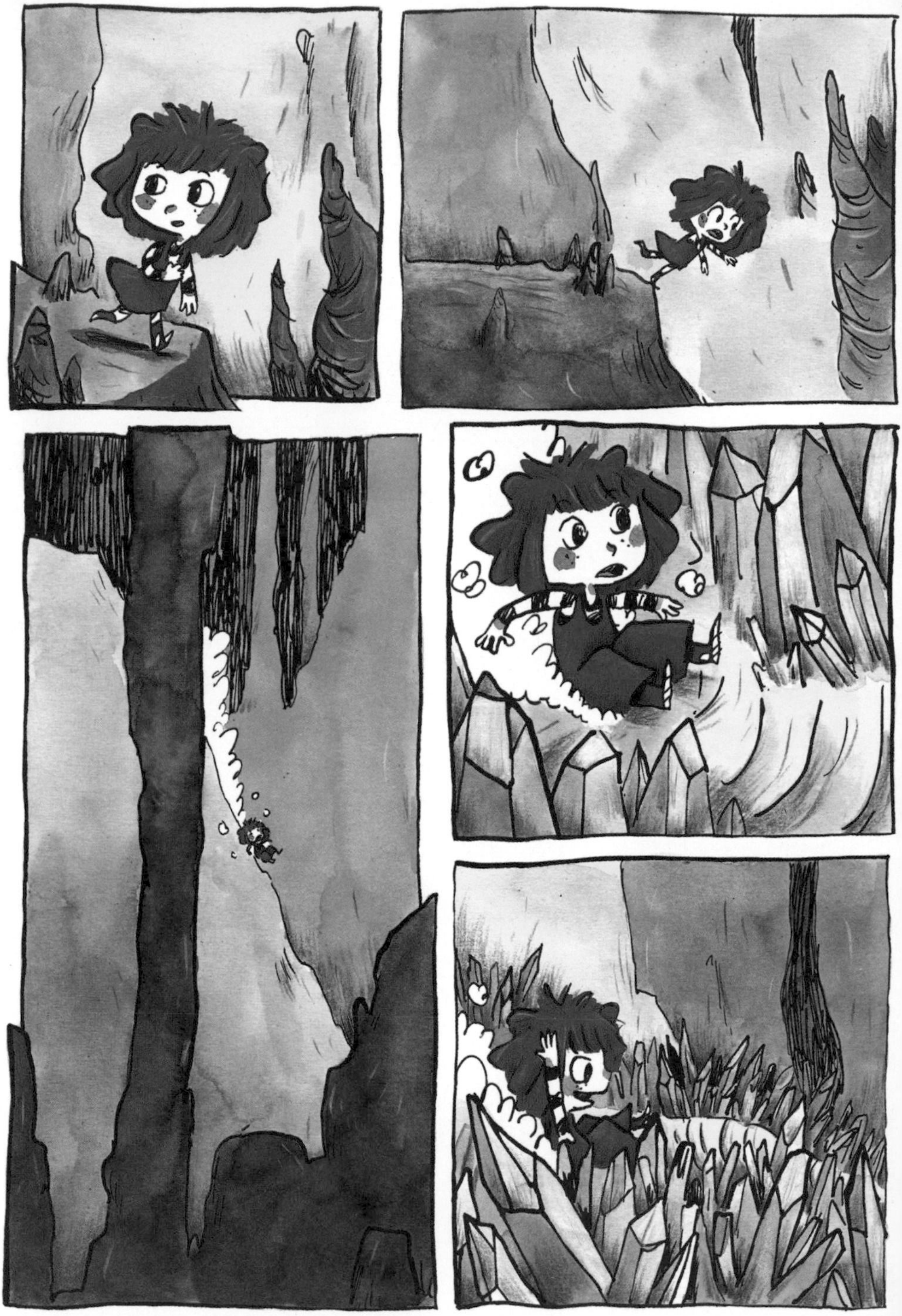

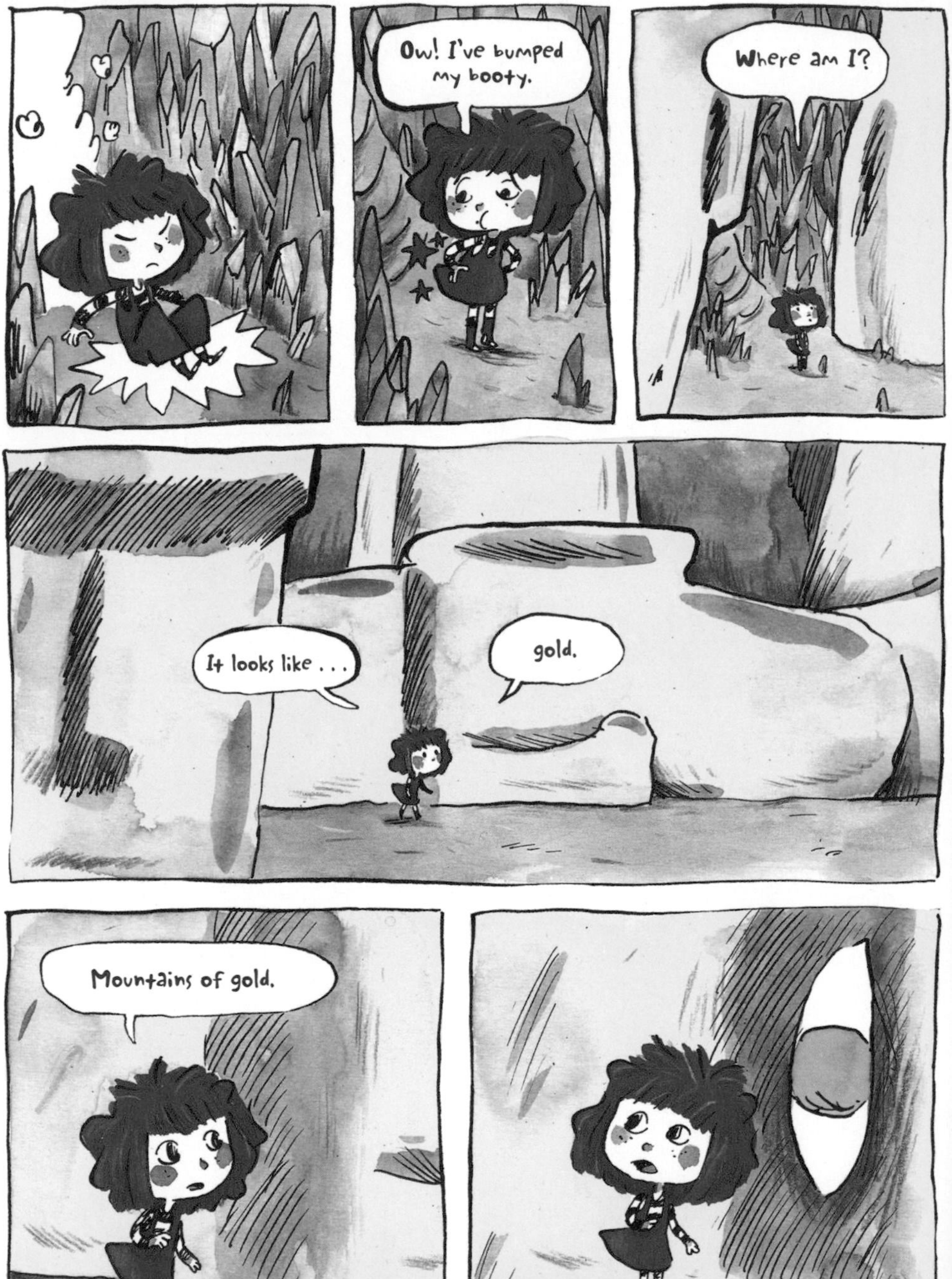
Ow! I've bumped my booty.
Where am I?
It looks like . . .
gold.
Mountains of gold.

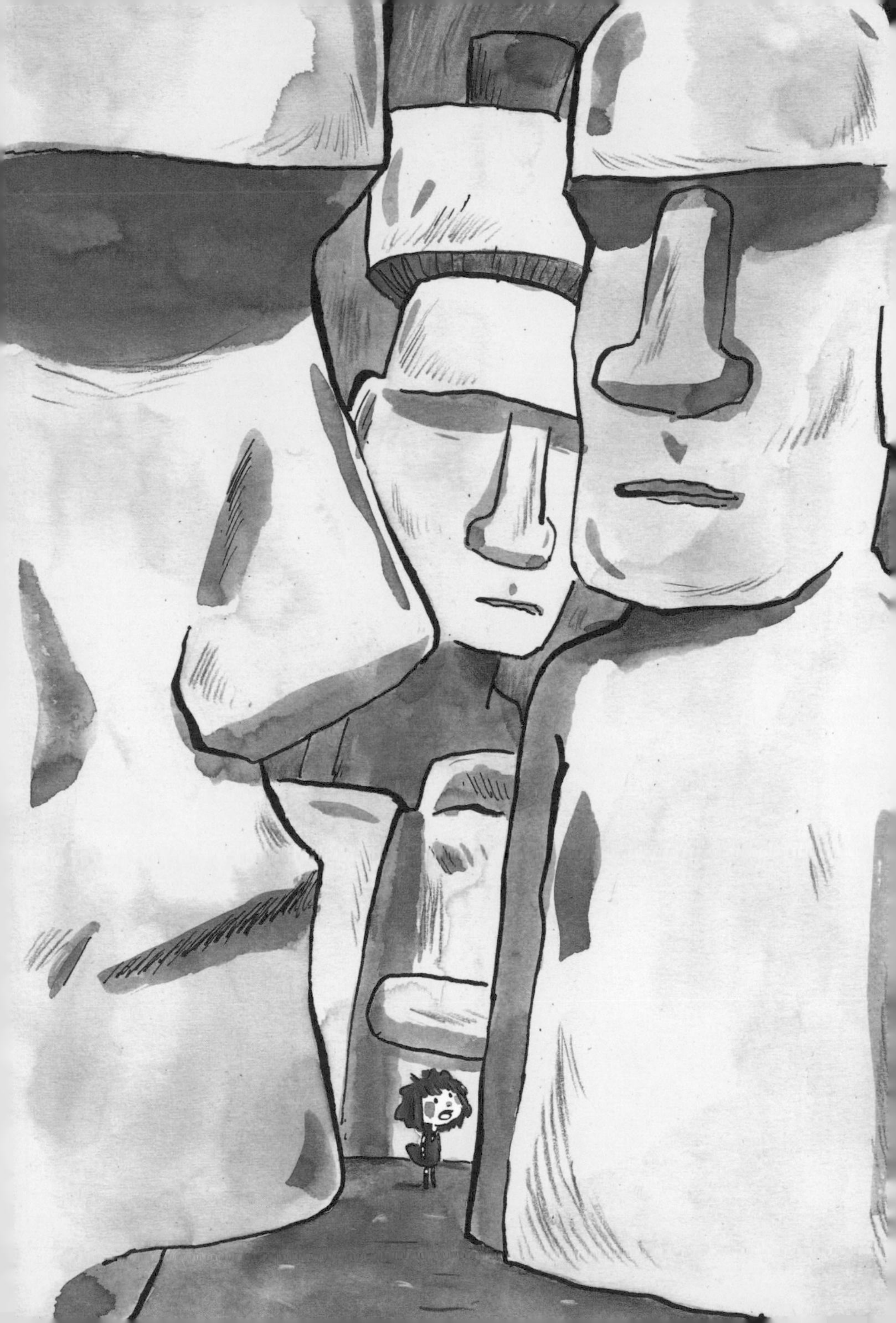

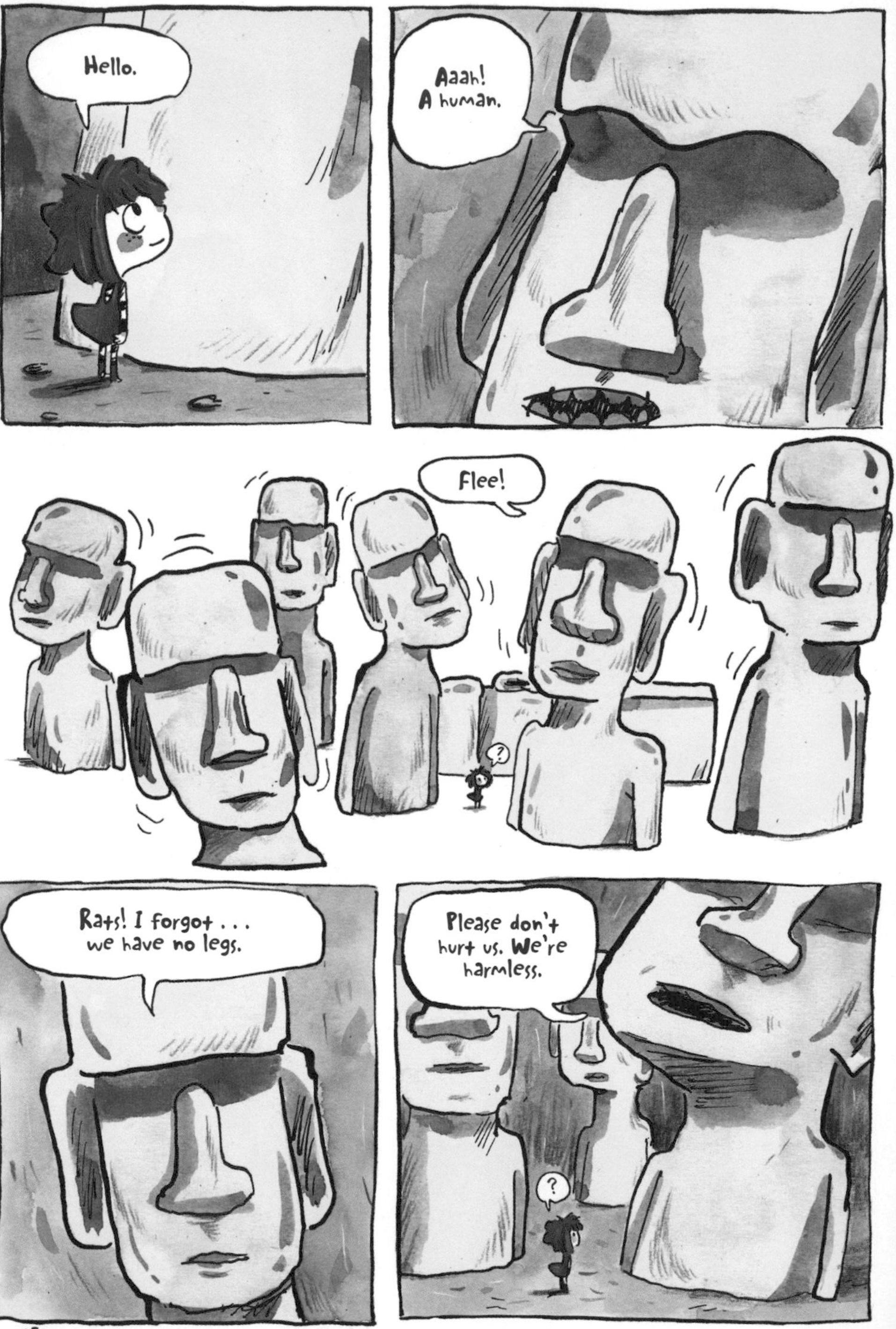
Hello.
Aaah! A human.
Flee!
?
Rats! I forgot . . . we have no legs.
Please don't hurt us. We're harmless.
?

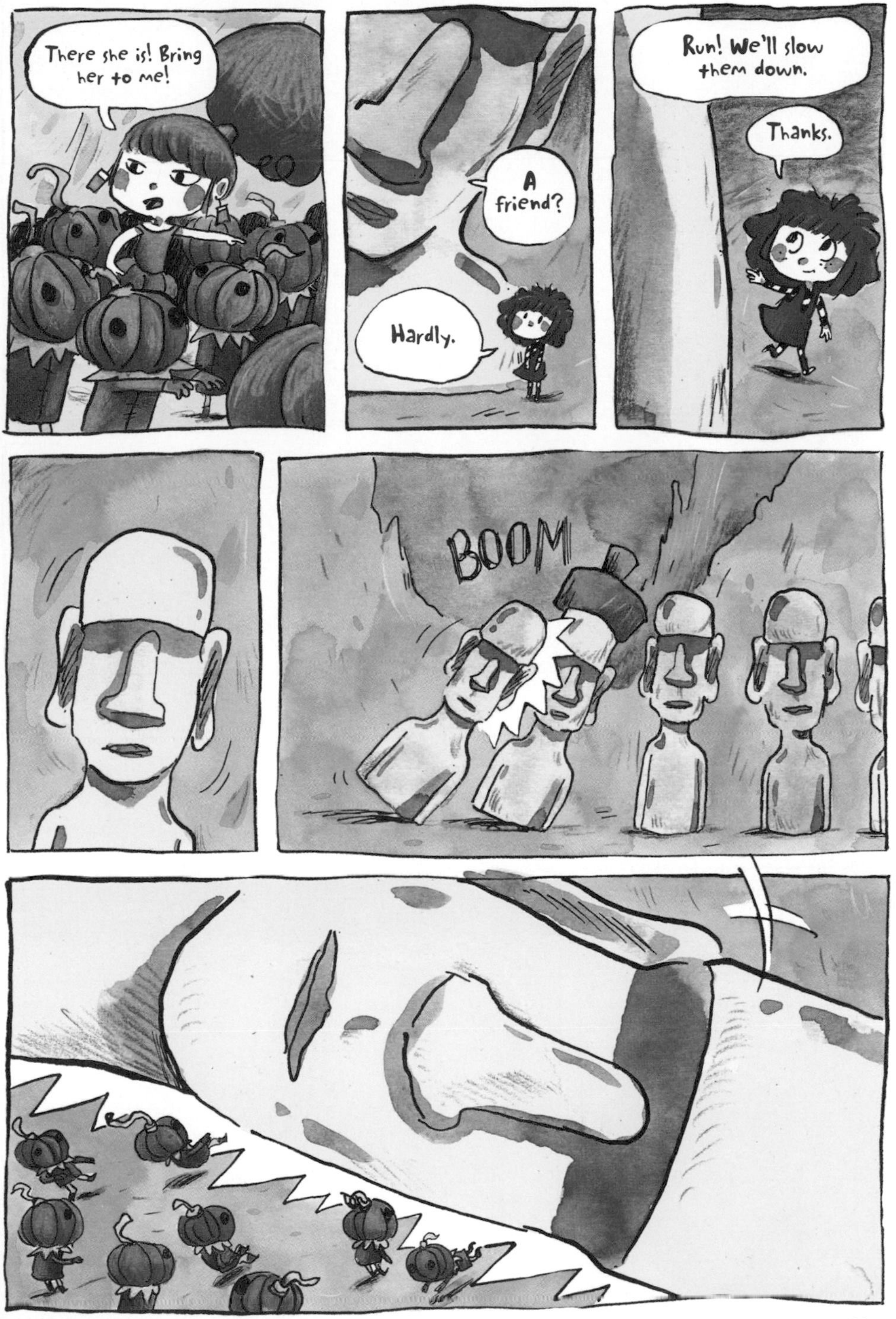
There she is! Bring her to me!
A friend?
Hardly.
Run! We'll slow them down.
Thanks.
BOOM

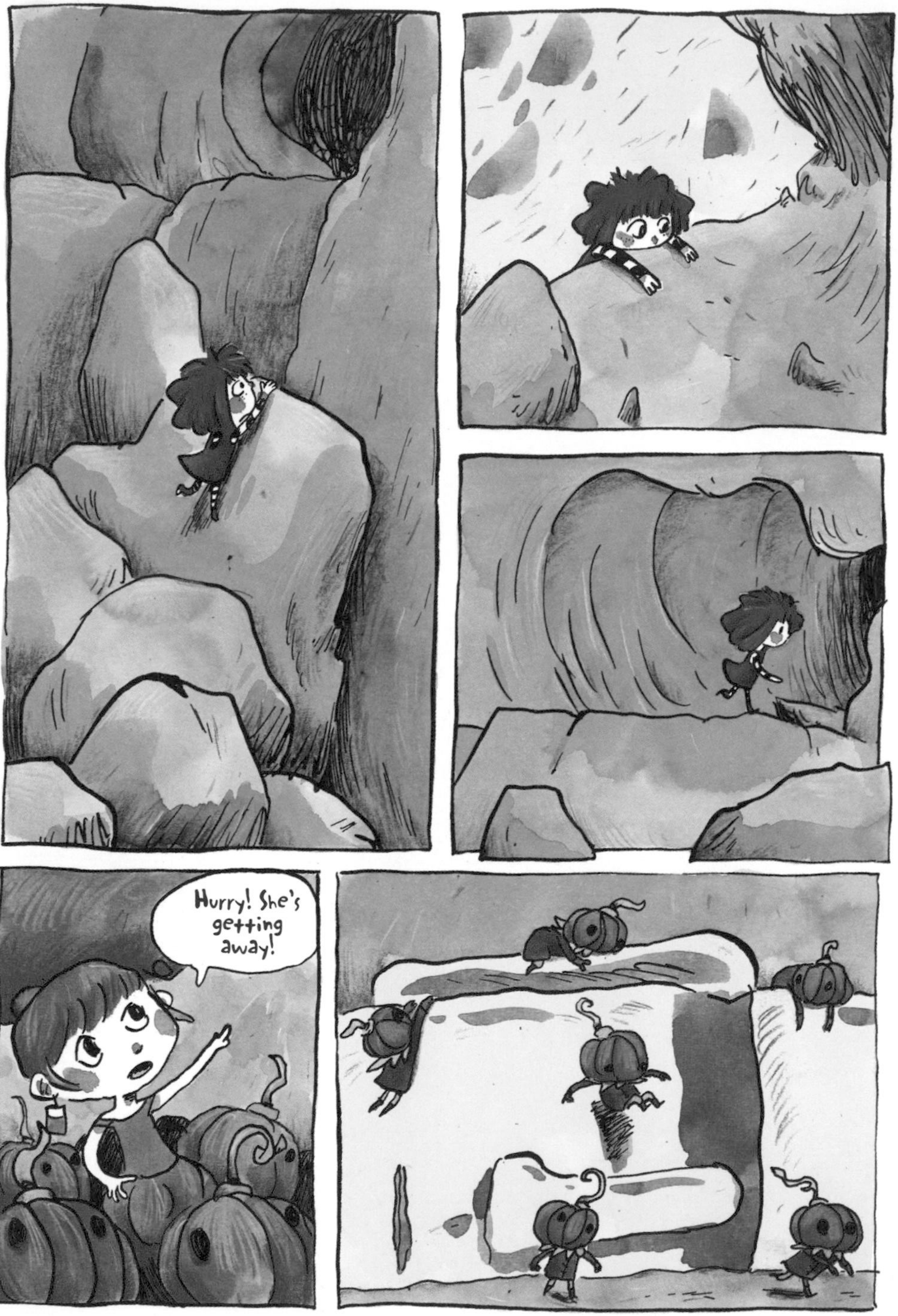
Hurry! She's getting away!

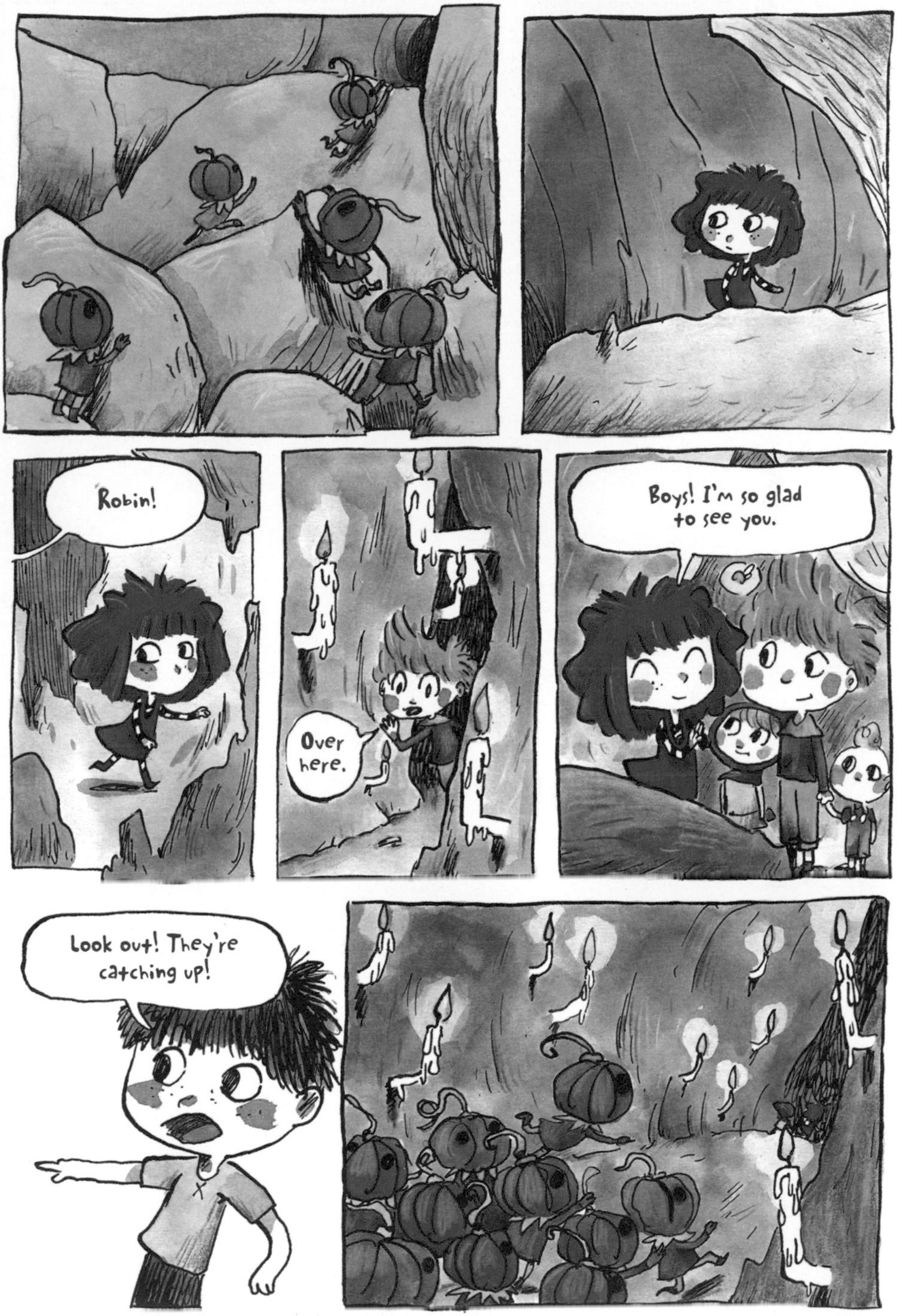

Robin!
Over here.
Boys! I'm so glad to see you.
Look out! They're catching up!

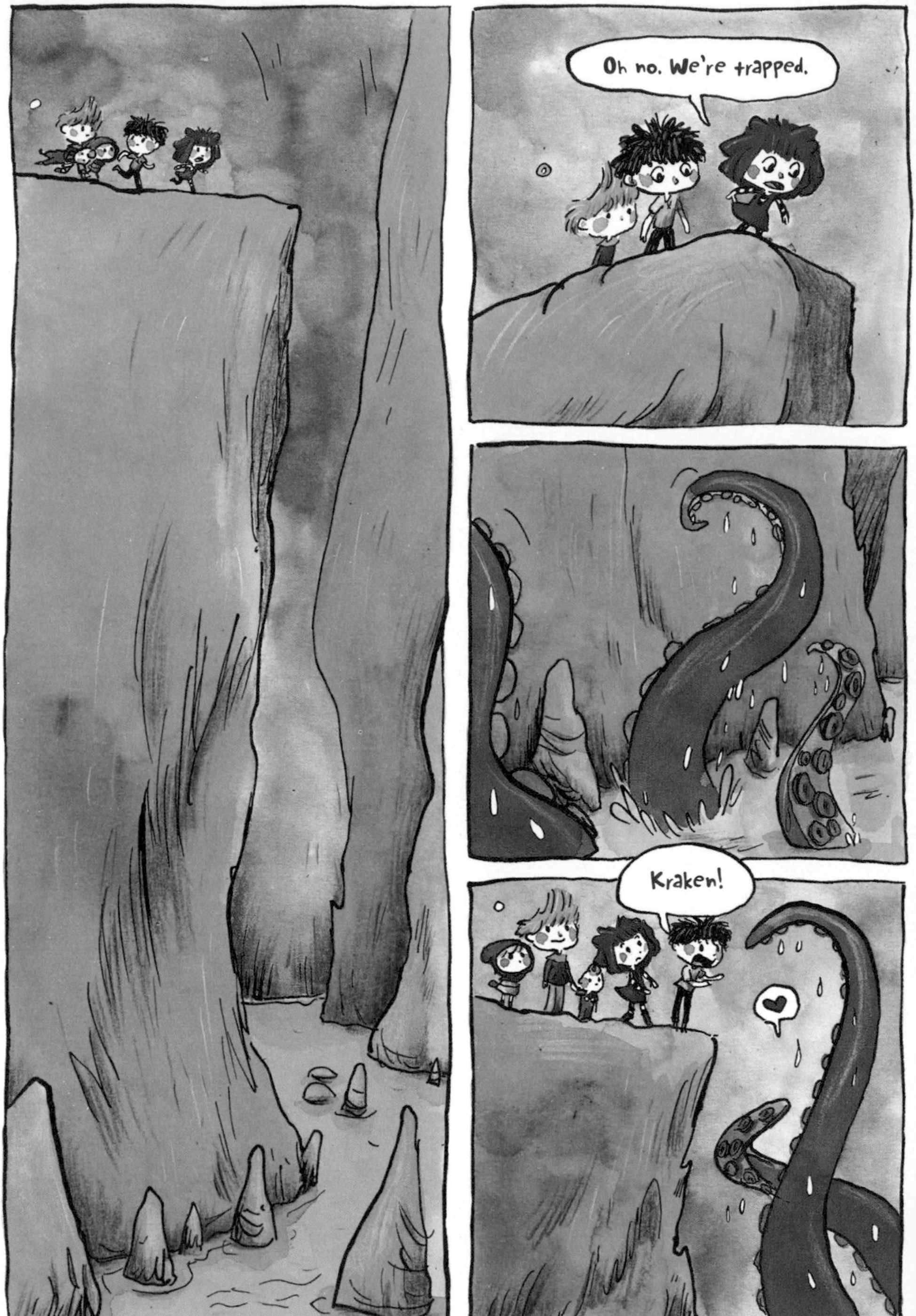
Oh no. We're trapped.
Kraken!

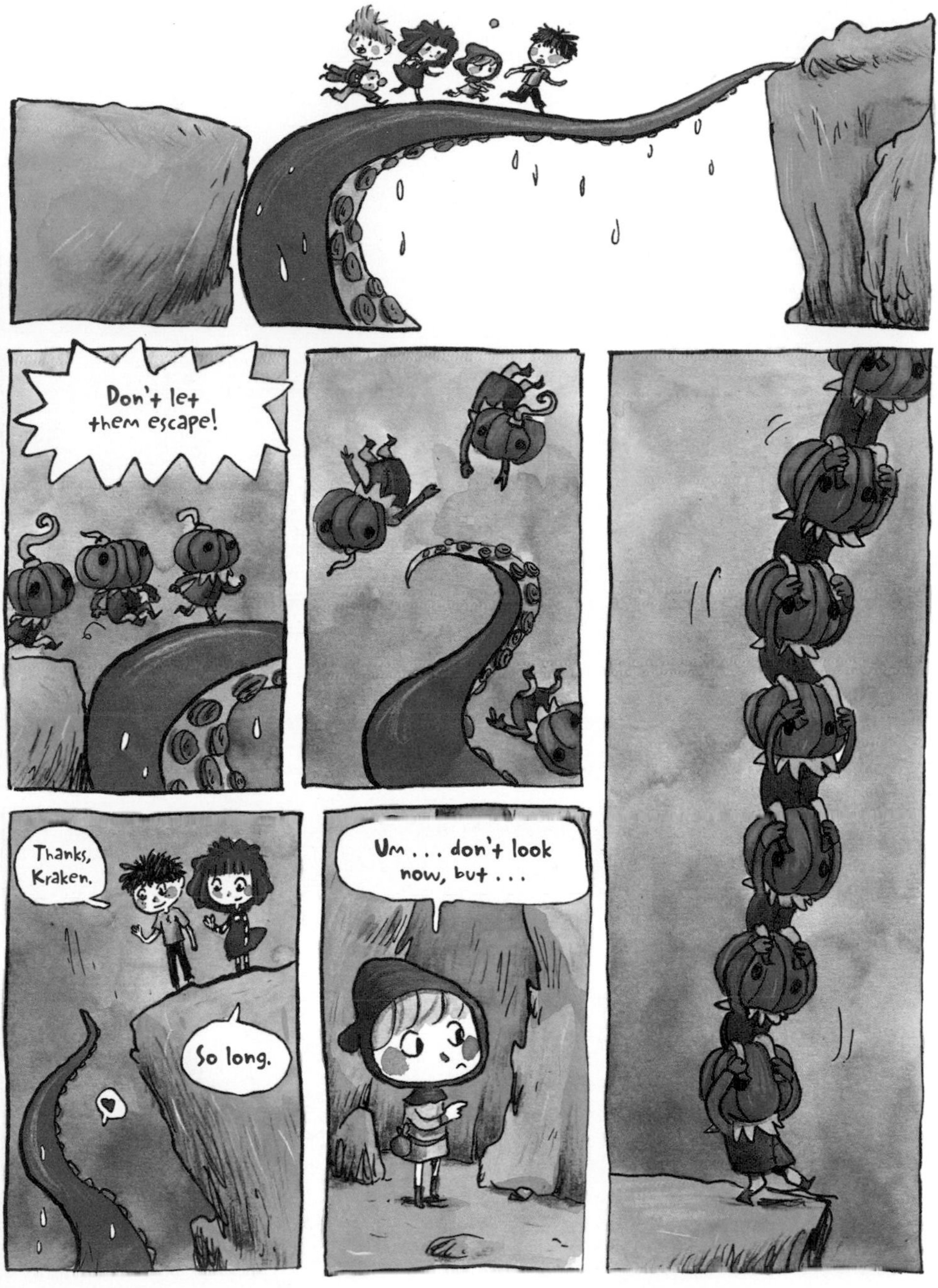
Don't let them escape!
Thanks, Kraken.
So long.
Um . . . don't look now, but . . .

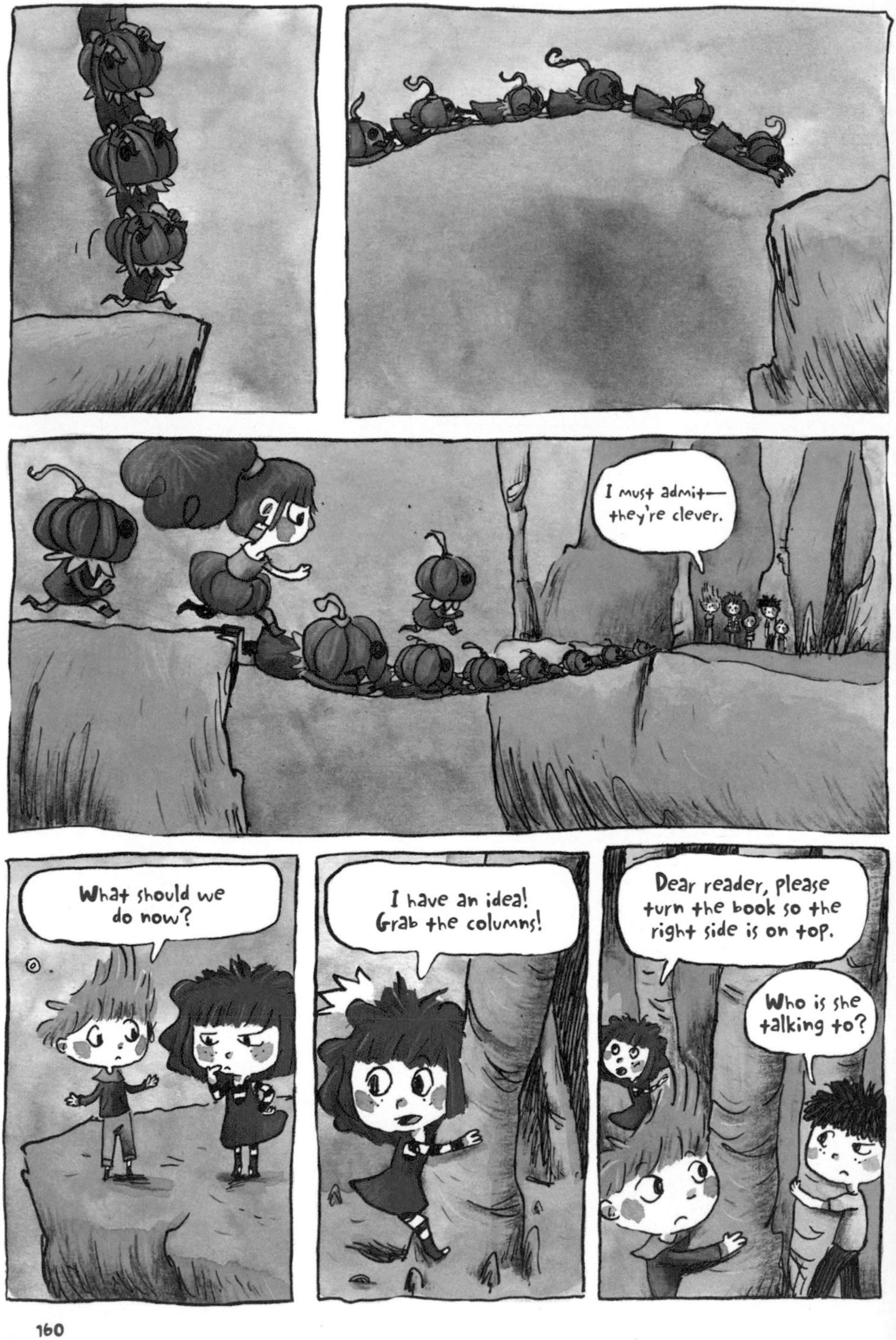
I must admit—
they're clever.
What should we do now?
I have an idea! Grab the columns!
Dear reader, please turn the book so the right side is on top.
Who is she talking to?

161

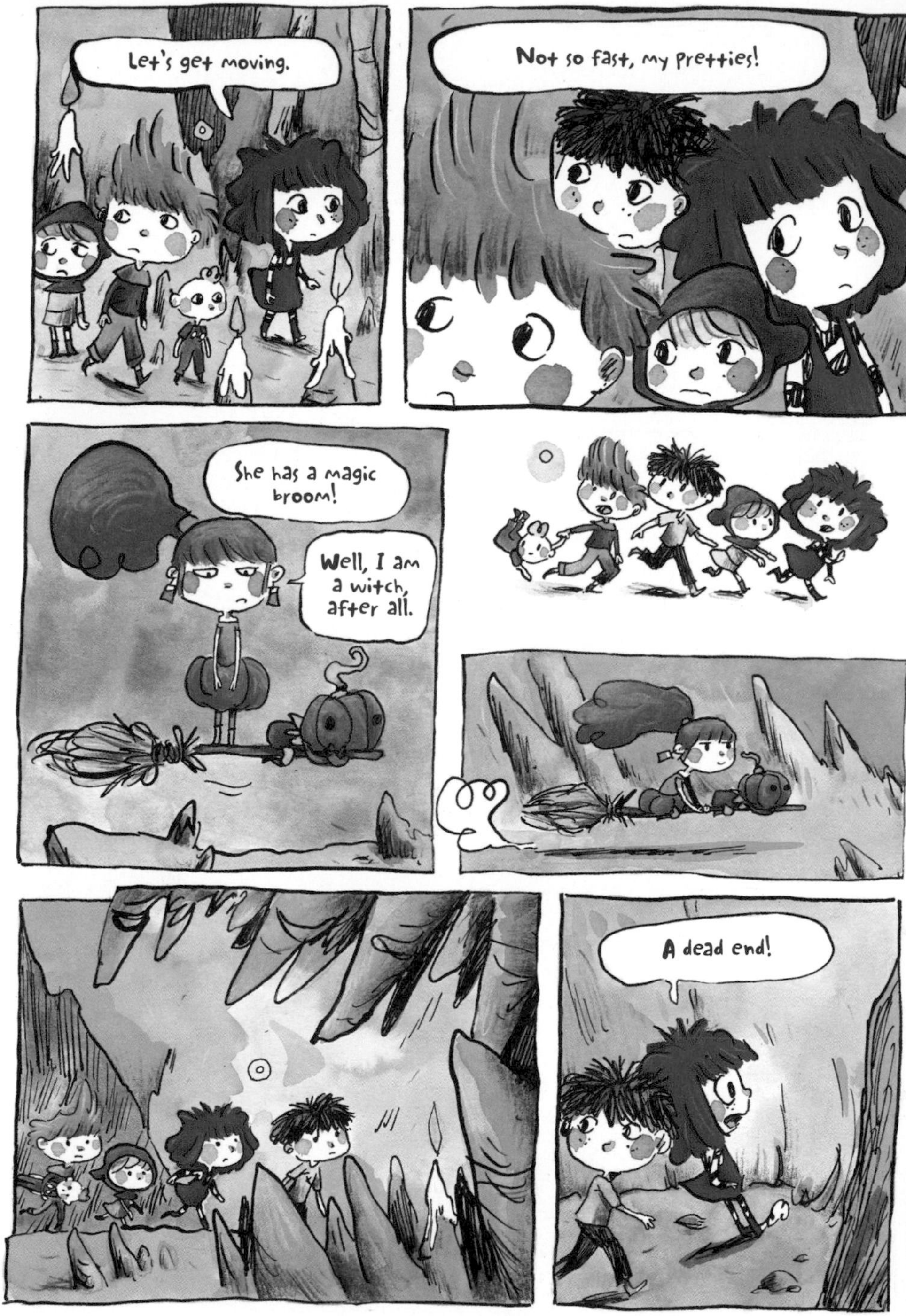
Let's get moving.
Not so fast, my pretties!
She has a magic broom!
Well, I am a witch, after all.
A dead end!

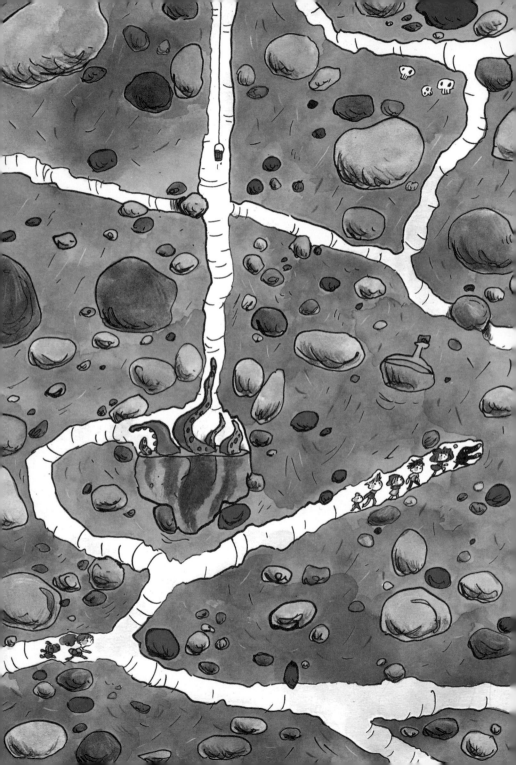

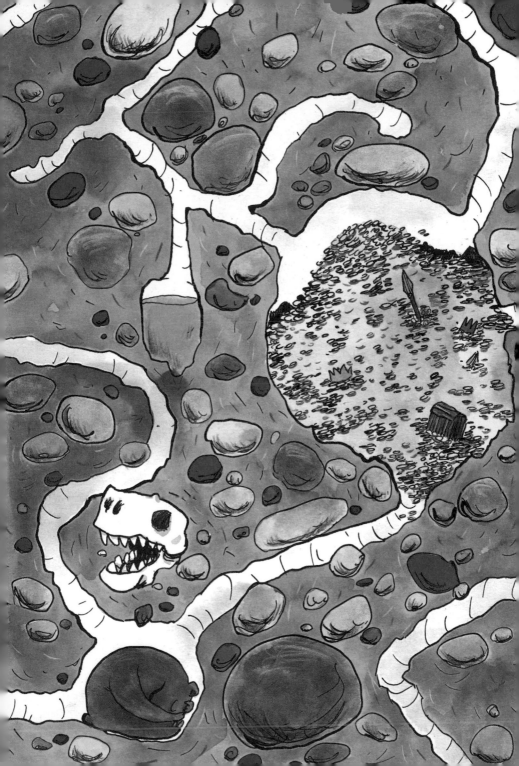

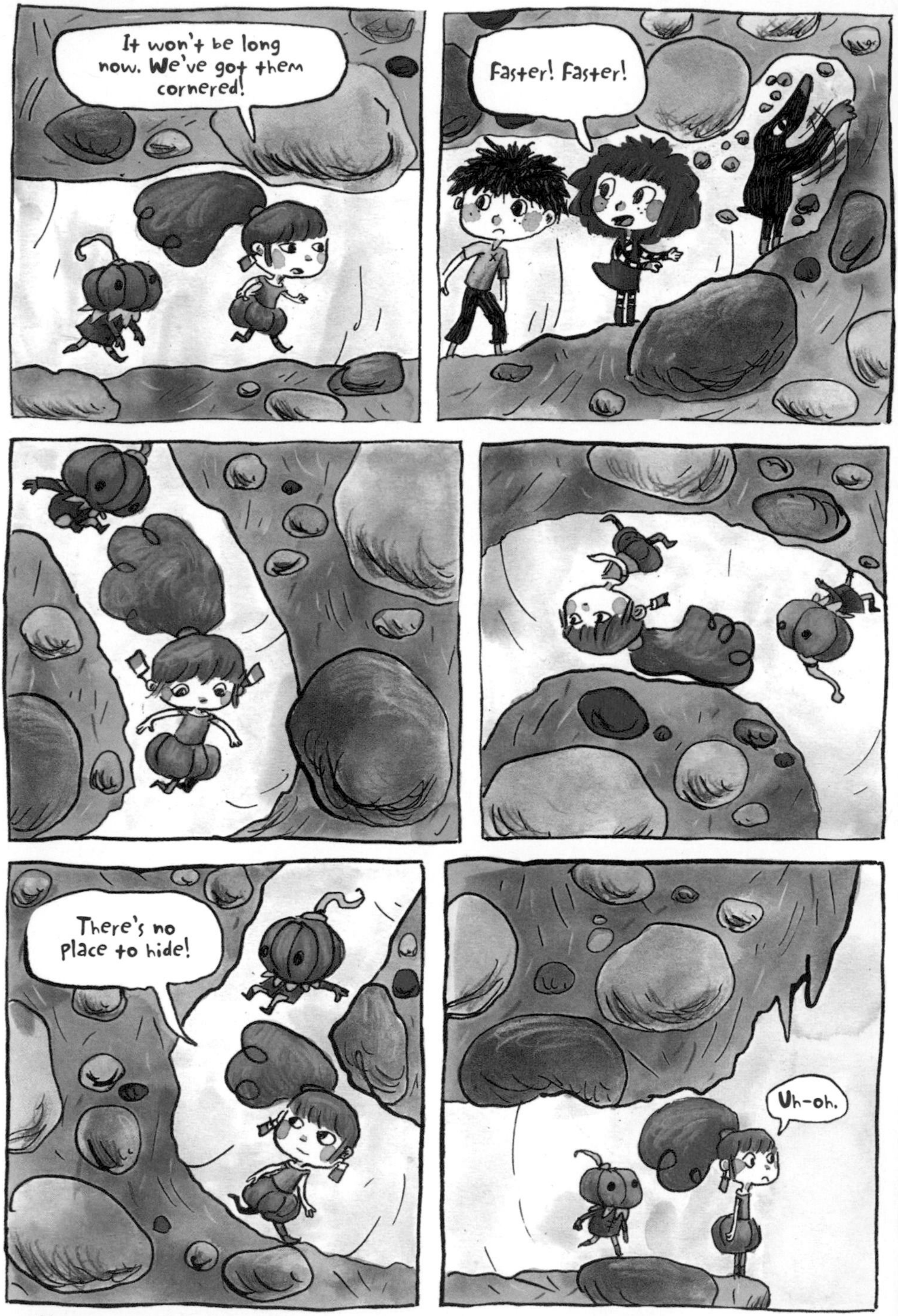
It won't be long now. We've got them cornered!
Faster! Faster!
There's no place to hide!
Uh-oh.

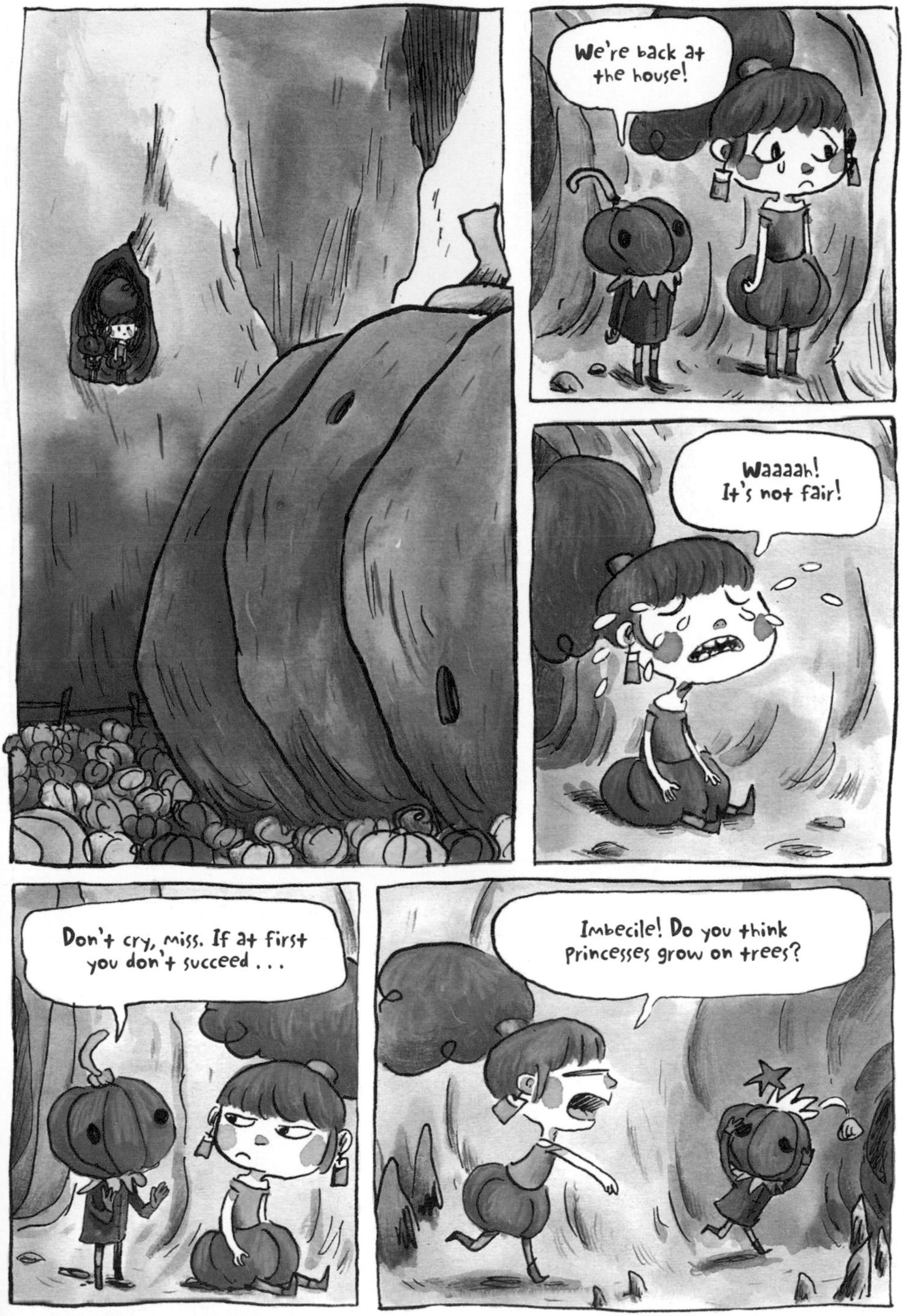
We're back at the house!
Waaaah! It's not fair!
Don't cry, miss. If at first you don't succeed . . .
Imbecile! Do you think Princesses grow on trees?

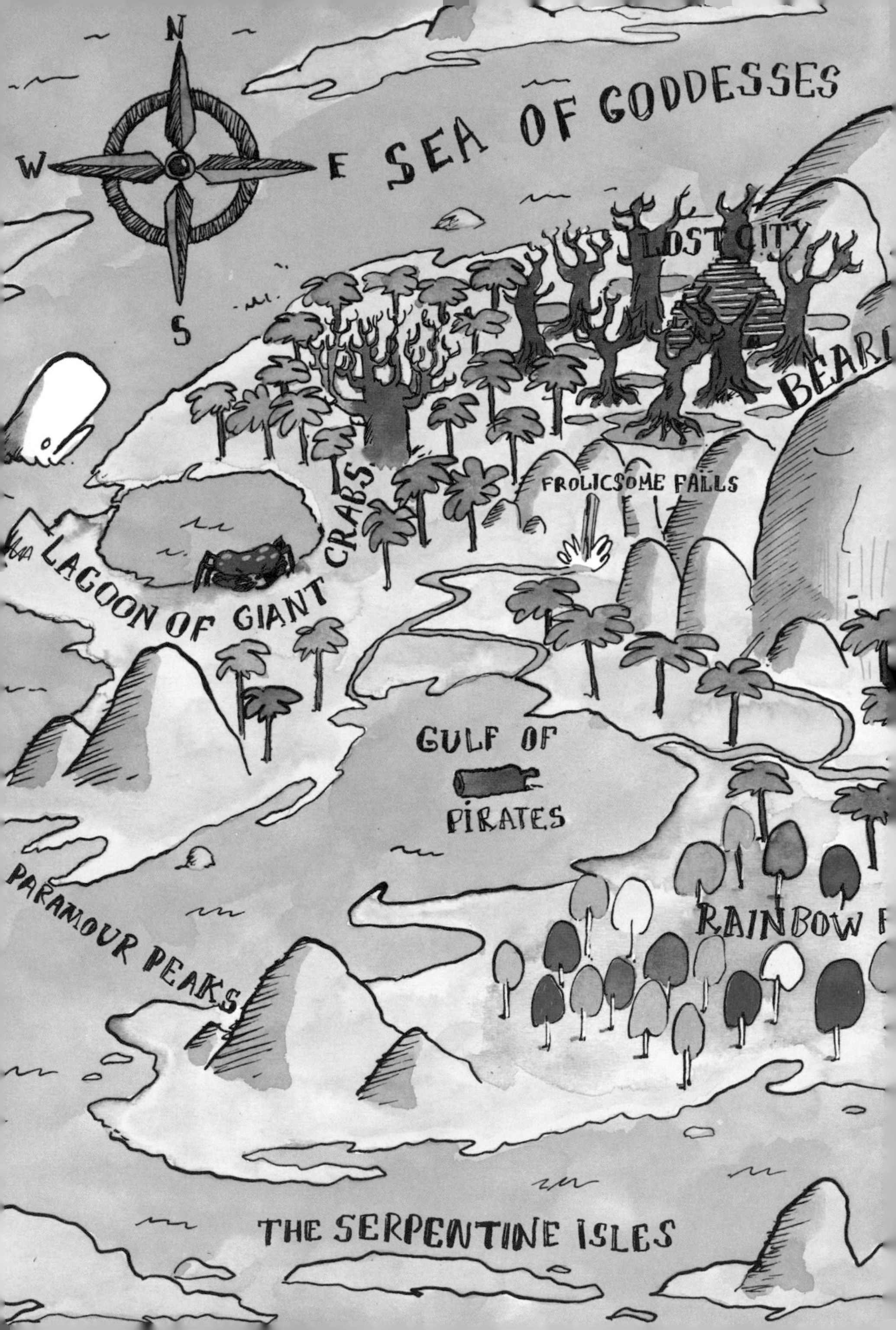
N
W
E
S
SEA OF GODDESSES
LOST CITY
BEARD
FROLICSOME FALLS
LAGOON OF GIANT CRABS
GULF OF PIRATES
RAINBOW
PARAMOUR PEAKS
THE SERPENTINE ISLES

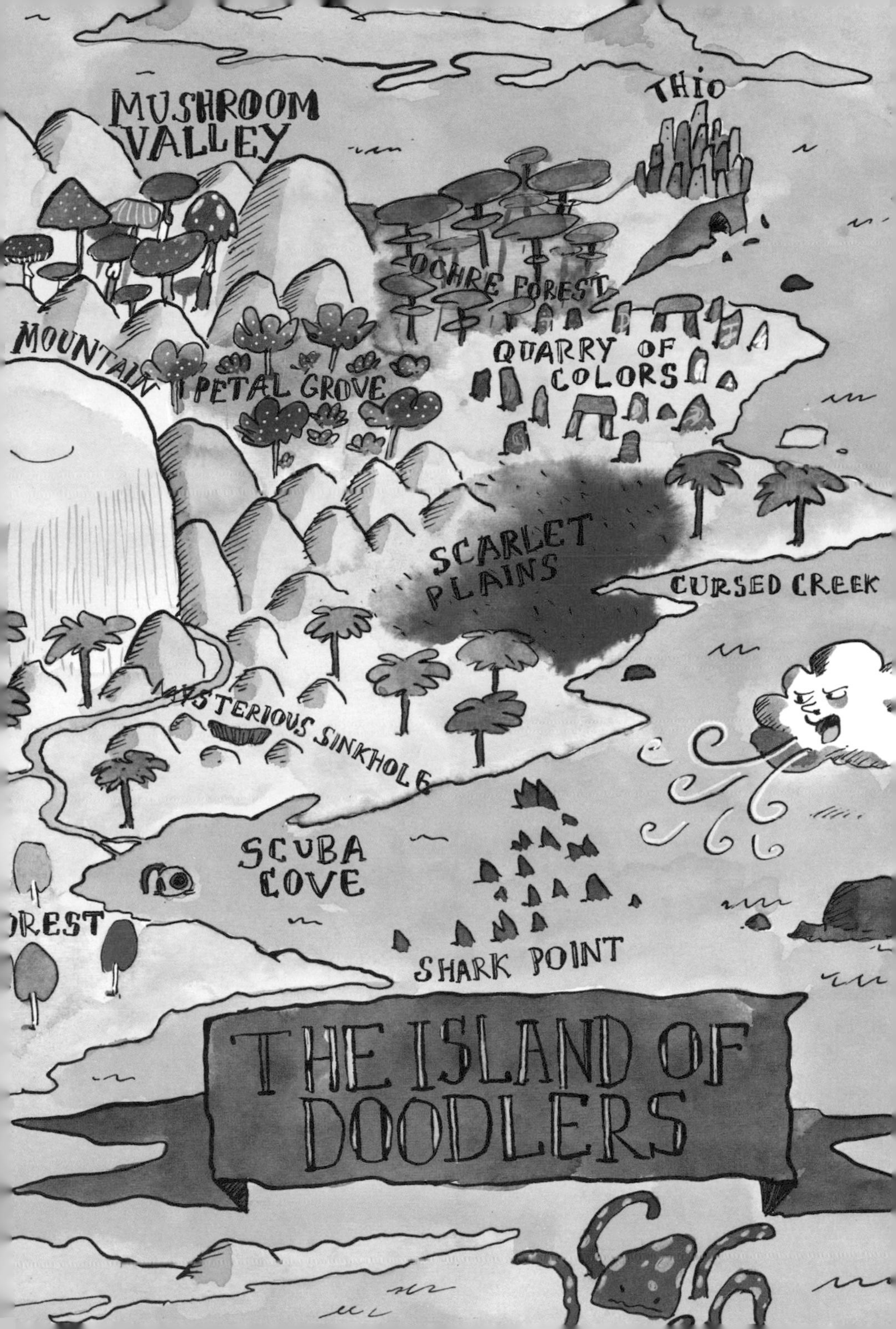
MUSHROOM VALLEY
THIO
OCHRE FOREST
QUARRY OF COLORS
MOUNTAIN
PETAL GROVE
SCARLET PLAINS
CURSED CREEK
MYSTERIOUS SINKHOLE
SCUBA COVE
OREST
SHARK POINT
THE ISLAND OF DOODLERS

THE PRINCESS

TRIES TO STAY IN ONE PLACE

(BUT THE WEATHER DOESN'T COOPERATE)

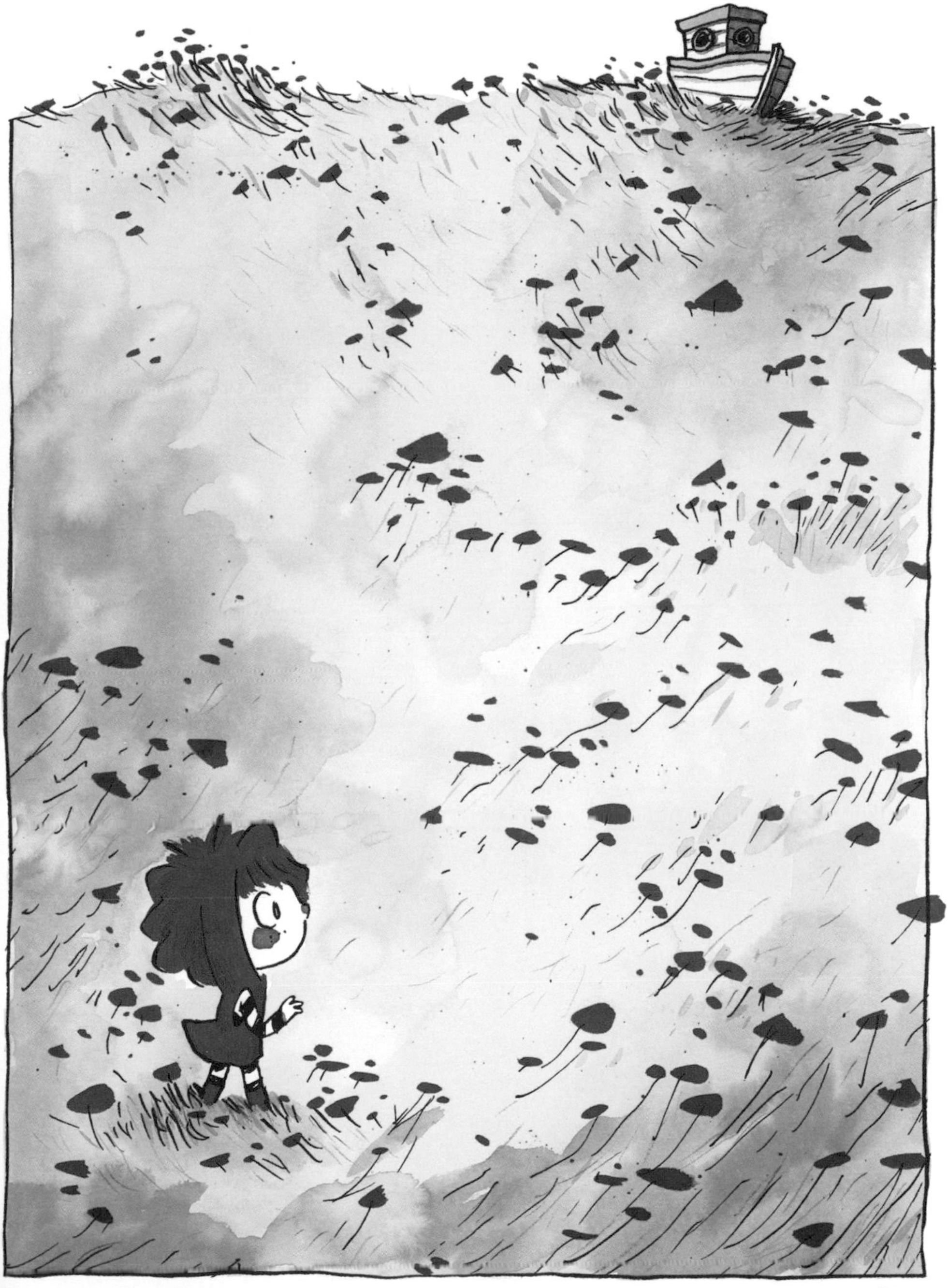

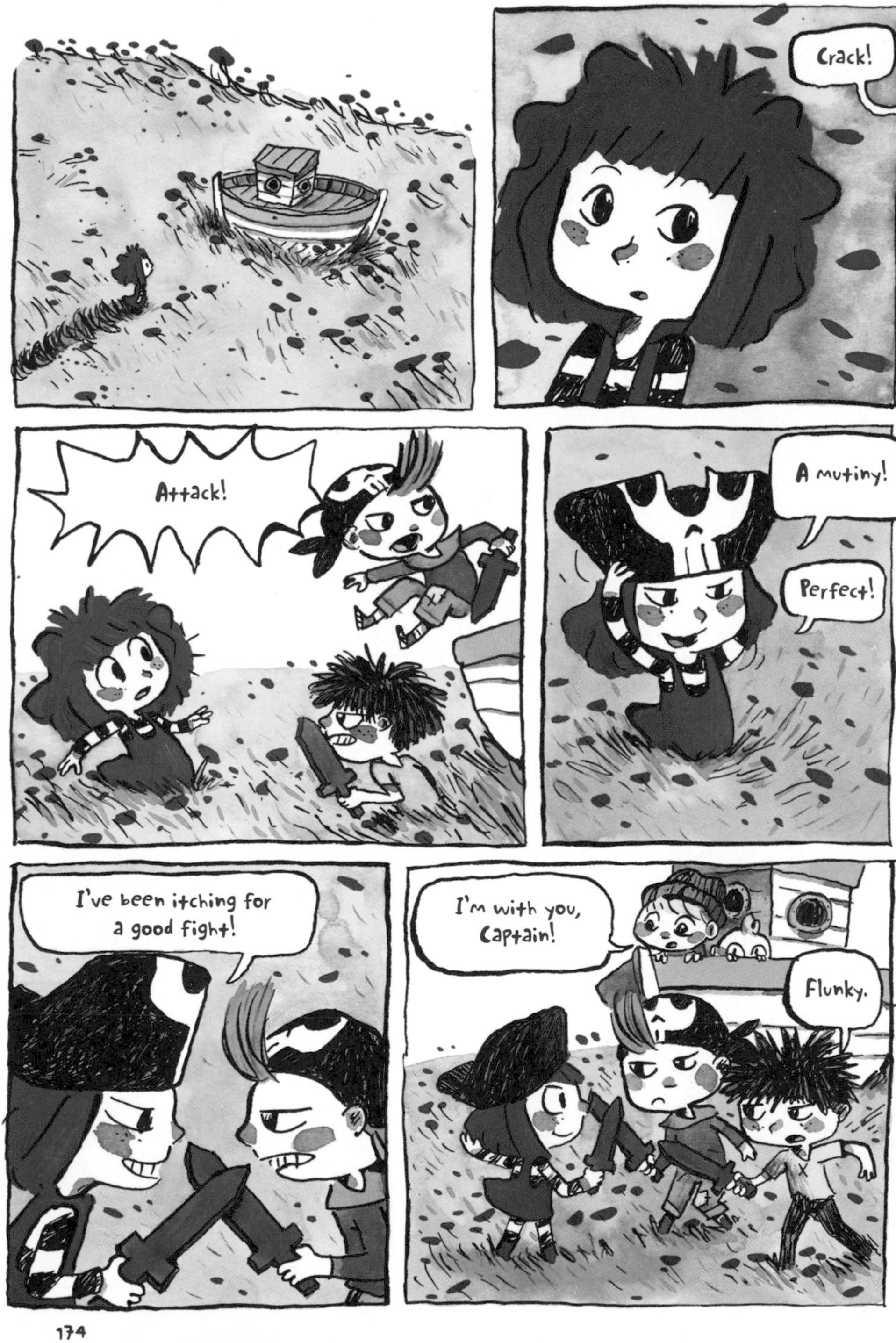
Crack!
Attack!
A mutiny!
Perfect!
I've been itching for a good fight!
I'm with you, Captain!
Flunky.

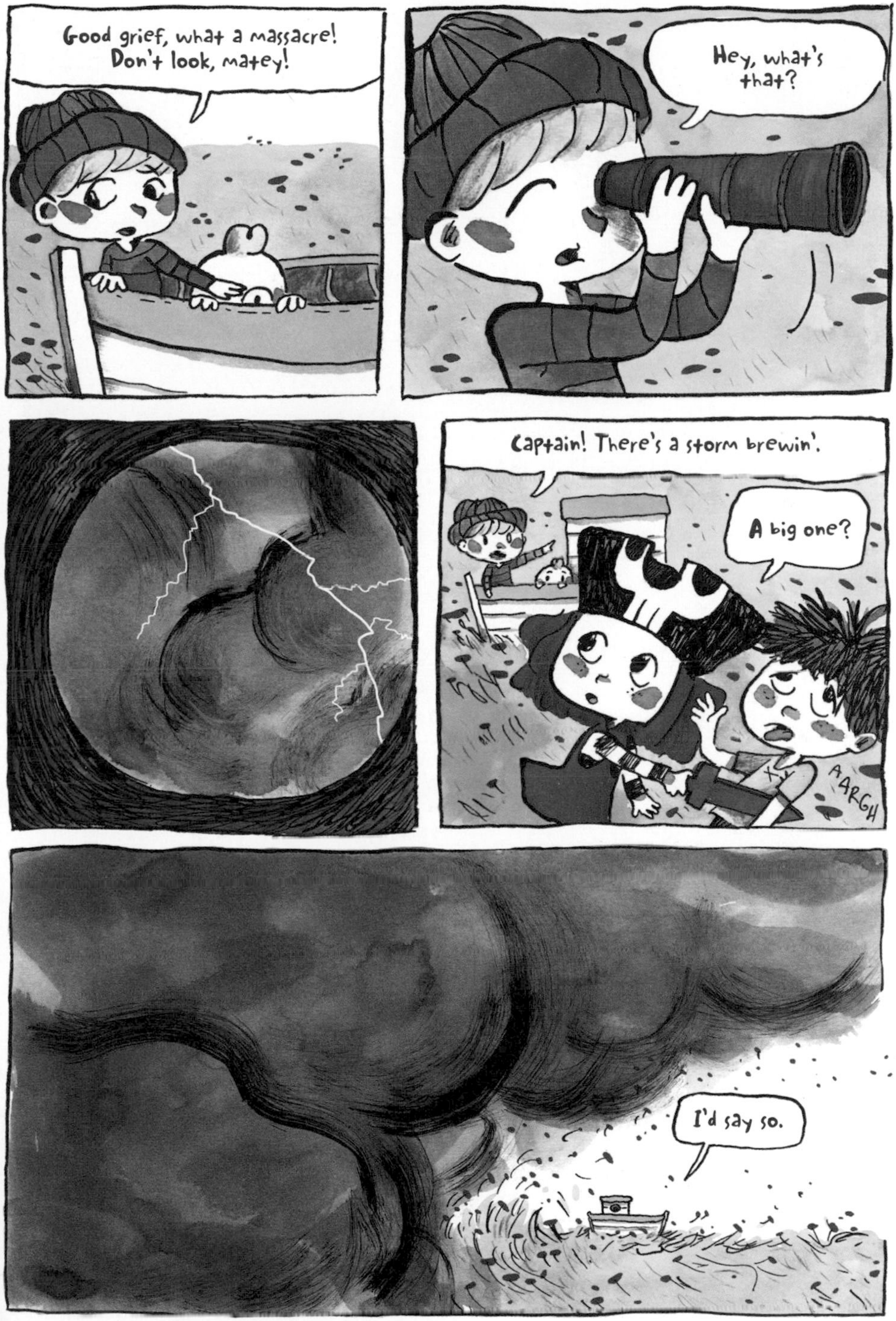
Good grief, what a massacre! Don't look, matey!
Hey, what's that?
Captain! There's a storm brewin'.
A big one?
AARGH
I'd say so.

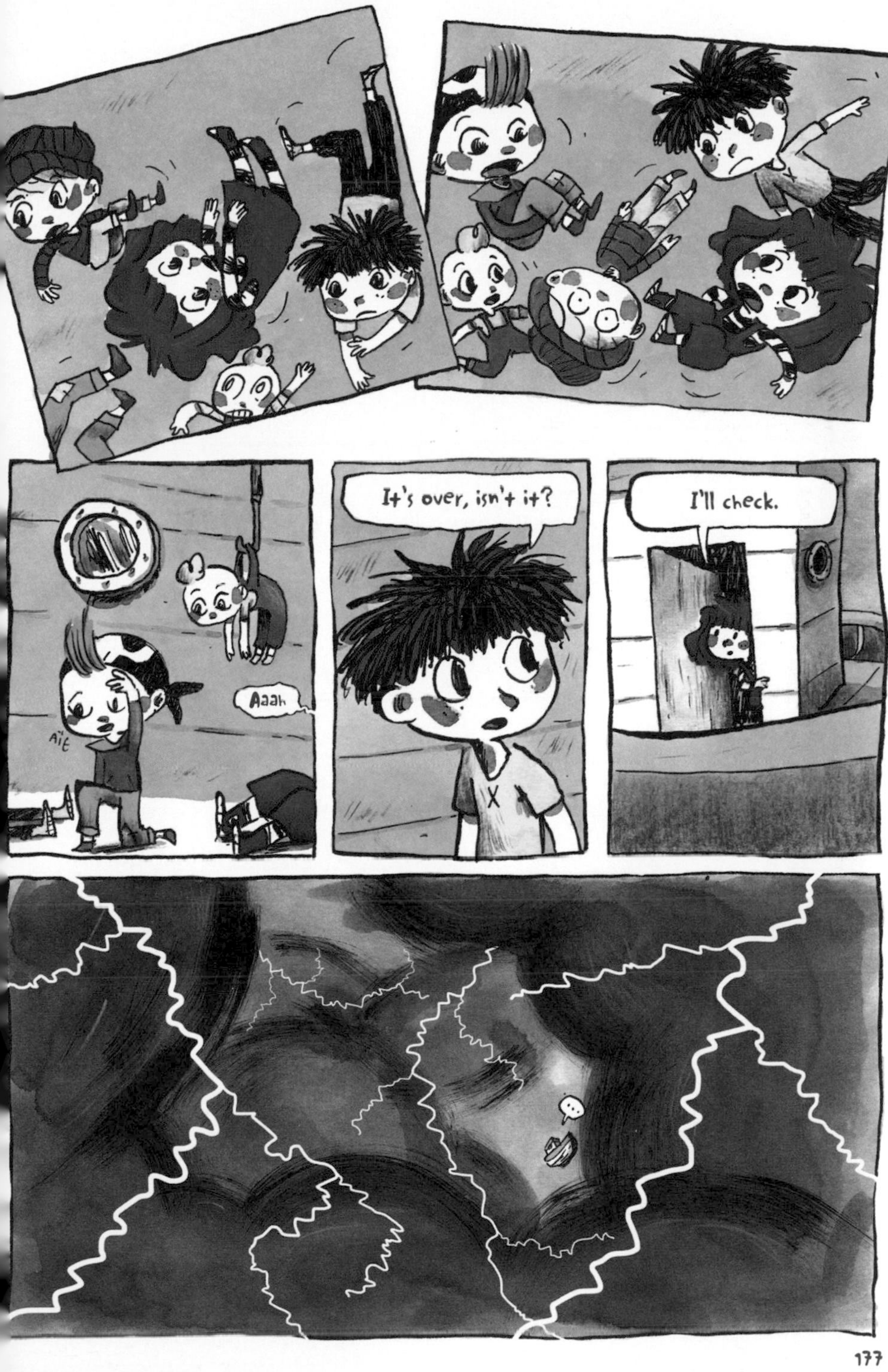
Aït
Aaah
It's over, isn't it?
I'll check.

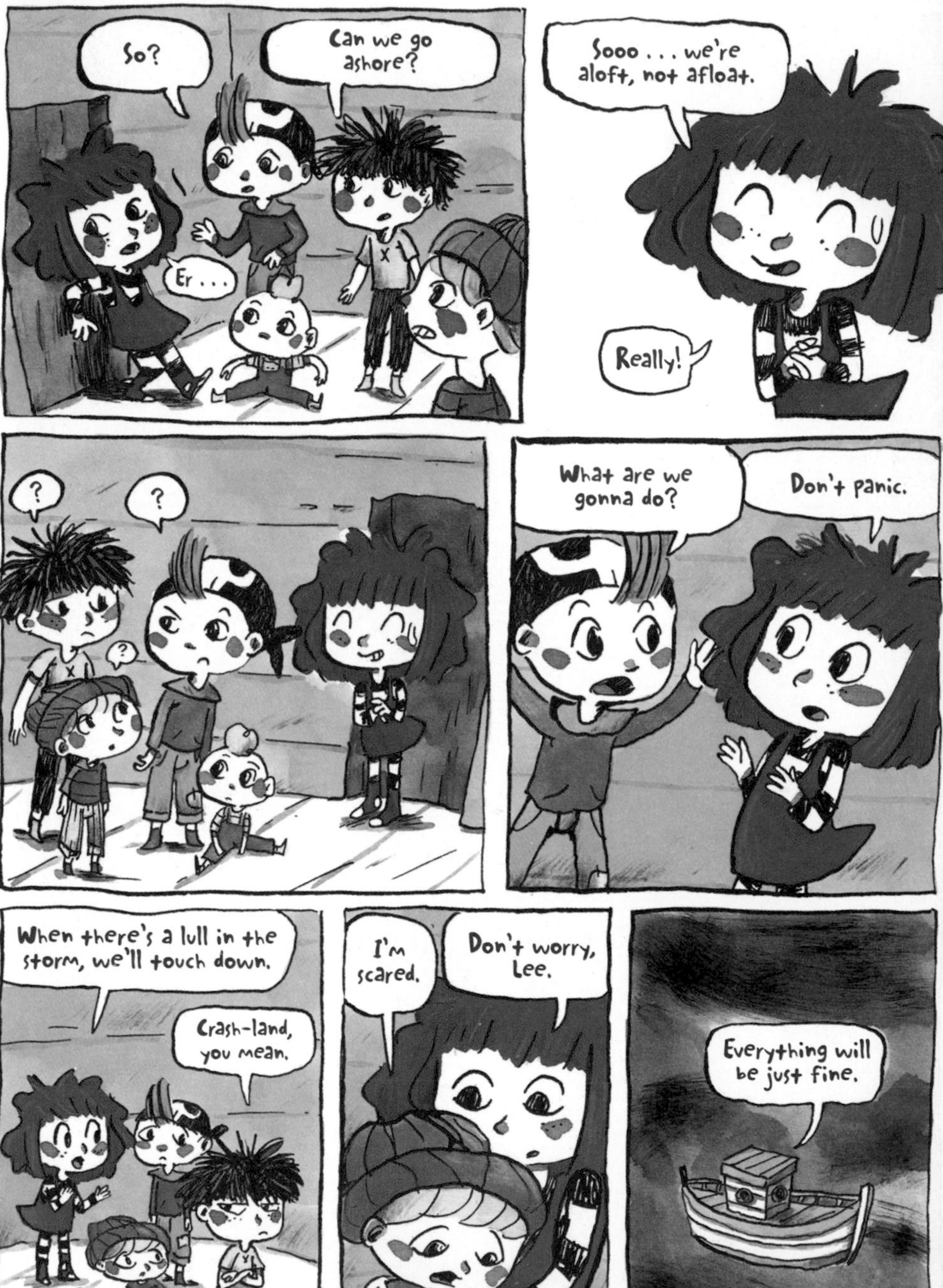
So?
Can we go ashore?
Er . . .
Sooo . . . we're aloft, not afloat.
Really!
?
?
?
What are we gonna do?
Don't panic.
When there's a lull in the storm, we'll touch down.
Crash-land, you mean.
Huh?
I'm scared.
Don't worry, Lee.
Everything will be just fine.

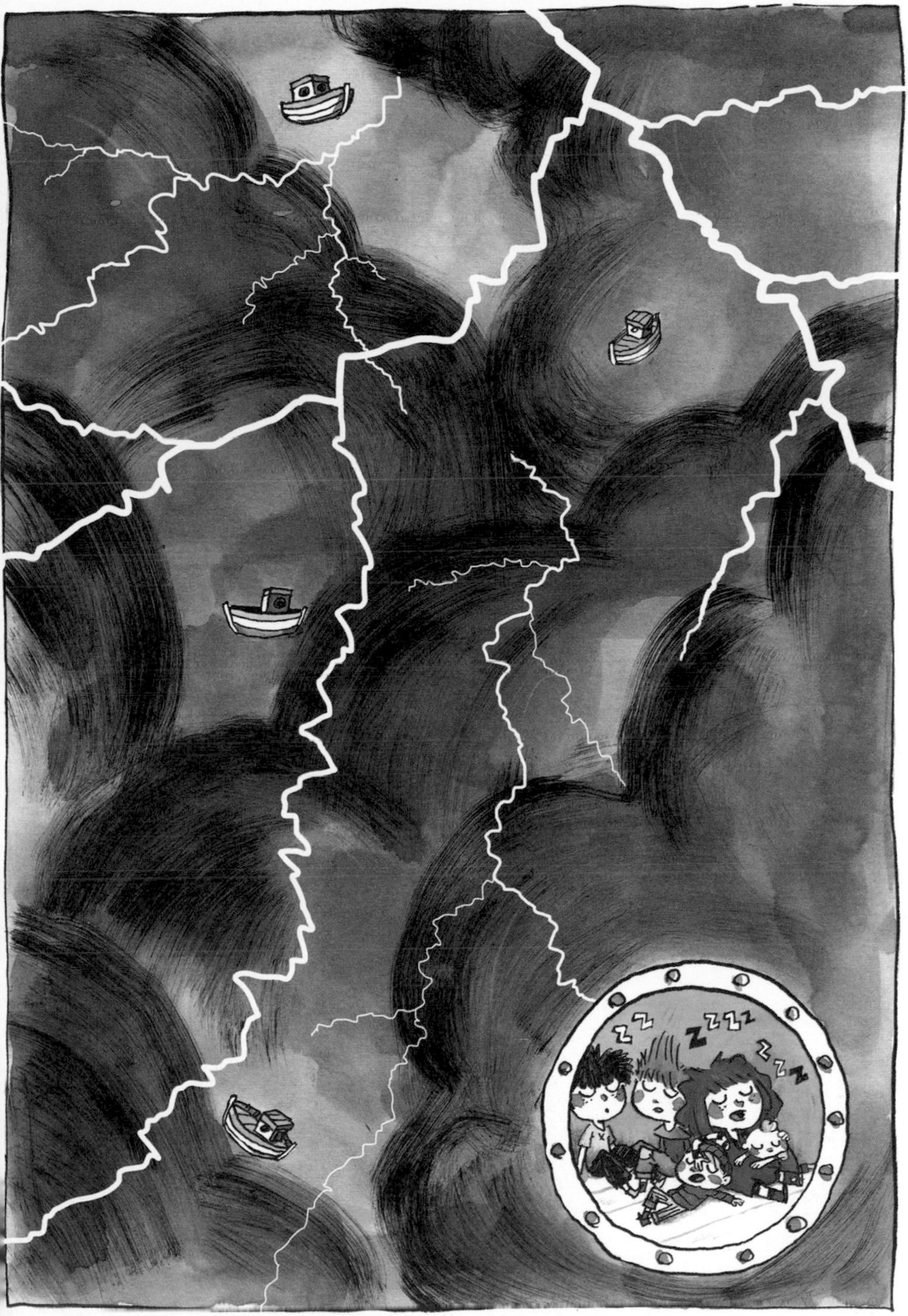
ZZ
ZZZZ
ZZZ

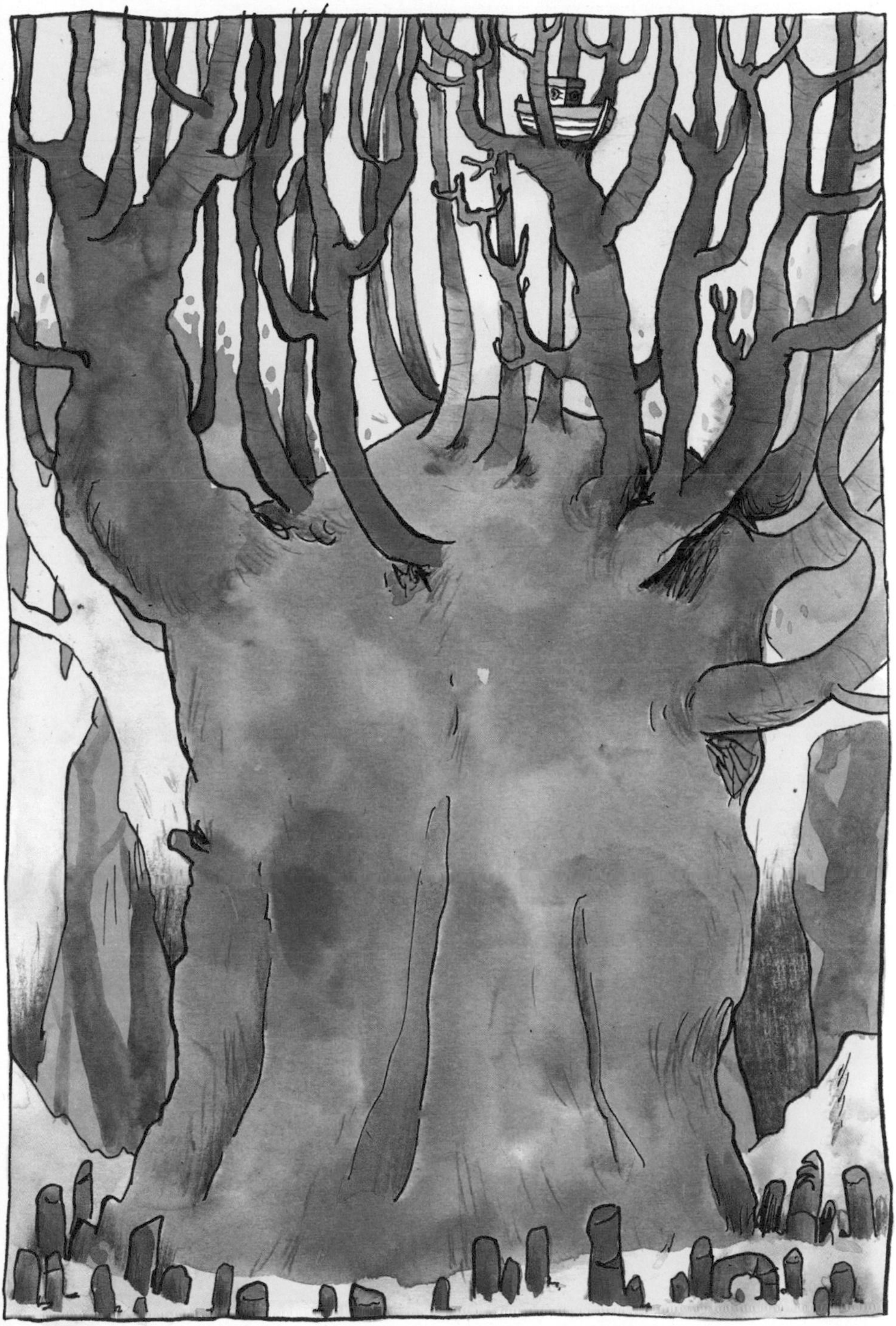

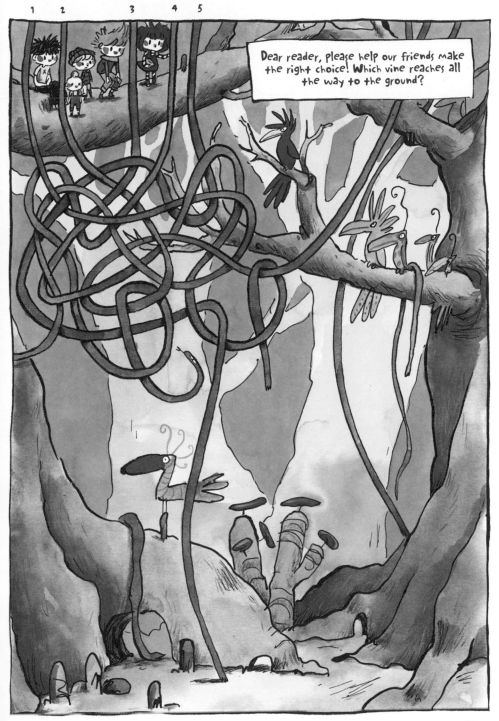

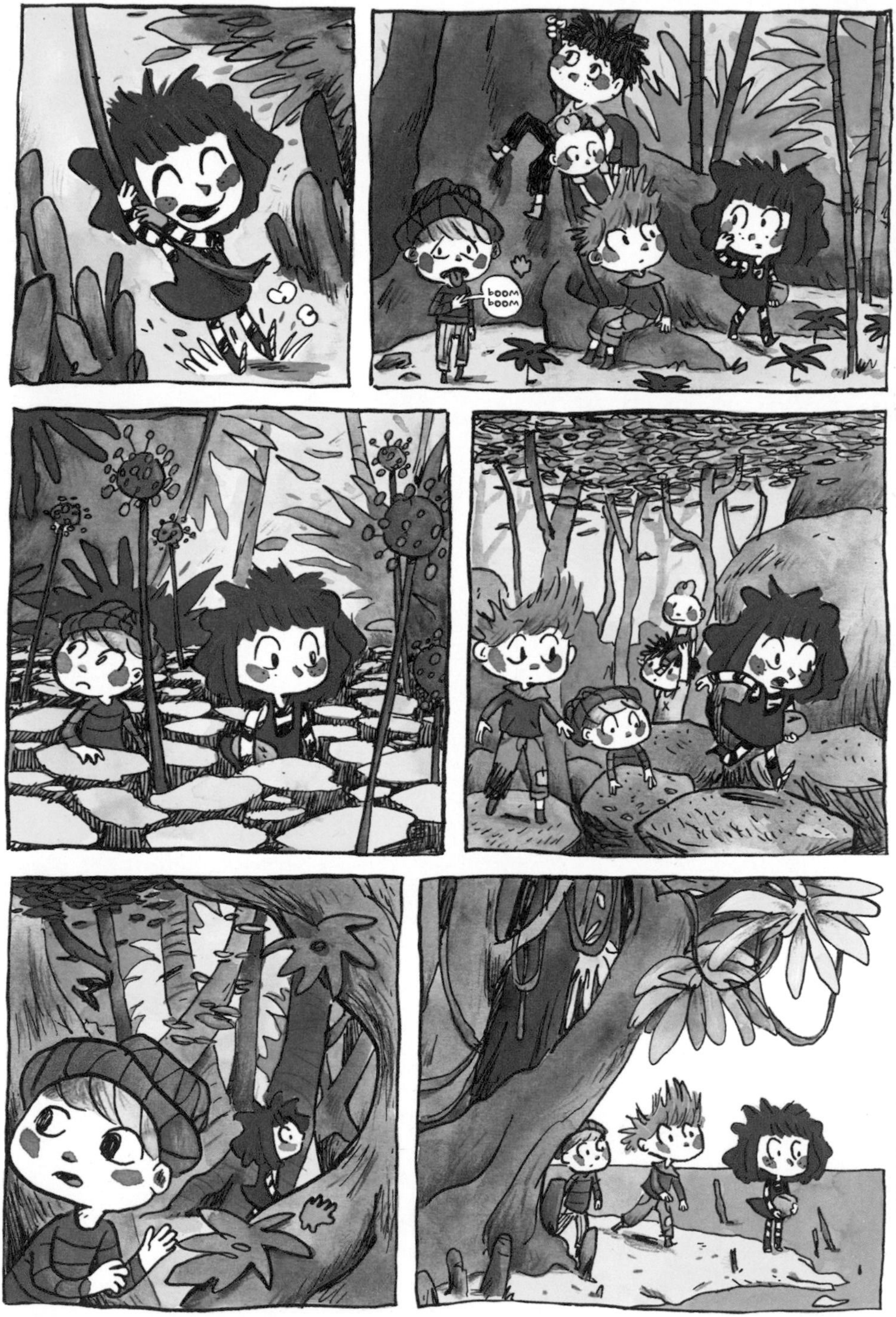
boom boom

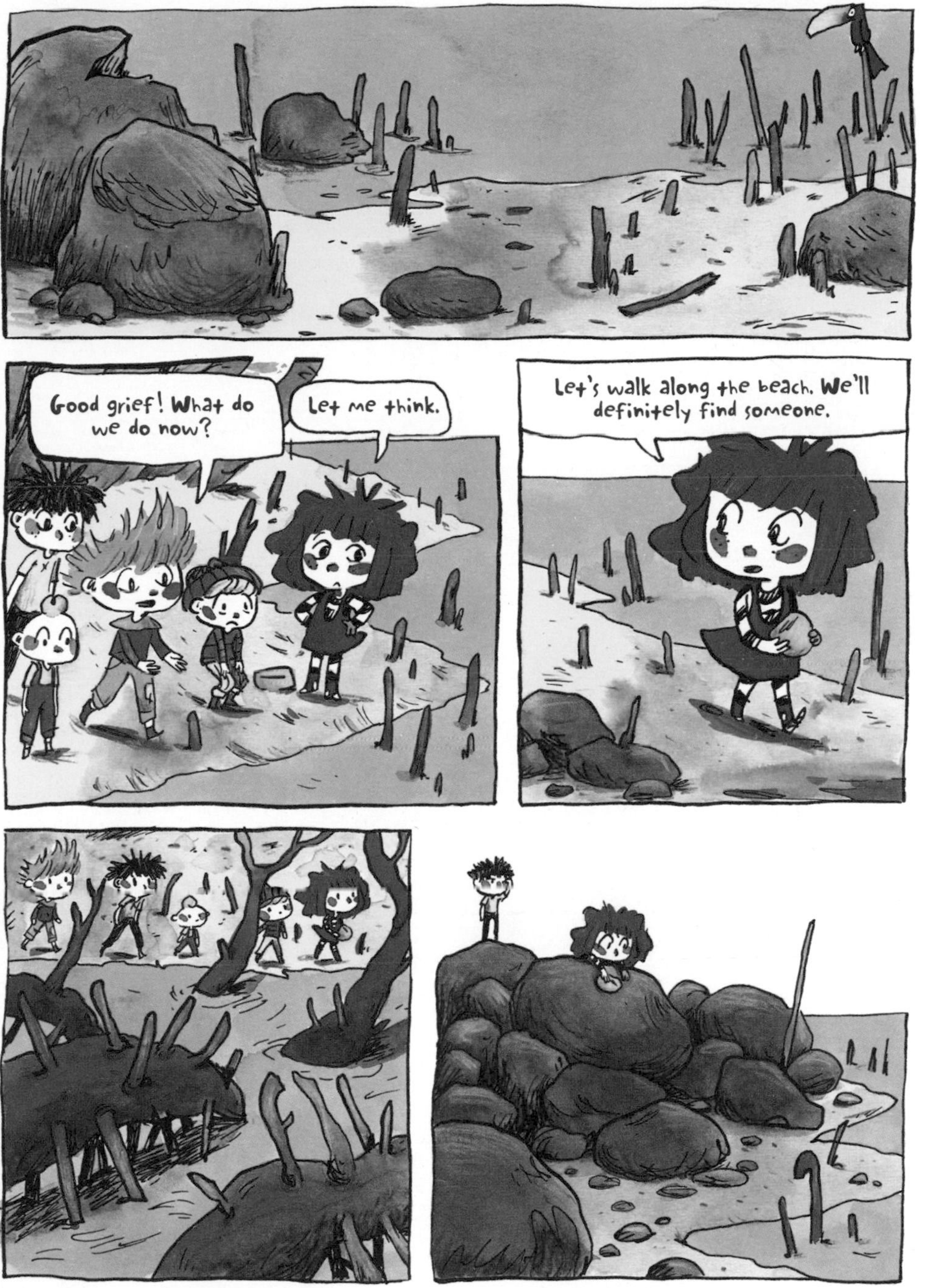
Good grief! What do we do now?
Let me think.
Let's walk along the beach. We'll definitely find someone.

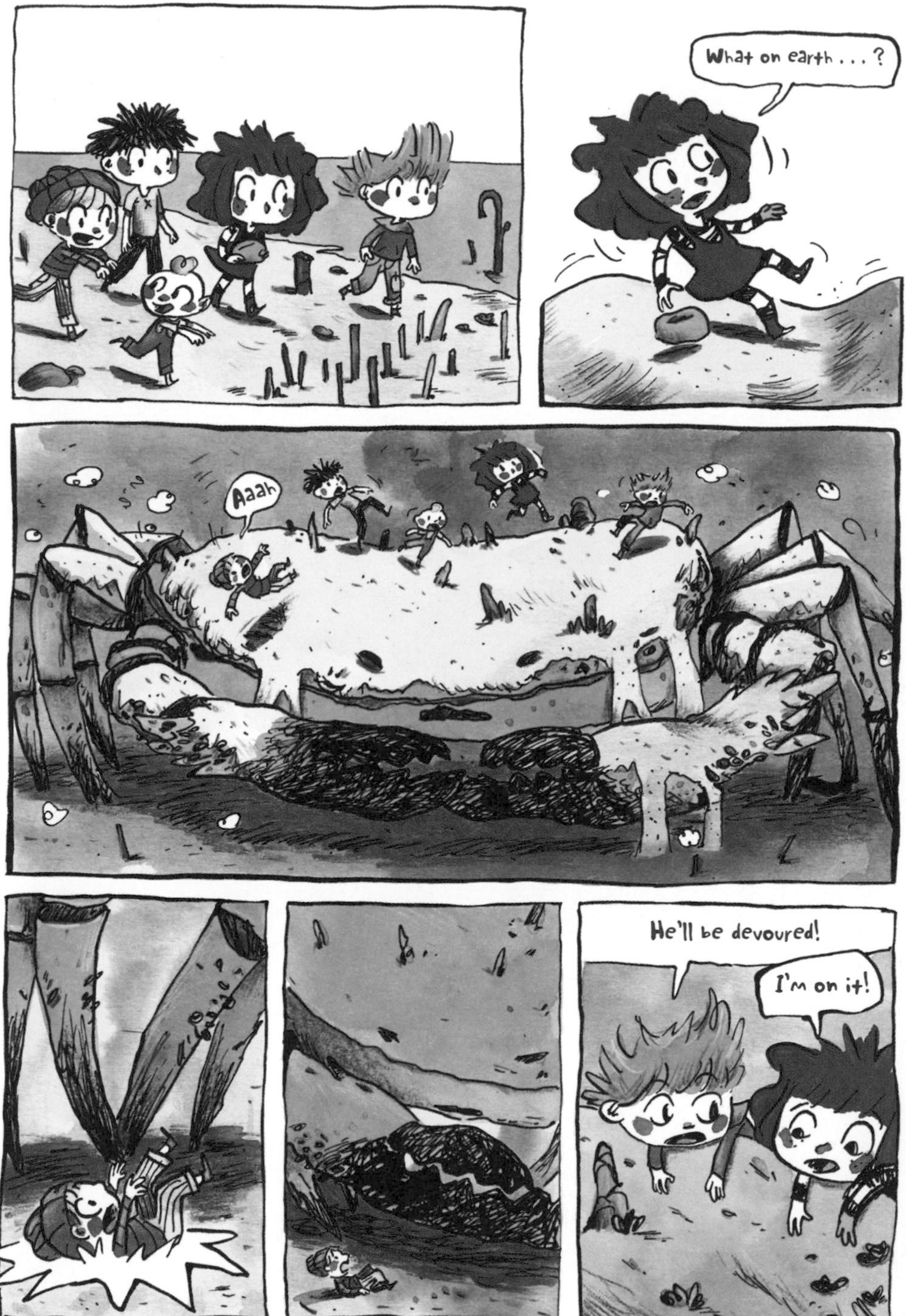
What on earth . . . ?
Aaah
He'll be devoured!
I'm on it!

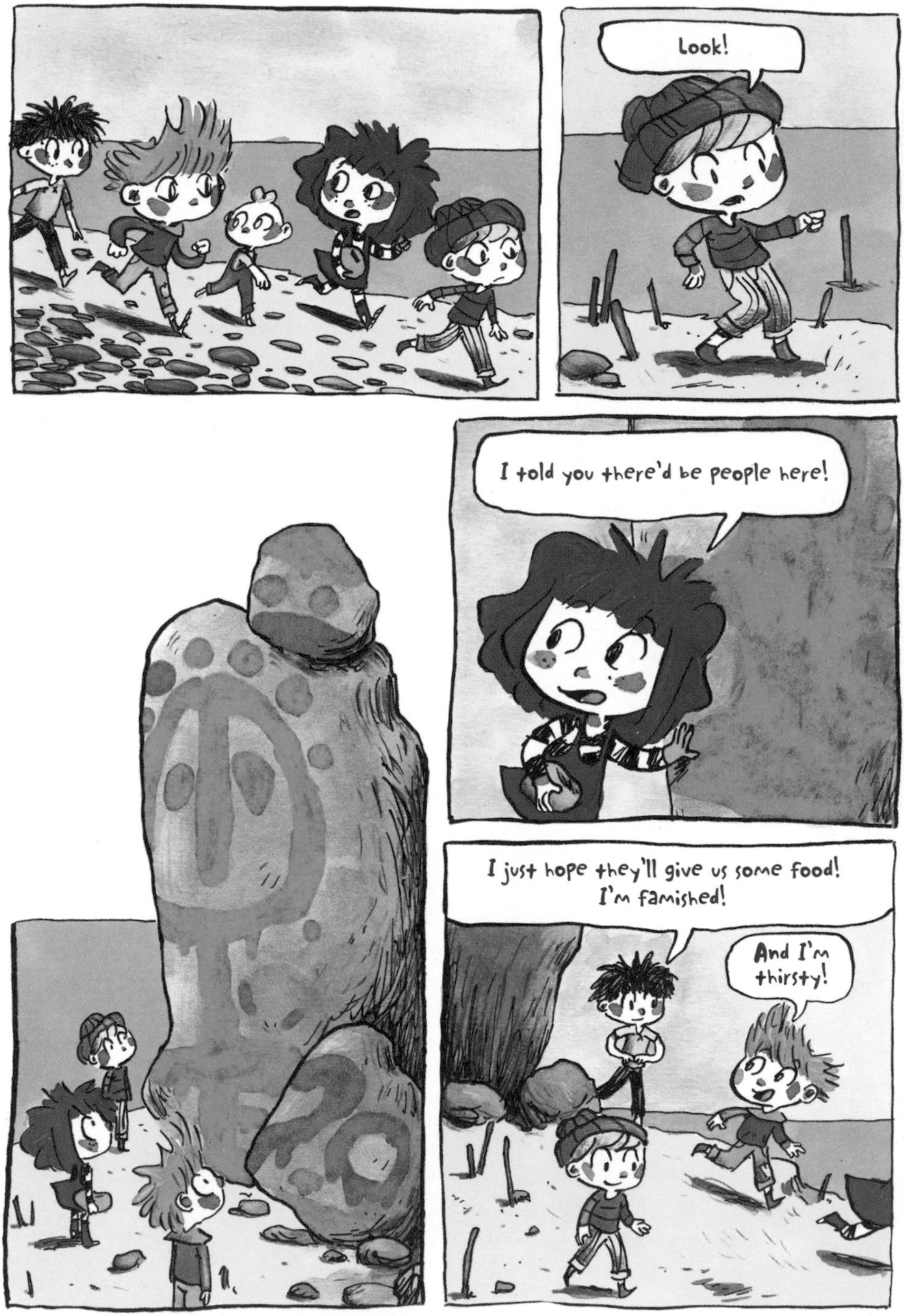
Look!
I told you there'd be people here!
I just hope they'll give us some food! I'm famished!
And I'm thirsty!

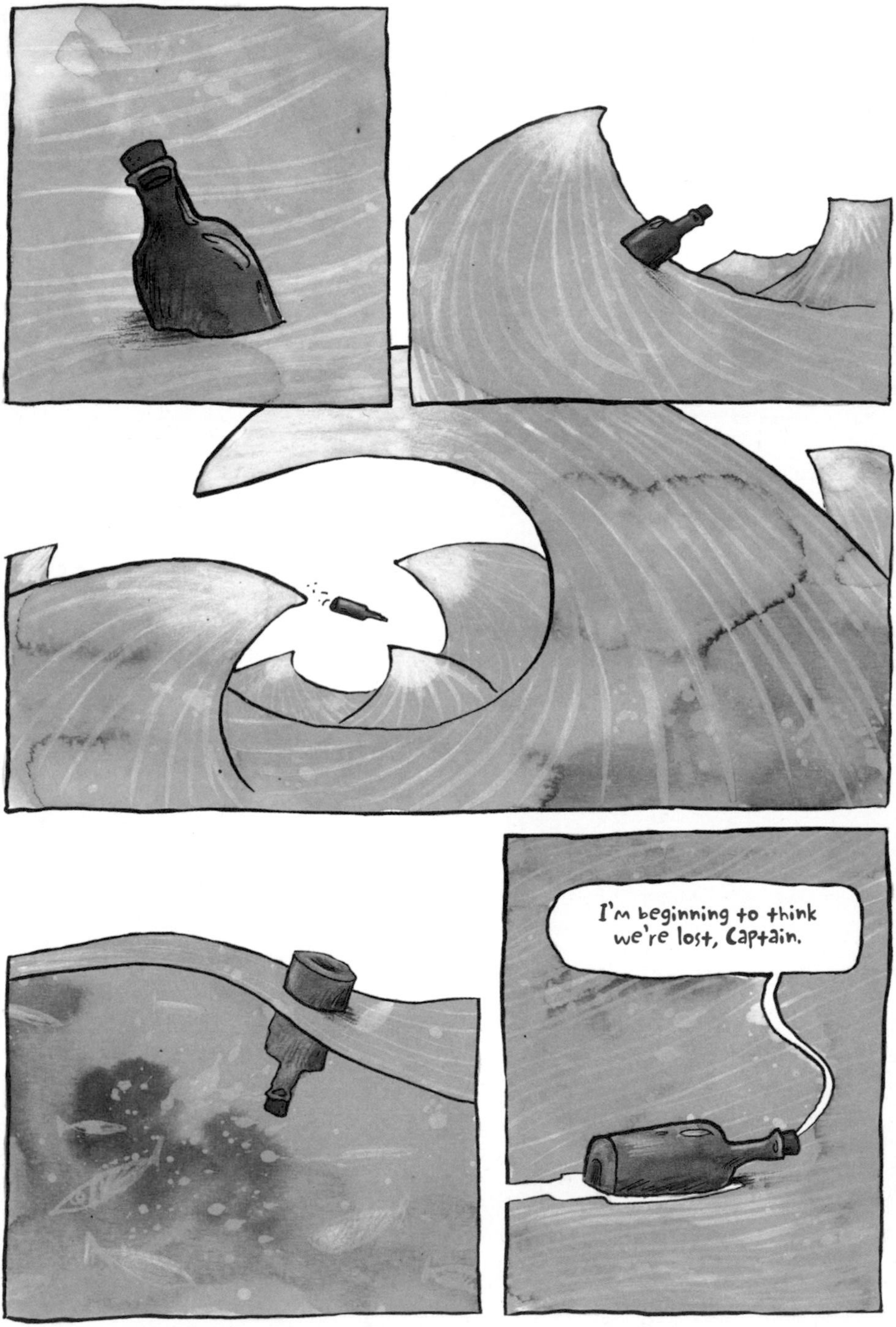
I'm beginning to think we're lost, Captain.

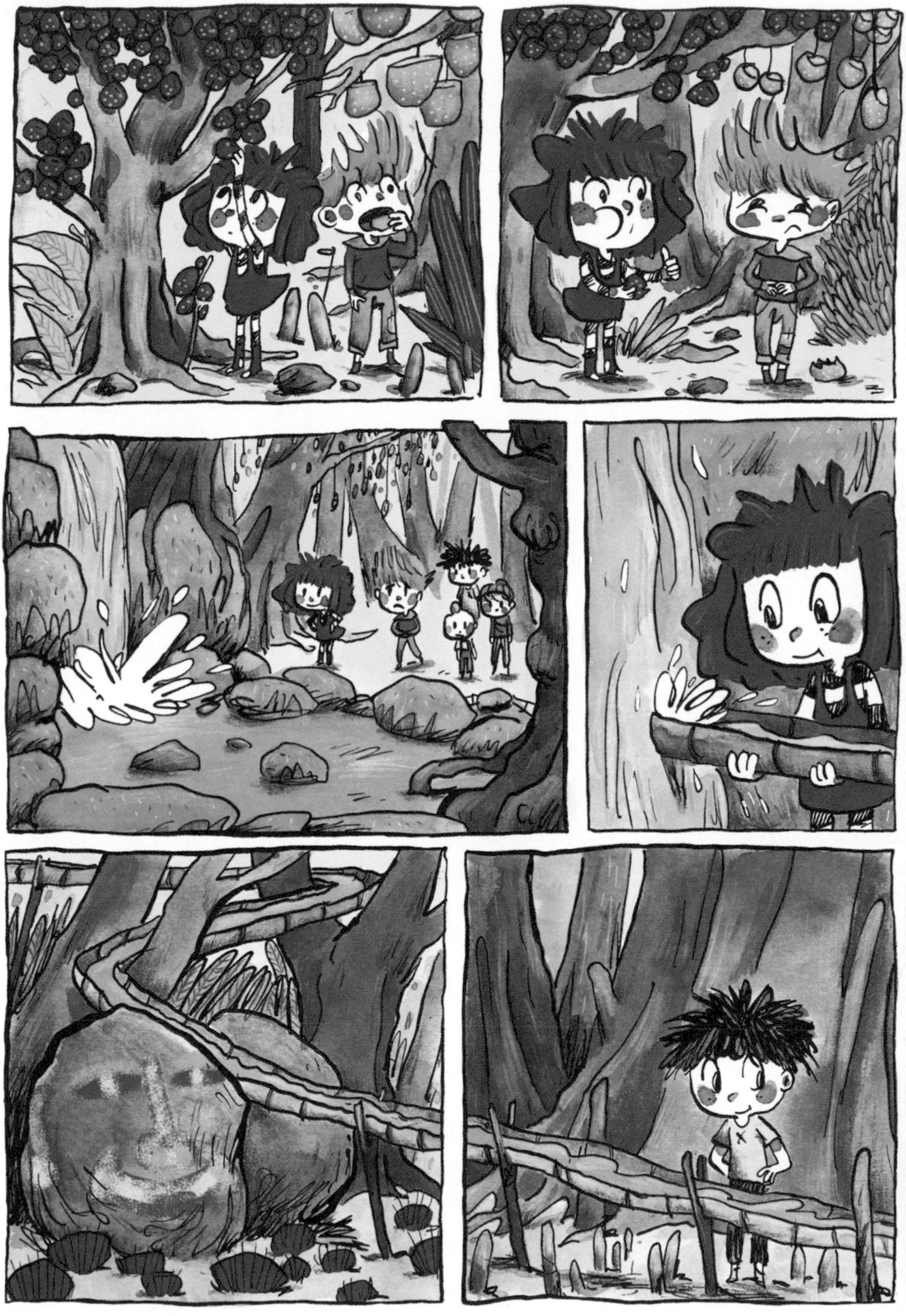

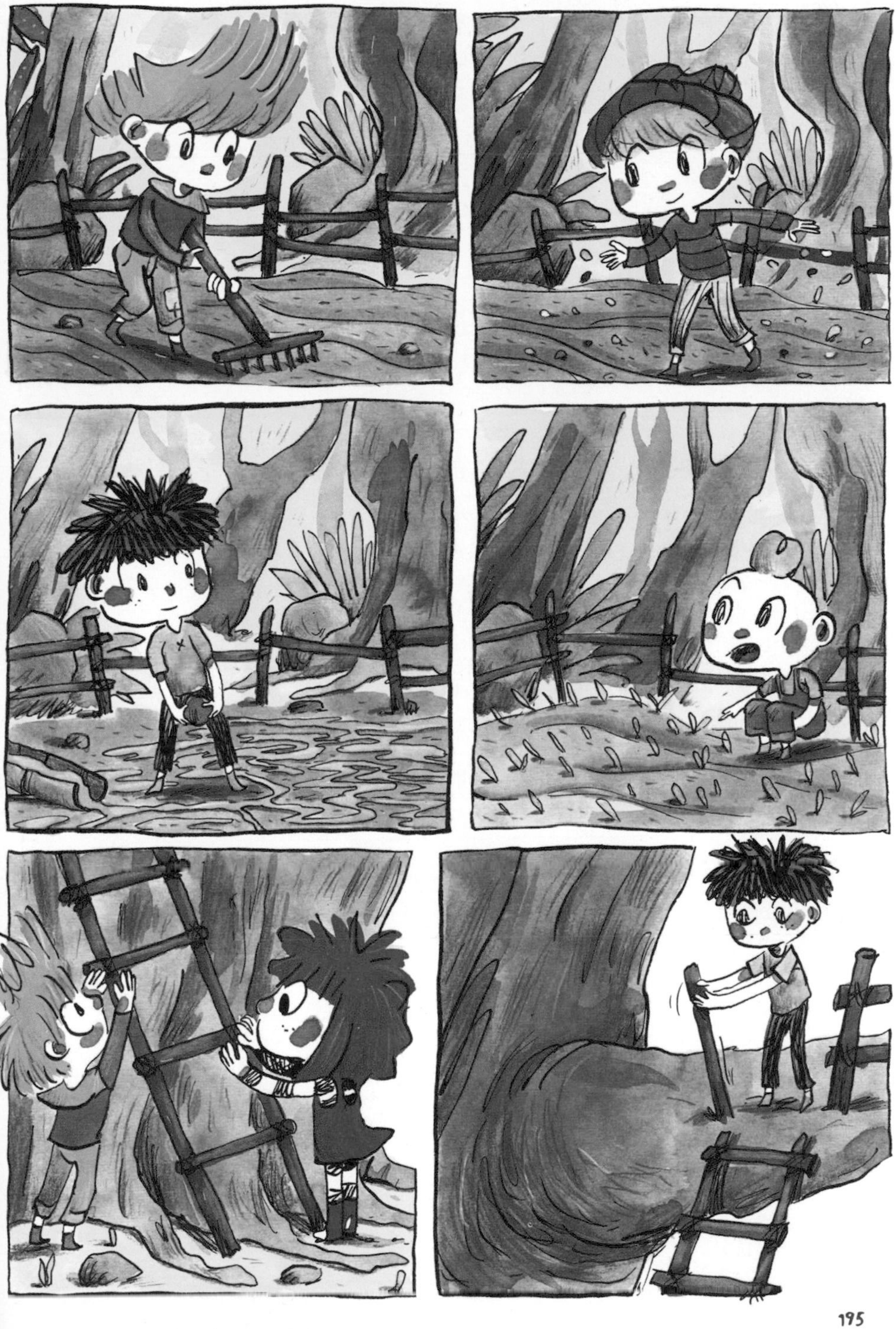

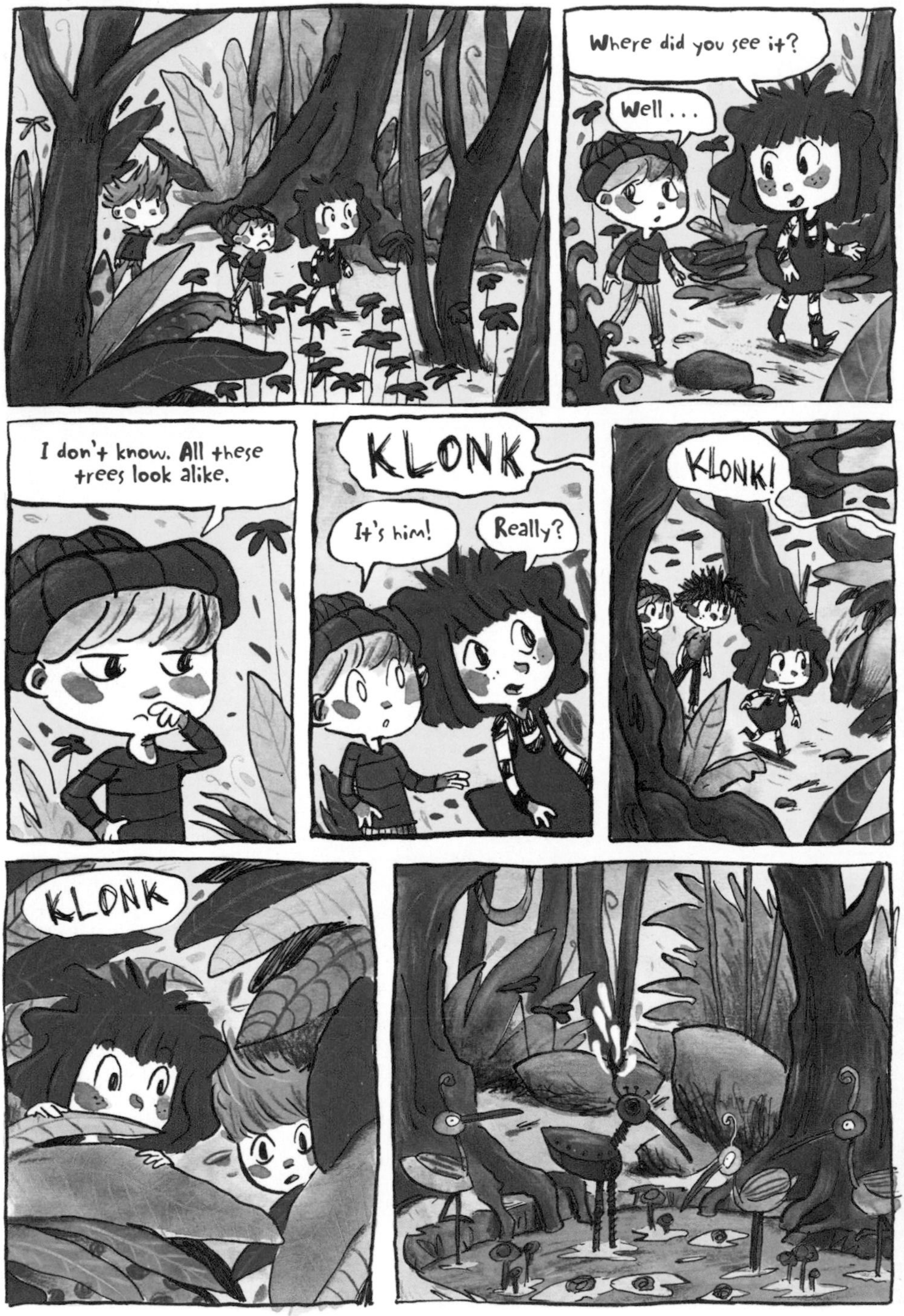
Where did you see it?
Well . . .
I don't know. All these trees look alike.
KLONK
It's him!
Really?
KLONK!
KLONK

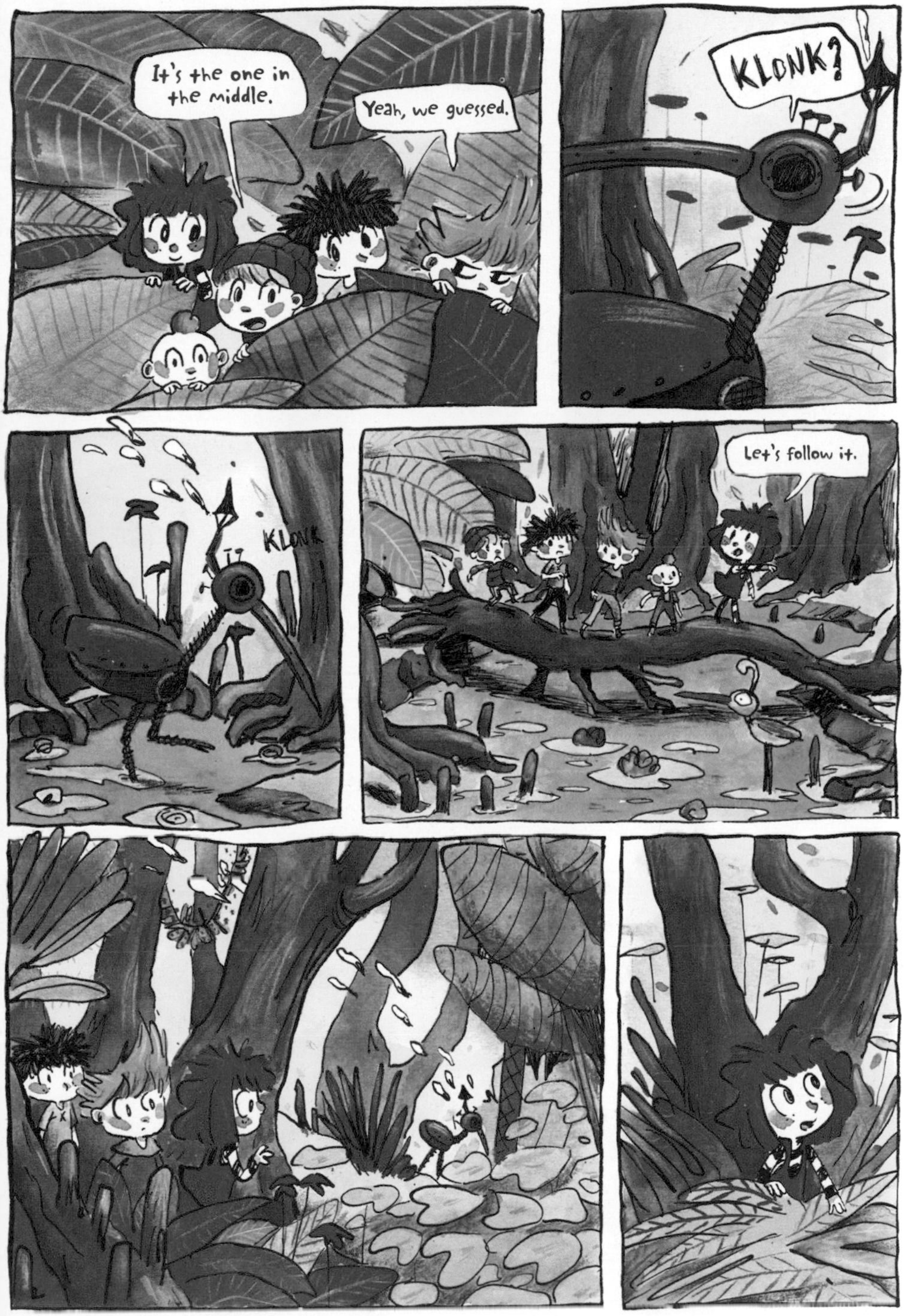
It's the one in the middle.
Yeah, we guessed.
KLONK?
KLONK
Let's follow it.

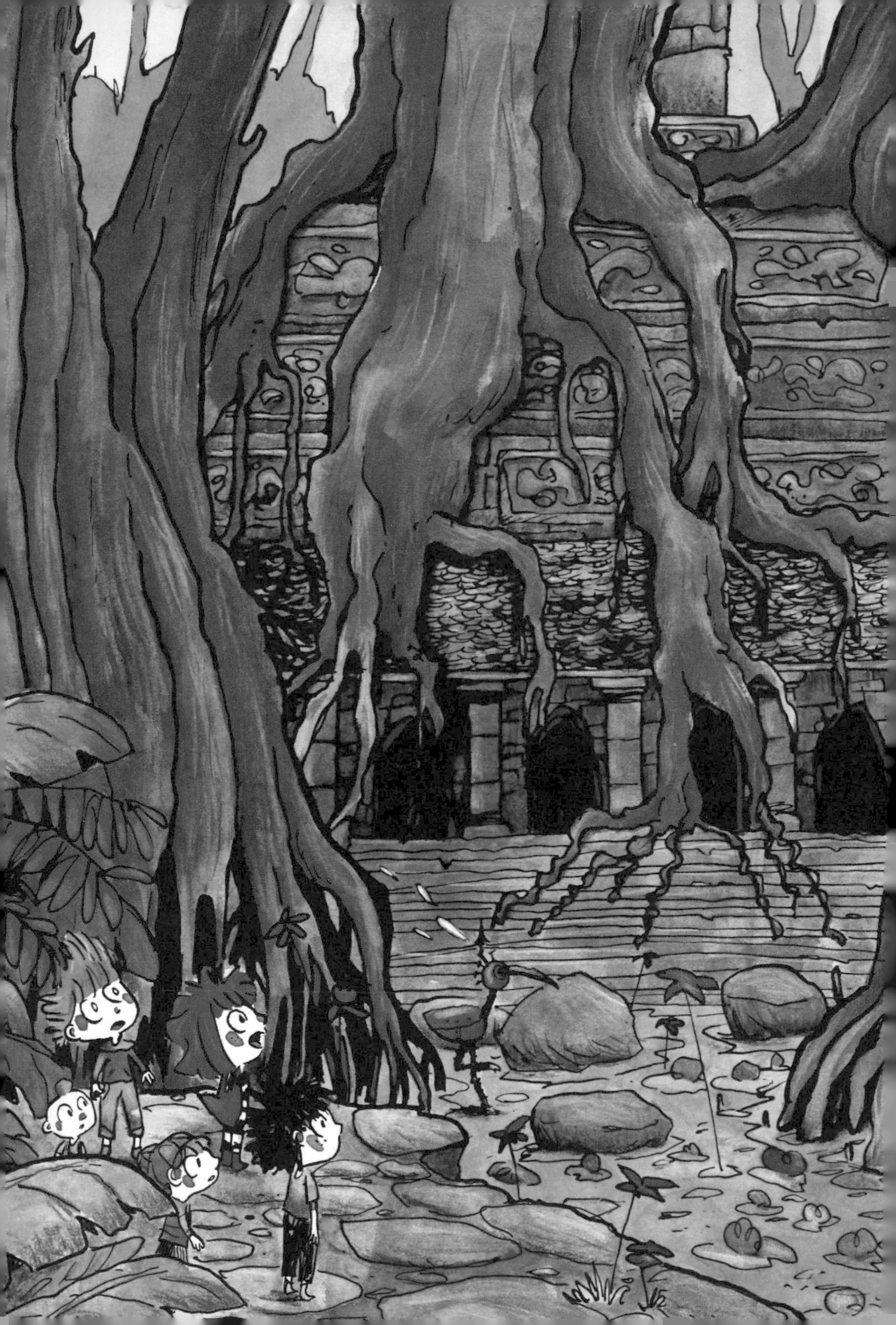

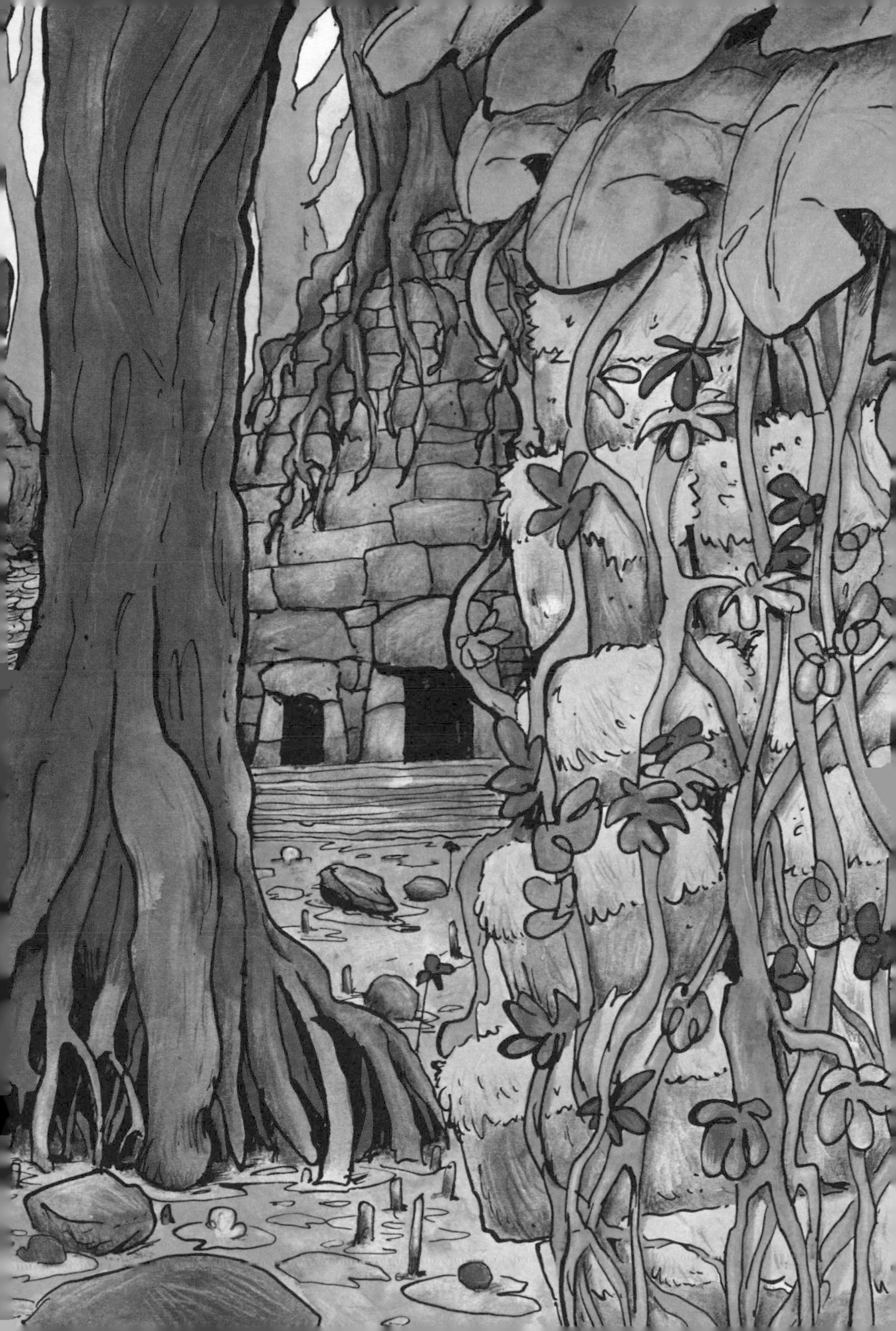

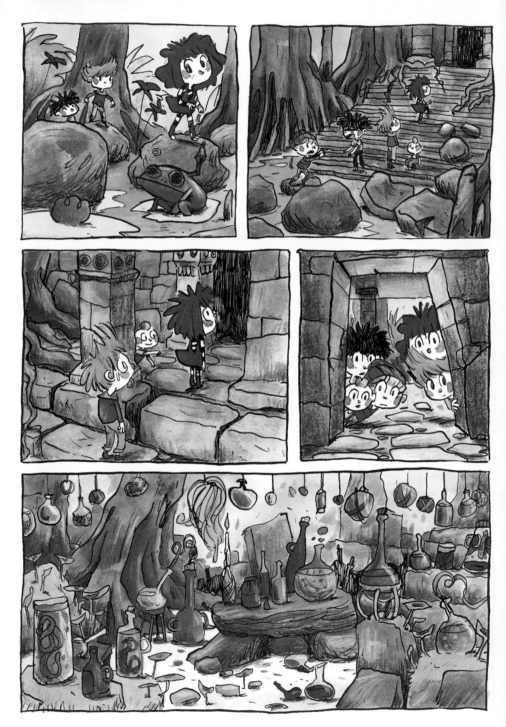

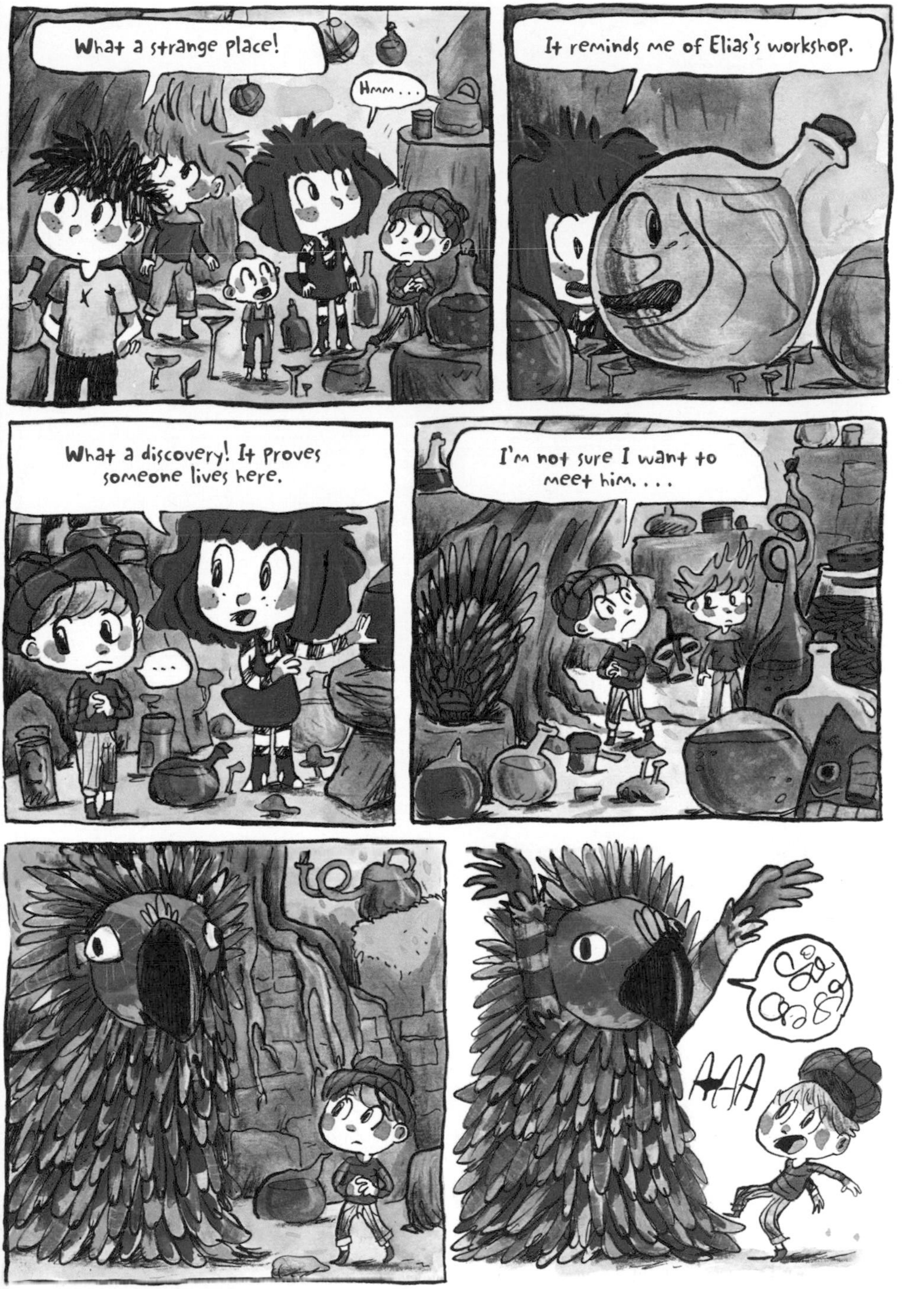
What a strange place!
Hmm . . .
It reminds me of Elias's workshop.
What a discovery! It proves someone lives here.
. . .
I'm not sure I want to meet him. . . .
AAA

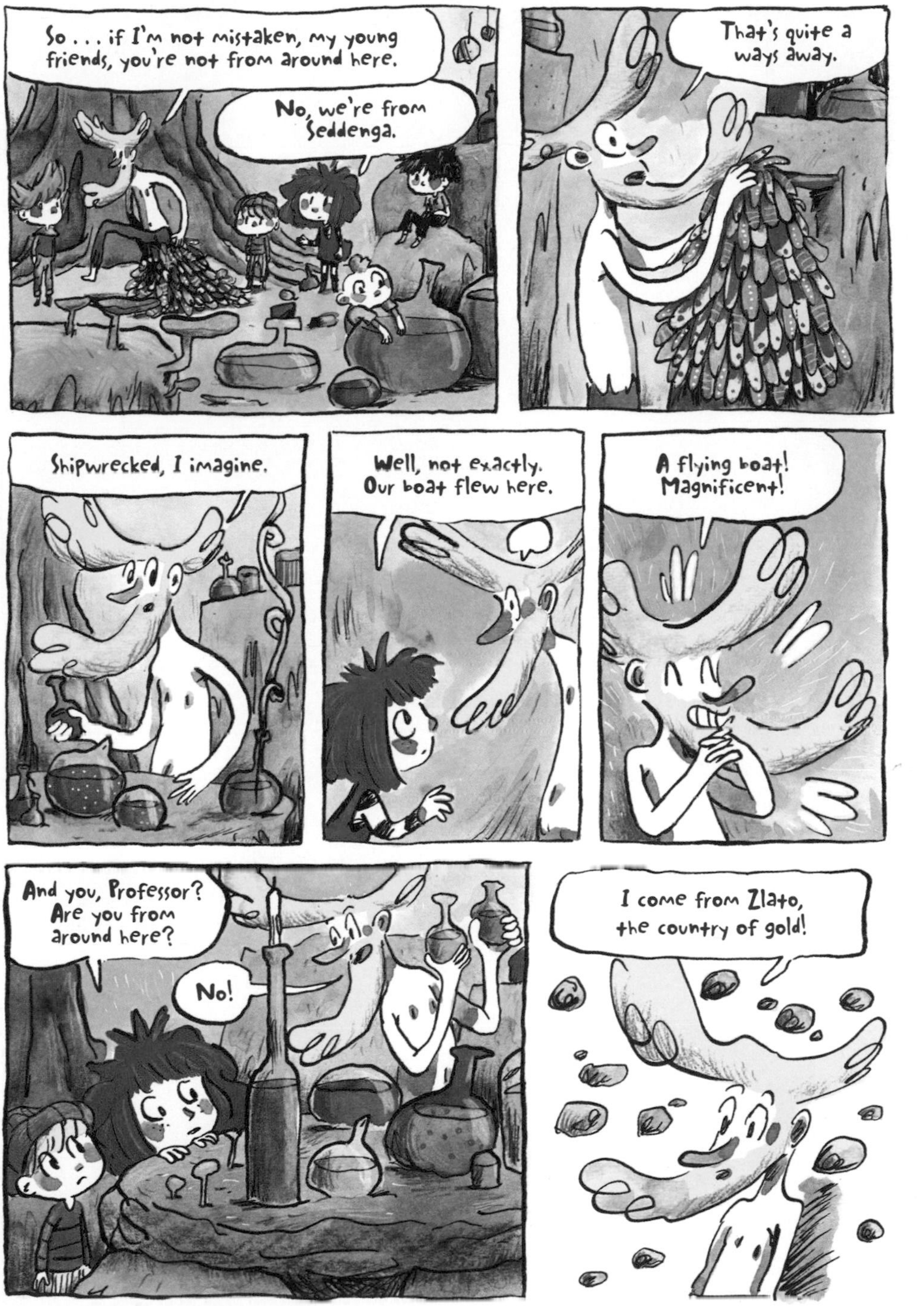
So . . . if I'm not mistaken, my young friends, you're not from around here.
No, we're from Seddenga.
That's quite a ways away.
Shipwrecked, I imagine.
Well, not exactly. Our boat flew here.
A flying boat! Magnificent!
And you, Professor? Are you from around here?
No!
I come from Zlato, the country of gold!

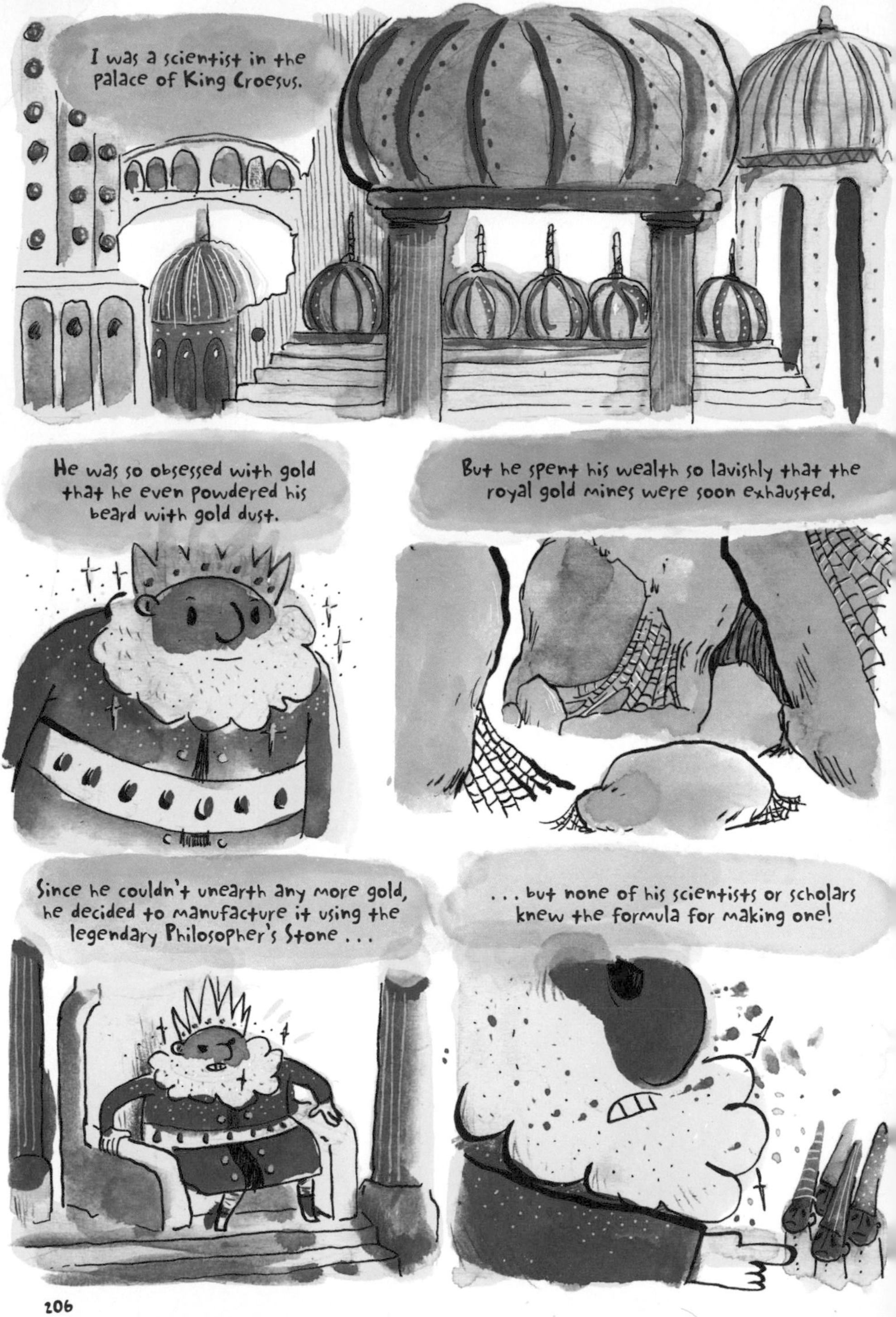
I was a scientist in the palace of King Croesus.
He was so obsessed with gold that he even powdered his beard with gold dust.
But he spent his wealth so lavishly that the royal gold mines were soon exhausted.
Since he couldn't unearth any more gold, he decided to manufacture it using the legendary Philosopher's Stone . . .
. . . but none of his scientists or scholars knew the formula for making one!

According to legend, a lonely giant sleeps there, awaiting the return of his sweetheart.
To reach the summit, we must cross the territory of the Klagoskas, who detest light and noise.
And so, dear reader, help us avoid their wrath by turning the page very quietly.

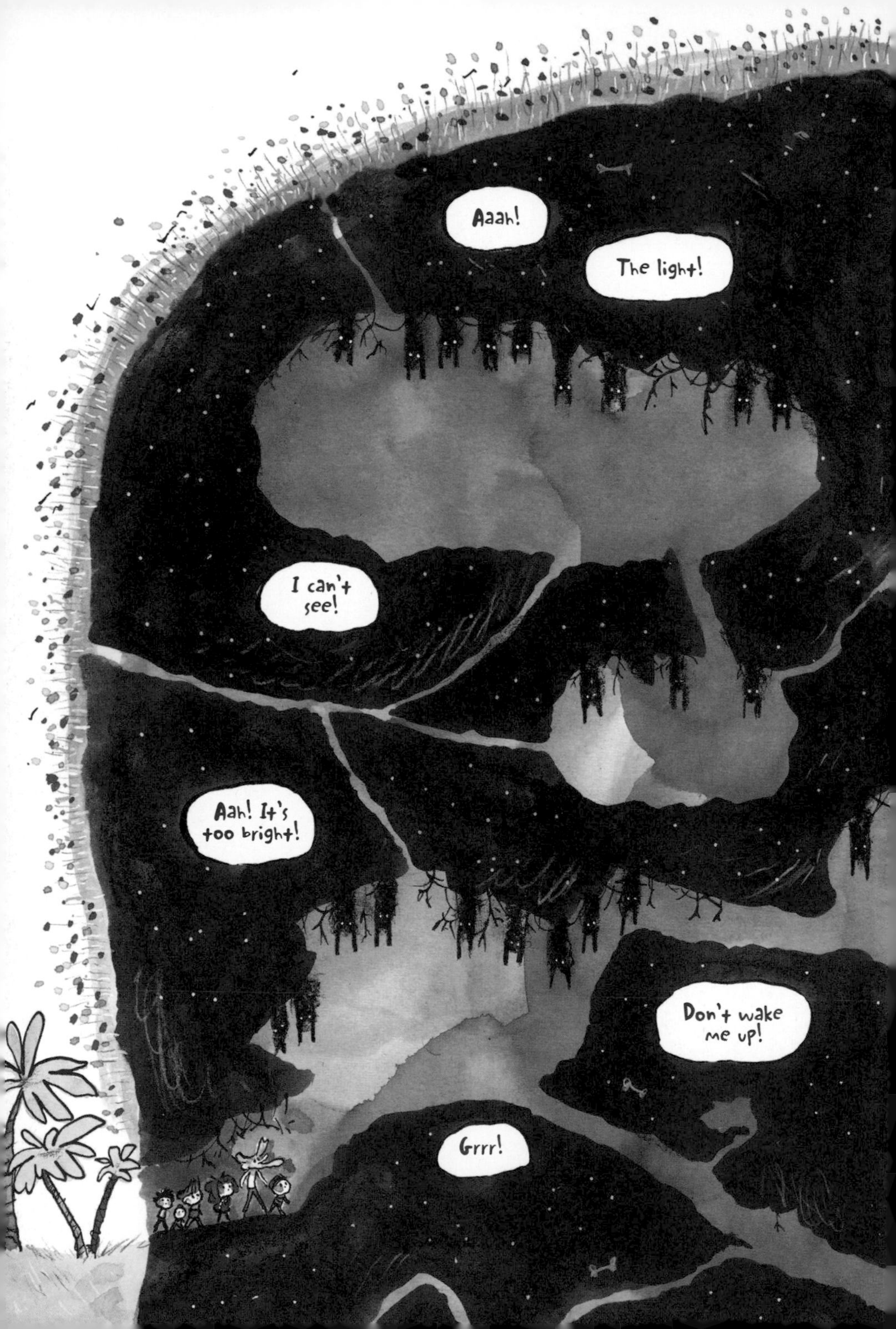

Aaah!
The light!
I can't see!
Aah! It's too bright!
Don't wake me up!
Grrr!

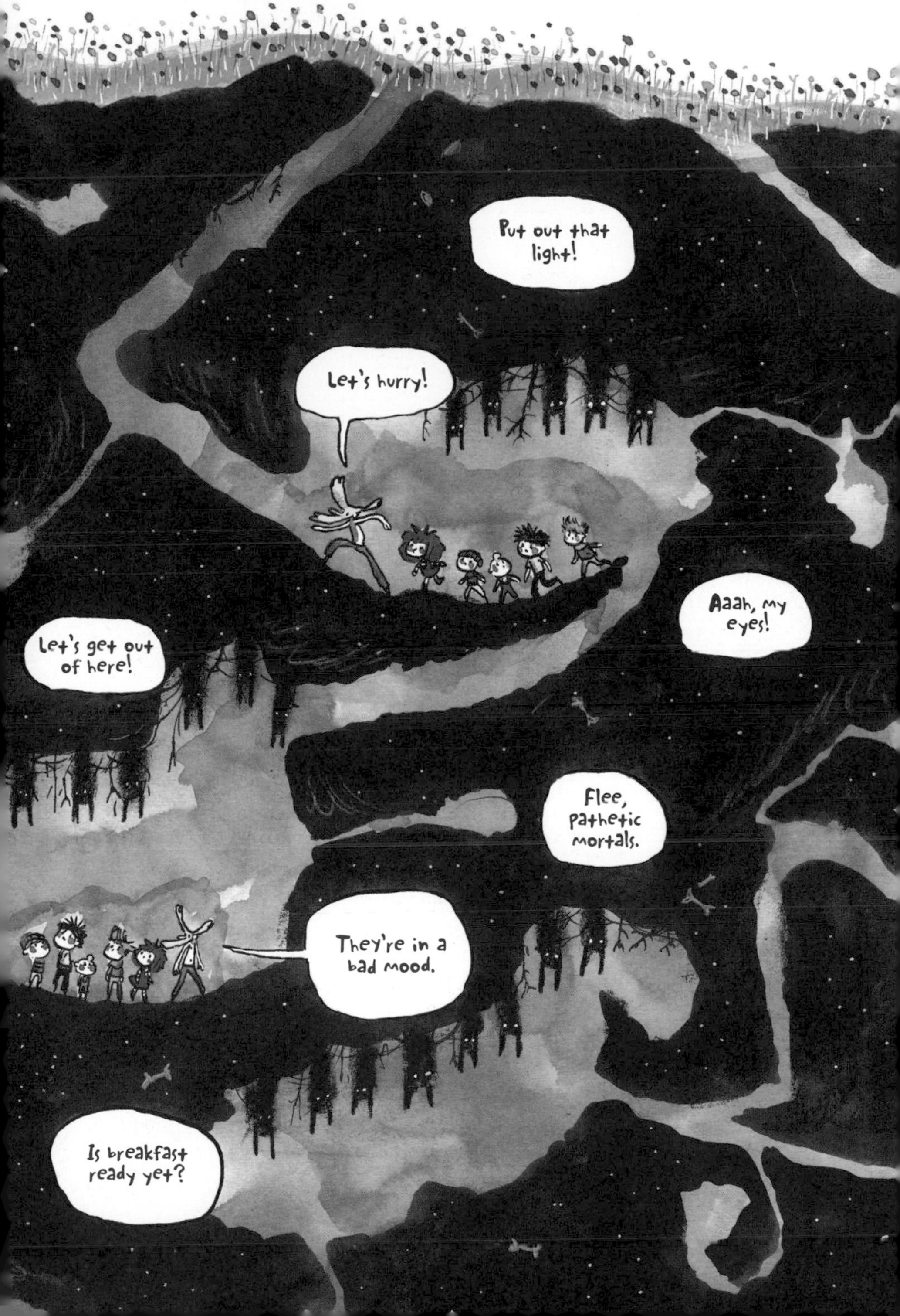
Put out that light!
Let's hurry!
Aaah, my eyes!
Let's get out of here!
Flee, pathetic mortals.
They're in a bad mood.
Is breakfast ready yet?

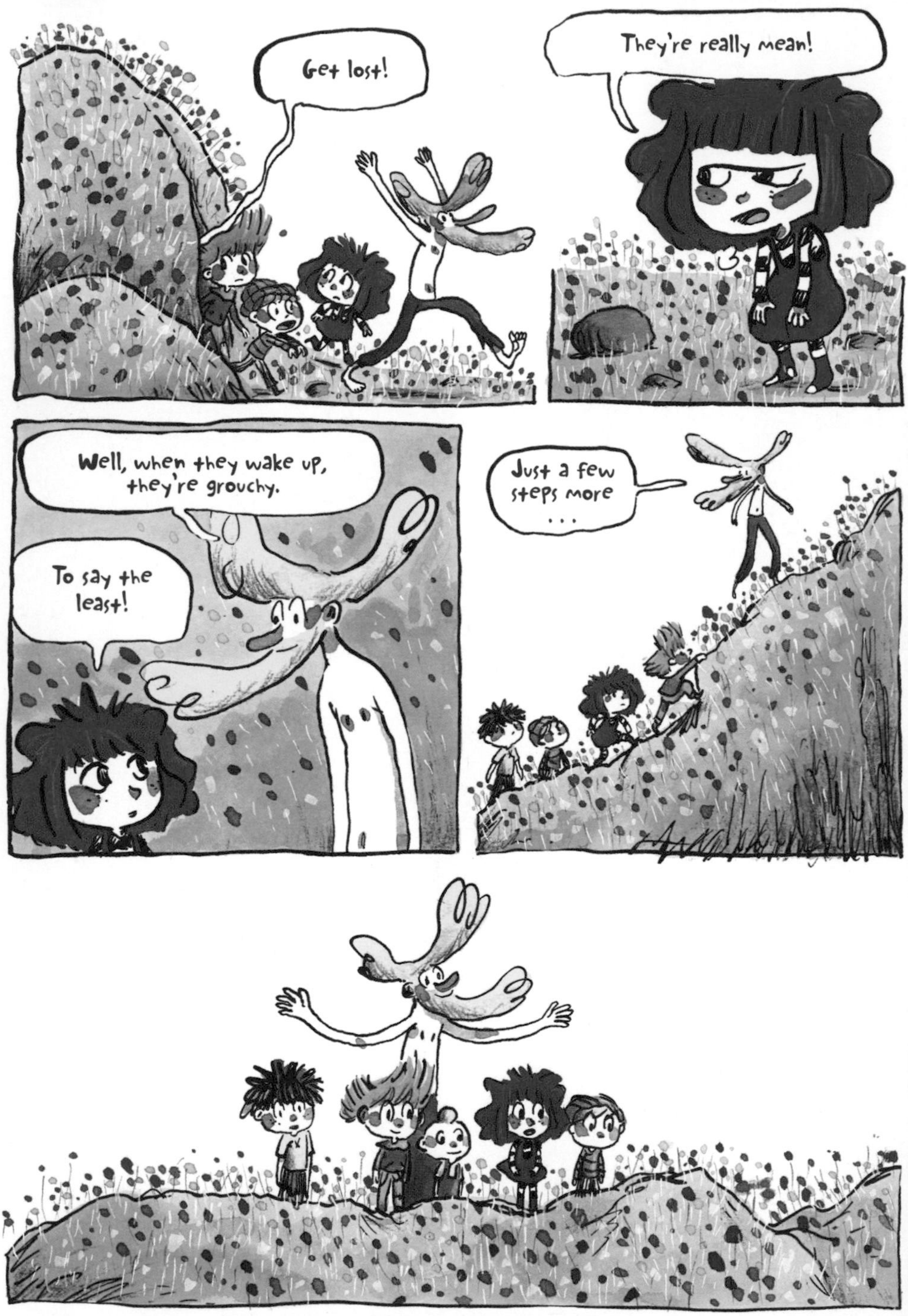
Get lost!
They're really mean!
Well, when they wake up, they're grouchy.
To say the least!
Just a few steps more . . .

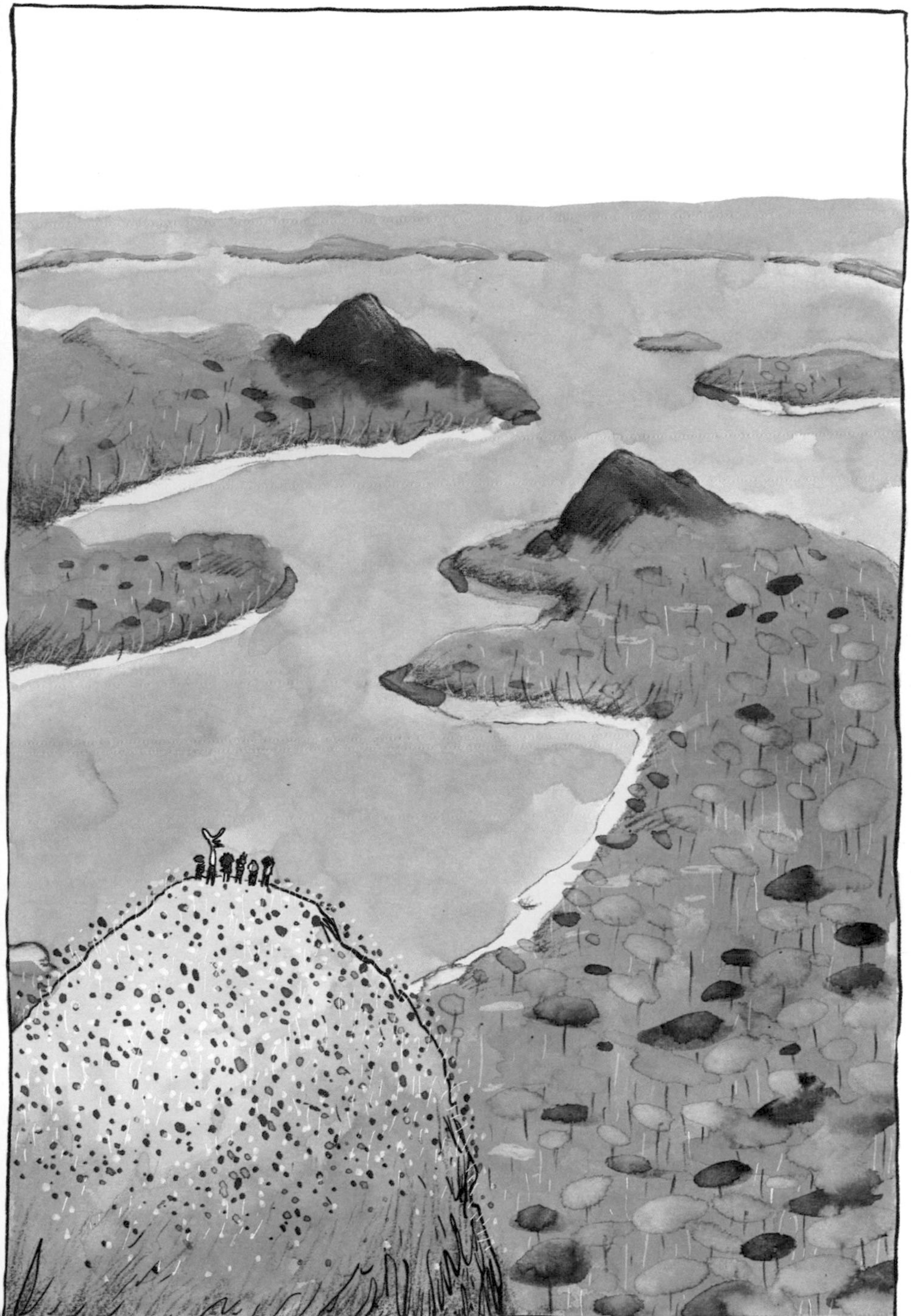

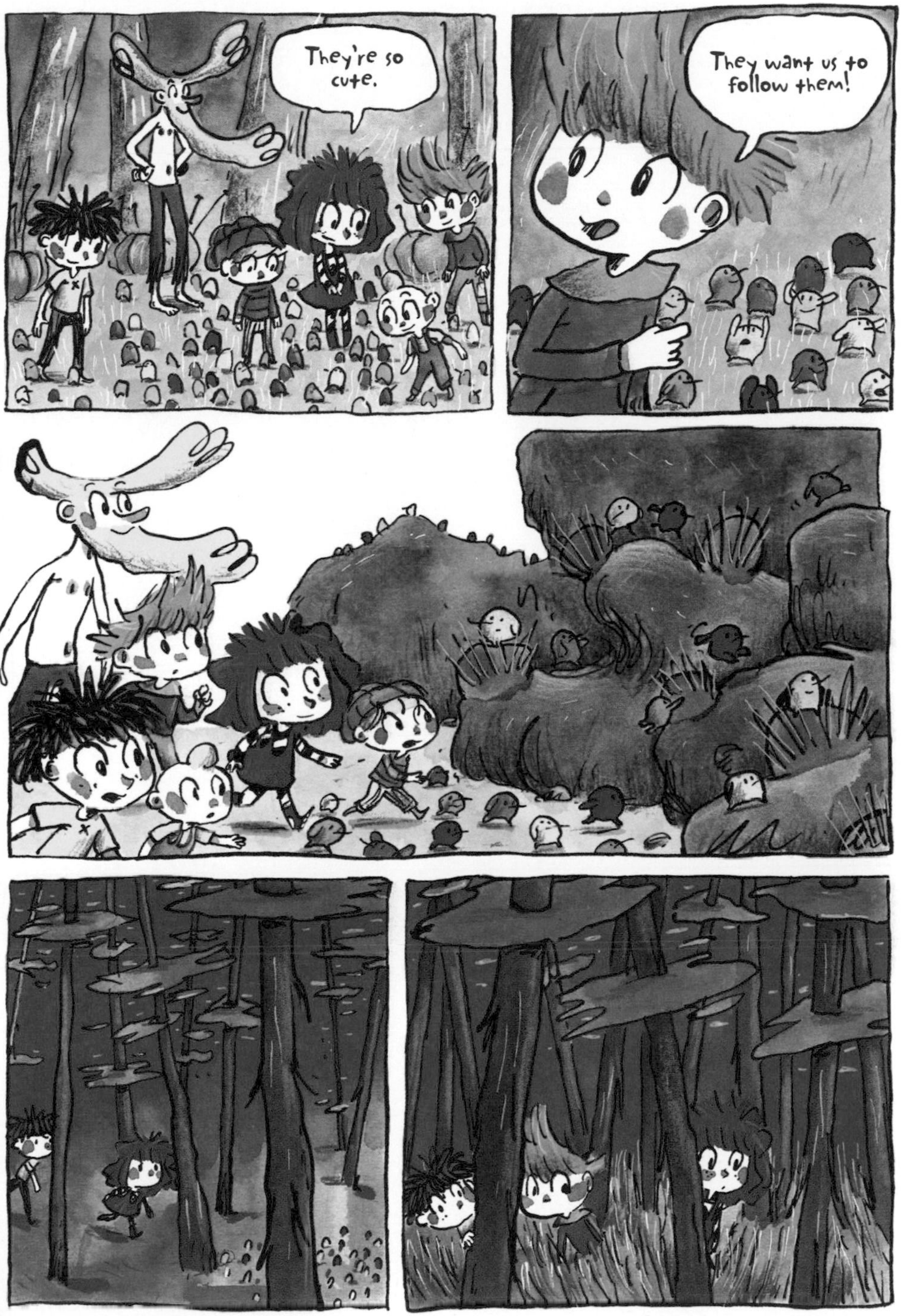
They're so cute.
They want us to follow them!

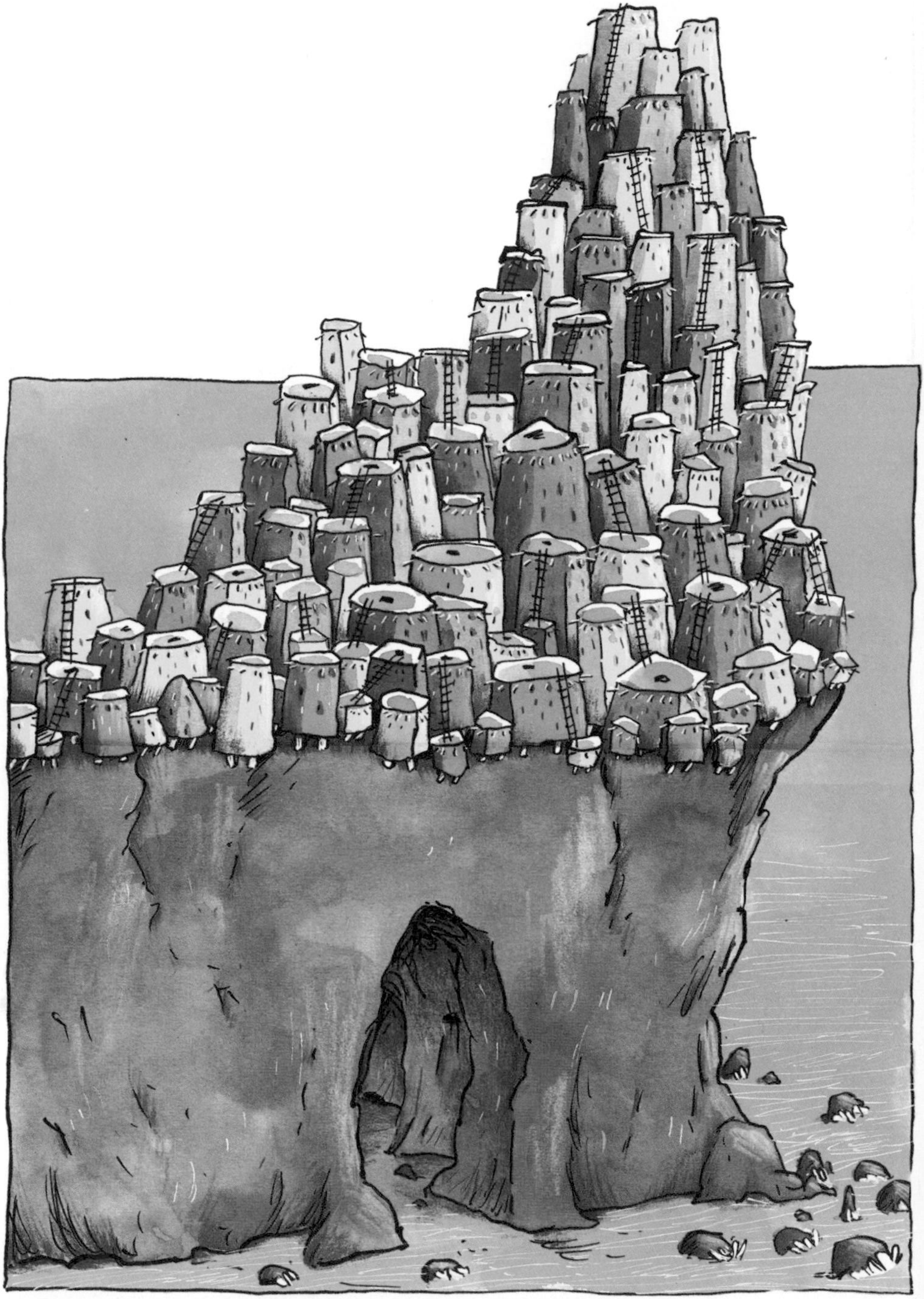

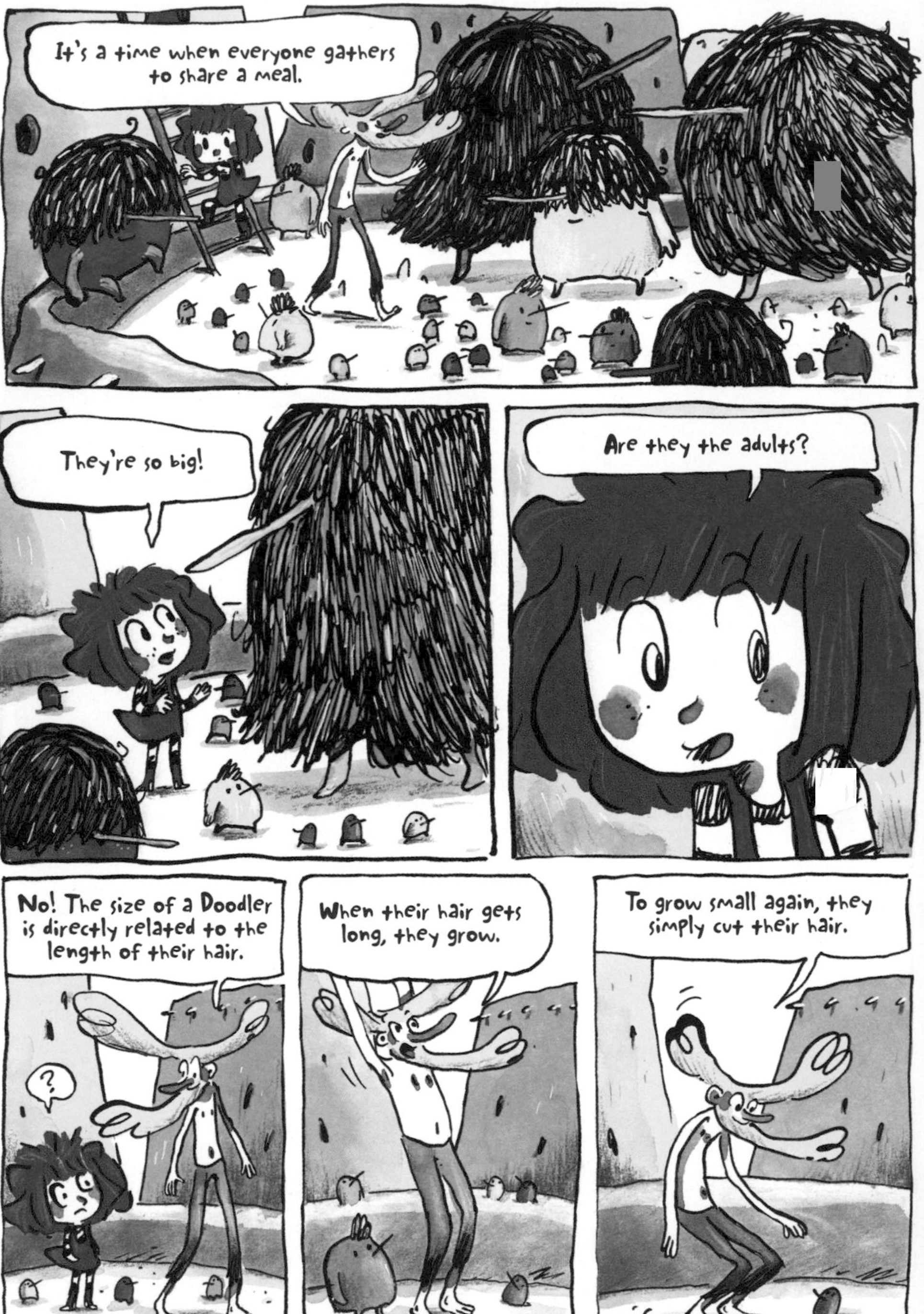
It's a time when everyone gathers to share a meal.
They're so big!
Are they the adults?
No! The size of a Doodler is directly related to the length of their hair.
?
When their hair gets long, they grow.
To grow small again, they simply cut their hair.

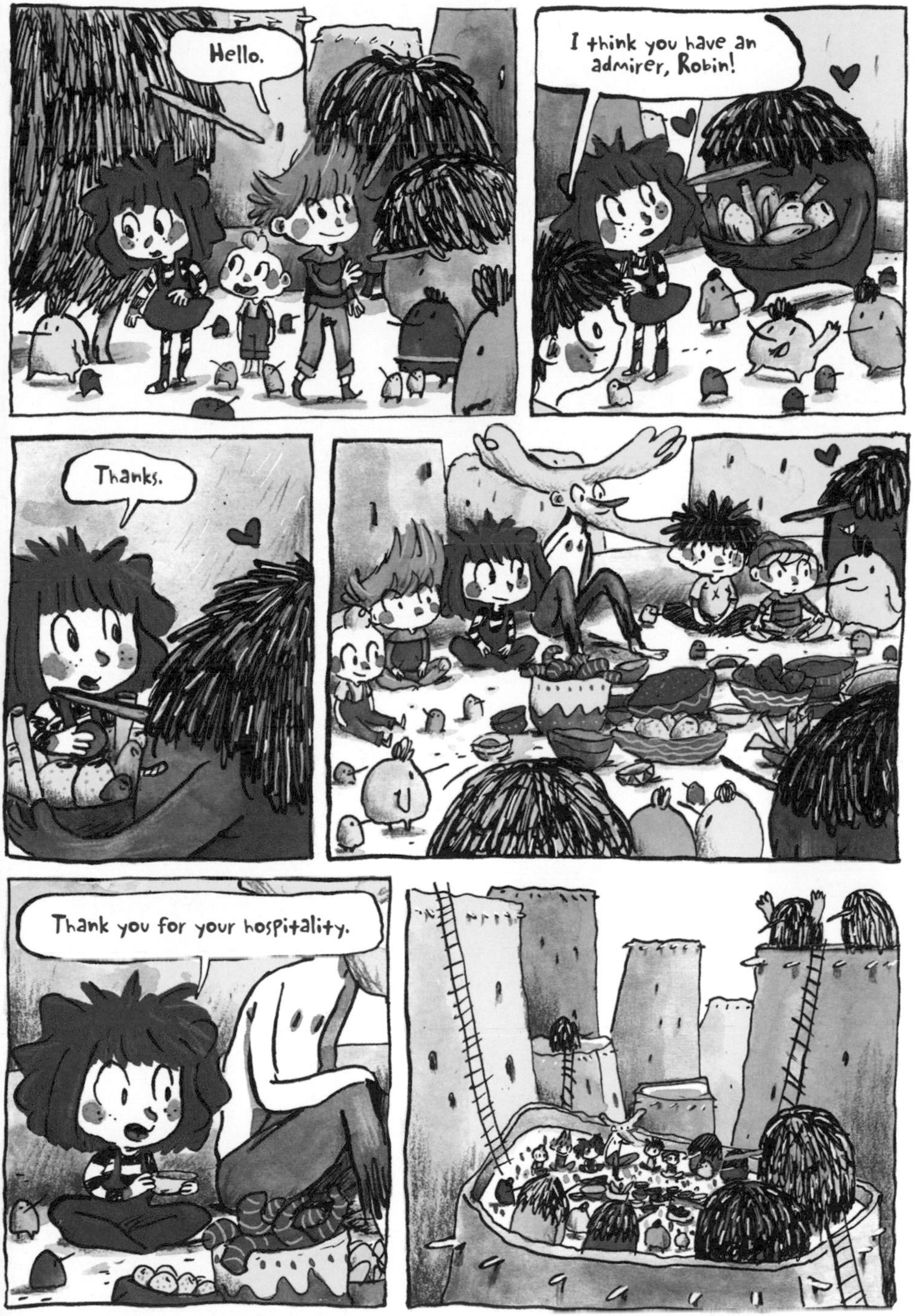
Hello.
I think you have an admirer, Robin!
Thanks.
Thank you for your hospitality.

Watch out!
He's about to attack!
Shoo.
GRRR...
He's ferocious!
AAAAAAAA

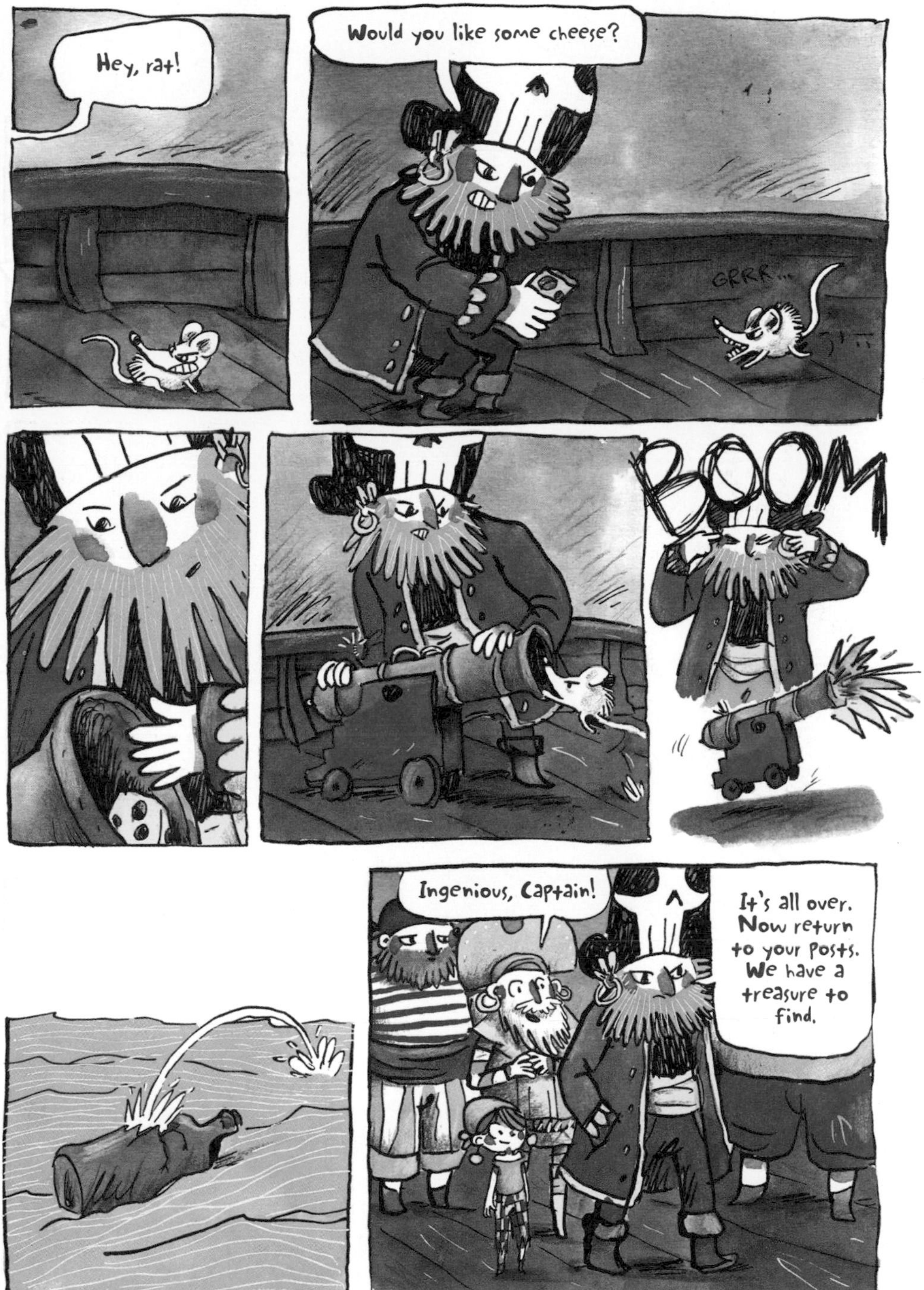
Hey, rat!
Would you like some cheese?
GRRR...
BOOM
Ingenious, Captain!
It's all over. Now return to your posts. We have a treasure to find.

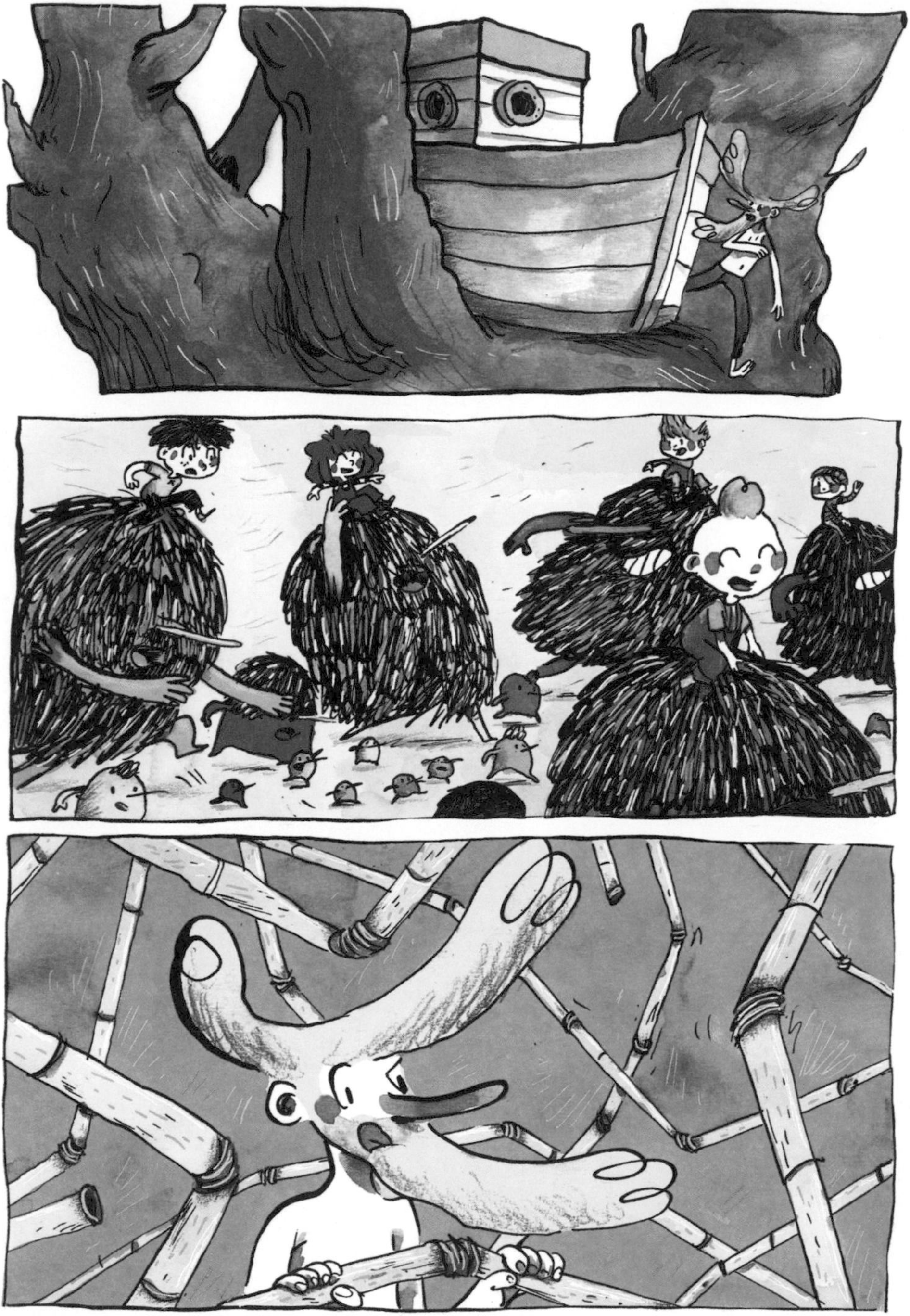

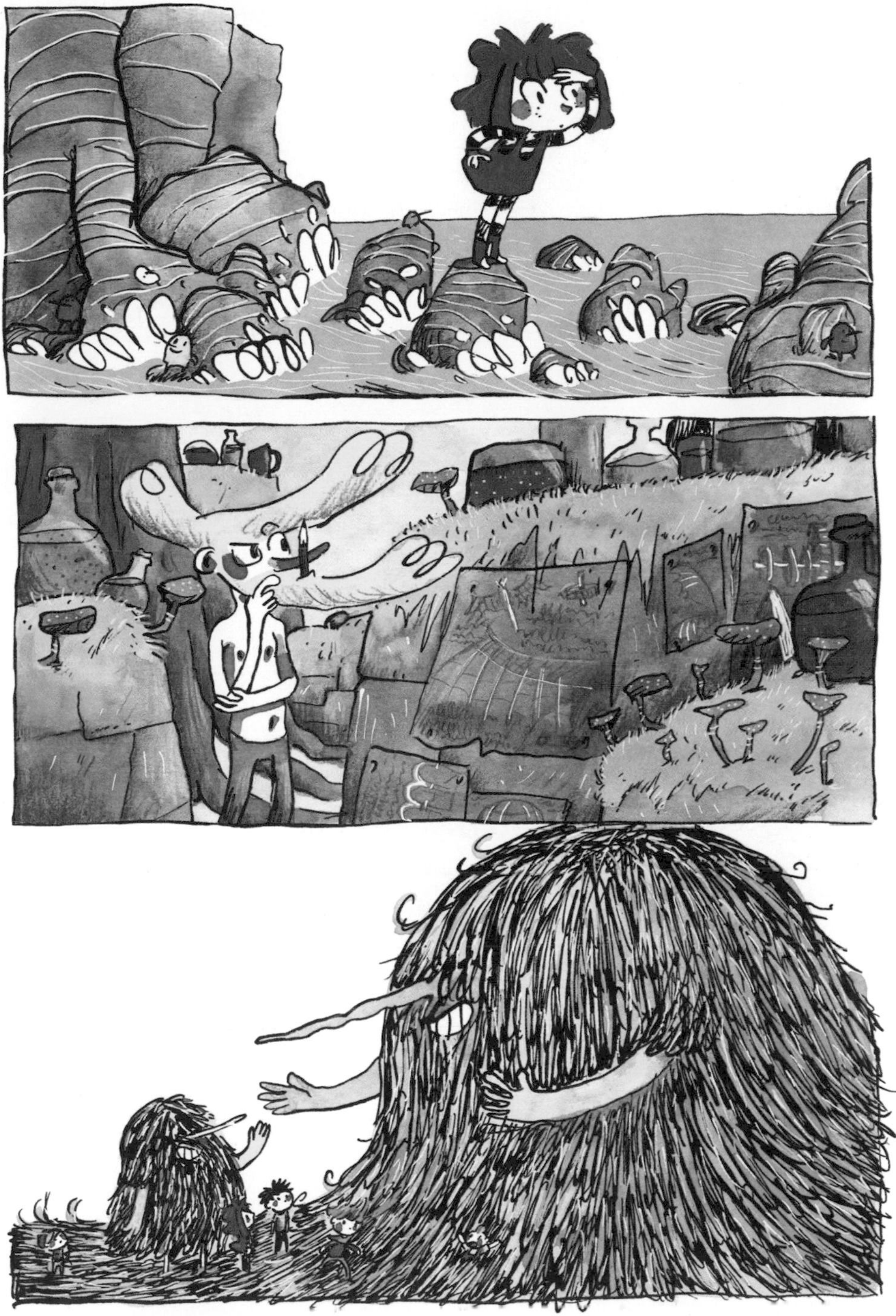

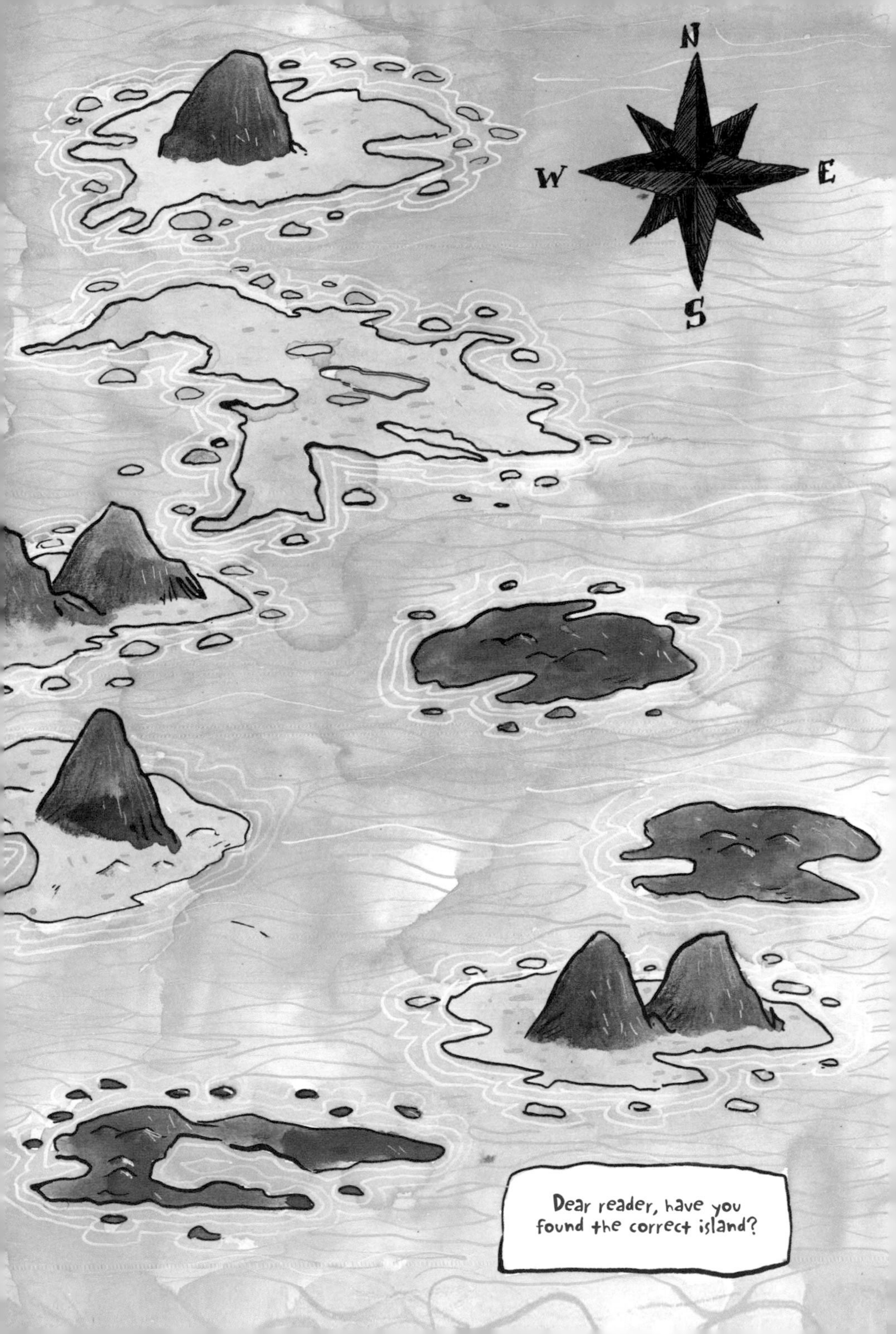
N
W
E
S
Dear reader, have you found the correct island?

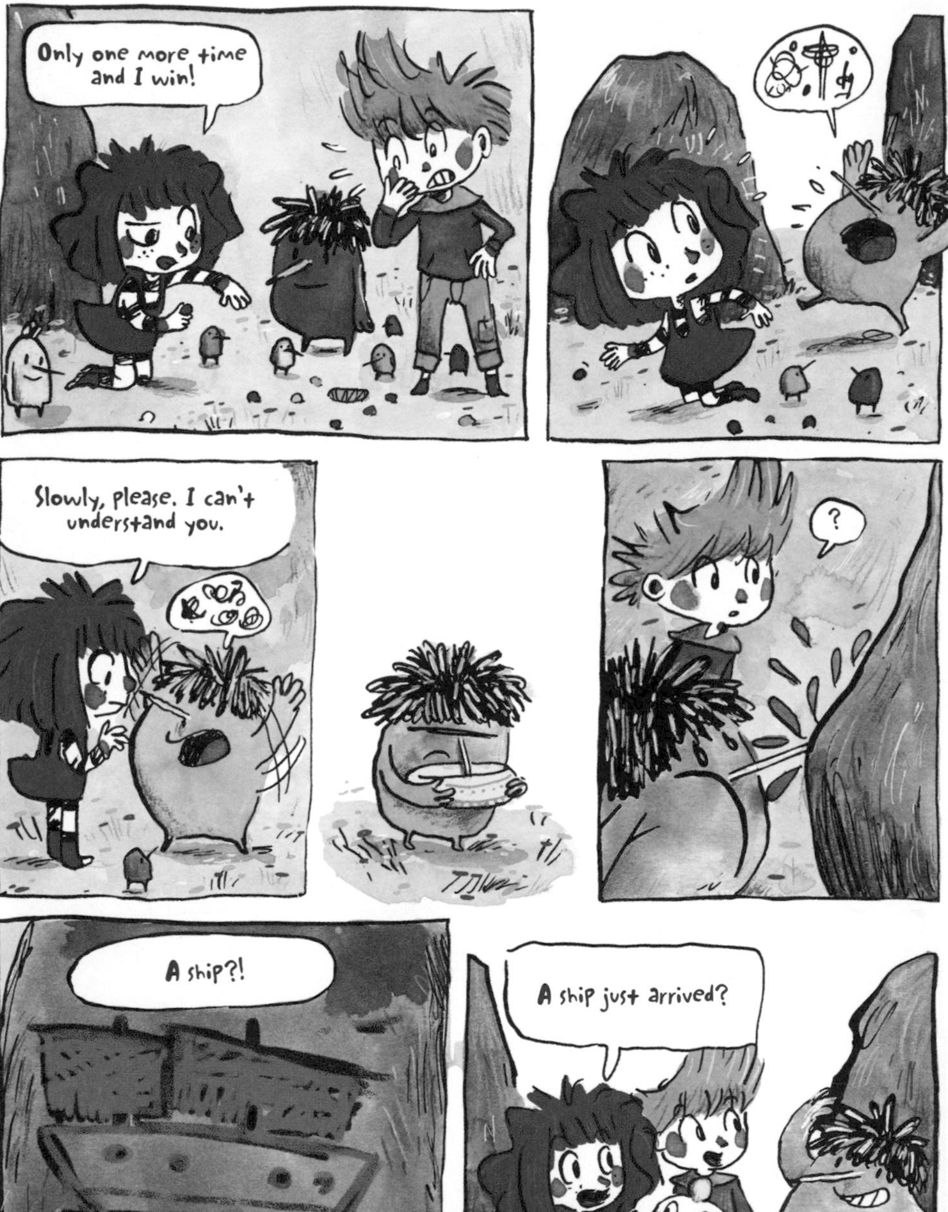
Only one more time and I win!
Slowly, please. I can't understand you.
?
A ship?!
A ship just arrived?

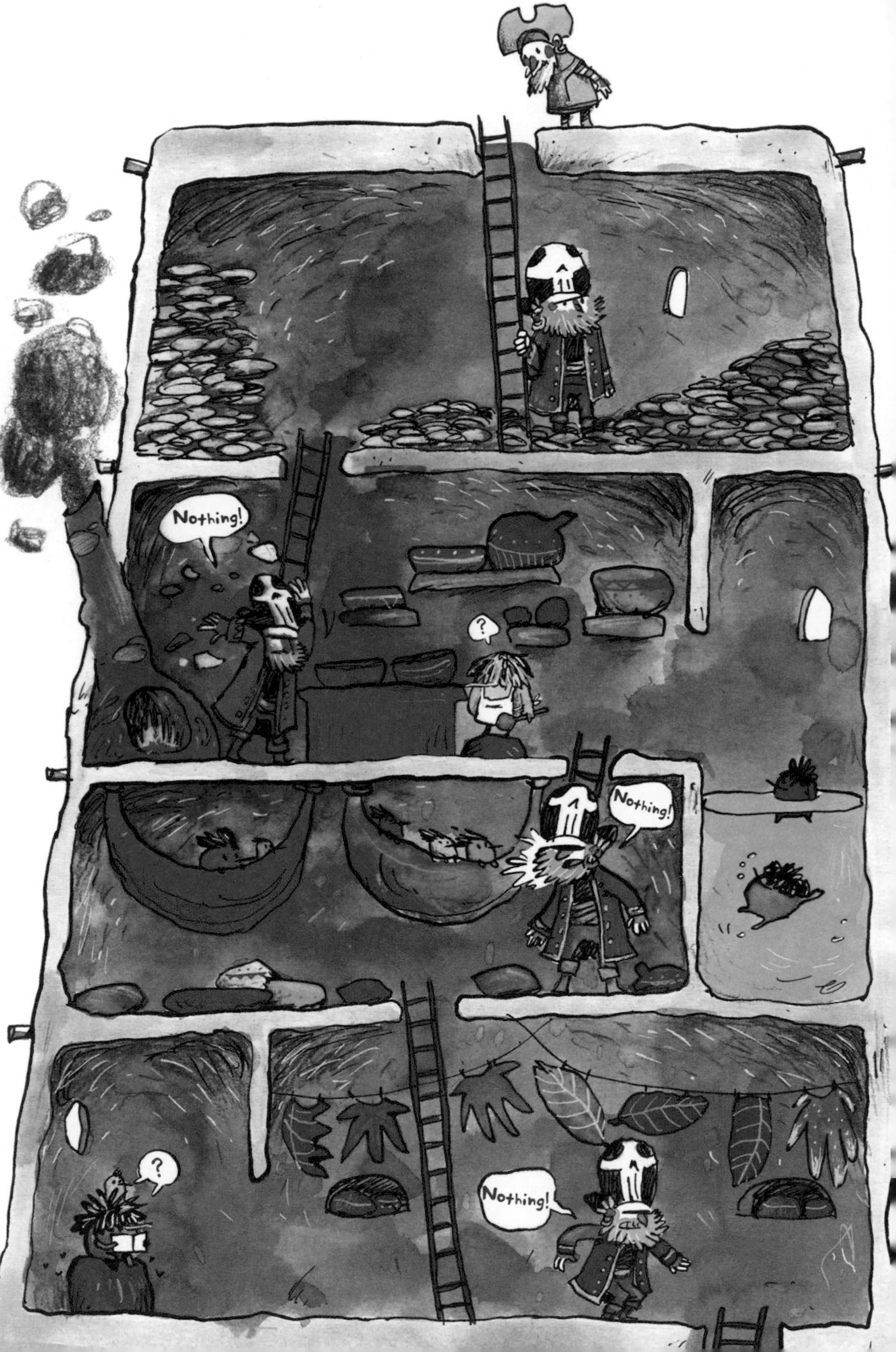
Nothing!
?
Nothing!
?
Nothing!

247

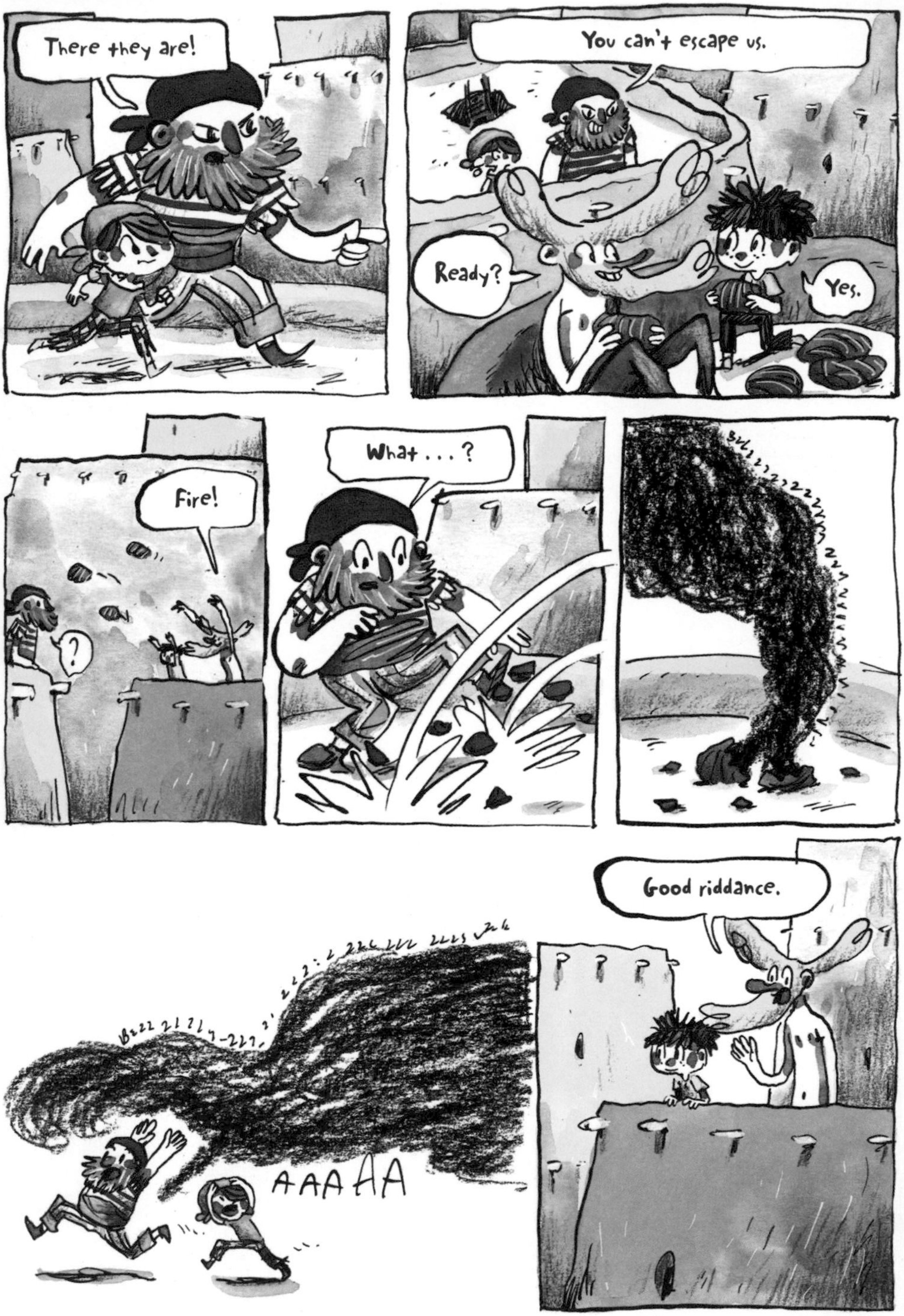
There they are!
You can't escape us.
Ready?
Yes.
Fire!
?
What . . . ?
Good riddance.
AAAAA

249

251

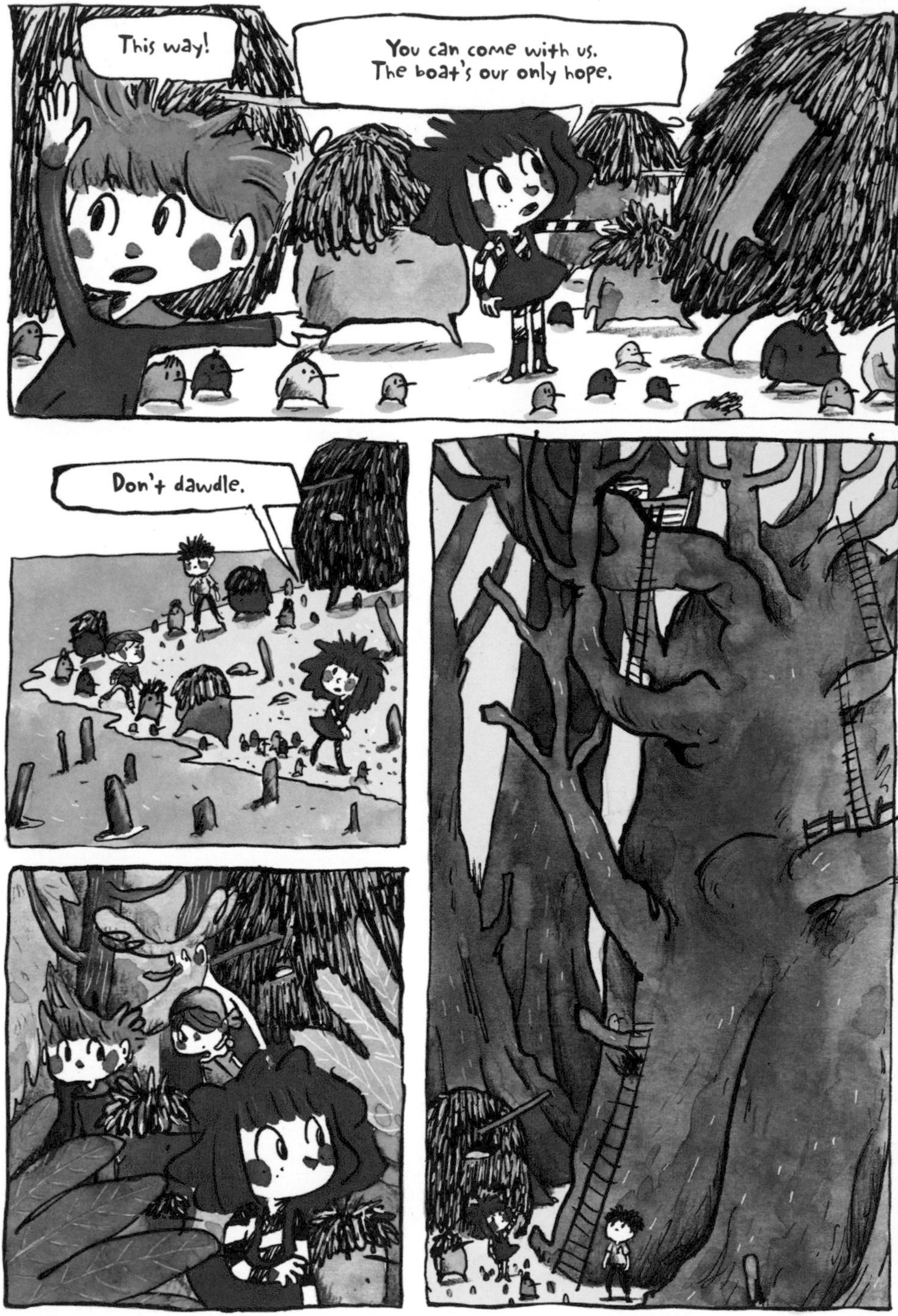
This way!
You can come with us. The boat's our only hope.
Don't dawdle.

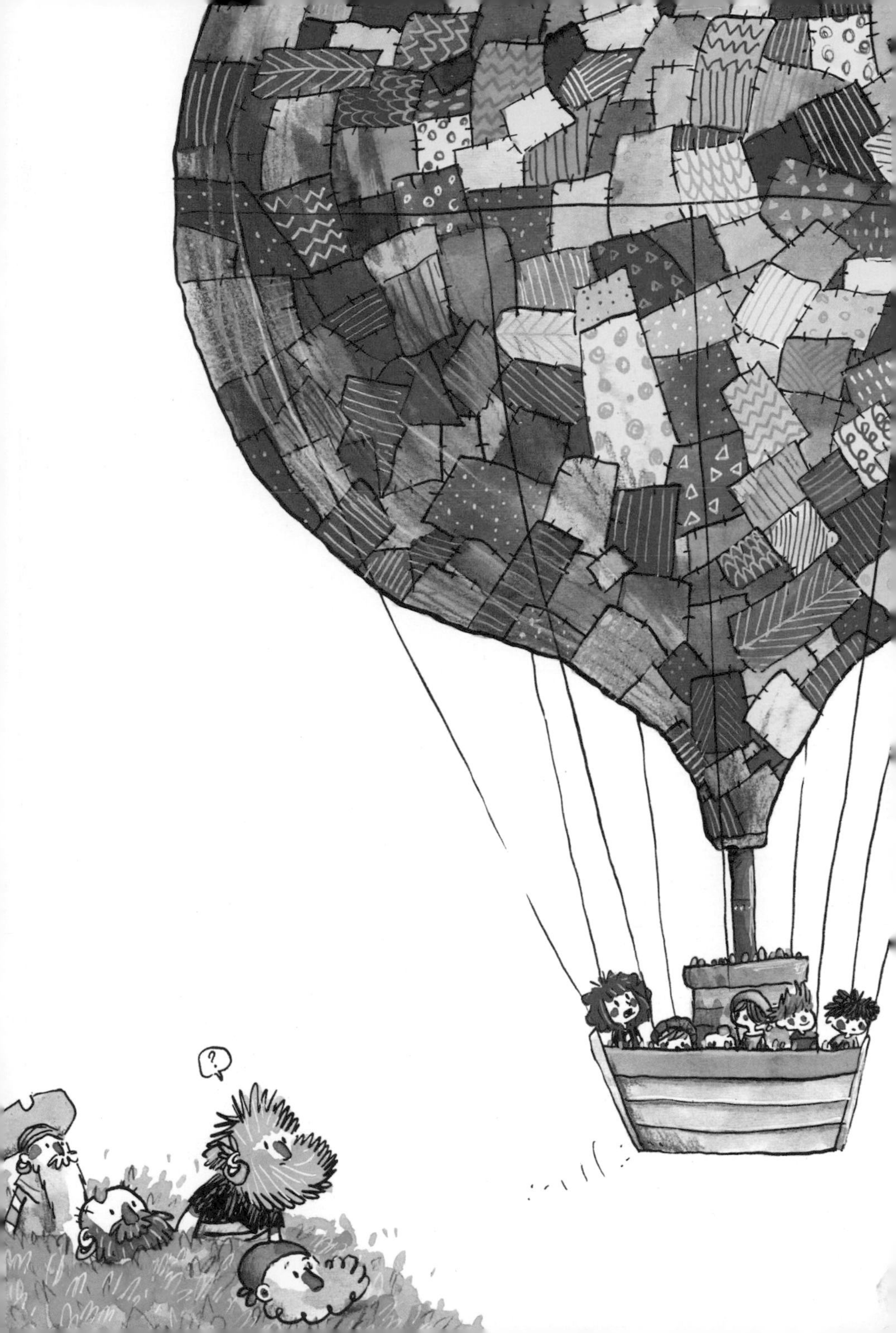
?

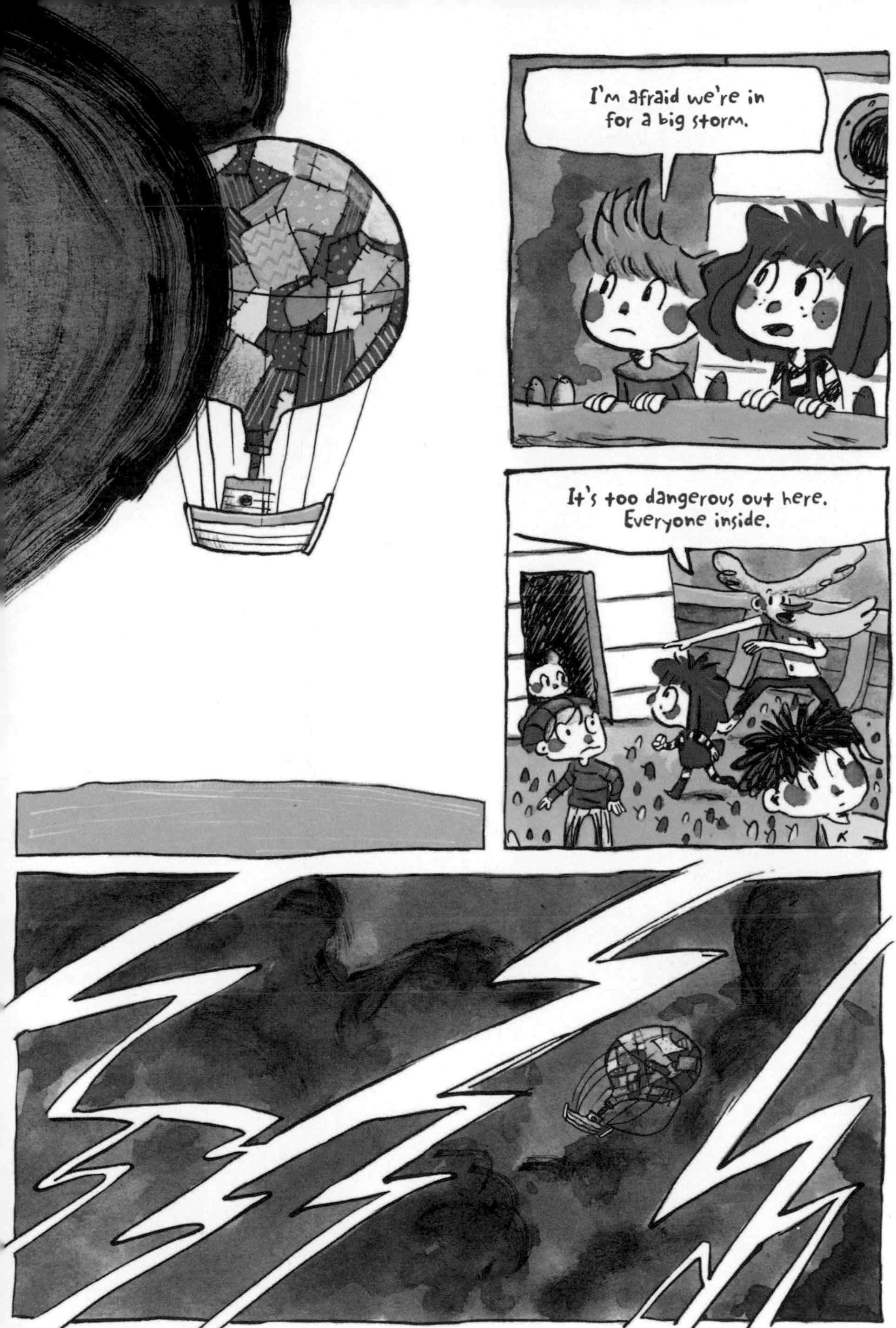
I'm afraid we're in for a big storm.
It's too dangerous out here. Everyone inside.

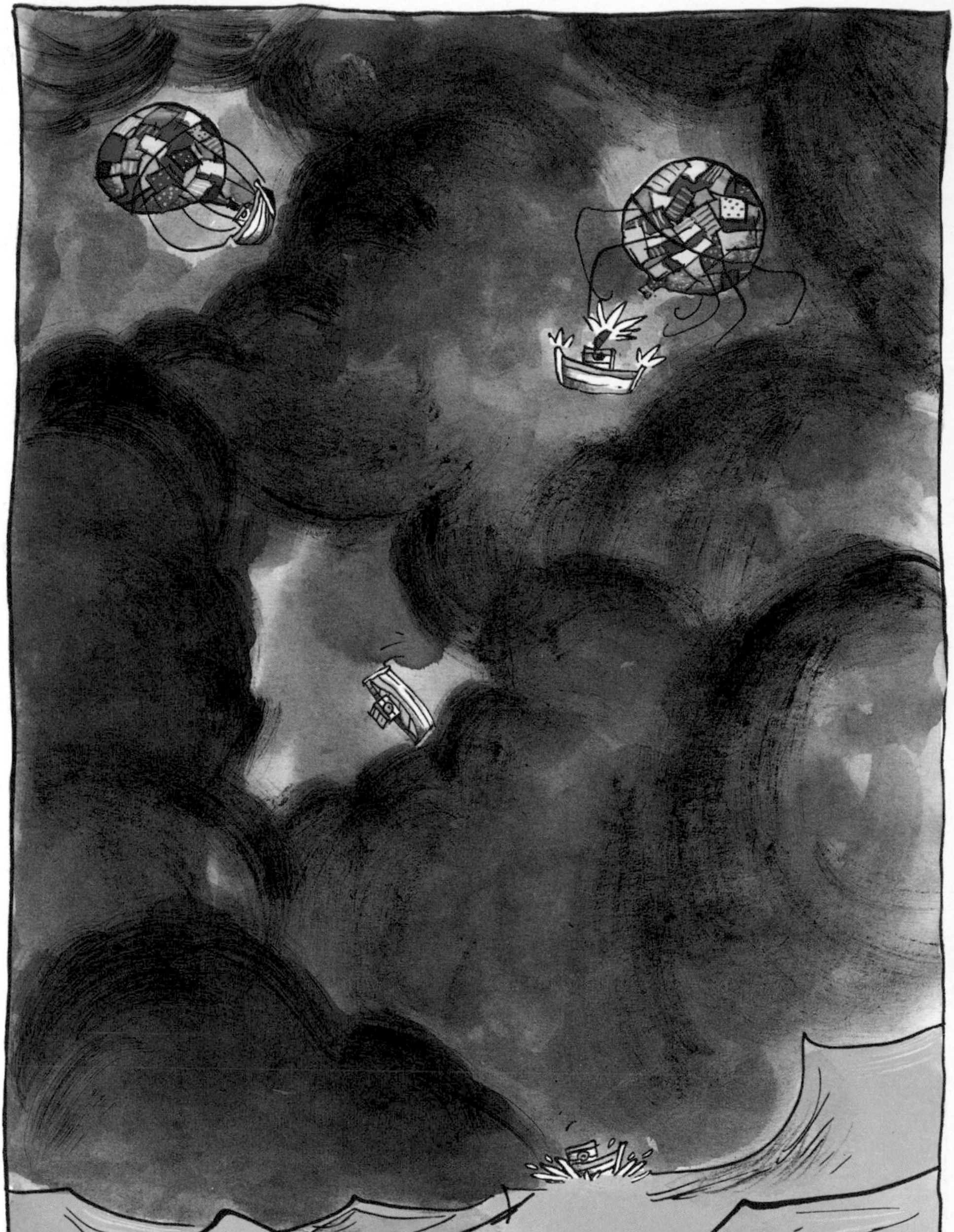

259

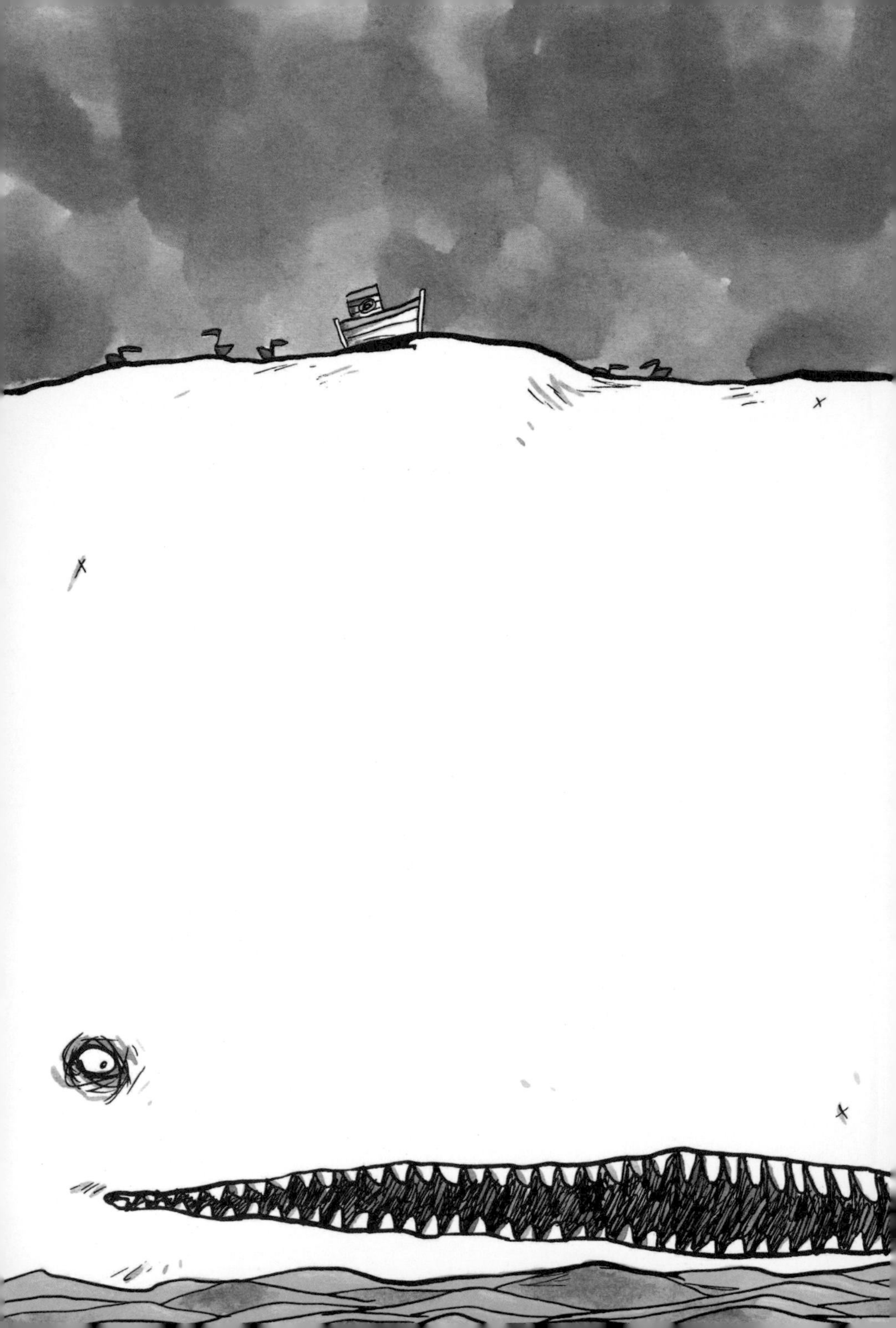

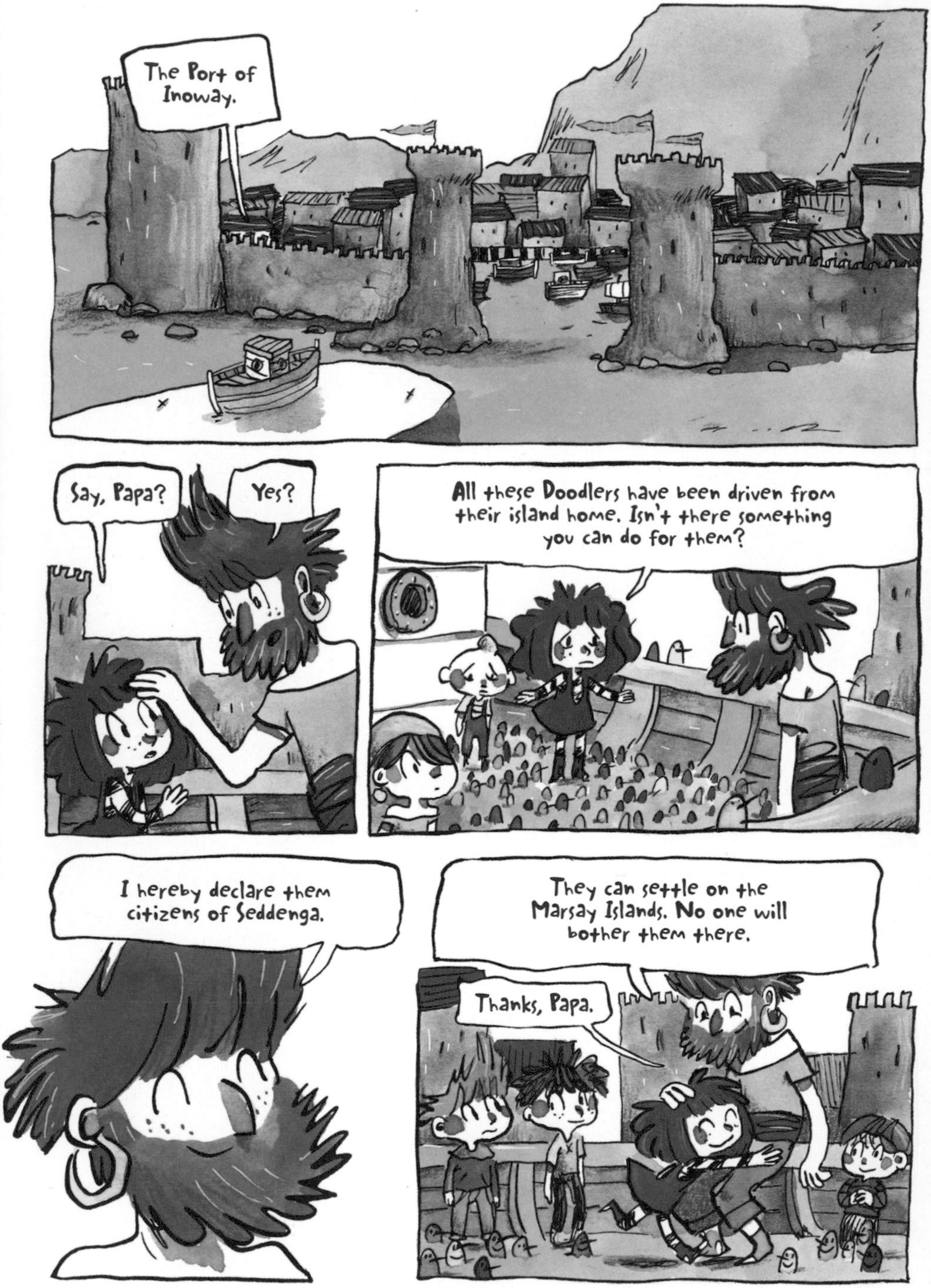
The Port of Inoway.
Say, Papa?
Yes?
All these Doodlers have been driven from their island home. Isn't there something you can do for them?
I hereby declare them citizens of Seddenga.
They can settle on the Marsay Islands. No one will bother them there.
Thanks, Papa.

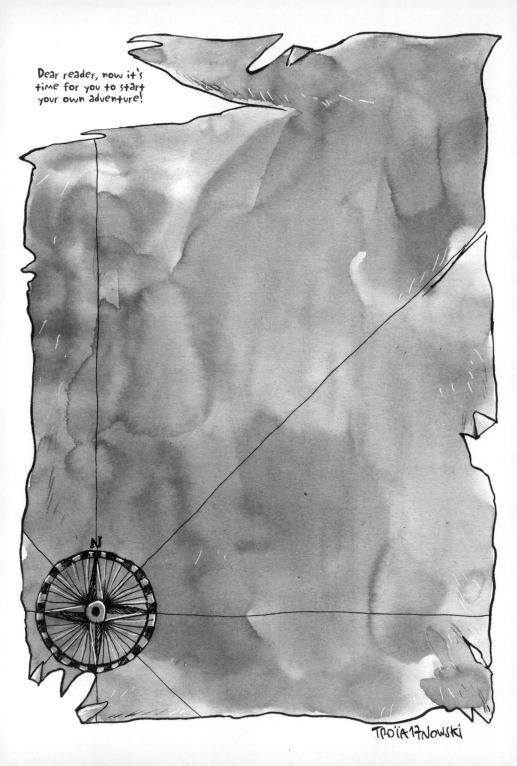

Dear reader, now it's time for you to start your own adventure!

TROÏA17NOWSKI

Character sketches

Behind the page! Original sketches

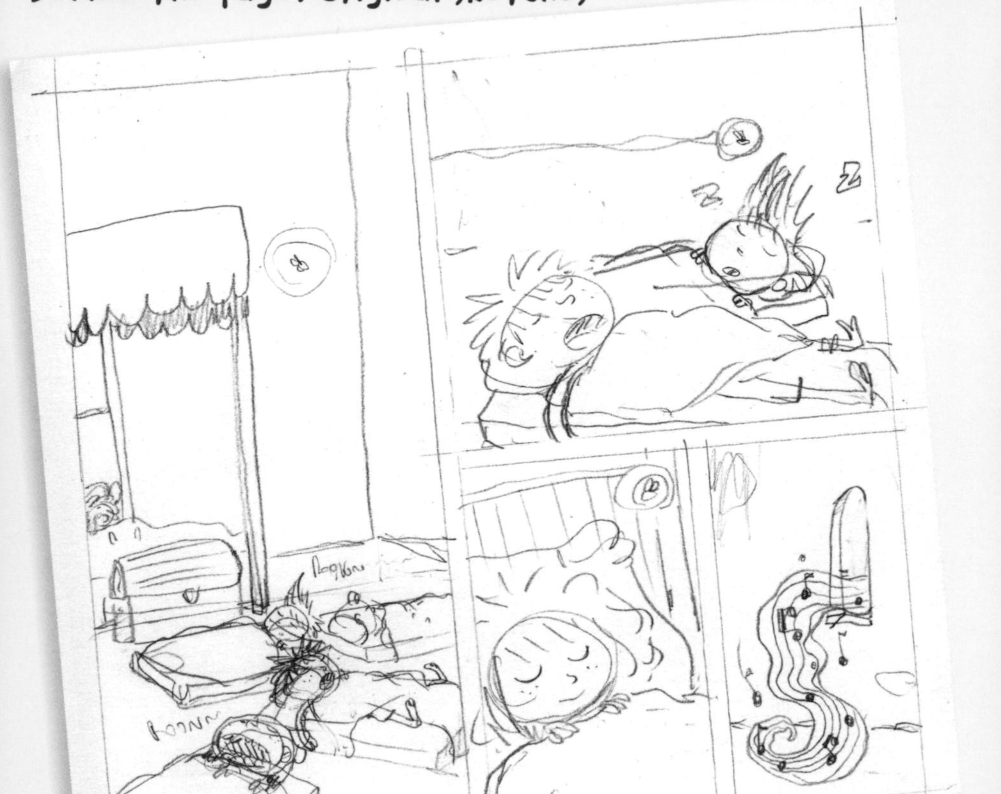

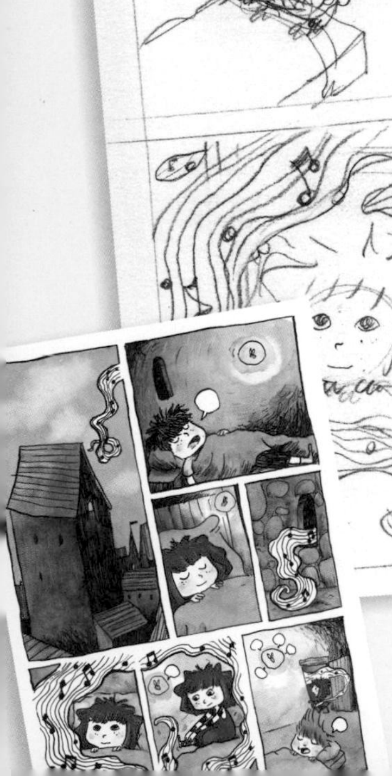

page 113

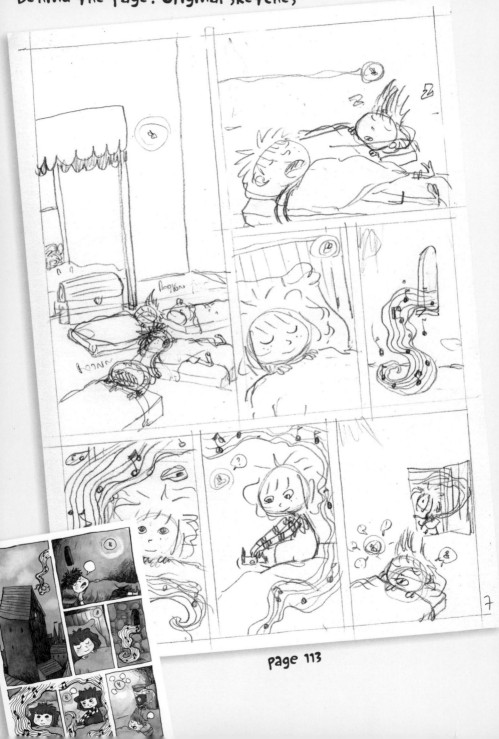

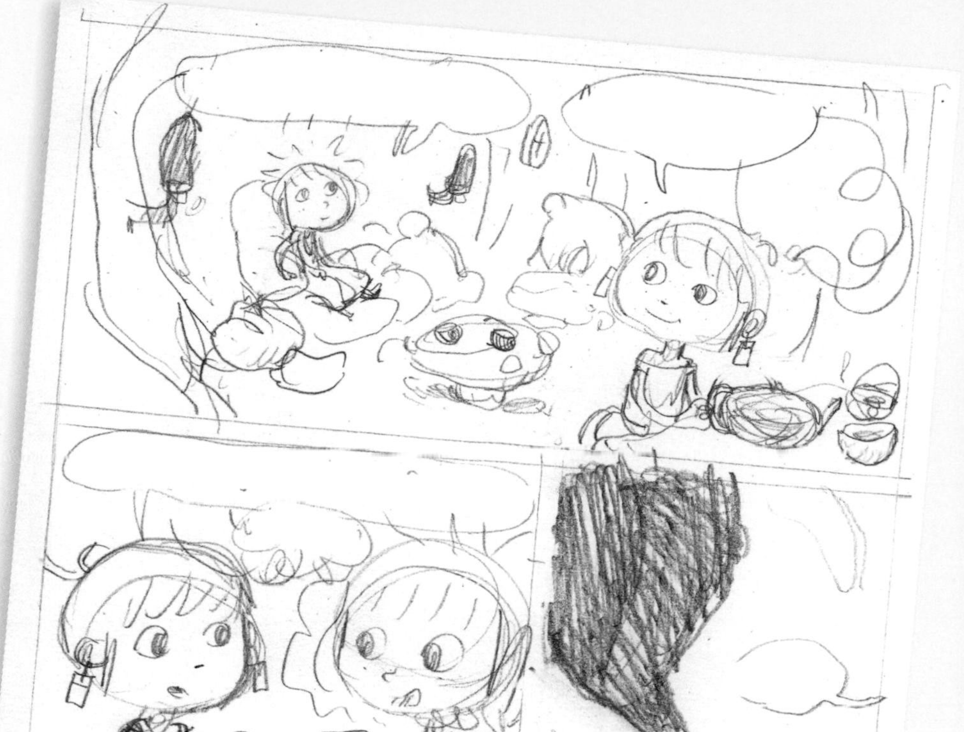

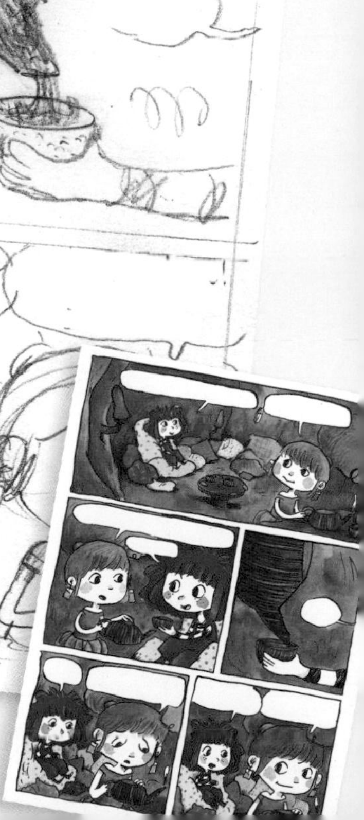

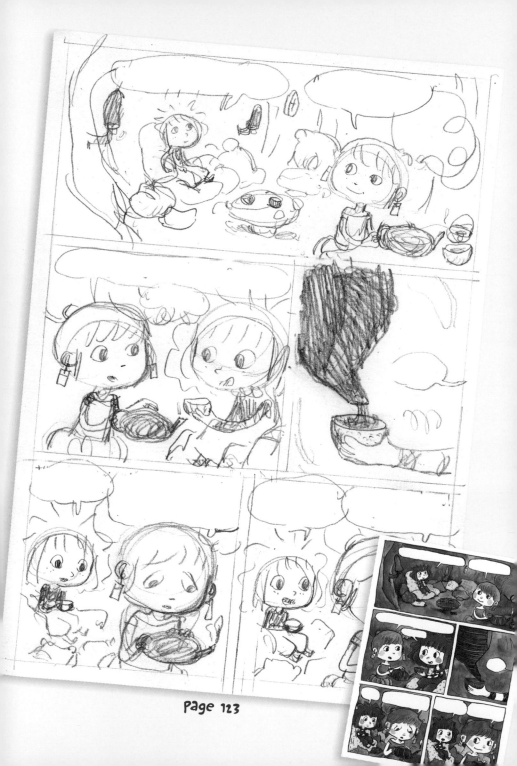

page 123

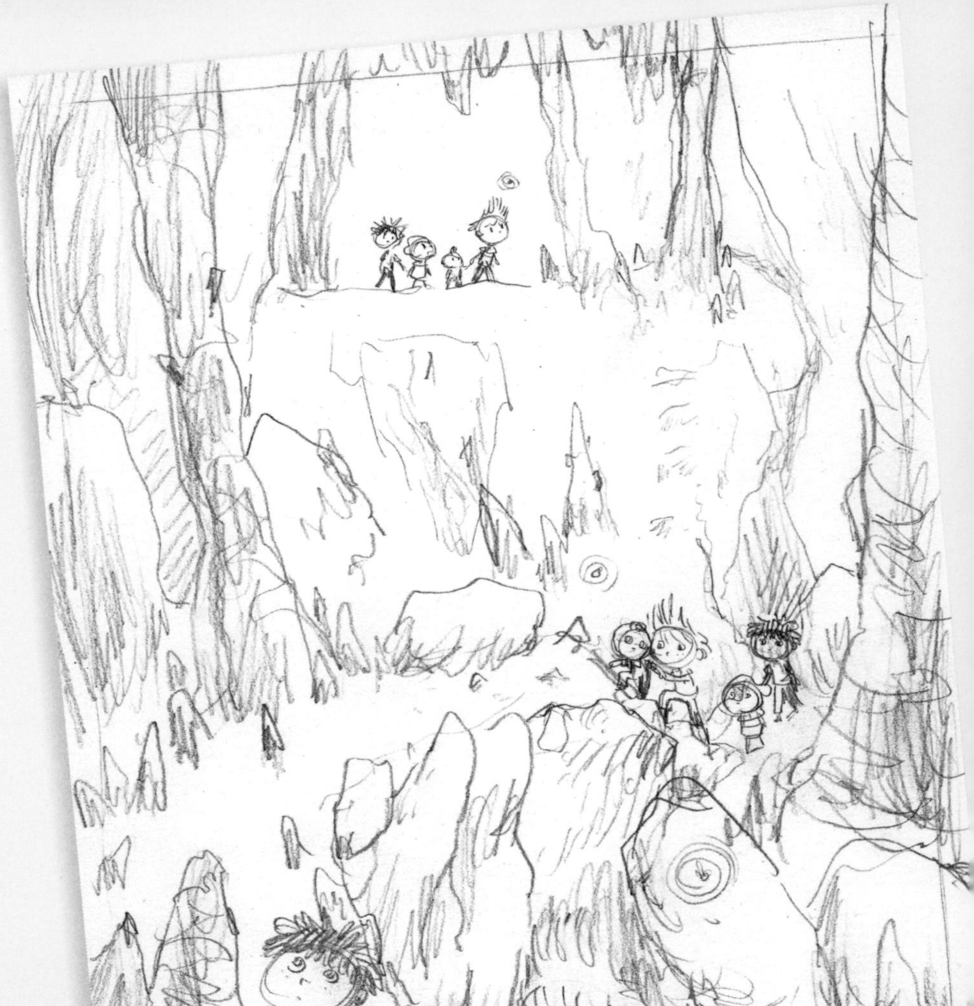

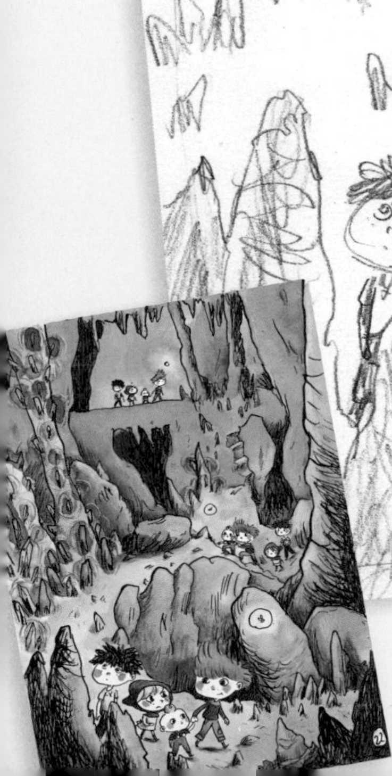

page 128

Page 146

RH GRAPHIC
THE DEBUT LIST

BUG BOYS
By Laura Knetzger

Bugs, friends, the world around us — this book has everything!
Come explore *Bug Boys* for a fun, thoughtful adventure about growing up and being yourself.

Chapter Book

THE RUNAWAY PRINCESS
By Johan Troïanowski

The castle is quiet.
And dull.
And boring.
Escape on a quest for excitement with our runaway princess, Robin!

Middle-Grade

ASTER AND THE ACCIDENTAL MAGIC
By Thom Pico & Karensac

Nothing fun ever happens in the middle of the country . . . except maybe . . . magic?
That's just the beginning of absolutely everything going wrong for Aster.

Middle-Grade

WITCHLIGHT
By Jessi Zabarsky

Lelek doesn't have any friends or family in the world. And then she meets Sanja. Swords, magic, falling in love . . . these characters come together in a journey to heal the wounds of the past.

Young Adult